Paramour

Desperation

FRANCIKA BENNETT

PatnisePublishing

ISBN-13: 9780991112913
ISBN-10: 0991112911

PROLOGUE

The apartment was dark and empty when Malcolm opened the door. It was depressing for him, given the fact that he had been expecting a happy reunion with Maggie when he returned home. Instead he would spend the night alone in their bed, not even knowing when he'd see her again.

Malcolm set the mail down on the kitchen island as he tossed his bag on the floor. He looked at the package on top of the stack of bills, frowning as he wondered what it was. He picked it up and noted that it was his name on the label adhered to the front. There was no return address, which only made him more curious. He picked it up with a yawn and gave it a shake, trying to determine what was inside. It was very light, but definitely contained something, as he could tell that something was inside moving around.

He walked over to the kitchen drawers and pulled out a pair of scissors, deciding to satisfy his curiosity. Cutting one end, he emptied the contents onto the kitchen counter. A small object fell out, wrapped in a considerable amount of bubble wrap. "Fuck it," he grumbled and picked it up, stabbing into the wrapping with the tip of the scissors. It came away fairly quickly, and within a moment or two an object fell onto the counter with a soft clang. He picked up the object and looked at it closer, his heart in his mouth as he recognized it. It was the Tiffany engagement ring that he'd given Maggie several weeks earlier.

Malcolm stared at the ring, unable to piece a logical explanation together for its sudden appearance. An anonymous package, addressed to him *not*

Maggie despite the fact that the ring was hers...what could it all mean? Was there a connection to Maggie's sudden trip to New York? Was there more to the trip than merely shopping? Malcolm's mind refused to consider that there was something going on, some dark secret lurking beneath the surface of these seemingly every day events. But the reality of the ring made it impossible to dismiss, impossible to ignore. *What the hell is going on?* He questioned. He'd had almost no sleep in the past 24 hours, and was hardly in a position to think logically. And yet, he knew he'd get no sleep now. Malcolm set down the ring and picked up the package it had arrived in to try and glean some information about its sender. The label had been printed, and contained no clue as to the person who'd created it. There was no return address, nor was there even postage. This package had been hand delivered, but by whom? None of it made any sense, and Malcolm knew that the only way he could truly uncover the truth was to talk to Maggie. But with no way of contacting her, no idea when she was returning from New York, he had very few avenues open to him. *I'll go to New York,* he decided. *I have to find out what's going on,* he vowed, unable to deny the ugly doubts that were bubbling up inside of him. Malcolm decided that he needed to try and sleep, and headed into the bathroom to find a sleep aide. He hadn't taken one in months, since Maggie had moved in with him, for she'd always lectured him about how dangerous they could become. Besides, with him in her bed, sleep had never been an issue for Malcolm. *Just one, just so I can sleep,* he vowed as he pulled the package from behind a bottle of nail polish remover. He took the pill, swallowing it down with a swig of water. Getting undressed, he left his clothes on the floor and got into bed, hoping that sleep would come to him easily and quickly.

One

Sleep did come quickly, but it was far from an easy rest that Malcolm had. Nightmares tore at him as his subconscious wrestled with the fear that his waking mind refused to acknowledge. And when he finally awoke, Malcolm felt as though he'd spent the night running a long, endless race. He was groggy, a common side effect of taking a sleeping pill, but he forced himself out of bed. The clock beside the bed read 4:23, but he had no idea if it was morning or afternoon. His body was still adjusting to the enormous time difference, and not doing a very good job of it. He picked up his cell phone and saw that it was in fact 4:23 PM, which meant he'd slept 12 hours. Malcolm checked his phone for messages, and was discouraged to find none. An idea struck him, however, and he searched through his contacts to find the number of someone who might have some answers for him. After a couple of rings, he heard Will's voice.

"Hello?"

"Hey Will, it's Malcolm."

"Hey Malcolm, you back from Australia?"

"Yeah, got in late last night. Listen Will, I haven't been able to get a hold of Maggie, and now I'm getting a message telling me her phone is no longer in service. Have you spoken to her since she and your mom went to New York?"

"I've spoken to Mum, but not Maggie. But I'm sure she's fine, Mum's said as much."

Will's answer served to relieve some of Malcolm's anxiety, but it wasn't enough. "Where are they staying?" he asked. "I'm heading down to New York in a little while. Can you give me the name of the hotel they're staying at?"

Will was silent for a moment, and then spoke up. "I don't know, Malcolm. Mum's never said where they are come to think of it."

Malcolm frowned, the anxiety assailing him again. "Don't you think that's weird?" Malcolm asked. "You don't know where they are?? Isn't your dad concerned?"

"He hasn't been," Will admitted. "But now that you mention it, it is a wee bit odd."

"Yeah, a *wee bit*," Malcolm replied. "Listen, I'm going to New York, and I mean to find Maggie. I don't care if I have to go to every goddamn hotel in the whole city, I *will* find her."

Will could hear the near-hysteria in Malcolm's voice. "Easy now, mate," he said. "You're getting yourself worked up for nothing. Mum and Maggie are fine," he said, but the words began to sound hollow to his own ears.

"Well I mean to find out that for myself," Malcolm told him. "Do me a favour Will. Next time your mom calls, ask her the name of the hotel she's at, then text it to me, okay?"

"Sure thing," Will replied. "Have a safe trip." Will ended the call and then sat for a moment thinking about what Malcolm had said. He hadn't questioned, nor had Will's father, any aspect of Maggie and Irene's shopping trip. But a few days had turned into a week, and then more than a week. *Was* there something going on? If so, what could it be? Will knew that his mother would be calling that very evening at precisely 9PM, just as she did every other night. But this time Will would make sure he asked her the questions that no one had bothered to ask. He only hoped that Malcolm's fears were unfounded, his worries unnecessary.

New York City was not far from Boston, just under four hours by car. But the distance seemed enormous given the level of desperation Malcolm felt.

Maggie was there, somewhere, in one of the hundreds of hotels spread over the enormous New York Metropolitan Area. Malcolm had been to New York, had attended boarding school there as a boy, but that gave him little by way of advantage given the magnitude of the task before him. Yet he was determined, and knew that if he needed to check each and every hotel, motel, bed and breakfast or inn in order to find Maggie, he would do just that. He didn't care how long it took; he would not rest until he found her. And then, only then, would he gain an understanding of the bizarre series of events that had been plaguing him since arriving in Sydney almost two weeks earlier.

As he packed a bag to take with him, Malcolm noticed something that did little to alleviate his anxiety; Maggie's luggage was missing. If she had gone to New York City for a few days, one of her suitcases would have sufficed. But all of them were gone; and as he looked through the closet for clean clothes to pack, he saw that her clothes were all but gone, with only a few items remaining.

"What the hell is going on??" he said aloud. He opened the dresser drawers next, noting the same thing that he'd seen in the closet: most of her things were gone.

It was as though she'd moved out, not just gone for a short trip. *But that can't be it,* he reasoned: *why would she leave? We're getting married, we're having babies... she loves me, she would never leave me!* But the evidence he was finding as he walked through the apartment was mounting: dirty dishes left in the dishwasher, a load of laundry left in the dryer. Malcolm knew Maggie well, and knew that she would never leave the apartment in such a state. She was organized and tidy, something he'd always enjoyed teasing her about. So why had she left dirty dishes and unfolded laundry? It appeared as though she'd left in a hurry, which seemed odd given the nature of her sojourn. None of it made sense. Clearly there was more going on than he knew, and Malcolm was determined to find out what that something was.

"Hey there Gerry," Malcolm said, offering the kindly doorman a half-hearted smile. "It's good to see you sir," Gerry replied. "When did you arrive home?" "Late last night," Malcolm replied. "And now I'm on my way to New York," he added. "Meeting up with Miss O'Toole?" Gerry asked with a smile.

"Hoping to, yeah," he replied. "Listen Gerry, did you see Maggie when she left?" "Yes sir," Gerry replied.

"How did she seem to you?" Malcolm asked.

"She wasn't herself, if you'll forgive me for saying so sir," Gerry replied.

"Was she upset?" Malcolm asked.

"Perhaps a little, yes," Gerry said, getting uncomfortable with Malcolm's questions.

Malcolm nodded. "Thanks Gerry," he replied. "I don't know when I'll be home, but do me a favour, will you?" he asked.

"Anything sir," Gerry replied.

"If Maggie comes home without me, or before me, give me a call," he said. "You have my cell phone number, right?"

I do sir," Gerry assured him. Malcolm headed to the parking garage at this point, leaving the doorman rather confused.

Malcolm had just pulled into the drive-through at the local Wendy's when his phone rang.

He answered it at once, hoping that it was Maggie. But it wasn't, it was his friend Dave. "Hi Dave," Malcolm said

"Hey Malcolm, you get a hold of Maggie yet?" Dave asked.

"No," Malcolm replied. "Hold on a sec," he said, and then placed his order. "I'm on my way to New York right now to find her."

"Are you crazy? You just got off a plane from Australia!" Dave reminded him.

"Yeah, so?" Malcolm replied, handing the girl at the take out window his money. "I need answers, Dave," he went on as he drove off. "There's too much weird shit going on, my gut is telling me that there's something wrong."

"You mean because you can't reach her?" Dave asked.

"That's part of it," Malcolm replied. "But there's more to it than just that," he went on, and then described the state of the apartment, the phone call with Will, and the ring that had arrived in an unmarked envelope.

"That *does* sound weird," Dave concurred. "And you know what? Carrie hasn't talked to her either," he went on. "Those two can't go more than a few hours without texting or talking."

"I know," Malcolm replied. "I'm going to find her, Dave. I'm going to get to the bottom of all this, I swear to God."

"If you need any help, or anything at all, you just let me know, okay dude?" Dave said.

"Thanks Dave," Malcolm replied. "I may just take you up on your offer. I'll talk to you soon."

Antigonish, Nova Scotia

Marilyn Calder looked up from the resume to the young woman who sat across from her. "Maggie, you have excellent qualifications," she said. "But I have to wonder why you're seeking employment as a cook rather than a nurse."

Maggie tugged at the collar of her blouse, finding the small room exceedingly hot. "I'm sure my cousin told you why," she replied pointedly.

Marilyn lived next door to Pat and Noreen MacPhee, and was aware that they'd taken in a relative from the States several weeks earlier. She hadn't wanted to pry, but clearly there was something unusual about the circumstances that had brought young Maggie to her neighbours' door.

"She told me that you were in a tight spot," Marilyn commented."But that's all."

Maggie sighed, not really wanting to get into the particulars of her rather complicated life. "I'm not a Canadian citizen," she began. "But I need to work. My cousin told me that you were starting a day care in your home, and that you were thinking of hiring a cook. I can cook," she went on. "I'm a very good cook, and would appreciate the chance to earn some money."

Marilyn looked at Maggie, then back on her resume, and then back at Maggie. "If you don't have your citizenship, then you can't apply for a social insurance number," Marilyn informed her. Paying her employers under the table wasn't an issue for her, but she had to make sure that Maggie wasn't a government agent sniffing around for non-compliance. The last thing she needed as she started up a new business was someone from Revenue Canada making life difficult for her.

Maggie sighed. "I don't know how long I'm going to be in Canada, so citizenship is sort of the last thing on my mind. Noreen thought you'd be able to help me out, but if you can't, I understand," she said, standing up. The small bump under her blouse gave Marilyn a small measure of guilt. Noreen had confided in her that the babies' father had abandoned Maggie, and circumstances had forced her to leave her home.

"Maggie wait," Marilyn said, standing up. "Don't go. I guess I'm just a little paranoid about government compliance," she explained.

"I understand," Maggie replied.

"But that doesn't mean that I'm going to turn my back on a person in need," Marilyn said. "The job is yours if you want it," she added.

Maggie wanted to cry with relief, and smiled. "Thank you, Mrs. Calder," she said. "I can't tell you how much I appreciate this."

Marilyn smiled warmly. "Please, call me Marilyn. Welcome aboard." Maggie smiled, as a small sliver of hope wormed its way into her traumatized heart.

Two

*H*aving checked into the Plaza Hotel, Malcolm made a plan of action. He had no desire to drive all over the city himself, and decided to engage the services of a driver. He figured that it would save him time as professional drivers were bound to know the city better than anyone. And with the state of mind that he was in, he wasn't sure that driving in a strange city was a good idea. After he had dropped his bag off in his room, he headed back down to the front desk to make a rather unusual request of the concierge.

"How may I help you, Mr. Sullivan?" The overly eager man asked.

"I need a list of all the hotels in the city," Malcolm said.

A look of panic spread over the man's face. "Is there something unsatisfactory, sir? Please let me see what I can do to..."

"No, there's nothing wrong," Malcolm assured him. "I'm looking for someone, and I don't know what hotel she's staying at."

The concierge was torn between the relief that he wasn't losing a client and concern that there was some nefarious reason for his search. "Er, well...I don't see how that's a problem," he said, opening his computer. "I trust that this woman will be happy to see you?" he asked.

Malcolm frowned. "She's my fiancée," he informed him. "So yeah, of course she'll be happy to see me."

The man's face reddened ever so slightly as he pulled up some information on his computer. "Well then I wish you well in your search sir," he said with a tight smile as sent the document to print.

Malcolm took the list and headed to the elevator, scanning over the list as he did so. There were easily more than 200, and that was just in New York City itself. And then there were the outlying areas, as well as bed and breakfasts, motels, inns...*how will I ever find her?* He thought with a moment of panic as the elevator doors closed on him and several other people. *I will find her,* he vowed, no *matter how long it takes, I'll find her.*

The next thing on Malcolm's to-do list was to find a driver. That search would prove to be a lot easier than the search for Maggie would be, without a doubt. He found a list of services quite easily online, and, after reading some of the reviews provided, selected one and phoned them. Within a short time, he'd engaged the services of a driver by the name of Gus Malone, who arranged to meet Malcolm in the bar, in one hour's time. That gave Malcolm enough time to jump in the shower and put on some fresh clothes.

As he sat waiting in the rather posh bar on the Plaza's main floor, Malcolm was overwhelmed with the urge to have a drink. Just one. His nerves were shot, and he knew that one would help calm him down. One couldn't hurt. So when the young woman serving tables asked him what he wanted, he ordered a Guinness. By the time Gus Malone was directed to his table 30 minutes later, he was on his second pint.

"Mr. Sullivan?"

Malcolm looked up. A man in his mid-fifties stood beside his table, and he guess him to be Gus. He wore a suit and tie, and had shortly cropped greying hair. "Gus?" Malcolm asked.

Gus nodded. "Yes sir, Gus Malone at your service," he said.

"Have a seat," Malcolm said. Gus hesitated for a moment, and then sat down, looking around somewhat nervously as he did so. He'd picked up many clients from the Plaza, but not once had he ever been invited to sit at the same table as any of them. He looked at the young man who had hired him, waiting expectantly for instructions.

"Malcolm Sullivan," Malcolm said, stretching his hand across the table. Gus shook his hand, growing rather perplexed. "You come highly recommended," Malcolm said.

"Yes sir," Gus replied. "I've lived in the City my whole life," he said. "Been driving for close to thirty years now."

"So you know this place like the back of your hand then," Malcolm said with a smile. The two pints had done a lot to alleviate his stress.

Gus smiled at his comment. "You could say so," he replied. "Is there somewhere you'd like to go tonight, sir?"

"Okay, let's get one thing straight right away," Malcolm said. "I don't want to be called sir, or Mr. Sullivan," he told an astonished Gus. "I have no use for that shit. Call me Malcolm, or call me Sully. Either one is fine with me. Got it?"

Gus nodded, starting to think his new client was either mad or drunk. "If you say so, sir...I mean, Malcolm."

Malcolm smiled. "Will you have a beer with me?" he asked as he beckoned the waitress. Gus hesitated, but when the waitress arrived at their table, he had no trouble at all ordering a Budweiser.

Malcolm and Gus sat in the bar drinking and eating together for a couple of hours, by the end of which time Malcolm had heard some of the funniest stories he'd ever heard. After he had a couple of pints in him, Gus became quite sociable, and Malcolm was quite sure that he had more life experience than anyone he'd had ever met.

"So tell me something," Gus asked as the waitress started clearing their table. "Why don't you know where she is?" Malcolm had told Gus about his situation, and how he'd come to New York to find his fiancée.

"I don't know the answer to that," Malcolm replied. "It's all a big fucking mess, my friend." Gus nodded.

"Youz two didn't have a fight, did youz?" Malcolm couldn't help but notice how the New York accent that Gus had managed to conceal was seeping out the more he drank.

"No," Malcolm replied. "Last time I saw her she was crying because I was going away for a few days," he explained. He shook his head as he downed the last of his beer. "It's the damnedest thing," he said. "None of it makes any sense. That's why I need to find her. She's the only one who can give me the answers to all my questions."

"Yeah, I guess so," Gus agreed. He looked at his watch. "Geez, the wife's gonna kick my butt if I'm not home soon," he bemoaned. "What time do you want me to pick you up?" he asked as Malcolm handed his credit card to the waitress.

"How about 9?" Malcolm suggested. "Hell of a lot of hotels to cover," he remarked.

"Sure is," Gus agreed as he stood up. "Okay, I'll meet you out front at 9 sharp," he said. He held his hand out to Malcolm. "Thanks for....all this," he said, gesturing the rather large collection of plates and glasses they'd emptied.

"Thanks for the company," Malcolm replied, shaking Gus's hand. "I'll see you in the morning." Malcolm headed upstairs to his room. He was more than a little tipsy as he rode up the elevator with some rather stuffy looking businessmen. *No way am I gonna be one of those,* he vowed to himself. *No freakin' way.*

The copious amount of alcohol in Malcolm's bloodstream made it easy for him to fall asleep, something for which he was grateful. But when he drifted into the depths of REM sleep, thoughts of Maggie found their way into his dreams.

It's my birthday, and Maggie surprised me with an amazing party. And even though my dad showed up, uninvited of course, I've never had such a happy birthday. And as if that wasn't enough! Maggie had one more surprise for me after everybody went home. Dressed in the sexiest nurse's costume I've ever seen, she rocked my world.

"Do you have any idea how much I love you?" I asked her, taking her face in his hands as she sat on my lap. Maggie smiled and nodded.

"Let's go in the bedroom. I want to hear you scream my name," I said. Maggie climbed off my lap and took my hand. I stood up and together we headed into the bedroom.

"Now I know it's your birthday," Maggie said as I lay on the bed. "But I want you to let me have control tonight." I had no problem with that! "Baby, you can do whatever you want," I said, smiling at her as she climbed on to the bed. I love it when she's aggressive, 'cause she hardly ever is. But as I watched her crawl up the bed towards me, I could see by the look in her eyes that she meant business.

"Are you having a happy birthday?" she asked as she ran her hands slowly up the length of my legs.

"Best one ever," I told her, watching her hands as they run over my thighs. Maggie smiled as her hands reached my groin. "I'm so glad," she said, grasping the base of my cock with one hand and running her tongue up the length of it. Fuck I love it when she does that! She kept her eyes on mine, watching the expression on my face. The sight of her red-lipsticked mouth closing over my cock, pulling me into her warm mouth slowly, almost made

me shoot my load right then and there. But I didn't, I kept eye contact with her, grabbing the quilt under me. And then she really went to work, using her hands and mouth to bring me to the brink. I knew that she wanted me to lose control. And it wasn't long before I did, helpless to stop it...

The intensity of Malcolm's dream woke him, the arousal he felt shaking him from sleep. It had been weeks since he'd been with Maggie. Dreaming of her only augmented his need for her. *We'll be together soon,* he told himself. *In a few days, a week tops.* Malcolm rolled over and did his best to force the images of his dream from his mind. But it wasn't easy, and it was a long time before he managed to find sleep again that night.

Antigonish, Nova Scotia

"Well that's wonderful," Irene said with a smile. "I'm so happy that Marilyn was able to help you out."

"Me too," Maggie replied as she sat down on the edge of her bed. She yawned. "I know it's early, but I'm just beat," she said.

"You haven't been sleeping well," Irene pointed out.

Maggie shook her head as she pulled her long hair out of its ponytail. "I'm still having dreams about him," she said quietly.

Irene nodded, not surprised at all. "That's to be expected," she said. "In time..." she didn't finish the sentence for she wasn't so sure that time would or even could change the way that Maggie felt about Malcolm. "Why don't you try to sleep now, love?" she suggested.

"I think I will," Maggie replied with a sigh. She looked down at the now visible bump, running a hand over it thoughtfully. She'd begun feeling the babies moving about, and it was an amazing feeling. And yet, the joy she felt each time she experienced the smallest movement was tempered with the knowledge that their father was not there to share it, would not be there to witness their birth, and would have no part in their lives.

Irene watched her daughter, knowing what was going through her mind, for it was always on her mind. It had been a month since she'd last seen Malcolm, and Irene knew that a year or even ten could pass, and Maggie would still feel the same sense of loss as she did right now. She glanced at her watch as Maggie got ready for bed, knowing that Mick would be expecting her call at 9PM sharp.

"Do you want some warm milk, Maggie?" Irene called through the bathroom door. "That helps you sleep."

That would be lovely, thanks Mum," Maggie called back.

I'll be right back," Irene responded, and then left their bedroom. She pulled out her phone as she walked to the kitchen and dialed her home number. It was Will who answered the phone.

"Hi Mum, how are you?"

"I'm good love, how are you?"

"Fine, just fine," Will replied. "Tired, you know, worked all day."

"Of course. I'm surprised you're still up, actually," Irene said.

"I stayed up so I could talk to you, Mum," Will said.

Irene's guard went up at once. "Well that was sweet of you, love," she said. "I miss you and the lads so much."

"We miss you too Mum. When are you coming home? It's been more than two weeks now," Will said.

Irene was not prepared for her son's questions, though in truth had been expecting such questions for some time now. "I'm not sure," she said. I was talking to Malcolm a few days ago," Will said. "He was asking a lot of questions about this trip you and Maggie took. Said he didn't know anything about it."

"Well it was kind of last minute," she explained uneasily.

"Yeah so you've said," Will said. "What hotel are you staying at?"

"Why do you ask?" Irene replied.

"Malcolm is in New York and wanted to visit Maggie," Will said. "He asked me to ask you."

Irene's heart started racing as she thought frantically of an answer that would satisfy her son. But she knew that whatever she said would be a lie, and Malcolm would find out the same thing soon enough. And then what? Her eyes darted around the kitchen, looking for an idea. She quickly scanned the newspaper which sat on the table in front of her and came up with a plausible sounding name. "The Breton," she said at last.

"Okay I'll let him know," Will said. "Dad's right here, so I'll let him talk to you. Give my love to Maggie." "I will," Irene said. "Goodnight son."

The rest of the phone call went smoothly, as Mick filled in his wife with the daily minutiae of the Hart and Hound. She listened patiently, assured him that they would be home soon and that Maggie sends her love. As she ended the call, she experienced the same measure of guilt that she did every night, every time she lied to her sons and her husband. *This has to end,* she told herself as she prepared Maggie's warm milk. *One way or other, this has to end.*

The warm milk helped Maggie to fall asleep, but it wasn't a restful sleep. And it wasn't long before she found herself in the midst of a vivid dream....

"Are they asleep?"

"Yeah, down for the count, both of them," Malcolm tells me with a smile. "We're all alone."

"For now. You know how early those wee lads of ours wake up in the morning." Malcolm nods as he climbs into bed. "Guess that means we'll just have to make the most of our time before they do."

I'm tired, but I don't want to tell him that. It's not often that we have a few minutes to ourselves. So when Malcolm pulls me close and runs his hands up under my nightgown, I simply let myself enjoy and not worry about the early morning we're sure to have. And when I feel his avid mouth on my bare skin, I know I'm helpless to resist him. His hands move in tandem with his mouth, caressing me, kissing me, sending me to that place where nothing matters but him and me. We have to be quiet now when we make love, for our twins tend to be light sleepers. But we have adapted, and have learned how to be quiet, how to be quick and take advantage of our time together before life as parents exerts its demands upon us once again.

Suddenly Malcolm looks up, and turns his head. "Did you hear that?" he asks I frown, frustrated that we've been interrupted so soon. "Awake already?" I groan. Malcolm shakes his head and looks back at me as he gets off the bed. "That's not what I hear," he tells me, and I grow alarmed.

"What is it?" I ask, sitting up in our bed. "Malcolm?"

But he doesn't answer, and simply heads to the door. Before he can open it, the door bursts open, and I scream, pulling the sheet up over me. It is Jack Sullivan standing in the doorway. "What the hell are you doing?" Malcolm shouts at his father.

"Taking care of business," he replies calmly, and then pulls a gun out. He aims it straight at me and fires.

"Maggie, Maggie wake up!"

Maggie's eyes flew open and she stared wide eyes at her mother, who was sitting on the edge of her bed.

"You were screaming," Irene told her, stroking Maggie's tousled hair. "You were screaming in your sleep, love."

Maggie nodded, as the terrible spectre of her nightmare filled her with fresh terror. "It was Jack," she told her mother tearfully. "He..." she didn't continue, and simply wrapped her arms around her mother's neck.

Irene held her, and did her best to comfort her. It was not the first time Maggie had awoken in such a state, and likely wouldn't be the last. "It was only a dream," she reminded her gently. Maggie knew this was true, but that did not negate the terror she felt, nor the feeling that Jack Sullivan would hold the key to her happiness forever in his grasp.

Three

Waking up with a headache was something Malcolm had vowed would never happen again. But when the phone beside his bed rang at precisely 8AM, he did just that. He groaned as he climbed out of bed, remembering all too well the feeling of having overindulged. For a moment, he sat on the side of his bed, holding his head in his hands. *Fucking idiot,* he berated himself. *Don't you ever learn?* He picked up his cell phone as he stood up and noticed that he had a text message. It was from Will. He pushed the pain of his headache aside as he checked the message, his hopes soaring when he read it. *Hey Malcolm. Mum says they're at the Breton. Tell Maggie to give me a call when you see her. Cheers.* Malcolm smiled as he sent a quick reply back. *Will do-- thanks a lot.*

He had a quick shower and headed downstairs for breakfast, happier than he'd been in weeks. He smiled when he thought back to his dream the previous night, feeling sure that he would be able to make it a reality very soon. Gus was on time, which did not surprise Malcolm in the least bit. He was all business as he opened the door for Malcolm and then disappeared into the front seat of the Cadillac. "Where to first?" Gus asked as he pulled away from the curb in front of the Plaza.

"The Breton," Malcolm replied as he buckled his seatbelt.

"The Breton?"

"Yeah," said Malcolm. "Maggie's brother texted me last night. That's the place." Gus didn't reply for a moment or two, and Malcolm figured he was busy locating the hotel on the car's GPS. He wasn't prepared for the next words that the driver spoke.

"There is no Breton Hotel in New York, Malcolm."

Malcolm frowned. "Well...maybe it's in another borough," he suggested. "Manhattan's a bit pricy," he went on.

"No, there's no Breton in *all* of New York," Gus informed him.

Malcolm refused to believe it. "There has to be!" he insisted. "Maggie's mother told Will that was where they were staying!"

"Do you have a computer with you?" Gus asked.

"Yeah."

"Google it. See if there is such a hotel in New York."

Malcolm opened up his iPad, anxious to prove Gus wrong. Why would Irene lie? There was simply no reason that she would lie. He entered the name Breton into the search engine, and found a number of sites that contained the name, but not one of them was a hotel in New York City. He clicked page after page, desperate to find it, but it soon became apparent that there simply was no such hotel in New York. Gus was right.

"Well?" Gus asked.

"Nothing," Malcolm said, the enthusiasm gone from his voice. "So...what now? Did she lie? Why would she lie?"

Gus had his own suspicions, but didn't want to say anything just yet. "Get out your list, Malcolm," he said. "We have a lot of hotels to get to."

Malcolm nodded and directed Gus to the first hotel on the list, the 70 Park Avenue Hotel. As Gus drove, Malcolm sent a text to Will. *There's no Breton hotel in NYC. Are you sure that's what she said?* He looked out the window as he waited for Will's reply, the exciting sights of the great city leaving him feeling empty inside. Within a few minutes, he felt his phone vibrate, and looked down to see Will's reply.

That's what she said mate. What the fuck is going on??

Malcolm frowned as he texted him back. *I don't know, but I'm sure as hell going to find out. I'll keep you posted.*

Malcolm had visited 14 hotels by evening, his mood sinking lower with each failure. No one had seen Maggie or Irene, no one had heard her name, or noticed a pair of red-haired women with strong accents. With each dead end, Malcolm's fight against his depression increased. And when Gus dropped him off at the Plaza at 9PM, it was all Malcolm could do not to drink himself stupid. He had a quiet supper in the dining room, fighting the urge to take up the offer of a glass of wine with his steak. As he ate, he looked around at the other patrons. A few of them were solitary diners like himself, but most were couples or families, laughing, enjoying their time together.

Seeing this did little to alleviate Malcolm's depression, but served to ruin his appetite. He signed for his meal, left a generous tip for the waitress, and then headed upstairs to spend a lonely evening in his large, luxurious suite.

Maggie would love this place, he mused as he sat his iPad case on the sofa. He sat down heavily, picking up the remote as he did so. He clicked through the channels, not seeing any of the hotel's many offerings as his mind drifted to a night in Scotland not so long ago...

"Best fuckin' bar in the whole goddamn world," I declare as the taxi leaves me and Maggie back at their hotel.

We're both really wasted.

Maggie says something as we stagger into the foyer of the hotel. It's funny how her accent is stronger now that she's pissed. In fact, I'm not even sure what she just said. I look at her with a smile as we step onto the elevator.

"What did you say?" I ask her.

Maggie frowns as I press the button for their floor. "You're too drunk to understand me," she says.

I understand her this time and laugh. "I'm too drunk? You're the one who's shit-faced, sweetheart."

Maggie giggles. "That's a funny expression," she said. "Shit faced," she says and laughs again.

I laugh too. "It is, isn't it? Shit faced." I laugh some more. "Do you remember what number our room is?" I ask her as we stumble out of the elevator.

"Nope," she replies. "Look at the bloomin' key," she suggested.

"Oh yeah," I laugh, making her laugh even more. We find our room and I drop the freakin' key, making her laugh even more.

"Ooo you have a nice bum," she says, giving my ass a pinch as I'm bent over to pick up the key. "I just want to bite it."

I pick up the key and manage to unlock the door. It isn't easy. "You can bite anything you want," I tell her as soon as the door's locked behind us.

"Can I?" she asks as I brace my hands beside her on the door.

"Yep," I tell her, getting hornier by the minute.

"Blimey now I'm horny," she says with a smile as I move closer.

"Good thing," I say as she starts removing her jacket.

"Why is that?" she asks.

"Cause you're about to get screwed," I tell her, moving closer and kissing her hard.

Our hands move recklessly to remove clothing, neither of us caring if our clothes get torn.

"You smell so fucking good," I tell her as I kiss her. I push onto a nearby table and move my mouth down to her breasts as my hands moved down the sides of her body, exploring aggressively as my tongue teases her nipples. As my body moves down over hers, I push her legs apart. Kneeling down before her, I pull her to me and run my tongue along the inside of one thigh. Maggie grips the edge of the table tightly, helpless. Glancing up at her, I smile. "You're so wet," I tell her, running a finger over her. "Looks like you've been thinking about this for a while."

Maggie props herself on her elbows and looks down at me. "Less talk," she says.

I laugh. "Whatever you say," I say, and bring my mouth down on her again. I can't get enough of the taste of her, and hearing Maggie moan only makes me more aggressive, my tongue going to work on her sweetness with renewed effort.

"Oh God," she moans, the wood of the table cracking under her tightening grasp. And then she cries out in ecstasy as she comes, her thighs squeezing my face between them as she writhes on the table....

Malcolm forced himself to stop thinking, to stop torturing himself with the memories of that perfect time. *I will find her,* he vowed to himself as he stood up. But doubt had begun to enter his mind, with depression hard on its heels. Drinking had always been his antidote for the depression he'd suffered from most of his life, but he refused to let himself down that path again. *I'm better than that now...I'm stronger than that now.* Deciding that he needed to direct his frustrations in a positive direction, Malcolm changed and headed down to the Plaza's rather extensive gym facilities. He worked out until he was exhausted, and then returned to his room, showered, and fell into a deep sleep.

Antigonish, Nova Scotia

Irene folded and refolded a pair of robin's egg blue cotton pants, her mind far from the task at hand. Maggie watched her, sitting on the edge of her bed. She could see how ambivalent her mother was; she shared her feelings.

"I don't know about this, Maggie," Irene muttered as she finally set the garment into her suitcase.

"Mum we've already talked about this," Maggie reminded her. "Dad and the lads need you as much as I do. You've been gone three weeks, they're bound to be concerned.

Irene frowned as she recalled the conversation she'd had with Will. "Will told me that Malcolm has been asking questions, Maggie," she said quietly. "He's gone to New York to look for you."

Maggie knew that she shouldn't be surprised by this, but was caught off guard nonetheless. "He has?" she asked, the strength gone from her voice.

Irene nodded. "He has," she replied as she set a blouse on top of the blue trousers. "Are you surprised? He must be frantic."

Maggie frowned. "I'm sure," she said quietly.

Irene looked up at her daughter, biting her tongue for the umpteenth time. "I have to tell them something, Maggie," she said. "Your father will want to know why you haven't returned. And when I come back in three weeks time... what then? I have to tell him something."

Maggie knew that this was true, but it had been one of those inconvenient truths that she'd managed to push aside for the past several weeks. But now, now that her mother was returning to Boston, it would not be ignored. There was no way that Mick O'Toole could be fooled into thinking that there was nothing amiss.

"Tell him...tell him we split up," Maggie said at last. "That's the truth, isn't it?"

Irene sighed. She had hoped that by now Maggie's outlook would have improved; but it had not. And, realistically, how could it ever improve?

She had lost the love of her life, had been ejected out of the comfortable, happy life she was enjoying by a man who cared for no one or nothing but the money that he was stockpiling.

"I think that's the only thing that he'll believe," Irene said.

Maggie nodded as a lump tightened in her throat. "You'll be back in three weeks, then?"

"Yes," Irene said.

"You won't tell Da where I am, will you?" Maggie asked. "It could get back to ...him."

"I won't tell him," Irene assured her as she closed her suitcase. She looked at her watch. "Well my bus leaves in 45 minutes," she said. "I'd best be off."

Maggie stood up. "Let me use the loo and I'll take you to the bus depot."

Irene gave her a smile, which faded as soon as Maggie had left the room. *Am I doing the right thing by leaving her now? And what state will I find her in when I return?*

"I'm ready," Maggie said as she rejoined her mother. She picked up her purse from the table beside her bed. "Let's go," she sighed.

It was raining as the Greyhound bus bound for Halifax left the small bus depot. From there Irene would take a connecting bus to Boston, arriving there around midnight. She hadn't given Mick any notice that she was coming, and was sure that he'd be shocked when she showed up at home out of the blue. No doubt he would be full of questions, particularly since Irene was alone. She hated to think of what she planned to tell her family, about how Malcolm and Maggie had split up. But it had been Maggie's idea. However, Irene knew her husband well enough to know that he would want an explanation. Given the fact that she and Malcolm had been engaged, given the fact that Maggie had gone through so much to be with Malcolm, it would not seem likely that she would end her relationship with him without a good reason. And to Irene's mind, there was only one reason that was feasible, but she hated to think of it.

She hated to think of how Mick and Maggie's three brothers would react to hearing it. *But there's no other way,* she reasoned as the bus trundled along the Trans-Canada towards Halifax. *And Maggie will just have to accept it.*

Boston

Mick O'Toole finished attaching a new keg to the spigot, tested it, and then hefted the spent keg to carry it out back. It was almost closing time, and he had half a mind to close early, as the place was nearly empty. The door opened just as he entered the kitchen, so he didn't see his wife enter their establishment.

Irene was tired, but wanted to go directly to the Hart, knowing that Mick would still be there. It was good to be back, and for a moment she simply took in the atmosphere of the comforting, familiar place. She looked around, not seeing any of her sons around, but given that it was late and a weeknight, that wasn't surprising.

Figuring that Mick was in the back, she headed in that direction, bracing herself for the conversation that she was dreading.

Mick was just returning from the back when Irene entered the kitchen, and for a moment he simply stared at her, almost as though he didn't believe she was really there. "Irene?"

Irene smiled. "Hello love," she said, walking over to him. "I've missed you," she told him, throwing her arms around him tightly. Mick returned her embrace, happy for the moment simply to have his darling wife home again.

"Why didn't you tell me you were coming home?" he asked.

"I wanted to surprise you," Irene said.

"Well you sure as hell did that," he said with a smile. He looked over her shoulder. "Is the lass with you?"

"No, Maggie's not here."

Mick frowned. "She went straight home, then?"

Irene shook her head. "She didn't come back to Boston with me, Mick. In fact, she won't be returning to Boston for a while."

"Why not?"

Irene sighed. "It's a long, sad story, love. Can we go home? I'll tell you all about it."

Mick nodded, a knot of uneasiness making its way into his gut. "I'll close up," he told her. "The lads will be happy to have you home."

"I've missed them," Irene told him. "I've missed you."

"You've been gone three weeks, Irene. Why so long? What the hell were you doing in bloody New York all this time?" he asked as they returned to the now empty bar.

Irene hesitated before responding. "We weren't in New York," she told him.

"Then where were you?" he asked as she helped him clean up.

"I'm afraid I can't tell you that. As I said, it's a long, complicated story."

Mick frowned. "I don't like this, Irene. My wife's been gone for three weeks, and now you're telling me you can't even tell me where you were all this time? What am I to think?"

Irene sighed. "It's because of Maggie, Mick."

"Is she okay?" He asked.

"No, I'm afraid not," she replied. "You see, she and Malcolm have broken up."

Mick stared at her with wide eyes. "They've *broken up?*" he asked in a shocked tone.

Irene nodded. "Aye, and she's broken hearted," she sighed. "She wants to stay away for a while, to get him out of her system. And she doesn't want any-one to know where she is, just in case it gets back to him."

Mick frowned. "What did the bastard do?" he asked.

Irene said nothing for a moment as Mick opened the car door for her. She waited for him to put her bag in the trunk and join her in the car. He looked at her expectantly as she summoned her nerve. "Tell me what he did, Irene," he asked once again.

"When he was in Australia he...he cheated on her," Irene said. "And Maggie found out. That's why she's left him, Mick. That's why she won't be coming home for a while."

Mick said nothing as he started up the car, and Irene knew that he was furious. "If that son-of-a-bitch sets foot in the Hart again, I'll tear him apart," Mick said quietly, his hands tightly gripping the steering wheel.

"I don't give a damn who his father is," he went on. "I'll castrate the bas-tard, Irene. I mean it. Didn't I say he was no good? Didn't I try to warn her?"

Irene didn't answer, and let him rail on. She looked out the window as they drove, fatigue and sadness washing over her. *I'm sorry Malcolm,* she thought as tears sprung to her eyes. *I'm so sorry I had to do this...*

The next morning

Will was up early, as was his custom, eating a bowl of Shredded Wheat when his mother joined him. He stared at her for a moment, his mouth full of cereal, before standing up and giving her a huge bear hug. Irene smiled and returned his embrace.

"When did you get back?" Will asked as Irene poured herself a cup of coffee.

"Late last night," Irene told him. "I didn't want to wake you and the lads up."

Will nodded and watched her as she sat down across from him at the small table. "Megs is home too, then?" he asked.

Irene looked up at her eldest. Will had always been very quick, almost as smart as his sister, and Irene knew that she would have to choose her words very carefully with him. She shook her head. "No, she isn't."

Will frowned. "Where have you been, Mum? And don't tell me New York. I know that's a lie."

"What do you mean, a lie?" Irene bridled.

Will looked at his mother, concerned that she was determined to stick to the story she'd fed him despite the obvious holes in it. "Did you know that Malcolm has been in New York looking for Maggie? He asked me to ask you the name of the hotel, and when I texted it to him, he told me there was no such hotel. How do you explain that, Mum?"

Irene sighed, and looked down into her coffee. "I'm sorry," she said quietly. "I...I had to lie, Will. I had good reason to lie."

Will frowned. "You taught us that lying was never justified, Mum," he reminded her. "So why did you do it? What reason could possibly justify it?"

Irene looked up at him. "Maggie has broken up with Malcolm," she told him. "And she doesn't want him to know where she is. She's afraid that if anyone knows where she is, that he could find out. That's why I lied, Will."

Will stared at his mother, her words not making any sense to him. Maggie *broke up with Malcolm?* How was that possible?

"I...I can't believe it," he said finally. "She's in love with him, she...she's engaged to him! Why would she break up with him? And why wouldn't Malcolm have said anything?"

"She found out something about him," Irene said. "He cheated on her when he was in Australia, and Maggie found out. That's why she broke it off."

"I don't believe it," Will said immediately. "That man worships Maggie. He would *never* do that to her. Not in a thousand years!"

Irene offered him a sad smile. "We all thought that, Will, especially Maggie. But it's true. I'm sorry, I know you and Malcolm are friends, but..."

"No, we *were* friends," Will retorted angrily, standing up. He put his bowl and spoon in the dishwasher, slamming the door shut. "If he's done this to Megs, then I'll rip his bloody arms off when I see him again."

Irene said nothing in reply, and simply watched as her son stormed from the room, hearing the front door slam behind him when he left for work. She sighed, wondering, not for the first time, how all of this would turn out in the end.

Four

Antigonish, Nova Scotia

The sounds of children at play penetrated through the thin walls as Maggie stood preparing lunch for the day care children. She was glad of the work, for it made her feel less dependent, less of a charity case. Her mother's cousins had been nothing but kind to her, but it still bothered her that she was dependent upon them. She'd considered leasing a small apartment for herself, but knew that the money she had from the sale of her car would need to be stretched far. She had no idea how long she'd be on her own, and once the babies came, she would need every penny. Working also took her mind off of her situation, off of Malcolm and how much she missed him. It gave her something to do to pass the long, lonely days. It had been even more difficult now that Irene had gone to Boston, even though she would be returning in a couple of weeks. Irene had been Maggie's anchor during this turbulent time, and she felt her absence keenly. But she also knew that Irene felt torn, that she missed the rest of the family, and felt compelled to return to them.

"Lunch ready?"

Maggie looked up to see Barb, one of the care givers, standing in the doorway. "Almost," she reported. "Five minutes, tops."

Barb nodded in understanding, and then disappeared again. Maggie brought out the small plates and started setting out the grilled cheese and cut up vegetables that she'd prepared for the children. As she finished her task, Marilyn entered the kitchen, a look of concern on her face.

"Something wrong?" Maggie asked as she picked up the tray that she'd set the plates on.

"Yes" Marilyn replied, following Maggie out to the small plastic picnic table where the children ate their meals. "Deb is sick, she needs to go home."

Maggie frowned as she started setting the plates down. "Well she shouldn't stay if she's sick," she pointed out.

"No, of course not," Marilyn agreed as she helped Maggie with the plates."But that leaves us shorthanded. I can't stay open with only me and Barb. Do you suppose you could help me out, Maggie?"

"Of course," Maggie replied. "I'd be happy to help."

Marilyn smiled with relief. "Thank you so much!" she said. "Don't do any heavy lifting, okay? I don't want you to hurt yourself."

"Okay I won't," Maggie assured her.

After the children had eaten their lunch, Maggie cleared the table set the dishes in the dishwasher. She was usually finished with her duties for the day by now, and would spend the next hour or two doing prep work for the next day and cleaning up. But that would have to be done later, as she was needed to help mind the small group of children in the adjacent room. Maggie liked children, and had got to know the names of the six children who came to the day care each day. She wasn't in the room long before a small girl named Tessie came up to her with a book in her hand.

"Will you read to me?" Tessie said, handing Maggie the picture book.

"Of course," Maggie replied, taking the picture book, If You Give A Mouse A Cookie, from the child's hand. They sat down on one of the sofas together as the other children settled down with books in various parts of the room. Tessie snuggled up close as Maggie read the story.

"Why do you have a big tummy?" Tessie asked quite nonchalantly.

Maggie looked down at the child in surprise. "Well...I'm having a baby," she explained.

"Really?" Tessie asked with wide eyes. "My mommy's having a baby too!"

Maggie smiled. "That's wonderful," she replied. "Shall we continue with the story?"

The rest of the afternoon was relatively uneventful, and Maggie got some experience with diaper changes and potty training. By six o'clock when the last child had been picked up, she was exhausted.

"You really did a great job today, Maggie," Marilyn told her as she helped Maggie clean up the kitchen. "You're going to be a great mom, you know that?"

Maggie smiled. "I hope so," she replied. "It's not going to be easy."

Marilyn nodded. "Parenting seldom is," she assured her.

"You're home late," Doreen commented as Maggie appeared in her kitchen. It was almost seven.

"Marilyn needed me to help out," she replied as she sat down at the small table. "One of the girls had to go home."

Doreen nodded in understanding. "Have you eaten?"

"No, but don't worry about me," Maggie assured her. "I can fend for myself."

Doreen smiled. "I know you can, lass," she replied. "But I've made supper, and there's plenty left over. Let me heat some up for you."

"Thank you," Maggie said, relenting at last. She had sensed that Doreen felt compelled to fill in for Irene in her absence.

"Did you talk to your mum today?" Doreen asked as she joined Maggie at the table.

Maggie shook her head as she began eating the chicken stew that her cousin had placed before her. "I spoke to her yesterday," she said. "She said she's coming back in another week."

Doreen nodded. "How did she explain your absence to your father? Did she say?"

Maggie frowned. "He thinks Malcolm and I have split," she explained. "That seems to be the only thing that was believable."

"I agree," Doreen replied. She watched Maggie for a few minutes. "I know how hard this is for you, Maggie. I know how much you love him."

Maggie nodded, trying not to cry. "I think I always will," she replied quietly. She took a moment to gain control of her emotions before looking up at her cousin. "Thank you for this," she said. "It was delicious," she added with a tight smile, and stood up to put her dishes in the dishwasher.

New York City

Malcolm had spent three weeks searching for Maggie in New York City. He and Gus had driven to every inn, hotel, bed and breakfast, motel in every borough of the Greater New York Region. And yet, he had not found her. With each dead end, Malcolm had sunk deeper into depression. The ugly truths that he'd been choosing to ignore were no longer unavoidable. Maggie had never been in New York, she had lied about where she was going. But why? What was *really* going on? He couldn't reconcile the strangeness of it all, and felt exhausted and defeated.

On the night before he departed from New York, he and Gus shared one last meal together. Malcolm had come to like Gus very much and considered him a friend by now. He enjoyed his frank, honest manner as well as his sense of humour.

"So what's next for you Malcolm?" Gus asked as they enjoyed their meal.

"I don't know, to be honest," Malcolm replied. "She clearly lied about coming here. But I don't know why," he went on. "I have no idea why. But I'm still determined to get answers."

Gus nodded as he stirred his coffee. He'd listened to Malcolm for the past 3 weeks talking about his relationship with Maggie, the ups and downs they'd gone through, the obstacles. And Gus had formed his own ideas and opinions, though he was unsure if he ought to share them with Malcolm. But it was clear that the young man was at a loss to understand what was going on; perhaps it was time for Gus to speak up.

"I have a theory, if you'd like to hear it," Gus said at last.

Malcolm looked up at him. "Yeah, shoot," he said.

Gus set his spoon down and looked at Malcolm, who was listening intently. "I think she was scared off," he said. "I think she was threatened, and told to leave."

Malcolm frowned, the thought of such a thing angering him immediately. "What makes you think that?" he demanded.

"Well, think of it," Gus went on. "You've said yourself that none of this make sense. The ring, her lying about being here, her phone being disconnected...it's pretty clear that there's something going on. A woman like Maggie doesn't walk away from a relationship without good cause. And if she's pregnant, then the reason would have to be a very serious one."

"Agreed," Malcolm replied. "But why do you think she was threatened? And by whom?"

"Think about it," Gus replied. "Who would love to see the two of you broken up?"

Malcolm knew at once who Gus was talking about. "My father," he said quietly.

Gus nodded. "Your father," he concurred. "Think about it, and tell me if I'm out of line suggesting such a thing."

Malcolm didn't want to think about it, he hated to think that his father could be so callous, so nefarious that he'd actually threaten Maggie in order to break them up. But how could he deny that it was completely plausible? He'd hated her from day one, saw her as nothing more than a gold digger.

"But how would I ever prove such a thing, even if it's true?" he asked at last.

Gus shook his head. "I don't know," he admitted. "I never said I had all the answers," he added with a smile.

"No, I don't have any either," Malcolm replied. "But I will, one way or another, I will."

Five

Malcolm left the Plaza Hotel the next morning with an ache in his heart. He had come to New York with such hope, certain that it was only a matter of time before he found Maggie. But he had not. And what was more, he had no idea where she was. The conversation he'd had with Gus the previous evening had occupied his thoughts a great deal; in fact, he'd slept very little because of it. In his mind he'd gone over each and every time his father had threatened to disinherit him because of his involvement with Maggie. *But would he really go this far??* Had he simply waited for Malcolm to leave the country to strike? *I have to find out...*he determined. *And if he has done something to her, then he's a dead man.*

The traffic on the interstate was heavy as Malcolm made his way north towards Boston. Cars, transport trucks, and all manner of vehicles filled every lane in both directions.

But the traffic was moving at least, for which Malcolm was grateful. He hated driving in such conditions, and knew that if he'd ever found himself in a position where he had to commute, he would surely go insane.

The steady drone of the traffic helped him to sort through his thoughts, most of them troubling. Gus's theory about his father predominated his mind, the possibility that Maggie's disappearance was his doing refused to be ignored. Malcolm had initially rejected the notion; granted, Jack didn't approve of Maggie, but would he really go so far as to force her out of

Malcolm's life? He couldn't accept that. He didn't want to accept that, for doing so would be to admit that Jack Sullivan was a cold-blooded monster. *He brutalized a pregnant woman...does it get much more cold blooded than that?* He reflected grimly. Malcolm frowned, conflicted by what he suspected to be true and what he wanted desperately not to be.

Brake lights began to pop up in front of him and the traffic slowed down. Eventually, inevitably, it stopped altogether.

"Fuck it," Malcolm grumbled as he geared down. There was no construction on the section of the highway he was on, so he reasoned that there must have been an accident. He came to a full stop, along with the cars on either side of him, and simply waited. "What's the fuckin' hold up," he muttered as he drummed his fingers impatiently on the steering wheel. Deciding to check his messages while he waited, he reached over and pulled his phone out of the glove compartment. There was a message from Dave asking how the search was going. Malcolm decided that conversation would be better in person, and replaced the phone in the glove compartment. He shut the compartment and glanced in the rear-view mirror as he did so. He was immediately alarmed to see an SUV heading towards him, seemingly unaware that traffic had stopped. Panic beset him as he realized that there was nothing he could do to get out of the vehicle's path. All he could do was hope that the driver noticed in time that the cars ahead were no longer moving. But the driver was too busy making an important business deal on his phone to notice until it was too late. He slammed on the brakes, but not soon enough to prevent him from rear-ending the black Ferrari in front of him, crumpling the car like it was an empty pop can.

Boston

"Malcolm and Maggie have split up?? Why?"

Irene looked at her husband, who simply scowled at the question.

"He cheated on her," Will spoke up. "That's why."

Quinn and Aidan exchanged a look.

"I can't believe he'd do that!" Quinn declared. "He loves her!"

"Apparently not," Mick said, helping himself to another piece of toast. "Seems Mr. Sullivan had us all fooled."

Irene sighed, hating that she'd essentially turned Maggie's family against the man she loved, a man who was as much a victim of all this as she was.

"So why isn't Maggie coming home then?" Aidan asked. "Why does she want to stay away?"

Mick looked at his wife, waiting for her answer. He'd yet to receive an explanation that made sense to him, and he wondered what she'd tell their sons.

"She's...well she's uncomfortable with the thought of living in the same city as him right now," she explained finally. "In time she'll..."

What aren't you telling us, Mum?" Will interrupted. "Cause I'm sure I'm not the only one who feels like you're holding back something."

Irene looked at her son, seeing in his eyes doubt. She had never lied to her children before, and hated herself for it. She hated the look in Will's eyes as he waited for her to answer his question.

"Maggie's pregnant," she said. "That's why she's staying away."

The shock wave was palpable as each male member of the family digested what they'd just been told.

"I *knew* that something like this would happen," Mick said. "God damn that son of a bitch! If I ever get my hands on him I'll rip him up in pieces. I swear to God!"

Irene sighed. "That would do nothing but land you in prison," she said quietly.

"Did he know before he went away?" Will asked.

"Aye, she's far enough along that he'd have known," Irene responded.

Will shook his head in disgust. "The bastard was screwing around even though he knew she was carrying his baby," he said.

"Babies," Irene told them. "She's expecting twins."

Mick said nothing, but stood up from the table and picked up his plate. Without a word he set them in the dishwasher and then left the room.

No one said anything as they finished their breakfast. Irene poked around with her fork, pushing the food around with no desire to eat it.

"Shouldn't she be here then?" Quinn asked finally. "I mean, won't she need help taking care of her babies?"

Irene looked at her son, wishing she had a convenient, easy answer for him. "She'll have help, love," she assured him. "Don't worry. I'll be helping her."

"You mean you're leaving again?" Aidan asked.

"Not for another week or so," Irene assured him. "I was planning on going back and forth."

"Where is she, Mum?" Will asked pointedly.

Irene looked at her son. "You know she wants that kept secret," she replied.

"Why?" Aidan asked.

"She's afraid Malcolm will find her," Irene replied.

"We wouldn't tell him," Quinn assured her. "Why would we?"

"I know you wouldn't," Irene said. "I'm only trying to honour her wishes. That's all."

While none of them liked it, the boys could see that their mother was in a very difficult position. Clearly she was very distraught about Maggie's situation. Will felt badly that he'd accused her of lying, for he could see, more so than his young brothers, that she was very conflicted about the entire state of affairs.

"She's lucky she has a mother like you," Will said, giving Irene a smile. "And I know she knows it too."

Irene smiled gratefully at him, her eyes misting over. "Thank you, Will," she said. "You have no idea how much I needed to hear that right now."

Will spent his Saturday as he did most Saturdays, tending bar at the Hart and Hound. He enjoyed it, but today he found that he was unable to stem the wave of memories that beset him there. Malcolm had been a regular here when he'd met Maggie, and Will felt sure that their love was real. It made the young man question everything he knew, or thought he knew, about relationships to see one such as theirs disintegrate like so much dust in the wind. His attention was diverted from his musings when a large, unfamiliar man sat down at the bar.

"Afternoon," Will said as he stepped up to where the man was seated. "What can I get you?"

"Scotch," the man grunted.

Will thought it was a little early in the day for the hard stuff, but decided not to say so. The man looked mean, and his mood was like a warning signal to back off or else. So he served up the drink, and watched the man down it with one pull.

"Gimme another."

Will frowned. "Are you sure about that, mate? That's pretty…"

"Just gimme the fuckin drink!"

Will wasn't about to get into an argument, and did as he was told. But as he set the second drink down, the man started talking to him.

"You got a woman?" he asked.

"Sure do," Will replied.

"You love her?"

"Yeah, I do," Will responded, a little weirded out by the turn of the conversation.

The man nodded. "I had a woman too," he said. "Treated her a like a queen. And you know what she did?"

Will shook his head.

"She dumped me. That's right, she dumped me for some asshole she works with. What the fuck is up with that?" he asked Will, the look in his eyes bespeaking his pain.

"Sorry mate," Will replied. "Women can be fickle."

"No shit," the man said, and then took a drink of his scotch. "This is good stuff," he commented. He looked around. "I think this'll be my new place, since I can't go to my own bar any more. *She* works there you see."

"I get it," Will replied.

The man looked back at Will, and then held out a meaty hand to him. "Hugh Wellman," he said.

"Will O'Toole," Will replied, shaking the man's hand. "Good to meet you."

"Yeah, you too," Hugh replied, looking at Will rather oddly. "You work for Sullivan, don't you?"

Will nodded his head, wondering how the man knew that. "You?"

"Yeah, I'm in administration," Hugh replied.

"Small world," Will commented with a smile. "Enjoy your drink, Hugh," he said, noticing more customers at the other end of the bar.

"Yeah, thanks," Hugh said. He watched Will walk away before pulling the bowl of nuts on the bar towards him and fishing around for the ones he liked. Cashews were his favourite.

The Country Club Golf Course

"Diversification, Jack, that's the name of the game."

Jack nodded, but said nothing as he focused on his shot. He waggled his club, took one last look toward the fairway, and then swung and hit the ball. He watched it as it flew straight and true. It was a good shot, for Jack was a good golfer. "You've been telling me that for years, Bill," he commented. "And I keep telling you, I don't trust my money to any goddamn foreigners. Good old American industry, that's the ticket."

"Yes but..." Bill stopped talking when he saw two uniformed police officers approaching them. "Jack, something going on?" he asked.

Jack looked over to where Bill's gaze had strayed and frowned. "Nothing I'm aware of," he commented as he set his club back in his bag. And then he began to worry. Had Maggie gone to the police? Were these officers here to arrest him for extortion? *She'll be sorry if she has,* he reflected as the officers approached. *She's a damn fool if she thinks she can best me.*

"Mr. Sullivan?" one of the officers asked. Jack noted that their uniforms were not that of the Boston PD, but rather Attleboro, a small town south west of Boston.

"That's me," Jack said. "What can I help you officers with?"

"We're here because of your son, sir," the second officer said. "I'm afraid he's been in a serious car accident."

Jack's immediate reaction was complete silence as he stared at the officers. "Which one?" he asked finally.

"I'm sorry?"

"Which son! Which one of my sons was in an accident," Jack explained impatiently.

"Malcolm sir," the first officer said. "It was Malcolm that was in the accident."

Jack nodded, feeling his heart starting to do double time. "Is he...he's not..."

"He survived the crash sir, but is in serious condition at South Shore Hospital," Jack was told. He nodded his understanding. He looked at his golfing companion, unable to process what he'd just been told.

"Go Jack," Bill told him, seeing that his friend was in a state of shock. "I'll take care of your clubs and settle up. Just go. Malcolm needs you."

"If you'd like we can escort you to the hospital, Mr. Sullivan," one of the officers offered.

"Yes, yes let's do that," Jack decided. He followed the officers off of the course and to their cruiser. He climbed in the backseat and pulled out his cell phone, sending a quick message to Rob and then Tom. *Malcolm's been in an accident. Meet me at South Shore Hospital.*

"What happened?" Jack asked the officers as they pulled out of the parking lot. "Was he drinking?"

The officers exchanged a look. "No, the accident was not caused by him," one of the officers informed him. "He was rear ended by someone talking on a cell phone."

Jack frowned. "How bad was it?"

"Well your son's car is a pile of junk," the second officer informed him. "So pretty bad."

"He's lucky to be alive from what we saw," the other officer commented. "Guess somebody up there likes him," she added.

Jack said nothing in response, and simply looked out the window as the police cruiser sped towards South Shore Hospital.

Six

om Sullivan drove to the hospital with his twin brother, and together they headed down the freeway towards the small hospital where their younger brother was in critical condition. They had very few details about the accident, only that it was very serious.

"I just hope Maggie wasn't with him when it happened," Tom commented as Rob drove.

"Good chance she was," Rob replied. "Dad didn't say."

Tom frowned. "He hates Maggie," he reminded his twin. "He wouldn't care if she was in the car."

Rob nodded. "To tell you the truth I'm surprised by how worried Dad sounded," he said. "It's not like he's ever really cared about Malcolm."

"No," Tom agreed. "But he *is* his son. Even the worst father would be worried."

Rob said nothing, but knew that Tom was right. "I've been thinking a lot about what Maggie said to us," he said. "About us being such shitty brothers."

"She never said that," Tom pointed out.

"Not in so many words, but that was the general sentiment," Rob replied. "She's right. We have been shitty to him. I just hope we get the chance to make it up to him," he said quietly.

Jack was in the waiting area of the small hospital's emergency room when his twin sons arrived.

"How is Malcolm? Have you seen him yet?" Tom asked.

"No, they're still with him," Jack replied. "Goddamn doctors won't tell me anything," he added.

"Was Maggie with him?" Rob asked.

"No, he was alone," Jack replied. "Though I blame her for this."

Tom frowned. "Why??"

Jack realized that he'd said too much, and didn't answer his son's question. "Do either of you know what he was doing down here?" he asked.

"Not a clue," Rob asked. "I haven't talked to him since he returned from Australia, have you?" he asked Tom.

"No," Tom replied. "How long have you been waiting here?" he asked Jack.

"Ten minutes," Jack replied. "The officers told me that Malcolm was brought in around 9."

Rob looked at his watch. "So he's been here over an hour," he commented. "I wonder what they're doing in there."

"Trying to save him," Tom said quietly, and for a moment all three fell silent as they contemplated what could be happening on the other side of the double doors that separated them from the ER department.

"Well this is unacceptable," Jack decided, walking over to the nurses' station. Tom and Rob followed, figuring if anyone could get some answers, it was their father.

"I want to know the condition of my son," Jack said to the nurse who was seated at the desk. "He's been in a car accident, and I haven't been told anything."

The nurse looked up at him. "His name?"

"Sullivan, Malcolm Sullivan," Jack replied. "He was brought in about 9 I'm told."

"Let me check," she told him, and stood up to confer with another nurse nearby. Jack waited, his patience wearing thin, as the two nurses talked for a few moments before the one he'd addressed returned to him.

"The doctors are doing everything they can to ..."

"Don't give me meaningless platitudes," Jack snapped. "I want to see my son!"

The nurse scowled, trying hard to bite her tongue. "Sir, you can't see him until the doctors have finished evaluating him," she said firmly. "I don't know what else I can say."

Jack scowled, and bit back a response. He turned to his sons. "I want to get him transferred to Mass General," he said, loudly enough for the nurse to hear.

"Dad, come and sit down," Tom suggested, seeing that his father was getting very worked up. "There's nothing we can do right now but wait. The doctors will let us know how he is when they can."

Jack wasn't happy about it, but decided to go along with Tom's suggestion for the time being.

It wasn't too much longer before a doctor in surgical garb approached Jack and his sons. They all stood up immediately once they realized that the moment of truth was upon them.

"Mr. Sullivan?"

"Yes, I'm Jack Sullivan," Jack said.

"Laurence Ryan," the doctor said, holding out a hand to Jack.

"How is Malcolm?" Jack asked, shaking the doctor's hand briefly.

"He's alive," Dr. Ryan replied. "Quite frankly he's lucky. If it hadn't been for the airbag, he might not have made it."

"Is he going to be okay, then?" Rob asked.

"It's too soon to say for sure," Ryan replied. "He's currently listed in critical condition," he went on. "There has been significant internal damage resulting in a lot of internal bleeding. His spleen was severely damaged, and we've removed it. However, the rest of his body needs to heal, and we've placed him in a coma in order to give him that chance."

"He's in a coma?" Tom asked.

"Yes," Ryan replied. "With trauma of this nature it's standard procedure."

Jack listened as the doctor described his son's injuries, as Tom and Rob asked questions. He wasn't quite sure how he felt, for there was an uncomfortable numbness inside of him that was far too reminiscent of the day that Malcolm's mother had died. He remembered all too well standing by, watching her slip away, helpless to stop it. Would he lose their son in the same manner?

"I want to see him," Jack stated.

Ryan nodded. "Very well," he replied. "Come with me."

Jack, Rob and Tom followed the physician through the double doors and down a corridor a short way until they arrived at the room where Malcolm had been brought. None of them were prepared for what awaited him.

"Sweet Jesus," Tom muttered as the three men stood at the foot of Malcolm's bed. He was on life support with a breathing tube inserted into his mouth. His face was swollen and bruised, almost unrecognizably so. It was shocking to see the energetic, outgoing young man so still, so vulnerable.

"I want him transferred to Mass General," Jack said. "Their facilities are the best in the state."

Dr. Ryan did not react openly to the veiled insult, but felt it nonetheless. "I understand your desire to do so," he said. "However it's not safe to do so at this point. You would jeopardize his life if you tried to move him now."

Jack frowned. "When will it be safe, then?"

"We'll keep him in a coma for no more than 48 hours," Dr. Ryan replied. "However, at this point it's impossible to predict what his condition will be once we revive him."

"We don't want to put him in danger," Rob spoke up. "If moving him will do that, then maybe we ought to keep him here for now, Dad," he suggested.

Jack begrudgingly concurred. "But as soon as it's safe to do so, I want him transferred."

"Understood," Ryan replied. "If you'll excuse me."

"One of us needs to contact Maggie," Rob said once the doctor had left them.

"Yes," Tom agreed. "But I don't think a phone call is quite appropriate, do you?"

"No," Rob replied. "Where would she be right now? Is she working at her family's pub?"

"I have no idea," Tom replied. "But if she isn't her family could tell us where she is. I'll go right now and talk to them."

"Okay," Rob said. "I'll stay here."

Jack had remained silent during the exchange between the two brothers, for he knew for a fact that they would not find Maggie at her family's pub. But he kept his mouth closed, not wanting to show his hand, not even to his sons.

Rob had noticed Jack's silence, and mistook it for deep concern for Malcolm. He walked over to where Jack sat beside Malcolm's bed, and put a hand on his shoulder. "You okay, Dad?" he asked.

"No," Jack replied. "I'm not. I won't be until your brother is out of this place."

Rob frowned. "He's being well taken care of," he pointed out. "The doctors saved his life."

But Jack didn't reply, and continued to watch his youngest son fight for his life.

Tom left the hospital and headed up to Boston. He felt knotted up inside as he considered the task before him. Maggie would undoubtedly be devastated, for Tom knew how much she loved Malcolm. It wouldn't be easy for her to learn of his accident, but she needed to know.

Will was at the bar when Tom arrived. He frowned when he recognized him as being one of Malcolm's brothers, and wondered how he had the nerve to come to the Hart.

"It's Will, right?" Tom asked as he stood at the bar.

"That's right," Will replied. "You're...."

"Tom Sullivan. Malcolm's brother," Tom said. "We met at the graduation party he threw."

"I remember," Will replied. "What brings you here?"

"I was hoping to talk to your sister," Tom said. "Is she here?"

Will frowned. "No she's not," he replied. "Your brother should know that."

Tom didn't understand the meaning of Will's comment, nor his hostility. "I need to talk to Maggie," he said. "It's urgent."

"Did Malcolm send you?" Will asked. "Cause if you did, I have a message for him. You tell that son-of-a bitch..."

"Malcolm is in a coma," Tom interjected. "He's been in a very serious car accident. *Now* can you tell me where I can find your sister?"

Will was too shocked to reply for a moment, for Tom's news was so unexpected that he didn't even know how to respond. Malcolm had been a good friend until recently, until he'd betrayed the trust of the woman he claimed to love.

"I'm sorry," Will said finally. "Really sorry to hear it. But I can't tell you where Maggie is. The truth is, I have no idea where she is."

Tom frowned. "You have no idea where your own sister is?" he asked, the disbelief clear in his voice.

"Nope," Will replied, folding his arms over his chest. "You see she and Malcolm have split up, or didn't you know that?"

Tom's eyes widened. "Split up?? Since when? Why?"

"Why? I'll tell you why," Will replied. "He cheated on her. That's why. The bastard cheated on his *pregnant* fiancée."

Tom stared at Will, unable to process what he'd just been told. "Maggie is pregnant??" he asked.

"Yeah she is," Will replied. "With twins. And the father of her babies was screwing around on her when he was in Australia. Pretty nice, eh?"

"I...I don't know what to say," Tom said. "I was so sure that he'd changed," he went on. "I can't believe he'd throw away what he had with Maggie."

"Well he did," Will replied. "Look, I'm sorry about his accident, but he'd better stay the hell away from my sister if he knows what's good for him."

Tom frowned. "He has a right to his children," he pointed out. "No matter what he's done, he's still their father."

Will had to concede the point. "I suppose," he said. "But if he has any decency in him, he'll leave her alone."

"I'm sure he will support them financially," Tom said. "Assuming of course he survives," he added quietly.

Will felt badly for Tom, for it was clear that he was very concerned about his brother. He knew that were one of his brothers in the same condition as Malcolm he would be inconsolable.

"I hope he does," Will said. "Truly I do."

Tom could tell that the young man was being honest, and offered him a small smile. "If there's any way of letting her know....I think she ought to know, regardless of what happened between them."

"I'll do what I can," Will said.

"I appreciate it," Tom said. And with that he turned and left the pub, leaving Will alone to consider the ramifications of the news he'd just learned.

Will was not alone in his ruminations. Tom was very contemplative as he drove back to the hospital. He wasn't sure why, but he didn't believe what Will had told him. He had seen Malcolm and Maggie together; he'd seen with his own eyes the devotion his brother had for this young woman. At one time, it would have been easy to believe that Malcolm could cheat on a woman he was involved with. But not now, not any more. Malcolm *had* changed, and the more he thought about it, the less sense it made to him. *So why has she ended their relationship?* The fact that she was pregnant was troubling to him as well, for he knew firsthand what grief Malcolm would endure from their father because of that. Tom's own wife had been pregnant when they'd been married, and Jack had harangued Tom for weeks because of it. Given the fact that Jack already had little regard for Malcolm, he would undoubtedly make his life hell should he know that Malcolm had impregnated Maggie, a woman that Jack had decided was all wrong for him.

Rob was in the elevator lobby on his cell phone when Tom arrived back at the hospital. He was speaking to his wife, explaining what had happened. Tom had phoned his own wife in the car. She had not been happy to hear that he was planning on staying at the hospital for the rest of the day, but Tom decided that he didn't care.

"Any change?" Tom asked as Rob ended his call.

"No," Rob replied. "I don't want him to be alone," he said, glancing back towards the doors to the critical care unit.

"Me neither," Tom agreed. "Maybe we should split the time, you know, I'll stay until midnight, you come back then or something like that. Shifts, you know."

Rob nodded. "Yes, let's do that," he said. "I'm going to cancel my appointments for the next few days. I suggest you do the same."

"Good idea," Tom said. "Is Dad still in with him?"

"Yeah," Rob replied. "He told me he has a business trip coming up in Seattle," he said. "Can you believe that?"

"Yes," Tom replied. "I'm surprised he's shown as much concern has he has over Malcolm, to tell you the truth," he said.

"Me too," Rob said. "I tell you, if he leaves and goes on some goddamn business trip..."

"He will," Tom assured him. "You know damn well that he will. Business comes first, Tom. Always has, always will."

Rob frowned. "Are we like him, Tom? I mean, when I think about how we've treated Malcolm....are we like him? Are we going to be like him with our kids when they're grown up?"

"No," Tom replied. "We're not him."

Rob nodded. "Come on," he said. "Let's get something to eat before we go back."

The Hart and Hound

Irene and Mick were in the kitchen when Will decided it was time to let them know about his visit from Tom Sullivan.

"Mum, Dad, there's something I need to tell you," Will said.

His parents looked up from what they were doing. Each of them could see that there was something greatly troubling their son.

"What is it?" Mick asked.

"Tom Sullivan was just here," Will told them. "One of Malcolm's brothers."

"What was he doing here?" Irene asked.

"Looking for Maggie," Will replied. "I told him that I didn't know where she was, told him about how they were split up. He was pretty shocked."

"Why was he looking for Maggie?" Mick asked. "Did his brother send him?"

"I thought that too," Will replied. "But it was to tell her something, something pretty bad. Malcolm's in the hospital. Had a car accident, pretty bad one too. Poor bastard's in a coma."

"Pity that," Mick said. He looked at Irene. "Will you tell her when you go back to see her?"

"I...I'm not sure what to do," she admitted. "If I tell her she may want to see him."

"But if you don't, and she finds out from someone else, she'll be mighty sore at you," Mick pointed out.

Irene nodded. "Aye, you're right," she said. "I suppose she ought to be told, then."

Will left them to return to the bar, and once he was gone, Mick turned to his wife. "Where is she, Irene?" he asked. "She's with Pat and Noreen, isn't she?"

Irene sighed. "Yes," she replied. "But you can't tell anyone, not even the lads," she told him.

"I won't tell anyone," Mick said. "But I know there's more to this than you're telling me, isn't there?"

Irene was tired of the lying, tired of hiding, and was sorely tempted to tell her husband the whole truth. Surely he had a right to know, after all; it was his son whose life was threatened, his daughter whose life had been shattered.

"There is," she admitted. "And it's so far reaching that I'm afraid if I tell you bad things will happen. So please trust me, Mick. And pray that everything works out in the end."

"Okay, I'll leave it alone," he told her. "For now. But I won't be content to do so forever, Irene. I promise you that."

Seven

*M*aggie looked at her watch once more, willing it to be 9:15, the time her mother's bus was due to arrive. She was tired, for she'd been on her feet from 6AM until 4PM, with very little break. As her pregnancy progressed, she was finding it more and more difficult. But then, just recently, she'd felt the first fluttering movements of her babies. It was an astonishing feeling, like the fluttering of butterfly wings, and it made her fall even deeper in love with her twins. The way she saw it, the three of them were in this together. And once they were born, as difficult as it would be, she knew that she'd never feel alone.

"You didn't need to come down here at this time of night," Irene said as Maggie drove her to their cousins' house.

"You should be in bed by now. I could have taken a cab."

"I wanted to meet you," Maggie replied. "I've missed you, Mum."

Irene smiled. "I've missed you too. Your bump is bigger, by the way."

Maggie ran a hand over her abdomen. "I've felt them move," she said. "What an incredible feeling that is."

"Yes it is," Irene agreed. "Your Da and brothers send their love. I told them about the babies, I hope you're okay with that."

"Well they're going to find out eventually," Maggie said. "How did Da take the news?"

"Not well," Irene told her. "He's very upset about all this, love. Especially since he thinks you and Malcolm have split up."

Maggie frowned. "Didn't they wonder why?" she asked.

"They did," Irene said.

"So what did you tell them?" she asked.

"You're not going to like what I told them," she said.

Maggie frowned. "What did you tell them?"

"I told them that Malcolm cheated on you when he was in Australia," Irene said. "I'm sorry love, but there was nothing else that they would accept as a valid reason for you breaking up with him."

Maggie said nothing for several minutes, and Irene could see that she was upset, but the way she saw it, there had been no other options.

"I can only imagine what they must think of him after hearing that," said Maggie finally. "Poor Malcolm! None of this was his doing, and now he'll be torn to pieces!"

"You can't concern yourself with what others think," Irene said. "You have your own situation to deal with."

Maggie nodded, but said nothing. She knew that her mother was right, but it didn't make her feel any better. Her life was a mess, plain and simple, all thanks to Jack Sullivan.

They drove in silence for the remainder of the trip, each of them lost in their own thoughts.

The house was quiet when they arrived, and both were ready to go to bed. Irene unpacked while Maggie got ready for bed. Irene had decided that Maggie needed to be told about Malcolm's accident, but at this point, had no idea how to tell her. Indeed, her insides were knotted as she considered the words she'd use to do so, knowing no matter how carefully she chose them, they would have the same effect on her daughter.

"You must be knackered after that long ride," said Maggie as she entered their small room. She brushed her hair as she sat down on the edge of her bed with a yawn. But when she noticed the look on her mother's face, she stopped brushing. "Something wrong?" she asked.

"I'm afraid so," Irene replied. "And there's no easy way to tell you, believe me I've been trying to think of one."

Maggie felt her mouth grow dry. "Tell me what?"

"Malcolm's been in a car accident. He's in critical condition."

The hairbrush fell with a soft thud to the carpet. Maggie felt her insides tighten, her mouth turn to sandpaper. "When? How? What happened?"

"I don't know all the details," said Irene. "His brother Tom came into the Hart. He wanted to talk to you, to tell you in person. Will spoke to him, told him he didn't know where you were. "

Maggie dropped her face into her hands and burst into tears. It was simply too much.

Irene went to her at once, sitting beside her and putting her arms around her. "I'm sorry, love, so sorry!"

"I don't know how much more I can take, Mum!" Maggie said. "How much can one person endure?"

"I know, you've had so much to contend with," Irene commiserated. "It's not fair."

"No, it isn't fair," Maggie agreed. "I have to go to him, Mum - I need to see him! What if he dies??"

"Now Maggie you have to think straight," Irene cautioned. "I know you're upset, you're hurting; but you have to remember why you came here, what's at stake."

Maggie looked at her mother, not wanting to hear what she was saying. She was hurting, she was tired, and she needed Malcolm. She needed to look after him, to make sure he was okay.

"This wouldn't have happened if I hadn't left him," she said.

Irene frowned. "If you hadn't left him your brother would be dead," she said.

That was what Maggie needed to hear to bring her back to the present. As much as she wanted, needed to go to him, she couldn't without jeopardizing Will's life. There was no doubt that Jack Sullivan would make true his threats, of that she was certain.

"You're right. I can't see him," Maggie relented at last. She closed her eyes as the tears rolled down her face. She felt defeated and helpless, and simply leaned her head on her mother's shoulder.

"Didn't you tell me that Carrie was working at Massachusetts General?" Irene said.

Maggie nodded.

"Then perhaps you could contact her, find out how he's doing," Irene suggested. "You could trust her with your secret, I'm sure of it."

Maggie considered this for a moment. "I don't know," she said. "What if she tells Dave? And what if he tells Malcolm?"

"I'm sure if you explained the situation, told her what Jack threatened to do, she would keep quiet," Irene said. "Don't you?"

Maggie was torn between her desperate need to learn of Malcolm's condition and her terror of Malcolm finding out what had happened, and the fall out of this discovery.

"Yes," she decided. "I think that she's totally trustworthy."

"So give her a call tomorrow," Irene said. "She can let you know how he is, I'm sure."

"Okay," Maggie said. She stood up to fetch a tissue.

"Well I'm for bed," Irene said, standing up. "And I think you ought to get to sleep as well."

Maggie nodded as she blew her nose. "I'll try," she said. "Not sure I'll be able to sleep now."

"All you can do is try," Irene said. "That's all any of us can ever do, love."

Boston

Carrie Robinson stirred cream into her coffee in the small nurses' lounge. She yawned, cursing herself once more for letting Dave talk her into going to a late movie the previous night. Working 12 hour shifts took a lot of energy, and at the moment she had very little.

"Yeah I heard all about it," sighed one of the older nurses. "We'll need to polish the silver and roll out the carpet for this one."

"Oh please," another said. "He won't be treated any different from any other patient on this floor."

"Dream on, Audrey."

"What's going on?" Carrie asked.

"Oh, there's some big shot's son being transferred here tomorrow morning," Audrey said. "And admin has told us that we're to be on our toes since the father is on the board of directors. As if we'd be anything but," she grumbled. "I hate that political crap."

"Who is it?" Carrie asked.

"Sullivan," one of the other nurses told her. "Malcolm Sullivan. Had a car accident on the freeway near Attleboro."

Carrie's widened in shock. "Malcolm was in a car accident?"

"You know him?" one of the nurses asked.

Carrie nodded, too stunned to explain how. "How seriously is he hurt?" she asked.

"Pretty seriously," one of the nurses said. "He's being airlifted here."

"Was he alone?" she asked, horrified to think that her pregnant best friend might have been in the car with him.

"As far as we know," Audrey told her.

"How do you know him?" another asked.

"He's engaged to my best friend," Carrie replied, though, in reality, she had no idea if that was still true.

"Sorry hon," Audrey said, putting a hand on Carrie's shoulder. "She must be going through hell right now."

Carrie nodded, not wanting to admit that she hadn't seen or heard from her best friend in weeks, and that she in fact had no idea where she was.

"I'm sure she is," Carrie said quietly, and then fell silent as she pondered the implications of what she'd just learned.

Antigonish, Nova Scotia

Maggie slept very little after learning of Malcolm's accident, and what little sleep she did manage was riddled with nightmares about him.

She'd thought long and hard about her mother's suggestion to contact Carrie, and had decided that she would do it. Carrie was working in the trauma unit of Mass General, that much she knew. Whether or not she would be able to tell her about Malcolm's condition remained to be seen.

Work seemed to drag on forever, with the worry of Malcolm weighing heavily on her mind. *Should I call him?* She wondered over and over. *What if he dies not knowing where I am or why I left? How would I ever live with myself? And what would I tell his children?* She pushed such thoughts from her mind. Malcolm would *not* die: he was strong, and young and in great physical condition. He would be fine, she resolved, determined not to let negative thoughts enter her mind.

By six o'clock all the children at the day care had gone home, and Maggie was dead tired. After she'd finished cleaning the small kitchen and prepping the meals for the next day, she sat down and pulled out her cell phone. With heart thudding in her chest, she entered Carrie's phone number, hoping that she'd catch her alone. *What if she's with Dave?? What if he finds out everything and goes to Malcolm? What if...*

"Hello?"

Maggie was unprepared for the emotional onslaught hearing her best friend's voice would bring, and for a moment she couldn't find her voice.

"Hello? Is there somebody there?"

"Carrie, it's Maggie."

Silence for a moment or two, which felt like hours to Maggie.

"Oh my God!" Carrie said. "Where are you?? What's going on? Are you okay?"

"I'm fine," Maggie replied. "It's so good to hear your voice!"

"Same here! I've been so worried! Where are you, Maggie? Why haven't you contacted anyone?"

"It's a very long story," Maggie said. "Where are you right now? Are you alone? Can you talk freely?"

"I'm at home, just got off work," Carrie told her. "And I'm alone. Why all the questions?"

"You'll understand why I'm being so cautious after I tell you everything," Maggie said.

Carrie listened in shocked silence as Maggie related the events of her encounter with Jack Sullivan several weeks earlier. By the end of Maggie's narrative, she had tears rolling down her face.

"Maggie, I...I don't know what to say," Carrie said. "Surely to God the police can do something!"

"Even if he were to be arrested, he would still have people ready to carry out his plan," Maggie assured her. "He has created an airtight plan, Carrie. I had no choice but to do as he says."

"And Malcolm knows none of this," Carrie said.

"He can never know."

Carrie frowned. "Maggie, you need to know something. Malcolm has been in a serious car accident."

"I know, my mother told me," replied Maggie quietly. "That's why I decided to call you," she went on. "I was hoping you could tell me something about his condition."

"I can't," Carrie said. "At least not yet."

"Why not?"

"He hasn't arrived at Mass yet," Carrie said. "He's being transferred here tomorrow."

"I see," Maggie said, disappointed. "Would you please call me when you know something?"

"Of course," Carrie replied. "I hate that you're in this situation, Megs. I hate that bastard that calls himself Malcolm's father."

"So do I," Maggie replied. "But you have to promise me that you'll not say a word of any of this to anyone," she went on. "Especially Dave."

"I promise," Carrie said. "If there's anything I can do, anything at all, please ask, okay?"

Maggie smiled. "Thank you," she replied.

"How are the babies?"

"They've started moving," Maggie replied. "It's an incredible feeling. I only wish..." she stopped, not wishing to finish the sentence, knowing what unwanted emotions doing so would herald.

"This will all work out, Maggie," Carrie said. "It has to. It's so unfair! You two belong together!"

"I know, but right now I don't know how that's possible. Jack Sullivan has won."

Carrie had no response for this, for it seemed that Maggie was correct. "Don't give up, Maggie," she said. "Sometimes when it seems like things are absolutely hopeless, something unexpected happens to change everything. Life's funny that way."

Maggie didn't want to disagree with her friend, but the past several weeks had drained away any traces of hope she had that things would work out. Malcolm's accident was the last straw, one last defeat in a long line of defeats that Maggie was struggling against.

"I have to go," Maggie said. "Please call me when you learn something about Malcolm."

"I will if you promise me something," Carrie responded.

Maggie immediately grew wary. "What's that?"

"Promise me that you'll keep in touch with me," Carrie said. "I've missed you so much, and I'm worried now that I know everything. Promise me we'll keep in touch."

"I can promise that," Maggie said. "I've missed you too, so much," she said, her voice breaking.

Carrie heard it, and felt her own emotions rising. "I love you Megs," she said. "Please take care of yourself and those sweet babies."

"I love you too," Maggie replied, wiping tears from her cheek. "And we will be in touch. I promise."

Eight

*M*alcolm was slowly weaned off of the life support, and, two days after he'd been admitted into the hospital, he was awake. His two brothers were present in the room when he opened his eyes for the first time in forty-eight hours.

"How are you doing, little brother?" Tom asked from the left side of his bed.

Malcolm was disoriented, and unsure of what had happened to land him in the hospital. "What happened?" he asked, alarmed at how much effort was required simply to utter two words.

"You were in a car accident," Rob said, from the right side of the bed. "A really bad one."

Malcolm turned his head slowly to look at him. "How?"

"Some ass-hole who was talking on his cell phone rear ended you on the freeway," Rob told him. "Your car was totalled."

"But don't worry," Tom spoke up. "Dad made sure the insurance paid for a new one. You can pick it up once you get out of the hospital."

Malcolm nodded, and looked around the room briefly. "Dad's not here?" he asked.

Tom and Rob exchanged a quick look.

"He had a meeting in Seattle," Rob told him. "He *was* here," he added.

Malcolm sighed, not at all surprised that his father would chose a business meeting over him. "How long have I been here?"

"You've been asleep for two days," Tom told him. "They're going to move you to Mass General this morning. Dad wanted you there, figured it's a better facility."

"I see," Malcolm said, closing his eyes. He felt exhausted, weak and disoriented. How was it he remembered nothing of the accident? All he remembered was leaving New York with a sense of hopelessness, having not found Maggie despite scouring the whole area.

"Malcolm, I went to the Hart and Hound," Tom told him. "I went to tell Maggie what had happened to you."

Malcolm's eyes snapped open. "You did?"

Tom nodded. "I didn't see her, but I spoke to her brother, Will. He told me something I'm having trouble believing. He told me that you two split up."

Malcolm frowned. "He told you *that?*"

"Yeah he did," Tom replied. But before he could continue, the doctor entered the room.

"Well Malcolm, how are you feeling?" Doctor Ryan asked.

"Been better," Malcolm replied.

Ryan smiled. "Yes I'm sure you have," he said. "But you're far better than you were two days ago, I assure you."

"How much longer will I be out of commission?" Malcolm asked.

"Not long," Ryan replied as he began listening to Malcolm's heart. "You're going to need some rehab to regain your strength, but you're in good shape. I don't think it'll be long before you can go home."

Malcolm nodded and let the doctor continue his examination. He looked at his brother, wanting to question him more about what Will had said. Is *that* what was going on? But why would she do such a thing? Why now, when they were engaged and expecting twins? *She loves me...she would never end our relationship...there has to be some mistake...*

"Well it looks to me like you're strong enough to be moved," Dr. Ryan said once he'd concluded his examination.

"Thanks for everything you've done, Doctor," Rob said, standing up. "We all appreciate the excellent care Malcolm has had while he's been here."

"You're quite welcome," Ryan replied. "I'll have Malcolm's records transferred to the trauma unit at Mass General right away," he said.

"Thank you," Tom said.

"Now tell me what Will said," Malcolm asked once the doctor has left the room.

"He told me that you'd cheated on Maggie while you were in Australia," Tom said. "And that's why she left you."

Malcolm felt as though someone had reached into his chest and ripped his heart out. "He said I *cheated on her?*" he cried. "I would *never* cheat on her! Why would he think such a thing?"

Both of Malcolm's brothers were greatly relieved that Will's information had been erroneous; but it only opened up a whole slew of questions.

"Where is she?" Rob asked. "You don't know, do you?"

Malcolm shook his head. "That's why I was in New York," he said. "I spent almost a week looking for her, thinking she was there shopping with her mother. But she wasn't. And now....why would she think such a thing? And why would she just take off without asking me if it's true?"

"I don't know," Rob replied. "It seems like there's more going on than you or anybody else knows, Malcolm."

Malcolm nodded, remembering what Gus had suggested. But he said nothing to his brothers, at least not for the moment. He needed to talk to Will O'Toole before he did anything, and find out where his information had come from. And somehow, some way, he'd get to the truth of it all.

Boston - Massachusetts General Hospital

Tension was high as the trauma unit welcomed their newest patient. Private nurses had been hired by the patient's wealthy father.

Carrie knew of course who the patient was, but being new on staff, she wasn't deemed experienced enough to care for the son of a Board member. However, that did not stop her from visiting Malcolm when she had a break.

Malcolm was sleeping when Carrie stepped into his room. She looked at his face, still bruised from the accident. She could only imagine what he'd been going through since Maggie had disappeared, and now this accident. *Why do bad things happen to good people?* She thought. *It just isn't right!*

"What are you doing in here?"

Carrie turned to see the head nurse in charge of Malcolm's case, a rather beefy woman named Marion, standing there, arms akimbo.

"He's a friend of mine," Carrie explained. "I just wanted to see how he is."

Marion's face softened a little, and she approached Malcolm's bed. "He's in fair shape," she said. "Looks to me like he was pretty lucky," she commented.

"So he's going to be okay?" Carrie asked.

The woman looked at Carrie and nodded. Given that it was strictly against every rule in the book for her to discuss Malcolm's prognosis with her, she felt it was okay to do that much.

"Is it okay if I visit him?" Carrie asked. "He's engaged to my best friend."

"A short visit," Marion said. "I'll give you five minutes," she said and then left the room.

Carrie was pleasantly surprised by the woman's compassion, but decided to take advantage of it nonetheless. Malcolm's eyes started to open as she watched from beside his bed. She gave him a smile when he looked at her.

"Carrie?"

"Hi there," she said. "I heard you had a bit of an accident."

"You could say so," Malcolm replied. "You're working here now?"

Carrie nodded. "Have been since graduation," she said.

"Nice," he said. "Have you spoken with Maggie lately?"

"As a matter of fact I have," Carrie said. "Just the other day."

Malcolm's eyes widened. "You did? Is she okay? Where is she?"

Carrie sighed. "She wouldn't tell me where she is," she said. "But she heard that you'd been in an accident and was crazy worried."

Malcolm looked up at her, her words not making sense to him. "If she's so worried, why doesn't she come to see me?"

"She has her reasons," Carrie told him. "Take my word for it."

Malcolm frowned. "She thinks I cheated on her," he said. "Doesn't she?"

"No! Why would you think that?" Carrie said.

"Will told my brother that," he said. "And that's the reason she's left me."

Carrie didn't know what to say. Why would Will say such a thing?

"She never said anything like that to me," Carrie said, choosing her words carefully. "I'm sure she knows you would never do that to her."

"Then why is she gone? Why has she left me?"

The look in his eyes made Carrie want to tell him everything, assure him that Maggie still loved him beyond words; but she knew that she couldn't do that. She had promised Maggie that she'd keep her secrets, and she meant to do just that.

"She has her reasons," she said again.

Malcolm could tell that she was holding something back; she knew why Maggie had left, but had undoubtedly been sworn to secrecy.

"So does she plan on letting me see my children?" he asked in a bitter tone that made Carrie cringe.

"Malcolm, I..."

"Never mind," he said, looking away from her. "I thought she loved me," he said quietly. "But clearly she doesn't. She was just waiting for me to leave the country before leaving me."

Carrie was about to assure him that she did love him, that being apart from him was tearing her apart; but given the fact that she could off no explanation for her disappearance, it seemed pointless.

"I'm sorry," she said finally. "So *so* sorry."

Malcolm said nothing, nor did he look at her. She left him without saying another word, fighting back tears as she did so.

Malcolm stared at the window, watching the summer rain as it pelted against the glass. He couldn't remember a time when he'd felt so low. All the things that had made his life worth living, all the things that made him happy and given his life meaning were gone. *Maybe it would have been better if that crash had killed me*, he thought morosely. *Maybe I'd be better off if it had...*

"You're awake!"

Malcolm turned to see his brother Tom enter the room, a smile on his face.

"Yeah, just woke up a few minutes ago," Malcolm said.

"How are you feeling?" Tom asked as he walked over to the bed.

"Okay I guess," Malcolm said. "Physically at least. I just had a visit from Maggie's friend Carrie."

"Oh? Did she tell you something upsetting?" Tom asked, pulling up a chair.

"She didn't tell me anything," Malcolm said. "Not a fucking thing. And I know she knows where Maggie is. She just won't tell me."

Tom frowned. "Did you tell her what Maggie's brother said?"

Malcolm nodded. "She didn't know anything about that," he said. "And was pretty shocked when I told her."

Tom shook his head. "This is getting really strange, Malcolm," he said. "None of it adds up."

Malcolm looked up at his brother. "I have to wonder if Dad is behind all this," he said, deciding to trust Tom.

"What do you mean, behind this?" Tom asked.

"I mean he said something to Maggie, I don't know what, but enough to make her leave town," Malcolm explained.

Tom frowned. "Why would he do that?"

"He hates her, for one thing," Malcolm said. "And he's convinced that she's a gold digger."

"That's ridiculous," Tom said. "She's a lovely young woman." He stopped as he remembered something. "You know, he said it was her fault that you'd had the accident," he said. "I didn't think anything of it at the time, but now I have to wonder if there was more to his comment than I'd originally thought."

Malcolm nodded, more convinced than ever that his father was behind the strange circumstances that had ripped Maggie from him. "But how do I prove it?"

"Not sure. It's not like he'd admit it," Tom said. "I think the only way you'll find out is to find Maggie."

"You're right," Malcolm replied. "Trouble is, I have no idea where she is."

Tom nodded. "That is a problem," he said. "Maybe if you talk to her brother you could learn something."

"Fat chance. He thinks I cheated on her, remember?" Malcolm said.

"Yes, but sometimes people give information away when they're emotionally charged," Tom said. "I see it all the time in the court room."

"I guess it's worth a shot," Malcolm replied.

"And when Dad gets back, I'll talk to him," Tom said. "I have a way of getting people to spill their secrets without them even knowing they're doing it."

Malcolm smiled. "You must be one hell of a lawyer," he commented.

Tom smiled.

Nine

It was quite late in the evening when Carrie called to give Maggie an update on Malcolm. Maggie had thought of little else, and had found it difficult to get through her work day.

"So how is he?"

"He's doing okay," Carrie told her. "It was a pretty bad accident, but he's out of the woods now."

"Did you get to talk to him?"

"For a few minutes, yeah."

"How is he?"

Carrie sighed. "How do you think he is, Megs? He's worried sick about you. He told me that Will said you'd left because you found out that he'd cheated on you."

"Oh no!" Maggie cried.

"Why would Will say such a thing?" Carrie asked.

"Because my mother said that was the reason I left," Maggie explained. "It was the only thing she could think of that would be believed by my family. And now Malcolm knows! He must be devastated!"

"Maggie, he's beyond devastated," Carrie said. "Your disappearance was enough, but now he thinks you believe he cheated on you!"

"What do you want me to do?" Maggie asked. "What choice do I have? What would you do in my place?"

Carrie sighed. "I can't even imagine being in your place," she admitted. "I'm sorry Megs, I didn't mean to question you, it's just that...he looked so sad."

Maggie closed her eyes as the tears rolled down her face. She knew that Malcolm had often been a victim of depression, and feared for him given this latest setback. "I wish I knew what to do," she said. "I wish none of this had ever happened, but it did happen. And maybe I'm not handling it the way I ought to be, but -"

"Maggie stop it," Carrie interjected. "You're doing the best that you can. No one should be in the position you're in, and hopefully one day Jack Sullivan will be brought to justice for what he's done to you and Malcolm. "

"Men like him are never brought to justice," she said. "They do whatever they please, and never have to face the consequences of their actions."

Carrie hated to admit it, but Maggie was absolutely right. "I'm sorry Megs," she said. "I really wish I could do something to help you, but - "

"You *are* doing something, Carrie," Maggie assured her. "Being able to talk to you again is wonderful, and hearing that Malcolm is going to be okay has alleviated a great deal of stress for me. I only wish I could talk to him myself," she said.

"Couldn't you just call him? Just to let him hear your voice?" Carrie asked.

"And what do I tell him when he asks why I left?" Maggie asked.

Carrie sighed. "I suppose you're right," she said. "Some day this will all be behind you, Megs. Hold on to that. Hold on to the thought of your sweet babies in a few months."

"Who will be raised without their father in their lives," Maggie said.

Carrie was worried by the depth of her best friend's bitterness, her sense of defeatism. It was so unlike Maggie; but who would feel any differently in her shoes?

"I have to get to bed," Maggie said. "Thanks for calling, Carrie. I'm sorry I'm so...emotional."

"Don't apologize," Carrie replied. "I'll call again in a few days, okay?"

"Okay. Goodnight Carrie."

"Goodnight Megs. Talk to you soon."

Boston

Malcolm spent a week in the hospital. His brothers visited him daily, even bringing Malcolm's nephew Jeremy on one occasion. Malcolm's father, however, was conspicuous by his absence. A business trip on the west coast was the only reason Tom had given Malcolm, who wasn't terribly surprised that his father had chosen business over him. It certainly wasn't the first time.

Little by little Malcolm regained his strength, but his heart remained heavy. He was given a regimen of exercises to regain his muscle mass and strength, but reasoned that he could do these on his own. Truthfully he was going stir crazy confined within the same four walls, and, despite his doctor's advice, left the hospital.

"I wish you'd reconsider this, Malcolm," Rob said as he drove Malcolm home. "It's been barely a week since you were in a coma."

"I'm fine," Malcolm assured his brother, looking out the window. "Didn't you say my new car is ready?"

Rob smiled. "Yes," he replied.

"At the dealership?"

Rob nodded.

"Sweet. Bang a right here and let's go get her," Malcolm said.

Rob complied, knowing that his brother desperately needed something to put a smile on his face. A brand new Ferrari just might do the trick.

Between his two brothers, Malcolm was kept busy for the next few days, for neither Rob nor Tom wanted to leave Malcolm alone for very long. They were both aware of his tendency to become depressed, and knew that his current circumstances were enough to drive him into a serious tailspin. But eventually they were obliged to return to their own lives, each of them having put their respective businesses on hold during their brother's crisis. They had arranged, however, to keep a close eye on him, particularly when their father returned to town.

As for Malcolm, he pushed himself hard with exercise, using the apartment's gym facilities daily as well as going for long swims. He hated returning to his empty apartment, for everywhere he looked he saw Maggie, every corner was haunted with memories of her. And at night, when he slept in the large bed alone, he was tortured with dreams of their life together...

Malcolm rolled over in bed, annoyed to find that he was alone. He frowned, and then relaxed when he heard singing coming from the bathroom. He loved hearing Maggie sing, loved how shy she was about doing so in front of anyone. Slipping out of bed he headed into the bathroom and slipped off his shorts. Maggie gave him a smile when he joined her in the shower.

"You were listening to me sing again, weren't you?" she asked as he wrapped his arms around her waist.

"Sure was," he responded, pulling her closer.

Maggie smiled. "Are you teasing me?"

Malcolm shook his head. "Not at all," he assured her. "You have an amazing voice. I love hearing you sing," he told her, bringing his mouth to her neck.

Maggie closed her eyes as his hands roamed over her bare, wet skin. "You love hearing me sing or you love hearing me scream?"

"Both actually," he murmured against her ear.

Maggie laughed. "You're incorrigible," she said, allowing him to push her up against the shower wall. Malcolm looked up at her briefly. "Totally," he agreed.

Maggie ran her hands into his wet hair as their mouths met in a hungry kiss. Malcolm's hands ran down the front of her body, over her breasts and then following the curves of hips. One hand meandered across her thigh, his fingers finding the heat between her legs. Maggie moaned into his mouth as he fingered her, her legs parting almost without her own volition. He slipped a finger inside of her as he looked down into her eyes, loving the wanton look in them. "You're so wet," he told her with a lustful smile.

"I'm in the shower," she teased.

Malcolm laughed. "Yeah well, showers don't usually get you wet inside, do they?" he asked.

Maggie wrapped one hand around his rigid penis that was pressed between their bodies. "They don't usually make you this hard either," she countered.

Malcolm smiled. "Maybe we ought to do something about that," he said.

"I couldn't agree more," she said.

Malcolm lifted her by the waist and positioned himself between her legs. Maggie braced herself against his shoulders as he pushed up into her, sliding easily to the hilt.

"Fuck that feels good," he said, pressing his mouth against her neck. Maggie brought her mouth to his ear, sucking his earlobe into her mouth in the way she knew made him crazy.

"Sing for me baby," he whispered against her ear. "I want to hear you sing..."

Maggie woke up as she did every night, needing to use the toilet. She'd dreamed of Malcolm again, of an intimate moment they'd shared one morning before he'd gone to Australia. It was impossible to believe that at one time she'd been utterly happy, completely at peace. And now all that was gone, all her happiness evaporated like morning mist under a summer sun. Maggie forced herself to push the images from her mind, but her body was another matter. She longed for Malcolm's touch, yearned to be with him in the most intimate of ways. He was her soul mate. How could she ever learn to live without him? How long would she have to endure the sweet agony of dreams of him? And how could she ever find true happiness again without him?

Maggie returned to bed, but sleep did not come easily. Her conversation with Carrie replayed in her mind endlessly as she thought of Malcolm. *He thinks I left him...he thinks I ended it...he thinks I don't trust him...I don't love him...* Maggie couldn't stem the tide of emotion, and ended up crying herself back into a troubled sleep.

The next morning, it was evident to all how little Maggie had slept. Irene had been aware of her daughter's restlessness during the night, and attributed it to the conversation Maggie had had with her friend Carrie.

"I think perhaps you should give Marilyn a call and tell her you can't come in today," Irene said. "You look exhausted, lass."

"I'm okay," Maggie said. "Just had a bit of a restless night is all."

"More than a bit," Irene said. "You barely slept at all, did you?"

Maggie shook her head.

"Marilyn is a kind woman," Noreen reminded her. "She'll understand if you call in sick, Maggie. You haven't missed a single day, after all, and have helped her out more than once when she's been in a pinch."

"I want to go in," Maggie said, looking down at her half-eaten toast. "Don't you see?" she went on, looking up at the two women. "I have to be occupied or else....I just think too much."

Irene and Noreen nodded in understanding, each of them concerned about Maggie's state of mind.

"You do what you feel is best," Irene said finally. "Would it help if I came with you today?"

Maggie nodded at once. "It would be a great help," she said.

Irene smiled. "Then that's what we'll do," she said. "And if you need to take a nap, I'll be there to pick up the slack. How does that sound?"

"It sounds wonderful," Maggie replied. "Thanks Mum. What would I do without you?"

Ten

Boston

*M*alcolm stepped out of the shower and reached for a towel when he heard his cell phone ringing. He walked into the bedroom and picked it up, not recognizing the number showing on the screen. Deciding to accept the call, he held the phone up to his ear with one hand while he towel dried his hair with the other.

"Hello?"

"Hi, is this Malcolm?" A rather nervous sounding female voice asked.

"Yeah, who's this?" Malcolm asked.

"My name is Robyn Gibson. You don't know me, but our fathers golf together, and ..."

"What can I do for you, Robyn?"

"Well like I was saying, your dad and my dad golf together, and I guess your dad thought you'd like it if I gave you a call so that we could...you know, get together some time?"

Malcolm frowned. "Sorry, not interested," he said, and ended the call. This was the second time he'd been solicited by a woman in the past week, and he was growing annoyed. It was clear that his father felt he needed to move on, but Malcolm knew that he simply couldn't do that. There were too many questions left unanswered to close the door on his relationship with Maggie.

And Malcolm was determined to get those answers. He'd decided to head over to the Hart and Hound later that evening when he knew that Will would be working. Will had always been a good friend, and Malcolm was hopeful that he would be willing to listen to what Malcolm had to say.

Elsewhere in Boston

Will sat eating his lunch with his coworkers. Normally he enjoyed the camaraderie and the laughs, but today he was in a pensive mood. Life had always been so straight forward for Will, running smoothly with very few bumps. He was a man of simple needs and simple pleasures, quite happy with the way his life was progressing. But what had happened to his sister had thrown a monkey wrench into the engine of his life, making him question what he thought he knew about relationships and life in general. He'd begun losing sleep as he worried about his sister, about her babies who would be born in a few short months. And then there was his mother, and her part in all this. He knew that she wasn't telling the family everything, and he had to wonder why. It bothered him that she was being devious, for his mother was the most steadfast, trustworthy person he knew. It shook him deeply that she was being less than truthful, that she was keeping secrets. She had always taught him to be honest, to tell the truth no matter what. Were all those teachings meaningless now?

"O'Toole, boss wants to see you."

Will looked up from his lunch to the doorway where Phil Cannon stood, the foreman of Will's crew.

"What for?" Will asked, standing up.

Cannon shrugged. "Beats me," he said. He'd known Will to be a reliable, hardworking young man for the past 3 years he'd been employed at Sullivan Construction. "Don't worry, Will," he said. "I'm sure it's nothing to concern yourself about."

Will nodded, but his foreman's assurances did nothing to prevent a knot from forming in his gut. He took a moment to wipe his mouth before leaving the lunch room and heading upstairs to where Phil's superior, Jeff Bradley's office was located.

"You wanted to see me, sir?" Will asked from the open doorway.

Bradley looked up. "Yes, come in O'Toole," he said. "Sit down."

Will came into the small office and took a seat. He wiped his sweaty palms on his thighs and waited for Bradley to speak.

"I'm afraid I have to cut your hours," Bradley said without preamble.

Will frowned. "Can I ask why?"

"Well we just brought another person on the crew, and..."

"And they get my hours?" Will interjected. "How is that fair?"

Bradley scowled. "Mind your mouth O'Toole," he warned. "You're just gonna have to live with it."

Will nodded, fighting to keep his cool. "I guess so," he said. "Though the union might have something to say about it."

"Don't think so," Bradley replied. "Newcomer's the daughter of the head of your local chapter, so I don't think the union will say a damn thing. Tough break, kid."

Will frowned. "Yeah, tough break," he muttered. He left the office without saying another word. His day had just got much, much worse.

On the way to the Hart and Hound, Will phoned Alli to tell her the bad news. They'd been talking about getting a place together, for Will was planning on proposing to her soon. But now those plans would have to be put on hold indefinitely.

"How can they do this to you?" Alli asked after Will had broken the news to her. He could hear the disappointment in her voice. "It's not fair!"

"I know it isn't," Will said. "But what can I do about it?"

"Can't you grieve it?" she asked.

"What would be the point of that?" Will asked. "It's the bloody union boss whose daughter has taken my hours. What good would grieving it to the union do?"

"You don't have to get annoyed with me," Alli said. "It was just an idea."

Will sighed. "I'm not annoyed with you, love," he said. "I'm just....pissed off."

"I know," she said. "I wish there was something I could do to make you feel better."

"So do I," Will said. "Believe me, so do I."

Will was sullen for the rest of the day, and when he arrived at the pub his father could see at once that something was wrong.

"You want to talk about it?" Mick asked as Will got ready for his shift at the bar.

"Bloody wanker cut my hours," Will grumbled as he donned an apron.

Mick frowned. "Are they cutting back, then? Seems unlikely given the amount of building that's going on around town."

"No, they're not cutting back, they're hiring," Will said as he cinched the strings of his apron with a quick jerk. "Hiring some Union big shot's kid, so going to the Union's useless."

"Sorry son," Mick said. "Guess you won't be able to get that flat you were looking at."

"Nope," Will replied. "Can't bloody afford it now. You go on Da, I know you've got Mum's shopping to do," he said. "I can take care of things."

"Okay," Mick replied. He gave his son a pat on the shoulder. "Sorry Will, I know you had your heart set on that place. Maybe things will pick up."

Will nodded, but didn't say anything as Mick left. Then he walked out to the bar to take up his duties.

It was Thursday, and business was fairly slow as the evening went on. Will had his two brothers to help him with waiting and bussing tables while his father did the weekly shopping for the bar. There was a baseball game on the television, and Will watched the Red Sox as they pummelled the Toronto Blue Jays. He didn't notice when someone came up to the bar and took a seat until he heard his name.

"Hi Will."

Will turned sharply, shocked to see Malcolm Sullivan sitting at the bar. His face still bore the signs of his recent car accident, but other than that, he seemed quite well.

"Sullivan," Will said, walking over to him. "Didn't think I'd see you in here again."

Malcolm was discouraged by the young man's coldness, but wasn't surprised by it. "I wanted to talk to you," he said. "Do you have a minute?"

Will looked around the bar, and decided that, since it was pretty quiet, he could take a few minutes to talk to Malcolm. He certainly had a lot he wanted to say to him. "Yeah sure thing," he said. "Come out back where we can have some privacy."

Malcolm nodded and stood up. He walked around the bar and followed Will out to the alley behind the bar.

"My brother Tom told me that you -" Malcolm sentence was cut off by Will's fist to his jaw.

"That's for what you did to my sister, you son-of-a-bitch," Will said.

Malcolm staggered back, and looked back at Will in shock, rubbing his jaw as he did so.

"Will you at least hear me out?" He asked.

"What for?" Will said. "Don't tell me you're gonna deny what you did!"

"Yes I am," Malcolm said in exasperation. "I don't know where you heard that I cheated on Maggie, but it's not true, I swear on my life, on the life of my children!"

Will didn't want to consider that this too was a lie, and put his fists up in a fighting stance. "Come on, let's go! Right now Sullivan, or don't you have the balls to hit me?"

"I don't want to fight you, Will!" Malcolm said. "You're one of my best friends, and I -" he was cut off by Will's right cross, and he fell down on the ground.

"Shut up!" Will shouted. "Just shut the fuck up! You're a liar, and a user and if you *ever* come near this place or my sister again, I'll break every bone in your body! Now get the hell outta here!"

Malcolm knew that Will was lost to him, and watched him as he returned to the bar, slamming the door behind him. Malcolm sat on the pavement surrounded by the stench of the nearby dumpster and his own misery. Will had been his last hope, his last chance to get the answers he so desperately needed. Dropping his face into his hands, Malcolm let go of all the emotions he'd held at bay for so many weeks, and simply wept alone in the dark.

Will returned to the pub, his mood even lower than it had been earlier. It bothered him that Malcolm would lie, that he wasn't man enough to own up to what he'd done. *But what if he's telling the truth?* A small voice deep inside of him asked. *What if all this is a lie?* Will pushed the thoughts from his mind. The situation was simple, Malcolm had cheated, and Maggie had ended it. Period. End of story. So why wouldn't that small kernel of doubt inside of him go away?

"Will, scotch neat for table 4," Aidan said, shaking Will's attention back to his surroundings.

"Sure, I'm on it," Will said, and moved at once to fill the order.

Malcolm made his way home, emotionally wrecked, physically exhausted. He'd never felt lower, and knew that if he did nothing to change that, he would never bounce back. He felt utterly alone, completely hopeless, and was having trouble finding a reason to go on. Alcohol, even drugs been his answer for depression, but he refused to go down that road again. He was better than that now, Maggie had made him a better man. But Maggie was gone, and he had little hope of finding her. What was more, she believed that he'd cheated on her. So what was there to live for now? But then a thought entered his mind, and a spark of hope entered his heart. *Scotland...I'll go to Scotland...I'll go to Nanna...* He knew that the doctors had advised him that he'd need another two weeks of rehab, but at this point he didn't care. He needed a soft place to land, and Scotland was the only place he knew that would afford him one.

By the time Malcolm went to bed that night, he'd booked a flight to Edinburgh for the next afternoon. He purchased a one way ticket.

The next morning...

"Scotland? You're going to *Scotland?*"

Malcolm heard the incredulity in his brother's voice and had to smile. "Yeah Rob, my flight leaves at 3," he said. "I need to see my Nanna. I'm just tired. I feel like I've been run over by a freight train."

"Well you just had a serious car accident," Rob reminded him. "It's rest you need Malcolm, not travel."

"I'll rest when I'm there," Malcolm assured him. "I just need to get away for a while. I ...I can't handle things right now."

"I understand," Rob said. "You've had a rough go, there's no doubt of that. Need a lift to the airport?"

"That'd be great Rob, thanks," Malcolm replied. He'd been very grateful for his brothers' support over the past few weeks, and knew that without it he'd have been far worse off than he was. But they were busy with their own lives, and Malcolm knew that they'd made a lot of sacrifices to spend time with him. He could ask no more of them.

Later...

"So how long are you staying in Scotland?" Rob asked as he drove his brother to the airport.

"Not sure," Malcolm replied. "Don't have much keeping me here right now."

Rob frowned. "You have me and Tom," he reminded him. "I know we haven't always been there for you Malcolm, but - "

"I know," Malcolm interrupted. "And I really appreciate all that you guys have done for me recently. I just need to get away from Boston. This place is too full of memories, Rob."

Rob nodded. "Just promise me you'll be back, Malcolm. Tom and I are going to talk to Dad, and try to get to the bottom of all this. If he's involved, we'll find out."

While Malcolm appreciated his brothers' intentions, he held out little hope that they would be able to get their father to admit to anything. Jack Sullivan was a man without conscience, without a moral centre. Lying to his sons would be nothing to a man like him.

The drive back to Boston afforded Rob time to think. He hated to think that his father was behind Maggie's disappearance, hated to think that he was capable of such cold-bloodedness. And if it was true, if Jack had been responsible for Maggie's disappearance, what then? What would Malcolm do to avenge such an act? *What would I do in Malcolm's shoes?* Rob realized that he could even imagine how Malcolm felt because Rob didn't love his wife the way Malcolm loved Maggie. He never had. Susan had been the daughter of a business associate of his father's, someone he was strongly encouraged to date and marry. And, being the obedient drone that he was, Rob had done just that. It wasn't that he didn't like his life: he had a nice house, beautiful children and a successful practice. They could afford to go to the Cape every summer and the Caribbean every winter. He drove a nice car, wore fine clothes; but what did all that mean, really? Rob knew without a doubt that Malcolm would give up everything he owned, every penny of his inheritance, every material luxury he had to be with Maggie. Could he say the same thing about his own wife? He loved his wife, but knew that he was not *in* love with her. And until he'd seen Malcolm and Maggie together, he didn't get that. But now he did, and it made him see his life in a whole new light. *Am I as shallow as my father? Will I be just like him in 30 years?* Rob had asked his twin brother that very questions only a short time ago, and Tom had responded immediately that they were not. But looking at his life, Rob wasn't so sure.

Annie Simms looked up from her computer to see Rob Sullivan standing before her.

"Good afternoon Dr. Sullivan," she said. "How can I help you?"

"Is my father in, Annie?" Rob asked. "I'd like to talk to him."

"He's in, but I think he's still on a conference call, let me check," she replied, turning in her swivel chair to do so. "No, he's finished. Go on in, I'll let him know you're here."

"Thanks Annie," Rob said, giving her a smile.

Annie simply nodded, surprised by his friendly manner.

Jack looked up when Rob entered his expansive office.

"What brings you by, Rob?" Jack asked, giving his son his full attention. "Shouldn't you be working this afternoon?"

"I just drove Malcolm to the airport, so I had Gladys reschedule my appointments," Rob explained.

Jack frowned. "Don't make a habit of putting off your clients. It's bad for business."

Rob sighed. "They're called patients Dad, and I don't make a habit of it."

"You took Malcolm to the airport?" Rob nodded. "Where the hell is he off to now?"

"Scotland," Rob replied. "He's very depressed. I'm worried about him. Tom is too."

"He's better off without her," Jack commented, picking up his cell phone and scrolling through messages. "I told him she'd only end up hurting him in the end."

"Well the whole thing seems kind of suspicious to me," Rob said, watching his father closely for a reaction. "It just doesn't add up."

Jack looked up at him instantly. "What do you mean, it doesn't add up?"

"Well it doesn't," Rob said, deciding to push a little further. "I mean, think of it. They had just gotten engaged, they're in love...what would make her up and leave like that? I can't imagine what could drive her away from him that way, can you?"

Jack was starting to grow uneasy with his son's questions. "I have no clue," he replied. "But as I said, he's better off without her. She's nothing but a gold digger."

"Well see, if that were true, why would she leave him *before* they got married?" Rob asked pointedly. "What does she stand to gain? If she was really after his money, she'd have married him first and *then* leave, right?"

Jack frowned, his son's logic giving him a headache. "Is there a reason you came by? I have a lot of work to do plus a personnel matter to resolve."

"No, just wanted to let you know that Malcolm is off to Scotland. I thought you might be interested," Rob said.

"Thanks for the news flash," Jack responded.

Rob frowned. "You know, he's a really remarkable person once you take the time to get to know him," he said. "*If* you take the time," he said, and then left his father's office.

Jack said nothing and watched his son leave, a feeling of uneasiness welling up inside of him. "Annie get Hugh Wellman on the phone," he said into the intercom. "Tell him I want him here in thirty minutes."

"Right away, sir."

Eleven

Boston

Will sat eating breakfast when his father joined him. Mick had been concerned about his first born, for he had been moody and sullen lately, which was very unlike Will. He knew that part of it was Will's frustration over his job, for he'd planned on moving out of the house. Will was twenty-four years old, and had grown tired of living at home. But now that his hours had been cut, it might not be possible. However Mick knew that there was more to Will's demeanour than his disappointment about his job. Will had always been very close to Maggie, very protective of her; and learning that she'd been cheated on by the man she'd given her heart to was a bitter pill to swallow.

"Morning lad," Mick said as he poured himself a cup of coffee.

"Morning," Will said.

"You're up early today," Mick commented as he sat down.

Will shrugged. "Was awake, so I got up."

Mick nodded. "It's really lousy what that bastard Bradley did to you, son," he said. "And I was thinking that you could put in some extra time at the Hart, you know, to help you out with getting your own flat."

Will looked up at his father. "That would be great, Da, thanks," he said.

"So how was business last night?" Mick asked.

"Pretty slow," Will replied. He frowned as he remembered one customer he could have done without. "Guess who showed up."

"Who?"

"Malcolm. The bastard wanted to talk to me. Had the balls to deny that he'd cheated on Megs," Will reported with a scowl.

Mick shook his head. "Figures," he said. "I hope you set him straight."

"I set him on his arse," Malcolm replied. "Right cross to the jaw. He didn't even fight back."

Mick nodded. As pleased as he was that Will had decked Malcolm, he worried about the consequences for his son. Malcolm was a Sullivan, after all, and the Sullivans were a powerful family in the Boston area.

"Just be careful, lad," Mick cautioned. "You never know what you'll unleash on yourself if you tangle with that family."

"I don't care," Will grumbled as he stood up with his dishes. "He had it coming."

Mick smiled. "Aye, he did at that."

Inverness, Scotland

A flood of memories bombarded Malcolm as he walked through the small airport. When last he'd been here he was full of excitement and hope as he and Maggie prepared to find his grandmother. And they had found her, and she was the reason he'd come back to Scotland. Malcolm felt as though he'd reached rock bottom, and knew that his grandmother would provide him the shoulder he needed so desperately. Betty had been very worried about Malcolm when he'd told her about his car accident, and was delighted when he'd called to let her know he was coming. And when she saw him coming through the arrivals gate in the small airport, her heart ached.

"Malcolm!" Betty cried as Malcolm met her and threw his arms around her. "It's so good to see you again!"

Malcolm didn't say anything in response for he was too tired, too emotionally exhausted to do so. Instead he simply held his grandmother, letting her gentle warmth surround him.

"Let's go home," Betty suggested, taking Malcolm's hand. "You looked right knackered."

Malcolm offered her a wan smile, and then let her lead him out of the airport to the small car park across the road.

"You're feeling well?" Betty asked as they drove along. "The accident didn't leave any permanent damage?"

"Well, I don't have a spleen anymore," Malcolm told her. "But other than that, nothing permanent."

Betty frowned. "It must have been serious, that accident," she commented.

"Yeah, pretty serious," he said, looking out the window. "I've missed you Nanna."

Betty glanced at him, concerned by his lethargic demeanour. When she'd seen him last he was so lively, so energetic and full of life. "I've missed you too," she said. "I'm glad you decided to come, Malcolm. You need some TLC right now I think."

Malcolm turned and looked at her. "I've never felt this way, Nanna," he told her. "I feel...empty inside."

"I know," Betty said. "And I know why. But we'll get through this lad, we'll get through this together. I promise."

Betty made a late supper when they arrived at her home, but Malcolm ate very little. He felt exhausted, and wanted nothing more than to climb into bed and escape from his life for a few hours.

"How long are you staying?" Betty asked him as she placed a piece of pie in front of him.

"I don't know," Malcolm replied. "I bought a one way ticket, actually. There isn't a lot in Boston for me anymore."

Betty nodded. "I know things look bad right now," she said, reaching over and putting her hand on his. "But life has a way of righting itself, usually when you least expect it to. Have faith that the Good Lord will see you through this, lad. Ask Him to help you get through it, and He will. Of that you can be certain."

Malcolm said nothing as he picked at his pie with his fork. He didn't want to tell his grandmother that he was having a very hard time believing that things would work out, that he'd become angry at God for taking Maggie from him. It didn't make sense to him; if there was a cosmic reason why all this was happening, it was beyond his ability to see it.

"Have you spoken to your granddad lately?" Betty asked, trying hard to get Malcolm to talk.

"I did when I got out of the hospital," Malcolm said.

"I imagine he was very concerned," Betty commented.

"He was," Malcolm agreed with a yawn. "I wish I could go visit him too; but I just don't have the energy to go that far."

Betty nodded. "It's a long way," she agreed. "Why don't you go on up to bed, love? You're exhausted."

Malcolm nodded. "I am," he agreed. "Sorry I didn't eat much, Nanna. It's delicious, but I'm just not that hungry right now."

"Don't worry about it," Betty said, standing up to clear the dishes. "You go on up to bed and sleep as long as you want."

Malcolm stood up and came around the table to give her a hug. "Thanks Nanna," he said. "Goodnight."

Antigonish

Nova Scotia, which is of course Latin for New Scotland, hosts a number of Highland Games in the summer. With the vast number of Scottish and Irish immigrants living in this part of Canada, the Games had become a part of the Nova Scotian culture and were always well attended.

Irene had always loved attending the games, and had even competed in dance competitions when she was a younger woman. So when she saw the ad in the paper for the Antigonish Highland Games, she got excited and told Maggie about it at once.

"We should go," Irene said over breakfast one Saturday morning. "You need something to lift your spirits, Maggie. You know how much you love the massed bands."

Maggie nodded. "Maybe," she said. "When is it?"

"Next weekend," Irene said. "Right here in Antigonish. I'm going to buy some tickets today," she said, knowing that if she did that, Maggie couldn't say no. "They'll probably have haggis!"

Maggie smiled. "Well you can have my share of that, Mum," she said. "You know I can't stand the stuff."

Irene laughed, pleased that Maggie seemed willing to go to the Games. It was the first time in weeks that she'd shown enthusiasm for anything, and it gave Irene a small measure of hope.

Maggie had no excuse to offer her mother the next weekend, for the weather was good, with a clear, cloudless sky. Irene had purchased tickets in advance, which also made it difficult for Maggie to refuse, and so they set off for the Northumberland Shore where the games were being held.

"Och, do you hear that glorious sound?" Irene asked as soon as they stepped out of the car. Maggie smiled, as she too heard the bagpipes in the distance. "I'm so glad you agreed to come," Irene said as she linked her arm in Maggie's. "This is going to be a wonderful day, I just know it."

Maggie leaned towards her mother and kissed her on the cheek. "Thanks Mum," she said. "I think you're right. This is just what I need right now."

Mother and daughter spent the day listening to the bagpipe competitions, watching Highland dancers, and enjoying the feats of the heavy athletes as they tossed cabers, hammers and stones in a competition of strength. The weather stayed clear and warm, enabling them to enjoy their supper outdoors.

"This has been lovely," Maggie said as she enjoyed her fish and chips.

"It has," Irene said. "It's like being in Scotland," she said, and then regretted her words. The only time Maggie had been to Scotland was with Malcolm, and Irene knew that Maggie had been trying valiantly not to think of him. "Sure you won't have some?" she asked, holding up a forkful of haggis.

"Quite sure," Maggie said. "But thanks anyway."

Boston

Saturday night was always busy at the Hart, and this one was no exception. Mick and Will worked the bar while the twins waited tables. Will's girlfriend Alli had started working on weekends to help them out in Maggie's absence.

"Your usual, mate?" Will asked the pub's newest regular.

"Make it a double," Hugh grunted.

Will frowned as he poured the drink. "Something wrong?"

Hugh nodded as he pulled the bowl of nuts closer. "Yeah, that fuckin' prick Sullivan canned me," he said, digging around for his beloved cashews.

"Sorry to hear it," Will said, setting the drink down. "Did he say why?"

"Yeah, said I was using company money to pay hospital bills for my mother," Hugh said. "Which is fuckin' bullshit. I took her to the hospital on a day I was supposed to work, but I used my own goddamn money to pay the bill."

"That's rough," Will said. "I got my hours cut recently myself," he said.

Hugh looked at him as he downed his drink. "Jack Sullivan is a cold-hearted son-of-a-bitch, and I don't care who hears me say it," he said.

"I only met him once, but he did seem a little...cold," Will said.

Hugh snorted. "He's an iceman, dude, a fuckin ice man," he said.

Will nodded in agreement. "Be right back," he said, noticing a customer waving him over at the other end of the bar.

"Bring me another!" Hugh called as Will moved away. He then proceeded to make his way through the bowl of nuts, pushing aside the unwanted peanuts and Brazil nuts to get to the preferred cashews. He picked one up and tossed it into his mouth. He did it again, but was distracted by the sound of loud laughter behind him, and the nut slid down his throat, lodging itself in his windpipe. Hugh grabbed his throat, gasping for breath as those around him watched in impotent alarm.

"He's choking!" someone shouted. "Somebody help him!"

Will heard the commotion and looked over to see Hugh turning purple. He ran around to the back of the man's barstool and whacked him on the back several times with the heel of his hand. This didn't work, so he reached around Hugh from behind. Circling his hands around the Hugh's abdomen, he used his fists to pull inward and upward, pressing into the man's abdomen quickly. The patrons of the bar stood around and watched as Will performed the Heimlich, cheering at last when the cashew flew out of Hugh's mouth and hit the mirror behind the bar.

"You okay, mate?" Will asked as he helped Hugh sit down.

Hugh was coughing mightily, but nodded that he was okay. Mick brought him a glass of water and stood watching with concern as the man's colour slowly returned to its normal hue.

"You saved my life!" Hugh said, turning to Will.

Will smiled. "Well, I was in the right place at the right time," he said.

Hugh took a drink of water as Will returned to his place behind the bar. "You're a goddamn hero, Will!" Hugh said.

Will was a little embarrassed by all the praise and simply smiled. "I wouldn't go that far," he said.

"I want to give you some money, you know, as a reward," Hugh said, pulling out his wallet.

Will held up a hand. "No, don't be daft," he said. "I don't need your money, Hugh. Put that away."

Hugh looked at Will, confused. He'd lived all his life living by the code that nobody gives a rat's ass about you but yourself; and here was this young man refusing payment for having saved his life.

"Listen, if you're looking for work, we could use a hand around here," Will said. "We've been short handed since my sister left."

"What kind of work?" Hugh asked. "You mean liked...bartending?"

"Actually we need a bouncer," Will told him. "I used to do it, but with Maggie gone I need to tend bar in her place. You look like a man who can handle that line of work."

Hugh nodded. "Yeah I've had...similar jobs," he remarked.

"So you interested?" Will asked.

Hugh shrugged. "Haven't got many prospects at the moment," he said. "So yeah, sure."

"Great," Will said. "I'll get my dad to talk to you about the details."

Hugh nodded, and watched Will walk away, amazed by the ironic turn of events.

Twelve

Scotland

Betty MacGregor was growing concerned. Malcolm had been in her home for close to a week, and he'd spent most of that time in the bedroom she'd shown him to on the day he arrived. He barely ate, said very little, and only left the room to use the bathroom. Betty hadn't wanted to push Malcolm, but was beginning to worry that he was getting worse rather than improving in his mental state. One evening she decided that she'd waited long enough.

"Malcolm?" she called through the door. "May I come in?"

"Yeah," was his response.

Betty opened the door, putting on a cheery smile. She looked around the small room, noting that the dinner that she'd brought him earlier had barley been touched. "How are you feeling?" she asked, sitting on the side of the bed.

Malcolm looked up at her, his large blue eyes telling her without need of words how he felt. She wanted to cry as he looked at her, but she knew she needed to be strong. He needed her too much for her to be anything but strong.

"Love, I'm worried about you," she said, running her fingers lightly through his tousled hair. "You need to get out of this room."

"I get out of the room all the time," he told her.

"I don't mean to use the loo," she said. "I know you're hurting, Malcolm. But you can't just stop living. And that's what you're doing, wasting away up here."

Malcolm said nothing, and turned away from her. He didn't want to go on living; that was the problem. The way he saw it, he had nothing to live for. "I don't know how to go on, Nanna," he said quietly. "I don't have the strength to go on."

Betty frowned, and fought the tears that sprung to her eyes. "Yes you do," she said. "You have to dig deep, Malcolm, but I know you have it inside of you. I want to help you, but you have to meet me half way."

Malcolm didn't respond for a few moments, and Betty began to think that her words had fallen short. But then he turned to look at her, and under the tears that filled his eyes, she saw a hint of a spark of the Malcolm she knew and loved. "Tell me what to do," he said.

Betty smiled. "Get up, get dressed, and come with me for a walk outside," she said.

Malcolm considered this for a minute. She had been very patient with him, more patient than anyone else would be. *Except for Maggie*, he reflected. *She was always patient with me...*

"Okay," he said. "I'll try."

Betty smiled. She left him so that he could get dressed, and headed downstairs. While she waited for him, she placed a long distance phone call to Australia. She'd resisted calling Norman, not wanting to alarm him; but knew that Malcolm needed all the support of those who loved him now, and she was going to make sure he had it.

As the days passed, Malcolm grew stronger. With the support of his grandmother, he forced himself out of his room, and had even begun taking small trips with Betty into town. Emotionally, however, he was still fragile; and Betty was almost certain that he was suffering from depression. She herself had known depression in her life; losing her only child at such a young age, being forced out of her grandchild's life had been hard on her. But she'd recovered. And now she was seeing the same symptoms in Malcolm. She'd wanted to talk to him about it, for she knew with certainty that his father had never addressed his problems. She knew from experience that depression wasn't something that went away on its own, and would only get worse if ignored. She was certain that Malcolm had become promiscuous and abusive of alcohol as a means of escaping how he felt. Maggie had helped him cope; she'd helped him to see that he was more than the worthless drunk that his father had believed him to be. But now that Maggie was gone, Malcolm was floundering. Not wanting to return to the lifestyle he'd rejected, he was at a loss to know how to cope. He needed help, and Betty was determined to make sure he got it.

"This is delicious Nanna, thanks," Malcolm said. "I loved this when I was a kid."

Betty smiled. "I remember," she said. "You'd have eaten mince pie every day if you'd had your way."

Malcolm nodded. "Yeah you're probably right," he agreed.

Betty watched him for a few minutes, trying to decide if she ought to speak her mind. "Malcolm, I think you need help," she said, deciding to put in all on the table. "I'm worried about you."

Malcolm looked up at her. "I'm okay, you don't need to worry."

Betty frowned. "Don't tell me you're okay," she countered. "I know depression when I see it, lad. I've struggled with it myself."

Malcolm said nothing, and for a moment they sat in awkward silence.

"It's nothing to be embarrassed about love," Betty went on. "But I know that if you don't do anything about it, it will only get worse."

"I don't want to take drugs," Malcolm said quietly, poking at his lunch with his fork.

"You don't have to," Betty assured him. "But I think talking to someone would do you a world of good. Would you at least consider it?"

Malcolm looked at his grandmother, seeing in her eyes her deep love and concern for his well being. How could he say no to her?

"I'll think about it," Malcolm said.

Betty smiled.

They spent the afternoon gardening. Betty's backyard was an oasis of flowers, trees and shrubs, and Malcolm had discovered that he'd inherited his grandmother's green thumb. He was finding the work therapeutic, giving him time to think. His grandmother's suggestion had given him pause; but once he'd started to think about it, he decided that she was right. Perhaps talking to someone would help; it certainly couldn't hurt.

"Nanna I'm going to take get the mulch from the car," Malcolm said as Betty weeded.

"All right love," she said. "Just set it down on the bench for now."

Malcolm headed around the side of the house and out the gate that lead to the street. He walked towards the driveway, and had just opened his grandmother's car when a taxi cab pulled up in front of the house. Curious, he turned to see who it was, and watched as a tall, white haired man stepped out of the back seat and onto the sidewalk. When the man turned, Malcolm forgot all about the mulch and ran to meet him.

"Grandpa!" Malcolm said, giving Norman a huge hug. "I'm so glad to see you!"

"Malcolm my boy!" Norman replied, returning Malcolm's embrace. "I've missed you!"

"What are you doing here?" Malcolm asked as the taxi driver drove off.

"I got a phone call from your grandmother a few days ago," Norman said as Malcolm picked up his suitcase. "She said you were in a bad way. So I came to see what I could do to get you straightened out."

Malcolm couldn't believe Norman would fly all the way from Australia just because he was worried about him. He reflected on how little concern his own father had shown recently, and a lump formed in his throat. "I can't believe you did this," he said emotionally. "I...I don't know what to say."

Norman smiled, and put an arm around him. "Come on," he said. "Let's go find your grandmother. I've been looking forward to seeing her again after all these years."

Malcolm and his grandparents spent the rest of the day getting caught up and looking over old photo albums. It was an emotional moment for Norman when he finally saw a photo of his first born.

"She was lovely," Norman said with a smile, admiring a photo of Judith taken on her third birthday. "What was she like, Betty?"

"She was a spitfire," Betty said. "A huge imagination and a mischievous side to go with it," she added with a smile.

Norman smiled. "Sounds familiar," he said. He flipped though a few more pages, literally watching his daughter grow up before his very eyes. "If only I'd known," he said quietly. He looked at Betty. "If only you'd had a way of telling me."

Betty smiled sadly. "If I had, you'd never have married your Nora, and you'd not have your children, your grandchildren," she said. "And I never would have gone to Boston, and we wouldn't have our Malcolm."

Norman looked at Malcolm and nodded. "I suppose you're right," he said, looking at his grandson fondly. "I suppose things happen for a reason."

"Aye, that they do," Betty agreed. "Who'd like another piece of pie?" She asked, standing up. Seeing Norman again after so long was dredging up a lot of old emotions, emotions she thought she'd learned to deal with. But looking at photos of their daughter together had opened up the old wounds caused by Judith's death. She knew that Malcolm was already emotionally fragile enough. The last thing he needed was to see her growing tearful. She needed to be strong, for she had become Malcolm's rock, his safe harbour. So when she left the living room to fetch a second piece of apple pie for Norman, she took a few moments to compose herself.

"Your grandmother has told me what happened with Maggie," Norman said as he set the photo album on the coffee table. "I can't tell you how sorry I am."

Malcolm nodded. "I still have so many questions," he said. "Part of me thinks my father had something to do with her disappearance," he said.

"What do you mean?" Norman asked.

"I told you how he hated Maggie," Malcolm said.

"Yeah you did," Norman said. "You really think he'd go that far?"

"I don't know," Malcolm said. "But none of it makes any sense, Grandpa. Why would she leave me? Why would she think I'd cheated on her? It doesn't add up."

Norman nodded thoughtfully, his dislike of Jack Sullivan growing. "No it doesn't," he said. He hoped that Malcolm was wrong, for what would it say about the man his eldest daughter had married if he was right? What kind of a monster *was* Jack Sullivan anyway?

Boston

"Thank you Hugh, just set the bags down on the counter," Irene said.

"No problem, Mrs. O," Hugh replied, and set the grocery bags down where she'd indicated. "Anything else I can do for you?"

Irene smiled. "Not right now, thanks," she said. "How's your mother doing?"

"About the same," Hugh replied. "I'm going to see her later."

"I'm sure it means a lot to her that you visit her every day," Irene said. "You're a good son, Hugh."

Hugh smiled, a little surprised and uncomfortable with the praise. "Thanks," he said, and then left her and returned to the bar. Since he'd been employed by the O'Toole family weeks earlier he'd become a very useful member of the Hart and Hound staff. Irene had been a little leery of him when she'd first met him, but she soon warmed up to him, for he'd shown her nothing but respect when she was around.

"Mum's back?" Will asked as Hugh joined him at the bar.

"Yeah, just helped her with the groceries," Hugh said. "She's a great gal, your ma."

Will smiled. "She's one in a million, that's for sure," he said.

Hugh nodded. "So how come she doesn't come in more often?" he asked. "I haven't seen her in weeks. She hasn't been sick has she?"

"No, nothing like that," Will said. "She's been staying with my sister who's out of town."

Hugh couldn't help but notice the look of concern that passed through Will's eyes when he spoke of his sister. "You're close? You and your sister?"

Will nodded. "Always have been," he said. "I remember when we were kids, back in Belfast," he said, "she was always thinking up the best games. We were always playing, her and me. Other blokes might think having a younger sister around was a pain in the arse, but not me. She was always my best friend when we were kids. Still is," he said, a frown creasing his brow.

Hugh nodded, a feeling of uneasiness welling up inside of him. "Sorry," he said.

Will looked up from the tray of glasses he was putting away. "Sorry for what?" He asked.

"Sorry that she's not here," Hugh said. "It's pretty obvious you miss her."

"I do," Will said, and then left to return the empty tray to the kitchen. Hugh watched him leave, an ugly feeling worming its way through his innards. The O'Toole family had been good to him, giving him a job, making him feel welcome, even having him over for dinner to their home. Will had saved his life. He felt a great debt of gratitude to them all, which made it all the harder to keep inside what he knew. Perhaps it was time to show his hand. Perhaps it was time that he came clean with what he knew about the disappearance of Will's beloved sister.

The Country Club Golf Course

"Nice shot Dad," Tom said as they watched Jack's ball soar through the air toward the fairway.

Jack smiled. "Thanks," he replied. "The fellow at the pro shop gave me a few pointers."

"Well it's working, whatever he told you," Tom remarked as he prepared to take his own shot.

Jack watched his son for a moment, frowning as he remembered what the pro had said about Malcolm. "You know that ungrateful brother of yours hasn't even bothered to show up for one single lesson?" He said after Tom had taken his shot.

"You mean Malcolm?" Tom asked.

"Who else?" Jack said. "I paid damn good money for those lessons, and he hasn't taken a single one. He's always been like that, ungrateful. Always wanting to do things his own way."

Tom resented his father's criticism of Malcolm. It seemed that no matter what he did, Malcolm could never measure up in his father's estimation.

"Malcolm's had a rough go lately," Tom said as they walked together along the course. "Quite frankly I'm worried about him. He's been in Scotland for weeks, and not a word from him."

Jack frowned. "He's soft, that's his problem," he said. "Can't take it when life gets tough. I tried to warn him that she'd break his heart. But would he listen? Oh no, never does."

Tom said nothing in response, as he was formulating his questions carefully, much as he would in the courtroom. He and his brothers seemed to think that Jack had been involved in Maggie's disappearance, but getting him to admit it would be impossible. No, he would have to be tricked into admitting his duplicity.

"Malcolm has changed Dad," Tom said. "Even you have to see that. And Maggie's the reason he changed. I'm just afraid that losing her will make him slip back to where he was before they met. I'm afraid he'll get so depressed he won't know how to bounce back."

Jack said nothing as he set his golf bag down. He selected a club and addressed the ball. "Depressed," he snorted as he waggled his club. "More like spoiled. Maybe this experience will toughen him up. God know he needs it. But if I know Betty MacGregror, she's coddling him and making things worse," he said with a frown. He stopped talking for a moment to take his shot. "He should have stayed right here in Boston. He needs to get on with his life. The moment she sent him back that ring should have been the kick in the ass he needed."

Tom looked at his father quickly. *What did he say?* "Yes," he said, wanting to get his father to elaborate. "That must have been tough."

Jack stuffed his club back in his bag. "That accident never would have happened if he'd just been smart enough to take the hint," he said.

"How do you figure that?" Tom asked as he prepared to take his shot.

"Well, he'd have had no reason to go to New York," Jack pointed out.

Tom took his shot, his mind racing a mile a minute. *How does he know she sent back the ring? Malcolm has never told any of us that...would he have told Dad something like that and not me and Rob?*

"No, I suppose not," Tom said as they watched his shot sail through the air. "So unlike her though, really," he said as they picked up their bags.

Jack looked at his son. "You don't know that, son," he said. "I don't think any of us really knew her, including Malcolm."

Tom said nothing, but made a mental note to call Malcolm as soon as possible. If he had said nothing about the ring to their father, then it would be impossible not to consider the possibility that Jack *had* been involved in Maggie's disappearance. And if that were the case, Tom couldn't even begin to imagine the fallout.

Thirteen

Inverness

*N*orman looked at his watch again, growing more restless as the minutes ticked by. Betty looked up from her magazine at him. "He's only been in there ten minutes, Norm," she reminded him

"I know," he said, glancing over at the door. *Dr. Peter Grant - Psychotherapist.* "I'm just worried about the lad."

Betty smiled. "We both are," she said. "But Dr. Grant is excellent. Malcolm couldn't be in better hands."

Norman nodded. "You really think this is necessary?"

"Absolutely."

Norman didn't want to question her, but he knew for a fact how uneasy Malcolm was about talking to a therapist. But he couldn't deny that Malcolm was not the same young man who'd come to visit him months earlier; he clearly needed something to bring him out of the doldrums he'd landed in.

"Tell me about Malcolm's father, Betty," Norman said. "I want to know about the man our daughter married."

Betty was half-expecting that Norman would ask about Jack at some point, but wasn't sure he was prepared to hear what she had to say about him.

"Hasn't Malcolm told you about him?" she asked.

"Some, yes," Norman replied. "But he's speaking as the man's son. Your view on him is bound to be more objective."

Betty frowned. "Don't be so sure," she said.

"You don't like him much, that much I know," Norman said. "Was he good to our girl? Did he treat her well?"

Betty sighed, wishing she could say yes. She knew that Norman already carried a certain amount of guilt about not being in Judith's life; how would he feel when he learned how she'd been treated by the man she'd given her heart to?

"She had a comfortable life with him," Betty said. "Jack Sullivan is very wealthy."

Norman could sense that she was holding back, and it troubled him. "I know that," he said. "What aren't you telling me?"

Betty was torn. She knew that Norman had every right to know how Judith had been treated, but in her heart she worried that it would only add to his feelings of regret. And after all, what could be done now to change things? Would knowing that Jack had been a cruel, controlling husband to Judith bring her back?

"Jack Sullivan is a cold man," Betty said. "Judith loved him, so I have to believe that she was happy. Was he good to her? In a material sense yes. But emotionally ...he's bereft of emotion, Norman. He has a heart of stone."

Norman's frown deepened as he listened to her. "What did he do to her, Betty?" he asked in a quiet voice.

Betty looked away from him, unable to keep the tears from her eyes. "You don't want to know, Norm," she said.

Norman was alarmed by her response, and stood up and walked over to sit beside her. Tentatively he took her hand. "Tell me," he said. "I need to know."

Betty looked up at him. "He tried to force her to have an abortion when she was carrying Malcolm," she said. "And when she refused, he gave her a black eye. That's the monster our precious lassie was married to."

A cold feeling blossomed inside of Norman as he sat in shocked silence. He cursed softly, as the shock slowly gave way to sadness. "I'm sorry you had to go through all that by yourself," he said, putting an arm around her shoulders. "If only I'd known..."

"You didn't know, and it wasn't your fault that you didn't," Betty said. She wiped the tears from her face. "She was happy at the end, she had her precious wee Malcolm."

Norman nodded, looking at the office door again. "I suppose he's all we have left of her," he said quietly.

Betty nodded. "He is," she said. "There's no one in the world I hold closer to my heart."

Malcolm was quiet as they drove to Betty's house later. Neither of his grandparents wanted to press the issue, for they both knew how uncomfortable he'd been about talking to a therapist. But they were both curious, both hopeful that Malcolm had found the session helpful. Finally Betty could contain her questions no more.

"So? How did it go?" she asked Malcolm. "Did you like him?"

"Yeah, he's pretty cool," Malcolm said.

"Do you think you'll want to go back then?" she asked.

Malcolm shrugged and looked out the window. "I don't know," he said. "It felt....weird talking to a stranger about personal stuff."

Betty nodded. "I know, but it will help," she said. "I promise."

Malcolm didn't want to disappoint his grandmother, for she had a lot of faith in the process. "I guess we'll see," he said.

Antigonish, Nova Scotia

"You didn't need to cut your visit home short Mum," Maggie said as they walked up to the clinic. "I could have gone on my own."

Irene smiled and took her hand. "Nonsense," she said. "Seeing my grandbabies before they're born was worth the drive, I promise you."

Maggie smiled. Truth be told she had been thrilled when Irene had shown up a week earlier than expected. The thought of going to her ultrasound alone had been difficult for her. Having her mother at her side would make it easier to bear Malcolm's absence.

Sitting in the waiting room, Maggie listened to Irene as she caught her up with the latest news from Boston. She was quite surprised to hear that her father had hired a new bouncer.

"Why isn't Will working as bouncer anymore?" Maggie asked.

"He's had to pick up more hours behind the bar since you left," Irene said. "And after getting his hours cut by Sullivan, he needs them more than ever."

Maggie frowned. "He had his hours cut?"

"Yes, by quite a lot," Irene said.

"I'll just bet Jack was behind that," Maggie said. "It would be just like him to do something like that."

Irene nodded. "You're probably right. He's quite low right now, poor Will. He was hoping to move out as you know, but won't be able to for a while now."

"I miss him so much," Maggie said. "I miss them all."

An uncomfortable silence fell on them as they leafed through magazines, neither of them paying much attention to the glossy adverts or out-dated articles. Finally Maggie's name was called and they headed into the examination room.

Maggie was unable to hold back the flood of memories as the technician prepared her for the ultrasound. She remembered how excited Malcolm was, how many questions he'd asked, and how they'd both been amazed when they finally saw their tiny babies for the first time. She pushed the memories from her mind, and focused on the screen, determined not to let the past ruin this special moment.

"Everything looks good," the technician said after a few moments. She pointed out where the babies' heads were, and then took a second look at the screen. "Did you want to know the gender of the babies? I can tell you if you wish."

Maggie looked up at her mother. "What do you think?" she asked.

"It's up to you, love," Irene said.

Maggie considered this for a moment, and then looked up at the technician. "I'd like to know," she decided.

The technician smiled. "You're having one of each, Maggie. A girl and a boy."

"Really? One of each?" Maggie asked, looking at the screen.

"Yes really," the technician assured her. "Here's your daughter," she said, pointing out the female fetus. "And your son."

A daughter and son, Maggie thought, tears filling her eyes. *That's exactly what Malcolm and I were hoping for...*

"How exciting!" Irene said, giving Maggie's hand a squeeze. "Now you can give them names."

Maggie nodded, wondering if her son would look like his father. "I suppose so," she said.

Maggie was pensive as they drove back to their cousins' home. It wasn't so long ago that she and Malcolm had been talking about names for their babies. And now, the task had fallen to her alone.

"So, any ideas for names?" Irene said, trying to draw Maggie out of her silence.

"No, well, I had originally wanted to name girls after you and ...his mother," she said.

"That's sweet of you," Irene said. "What was her name? Malcolm's mother?"

"Judith."

Irene nodded. "That's a lovely name," she said. "You could still use both names, you know," she said. "Just make one the middle name. Judith Irene, sounds lovely."

"Or Irene Judith," Maggie said.

"No, I think it's better the other way," Irene said.

Maggie sighed. "I don't even know if I want to use her name now," she said quietly. "It would be a constant reminder of him."

Irene frowned and looked out the window. "You're going to have his children, Maggie," she said. "How can you help being reminded of him?"

Maggie didn't like her mother's remark, but said nothing. She was, after all, quite right. She remembered having a dream before all of this had happened, a dream of holding a baby boy with blond hair. What if they both looked like Malcolm? What if they both had his big blue eyes? How could she ever learn to live without him then? They drove in silence for the remainder of the trip, each of them frustrated and tense.

Fourteen

Inverness

Malcolm drummed his fingers on the armrest of the leather chair he sat in. He'd been to several sessions with Dr. Grant by now, and was starting to feel more comfortable talking to the man about his personal demons. He'd never spoken to anyone about his childhood, except for Maggie. As he sat waiting for the doctor his mind hearkened back to that glorious trip to St. Lucia long ago...

"I've always wanted to live in Scotland, actually. My grandparents live there, as you know. It's so beautiful and peaceful up in the highlands," Maggie tells me.

"I've never been to Scotland," I reply. "I've been to lots of places in Europe, but not there."

"Did you travel with your family?"

"School trips mostly. I went to a private prep school in New York," I say. "From the age of eight to seventeen I lived away from home."

"Really? That must have been hard," she says, sounding pretty shocked. "Did you go home for holidays at least?"

"Sometimes," I say, picking up a strand of her hair and playing with it. I don't really want to talk about this, my past isn't exactly full of happy memories. "I spent a few at the school, hanging out with the other kids whose parents didn't want them around," I tell her, admiring the gorgeous lock of hair between my finger and thumb.

"I'm sorry," she says, reaching out and stroking my face. "I didn't mean to open old wounds."

I look back at her. I've never been able to open up to anyone since Nanna was forced out of my life. But I know that I can tell Maggie anything, trust her with my deepest secrets, my greatest fears. Maggie loves me, she cares about me, she has a right to know all about me. God knows I know all about her. But this is supposed to be a fun time, not a time to burden her with all my baggage. And so I just smile, and push the flood of bad memories back down deep inside of me once more.

"I don't know about you, but I'm starving," I say. "You want to head downstairs? Or order in? This place has 24 hour room service."

Maggie must see that she'd struck a nerve, and backs off. "I'd like to go down to the beach, actually. Can we eat down there?"

"Sweetheart, you can do whatever your heart desires," I tell her, leaning over and kissing her. "I'm gonna jump in the shower first though. I really worked up a sweat earlier."

"So did I," she says as she climbs off of the bed. "Mind if I join you?"

"Mind? Hell no," I say, holding out my hand to her. "After you, gorgeous."

We step into the huge shower stall, and I turn on the water as Maggie wraps her arms around me.

"Come here," I say, turning around to face her. I pull her closer, feeling myself growing hard again by our contact. Bending to kiss her, my hands roam over her body as her hands do the same to mine. Even though we've just had sex, I'm ready to take her again. I know I'll never get enough of her. I lift her easily around the waist, and hold her for a moment as I position myself between her legs. Maggie moans with pleasure as I slide into her again. "This was definitely a good idea," she sighs.

"Good morning Malcolm," Dr. Grant said as he entered the room. "Sorry about the hold up."

"No problem," Malcolm said, grateful to have his train of thought derailed.

"Minor family crisis," Grant said with a smile.

"Everything okay?" Malcolm asked.

"Oh yes, perfectly," Grant said as he sat down facing Malcolm. He looked at him for a moment, as though sizing him up. "So how are you doing today?"

Malcolm shrugged. "Okay I guess," he said.

Grant nodded. "Did you sleep last night?"

"A little."

"Did you try the relaxation exercises I showed you?" Grant asked.

Malcolm hadn't, but was reluctant to tell the doctor so. "No, sorry," he said.

Grant wasn't surprised. Malcolm was one of the biggest challenges he'd known as a psychologist. It was clear that he had a lot of emotional baggage, but was very reluctant to talk about anything from his past. And Grant knew that if he couldn't get the young man to confide in him, then it would be very difficult to help him through his current state of depression.

"Not to worry," Grant said. "Look, I know how reluctant you were about coming here," he said. "I know you're doing it because of your grandmother. Am I right?"

"Pretty much," Malcolm said, not feeling the need to deny it.

"Fair enough," Grant said. "But if you give me a chance, I promise that you won't regret it. All I'm asking is for you to talk to me, about anything you want."

Malcolm sighed, and fought the urge to look at his watch. "How's that gonna help?" he asked.

Grant smiled. "I know what I'm talking about, Malcolm. Trust me."

"Okay," Malcolm said, though still felt rather ambivalent. "What do you want to talk about?"

Grant thought about this for a moment. "Tell me about the summer your grandmother left Boston," he said, he felt quite certain that was the event that marked a water shed moment in Malcolm's life.

Malcolm frowned, and looked away. "I don't see what that's got to do with how I'm feeling now," he said.

"You lost someone in your life whom you loved," Grant pointed out. "Someone who loved you. Sound familiar?"

Malcolm looked back at the doctor. "It's not the same," he said.

"Perhaps not on the surface," Grant agreed. "Go on. I want to know about that summer."

Malcolm sighed, trying to keep control of the flood of emotions thinking about that summer heralded. "I'm sure she already told you what happened," he said.

"She did," Grant said. "She was given a court order to stay away from you, including phone calls," he said. "And then she came back here. What I don't know is your perspective."

Malcolm stared at the man, fighting his anger. "I think you can guess," he said. "How the fuck do you think I felt?"

Grant ignored Malcolm's anger and pressed on. "I'm sure I can imagine," he said. "Tell me about that summer."

Malcolm resented the man for pressing, but judged that it was his job to do so.

"I was heartbroken," Malcolm said. "I probably cried for a week straight. Didn't eat, couldn't sleep. Kind of like now."

Grant nodded. "And how did your father handle your behaviour?" he asked. "Did he try to reason with you?"

"Reason with me?" Malcolm asked with a bitter smile. "No, he didn't. He just shipped me off to boarding school. *That's* how he dealt with my behaviour."

Grant frowned, not expecting this. "He sent you to boarding school?"

"Yeah," Malcolm said. "Even though I begged him not to, he did it anyway. Put me on a train by myself headed for New York. School hadn't even started yet, but he wanted to get rid of me. And once my grandmother was gone, he figured he could do whatever he wanted since she wasn't there to look out for me anymore."

Grant sat quietly for a moment, writing down a few notes. He'd suspected that Malcolm's relationship with his father wasn't a good one, and what he'd just learned only added credence to this belief.

"Tell me about boarding school," Grant said, looking back up at Malcolm. "Did you make friends there?"

"Yeah sure," Malcolm said. "Lots of them. But I got in trouble a lot. The teachers were pretty strict."

"I'm sure," Grant said. "What kind of trouble did you get into?"

Malcolm shrugged. "The usual shit," he said. "I never did anything bad enough to get suspended or anything like that," he said. "Just ....stupid stuff."

Grant nodded in understanding. "Did the teachers tell your father?"

"Of course," Malcolm said. "Every single time."

"And what was his reaction?"

"Most of the time he'd just call and yell at me," Malcolm said. "Then there was that one year he wouldn't let me come home for Christmas."

Grant frowned. "How old were you?" he asked.

"Ten," Malcolm said. "I spent Christmas holidays in the boarding school residence," he said. "Me and a couple of foreign exchange students. I guess he figured I'd behave if I missed Christmas."

"And did you?"

"Not really," Malcolm said. "It only made things worse, made me mad at him. I didn't really care anymore what he thought."

Grant felt quite sure that this wasn't true; in fact, he'd be willing to bet that the opposite was. Malcolm had never been able to please his father, and pretended that he didn't care about his opinion as a defense mechanism. The more he got to know him, the more layers Grant discovered. Clearly Malcolm Sullivan was a complicated young man.

After leaving Dr. Grant's office, Malcolm stood outside on the sidewalk for a long time. It was a grey, wet day, and people were walking about with umbrellas. Malcolm stood, struggling with the anxiety inside of him. He hadn't thought about those years at boarding school in a long time, and now that he'd spoken of them again, the feelings he'd learned to sublimate were threatening to overwhelm him. The night his father had called him to tell him he wasn't sending him a train ticket to come home for the holidays came back to him, despite his efforts to hold the memory of it at bay...

I don't know what the hell you were thinking, boy. Why would you do such a stupid thing? Putting frogs in the girls' dormitory? Have you got shit for brains or what?

It was just a joke, Dad. I didn't mean to scare them. I wanted to make them laugh.

You're an idiot, you know that? Since when do girls find frogs in their bed funny?

I don't know...I guess I wasn't thinking.

That's your problem, Malcolm. You never think.

I'm sorry.

Sorry doesn't cut it, not this time. You're staying there for the break. Maybe that will teach you to think.

You mean I'm not coming home for Thanksgiving? For Christmas?

That's right, genius. Maybe some time alone up there will straighten you up.

Please let me come home, Dad! I promise I'll never do anything bad again! Please don't leave me alone up here! I'm sorry!

Too late. I'm not sending you a ticket, and that's final. Don't worry, maybe Santa Claus will be able to find up you up there....

I need a drink, Malcolm thought, not even trying to fight the old urges. *I need a drink right now.* Taking his phone out of his jacket pocket, he located a nearby pub. According to the map, it was only a couple of blocks away. Shoving his phone back in his pocket, Malcolm headed there at once.

Norman and Betty were in the garden working while they waited for Malcolm to return from town. He'd asked them to wait at home, for having them wait for him at the doctor's office was making him feel awkward and uncomfortable. They agreed, but both were anxious as they waited for him to return. And as the time passed with no sign of him, their anxiety only worsened.

"It's almost 5," Betty said, looking at her watch. She looked at Norman, the worry evident on her face. "Where could he be? His session ended at 3:30."

Norman nodded as he wiped his hands on an old towel. "I'll go have a walk downtown," he said. "Maybe he's gone into the shops."

"Maybe," Betty said doubtfully. Neither one voiced their fears, but they were both thinking the same thing: he's drinking again.

"I'll be back soon," Norman said. After a moment's thought he gave her a peck on the cheek. "Don't worry, Betty. He's fine."

Betty nodded, and then watched Norman head into the house. Malcolm hadn't been fine since he'd arrived more than a month ago. She was sure it would be a long time before he was again.

After washing up, Norman headed towards town. It wasn't a far walk, as Inverness was a rather small place. Norman had a good idea where he'd find Malcolm, but hadn't told Betty. He knew how worried she was about their grandson, and didn't want to add to her worries. But Norman knew that Malcolm had struggled with drinking for a good part of his adult life. With all that was going on in his life, it wouldn't be surprising if Malcolm was wrestling with those demons again.

The Thistle Inn was a few minutes' walk down the road from Betty's house, and it was there that Norman headed to find his grandson. It was already quite busy inside, for the dinner hour had begun and the pub served full dinners as well as a variety of alcoholic beverages. Norman looked around the pub, and then spotted Malcolm sitting at the bar. He walked over to him at once.

"Another pint, love?" the barmaid asked Malcolm, giving him a warm smile. She'd been interested in him since he set foot in the door. The fact that he had an exotic American accent only added to his charm.

"Yeah sure," Malcolm said.

"That accent of yours," the barmaid asked as she drew another pint of Guinness, "what part of America is that from?"

"Boston," Malcolm said as she set a fresh pint in front of him.

"It's lovely," she said. "What are you doing here? Vacation?"

"Something like that," Malcolm said.

"I'll have one as well, miss." Malcolm turned to see his grandfather sitting in the barstool beside him. Norman turned to Malcolm with a smile. "You don't mine if I join you, do you lad?" he asked.

"No," Malcolm said. "Just as long as you don't lecture me about drinking," he said, turning back to this pint.

"That's not why I'm here," Norman said as he accepted his own drink.

Malcolm was grateful to hear this and turned back to his grandfather. "So why are you here?"

Norman frowned. "Do I need a reason to share a pint with my grandson?"

Malcolm felt badly for his question. After all, his grandparents had been nothing but supportive of him. "No, of course not," he said. "Sorry Grandpa, I'm just feeling pretty low."

"Rough session today?" Norman asked.

"Yeah," Malcolm said, taking a drink of his beer. "The worst."

"Sorry to hear it, lad," Norman said. They sat in silence for a few minutes, simply drinking their beer and watching the football match on the television over the bar. "Celtic's doing well this season," he commented.

"Sure are," Malcolm agreed, grateful that his grandfather wasn't questioning him about his session with Dr. Grant. "We should get to a game some time," he said. "Check out when they're playing up here."

"That would be fun," Norman said. "You ever play? Footie?"

"No, hockey was always my game," Malcolm said.

"Of course," Norman said. "Boston Bruins' fan, right?"

Malcolm smiled. "Yeah, good memory," he said. "Bastards bowed out of the playoffs early this year," he said. "Not the champs anymore."

"Sorry to hear it," Norman said. "Maybe next year, eh?"

"Maybe," Malcolm said, taking a drink of beer. "Not holdin' my breath though."

Norman laughed, and took a drink of his own beer, content for now simply to be there for his grandson.

Boston

Closing time had come to the Hart and Hound. It was Saturday night, so Mick, Hugh and Will were kept busy as they made their rounds to ensure that everyone was out of the establishment before locking up.

"Can's clear," Hugh said as he started helping Will stack chairs.

"Okay good," Mick said as he took the day's earnings out of the till.

"Something wrong?" Hugh asked, noticing how quiet Will had become.

"Just remembering," Will said.

"Remembering what?" Hugh asked.

Will looked towards the restrooms. "How many times I hauled Malcolm out of there," he said. "Before he started dating my sister he was pissed out of his gourd every night." He frowned. "Guess he didn't change nearly as much as we all thought he had."

Hugh said nothing, as he continued putting up chairs. He'd been thinking a lot lately about what the O'Toole family had been going through. They were good people, he'd decided, and didn't deserve what had befallen them. He knew he was risking much by speaking up, but his conscious had been bothering him of late. It wasn't a feeling he was used to, and found it very inconvenient. But it wouldn't be ignored, not any more.

"Hey Will, you got a minute?" Hugh said as Will made a last check behind the bar.

"A minute? What for?" Will asked.

Hugh looked at him, and then at Mick who had just emerged from the kitchen. "I need to tell you guys something. Something real important."

"What's that?" Will asked.

"It's about your sister," Hugh said, gaining Will's immediate attention. "I know why she left town."

Will grew tense at the mention of Maggie, and stepped closer to Hugh. "What do you know about my sister?"

"Plenty," Hugh said. "Old man Sullivan ran her out of town," he said. "Blackmailed her to leave. That's why she's gone."

Will frowned and exchanged a look with his father. Each of them were having a hard time believing the man's story. "Why would he do that?" Mick asked.

"She was engaged to his son," Hugh said. "You know that I'm sure. But what you might not know is that the old man was dead set against it. Figured your sister was only after the family fortune. So he forced her to leave and never come back."

"How?" Will asked. "Maggie loved Malcolm, she would never be forced out of his life."

"Well she isn't here now, is she?" Hugh asked.

"She left because the bastard cheated on her," Mick said, starting to have doubts.

Hugh shook his head. "No, that wasn't why she left. She left because the old man said he'd arrange for someone she loved to have an accident if she didn't."

Will's eyes widened in shock. "What? He threatened to *kill* Malcolm if she didn't leave him?"

"No, it wasn't Malcolm's life he threatened. It was yours, Will."

Will stood transfixed, as though he'd had the wind knocked clear out of him.

"How...how do you know all this?" Mick asked.

A look passed through Hugh's eyes, a look of shame. "I know because I was there when he did it."

Hugh then proceeded to tell the two men the whole story, including his part in Maggie's abduction.

"You took my daughter by force to that monster?" Mick asked once Hugh had finished his narrative.

"Yes sir, I did," Hugh admitted, unable to look Mick in the eye. "I didn't hurt her, it was just a job, I did as I was told."

Mick didn't reply, but his steely gaze didn't leave Hugh.

"So Malcolm *didn't* cheat on Maggie," said Will, awash with guilt when he considered the last time he'd seen Malcolm. "I should have believed him when he told me that!"

"So assuming all this is true, what's to prevent me from calling the cops right now and having you arrested for your part in all this?" Mick asked.

"Because if you ever want Jack Sullivan to be brought to justice, you're gonna need me to do it," Hugh replied.

"He has a point," Will pointed out. "But if Sullivan's got all kinds of paid thugs, how can we make sure he won't do something now that the cat is out of the bag?"

"We can't let him know that we know," Mick said. "But we have to tell Malcolm. The poor lad's suffered enough in all this. You have his number, don't you?" He asked Will.

"Yeah I do," Will replied, pulling out his cell phone. "He's going to be royally pissed when he finds out all this."

"Good," Mick said. "Then maybe that bastard of a father of his will get what he has coming to him."

Will scrolled through his contact list and found Malcolm's number. He clicked on it, but only got Malcolm's voice mail. He sighed in exasperation and waited for the recorded message to conclude before speaking. "Malcolm it's Will. Call me as soon as you get this message, it's urgent." Will looked up at his father. "Not answering. Maybe I should go over to his place and talk to him."

Mick nodded. "Good idea," he said. "And while you do that, I'm going to call your mother. I need to let her know that we know everything," he said. He frowned as he reflected on how oddly Irene had been acting, how secretive. Now he understood why, and realized that she'd had no choice. She was protecting both Maggie and Will, and doing it in the only way she knew how. "That bloody bastard has gone too far," he said. "There's not a doubt in me mind that Sullivan will follow through on his threats against you Will. I think you should quit your job before he has the chance to arrange for an accident."

"I agree with your dad, Will, " Hugh said. "Sullivan's ruthless. Knocking you off would be nothing for him."

Will nodded. "I think you're right," he said. He shook his head. "I can't believe the old man would go to such lengths to keep Maggie and Malcolm apart."

Mick frowned. "He's a soulless man," he said. "I knew that the first time I met him."

"You're right," Hugh said. "He's a man used to getting his way, and will stop at nothing to make sure he does."

Will headed directly over to Malcolm and Maggie's apartment complex. It was very late at night, but what Will had to say would not wait. He only hoped that Malcolm would be forgiving, and understand why Will had acted the he had the last time they'd seen one another. *I never should have believed that,* Will admonished himself as he parked his truck. *How could I think such a thing of one of my best friends?*

It was raining as Will entered the complex, and was met immediately by the night doorman, Gerry.

"Good evening, Mr. O'Toole," Gerry said, recognizing Will at once.

"Hi," Will said, not remembering the man's name. "I know it's late, but I really need to talk to Malcolm."

Gerry frowned ever so slightly. "I'm sorry, Mr. O'Toole, but Mr. Sullivan isn't home."

"Oh," Will said, disappointed. "Guess you have no idea when he'll be back, do you?"

Gerry was rather surprised that one of Malcolm's friends didn't know that he'd been out of the country for close to two months, and debated telling him what he knew. "I'm afraid not," Gerry said finally, deciding that discretion was the better part of valour. "I'm sorry."

"It's okay," Will said. "Guess I'll just have to come back tomorrow."

Gerry said nothing, and simply gave Will a pleasant smile as the young man exited the building.

Fifteen

Antigonish

It was past midnight when Irene's cell phone began to ring. It startled both women awake, each of them alarmed by the lateness of the call. Irene picked up the phone, frowning when she saw the number.

"Who is it?" Maggie asked.

"Your father," Irene said.

Maggie's heart jumped to her throat. Had something happened to Will? Why would Mick be calling so late?

"Hello?"

"Hi love, it's me," Mick said. "I'm sorry I woke you, but I needed to talk to you right away."

"You're scaring me Mick," Irene said. "What's happened? What's wrong?"

"I know what happened, Irene," Mick said. "I know the whole story."

Irene's eyes darted nervously to Maggie, who sat on the edge of her bed, listening intently. "What do you know?" she asked.

"I know that Jack Sullivan forced Maggie out of Boston," Mick said. "I know that he threatened to kill Will if she didn't do it."

Irene closed her eyes. Part of her was relieved that it was all out in the open; but part of her was still terrified that harm would come to her first born. "How did you find out?" she asked quietly.

104

"Our new bouncer told us," Mick said. "Turns out he was one of the goons that helped Sullivan carry out his plan."

"You mean Hugh?" she asked, shocked that the man she'd come to trust and like had done such a thing. "If he's one of Sullivan's thugs, then why would he tell you?" Irene said. "Why would he do that?"

"I guess he feels guilty," Mick said. "And he got sacked by the old man recently, so maybe some of it is revenge. But now that we have him on our side, we can use him to nail that bastard to the wall."

Irene glanced at Maggie, who had gleaned enough of the conversation to know what had happened. "You haven't told Malcolm, have you?" Irene asked.

"No, not yet," Mick replied. "Will went over to see him earlier, but after what happened the last time they saw each other, I'm not sure how that well that will go."

"What happened the last time they saw each other?" Irene asked.

"Will put him on his arse with a right cross," Mick said.

"Oh no," Irene sighed. "Well perhaps it's better if Will isn't the one to tell him. Besides, Maggie is sure that if Malcolm learns of this he'll go after his father and do something that could land him in prison."

"Well the bastard deserves whatever Malcolm gives him, in my opinion," Mick said.

"We have to make sure that Will is safe, Mick" Irene said. "That's more important than anything else right now."

"Of course. I've convinced him to quit his job," Mick said. "He's pretty rattled by all this, as you can imagine. We all are. I can't believe you and Maggie have been carrying this alone all this time," he said. "The poor lass!"

"Aye, and poor Malcolm," Irene said, relieved that she could discuss the situation openly with her husband. "He's suffered as much as Maggie in all this. But he has no idea what's going on. Imagine how he must feel."

"I know," Mick said. "I'm going to come up there with the lads, Irene," he said. "We need to talk about how we're going to handle all this."

"Okay love, if you think that's best," Irene said. "I'm happy you know, Mick. It's been terrible having to lie to you and the lads all this time."

"You had no choice darlin', I know that now," he said. "But now that I do know, we're going to handle this together. And some way we'll find a solution to all this."

Maggie sat as still as a statue as she tried to glean the content of the conversation her mother and father were having. Somehow they knew, somehow they had found out. But how? And, more importantly, did Jack Sullivan know that they knew?

"What's happened?" Maggie asked her mother as soon as Irene had ended her conversation.

"They know everything," Irene said. "And they're coming up here. I think that's best, don't you?"

Maggie nodded, her mind racing as she contemplated the possible implications of this unexpected turn of events. "How did they find out?" she asked.

"A wee bit of luck," Irene said. "Remember that new bouncer your Da hired?"

Maggie nodded.

"Turned out he was one of the thugs who'd taken you to see Sullivan," Irene said.

"What?" Maggie said. "Why would one of those thugs rat Jack out? They did anything he asked without question."

"Hugh, that's the man's name, was fired by Sullivan some time ago," Irene explained. "That's how he came to land a job at the Hart. I think part of his reasoning was revenge, pure and simple. But I think the larger part was that he got to know Will and saw what a good man he is. Will became his friend, and I think Hugh felt that it was the right thing to do, telling him and your father."

Maggie shook her head in astonishment. "I can't believe it," she said. "Those men who took me were so cold, so frightening. I can't even imagine that either of them would have any good in them at all."

Irene smiled. "Hugh is a good person once you get to know him," she said. "I suppose he was a victim of circumstance."

"Maybe so," Maggie said.

"Didn't I tell you that the Good Lord has a way of making things work out?" Irene said. "And sometimes it's in the least likely manner imaginable."

Boston

Will tried once again to see Malcolm, but was told by a different doormen that Malcolm wasn't home. Will began to worry that Malcolm had left word with the doormen not to allow him entry; he'd certainly have just cause to do so. But this didn't solve Will's immediate problem: how to contact Malcolm. He decided to try again throughout the day, but after many disappointments, decided that the best he could do for now was leave another message on Malcolm's voice mail. He only hoped that Malcolm would hear his messages sooner rather than later.

"You don't know how long you'll be gone?" Hugh asked. Mick had been loath to tell him that the job he'd so desperately needed was now gone, but with the present situation, there was no choice.

"No, I'm afraid not," Mick replied. "We're not sure how long it will take for all this to be sorted out. I'm sorry about the job, but..."

"Don't apologize sir," Hugh said. "I get it. I can find something else, don't worry about me."

Mick nodded. "I want to thank you for coming forward the way you did," he said, extending a hand to Hugh. "That took courage."

Hugh shrugged. "Just doing what I thought was right."

"We'll be in touch," Mick said. "Good luck to you, Hugh."

"Thanks. Good luck to you too," Hugh said. "Hope that son of a bitch Sullivan gets what's coming to him."

Mick smiled. "We all do."

Mick and his three sons and Will's girlfriend, Alli, made the long drive up to Antigonish the next day. Mick had considered asking his uncle to take over the pub in their absence; but given the fact that they had no idea how long they'd be gone, decided against it. Ted wasn't a young man after all, and the business was just too much for him to handle on his own for long.

It was quite late at night when they arrived at Pat and Noreen's house. Maggie was excited at the prospect of seeing her father and brothers again after so long. And when the door opened, she couldn't help but run to meet them.

"My poor girl," Mick said, holding Maggie tightly. "I hate to think of what you've gone through all this time!"

Maggie couldn't say anything in response, for the lump in her throat was too tight. She simply hugged her father tightly, overcome with emotion by their reunion.

"You did all this for me, didn't you?" Will said when it was his turn to greet his sister. "I'm so sorry you were put through this, Megs," he said, holding her tightly. "But it's all over now. That bastard Sullivan can't hurt any of us now."

I really wish I could believe that, Maggie thought.

After reuniting with her younger brothers, the family sat down around the kitchen table, along with Pat and Noreen, and had a late snack of tea and cookies.

"You look wonderful, Megs," Alli said.

"Thanks," Maggie said. "It was such a relief when the morning sickness subsided."

"You look like you swallowed a basketball," Quinn said with a smile.

Maggie smiled, and looked down at her rather round belly. "Did Mum tell you that I'm having twins?" She asked.

"She did," Mick said. "I hope you're back with Malcolm before they're born," he said.

"I called him, Megs," Will said. "And I went over to see him a few times, but he was never home. I left messages asking him to call me, but I'm not sure he will."

"Why wouldn't he?" Maggie asked.

Will looked guilty for a moment. "Well, the last time we saw each other things got kinda...ugly between us."

Maggie frowned. "What do you mean, ugly? What happened?"

"I punched him," Will said. "I thought he'd cheated on you, Megs, and I was really pissed off at him. And when he denied it, I lost it. I dropped him, and I feel terrible about it now that I know the truth."

"Poor Malcolm," she said softly. "He's suffered so much because of all this. I can't imagine how confused his is right now, how hurt!"

"Well as soon as we find him you can tell him everything," Irene said.

Maggie shook her head. "How can I tell him? He'll go after his father and end up in prison!"

"Malcolm is smarter than that, Megs," Will said. "He has to be told. This has gone on long enough. He's miserable and lost without you. And he deserves to be a part of his children's life."

His words hit her hard, and the tears that seemed to come so easily to her these days filled her eyes. "You're right," she said softly. "He does. I need him so much. I can't imagine raising these two babies without him. I'm just so worried about his reaction to all this."

"Malcolm knows that you need him, love," Irene said. "He's not going to jeopardize a future with you and the wee bairns, no matter how angry he is. Have faith that he'll do the right thing."

Maggie nodded, not really seeing that she had any option but to do so.

"You should call him, Megs," Alli suggested. "Tell him where you are."

Maggie nodded. "I think so," she said. She stood up. "I'll ring him right now," she said, and left her family to make the most important phone call of her life.

With trembling hands Maggie entered Malcolm's number. He mouth was dry as she waited to hear his voice, a voice she'd heard in her dreams for months now. The phone didn't even right three times before her call was sent to his voice mail. *Hi, this is Malcolm Sullivan. When you hear the beep you'll know what to do.* She smiled through her tears, the sound of his voice making her heart race. But before she could even say hello, an automated message dashed her hopes. *The mailbox you are trying to reach is full. No new messages may be received at this time.* Deciding she's just have to try again, Maggie tried not to be discouraged by this setback. *I'll talk to him tomorrow,* she told herself. *And we'll be together again very soon.*

Sixteen

$\mathcal{M}$alcolm's therapy continued, and with each session he grew a little more comfortable, a little less embarrassed. He discovered that therapy did help, that talking out his feelings wasn't as much of a waste of time as he'd originally thought. In addition to his therapy, Malcolm had decided to remove all outside distractions, so he'd turned his phone off, and hadn't been online for weeks. At first it had been difficult to cut himself off from the world that way; but as time passed he found that it afforded him a nice cocoon in which he could heal and regain his strength.

Time spent in Inverness with his grandparents had proven to be just as therapeutic as the long talks he had with Dr. Grant. He spent his mornings gardening with his grandmother, and in the evenings he went for long walks with his grandfather. They would walk for an hour or more, talking about everything, growing closer with each passing day.

Has he'd planned, Malcolm procured tickets for an Inverness Caledonian Thistle's football match. Betty had declined the invitation to attend, deciding that Malcolm needed the time with his grandfather alone. Malcolm was a little disappointed that she hadn't come with them, but decided he'd have a good time with his grandfather nonetheless.

It was a warm afternoon when Norman and Malcolm arrived at Tulloch Caledonian Stadium.

"Should be a good one," Malcolm said as they took their seats. "Aberdeen's only a point behind them in the standings."

Norm nodded as he took a drink of his beer. He was pleased that Malcolm had taken such an interest in the local sports team, for it helped him keep his mind off of his problems. "Should be," Norm said. "But without Draper they'll be hard pressed."

"McCay's a beast," Malcolm said as the players filed out onto the pitch. "They'll win."

Norm smiled. "Care to make a wager? Winner buys loser a pint at the Thistle after the match."

Malcolm smiled with a nod. "You got yourself a deal," he said.

"Guess you've never seen a hockey game, have you?" Malcolm asked as they watched the action.

"Can't say that I have, no," Norm replied. "Not much hockey down under."

"Didn't think so," Malcolm said. "You'd love it, though. It's so fast, lots of action."

"Lots of fighting from what I've heard about it," Norm commented.

Malcolm nodded. "Yeah, there's that too," he said. "Just a part of the game."

Norman frowned. "Seems strange," he said. "You played hockey in college. You ever fight?"

Malcolm smiled. "More times than I like to admit," he said. "I'm kind of a hot head sometimes."

Norman laughed. "Must be the Scottish in you," he said. "Don't tell your Nan I said that though," he was quick to add.

Malcolm laughed. "I won't say a word."

Aberdeen ending up winning the match 2-1, and so it was Malcolm who was buying as he and his grandfather headed to what had become their favourite watering hole.

"Better luck next time, lad," Norm said as he saluted his grandson with his pint of beer.

Malcolm smiled as he took a drink of his own pint. "Yeah sure," he said. He looked around the pub, many of the faces now familiar to him. He appreciated that his grandfather didn't lecture him about drinking, and let him enjoy the occasional pint. Malcolm was well aware of his tendency to overdo it where alcohol was concerned, and was making a concerted effort to drink in moderation. As time went on, the easier it became. The therapy was helping him tremendously, the bonds he was forging with this grandparents even more so. But Malcolm knew that this time would come to an end. Norman had a family in Australia who missed him, and with the Australian spring about to start, a farm to look after. As for Malcolm, he knew that he needed to return to the life he'd left in Boston. He was better now, physically and emotionally, and knew that his problems had to be faced, not avoided.

"So what are your plans, Malcolm?" Norm asked as they sat side by side at the bar. "Have you given any thought to the future?"

Malcolm nodded. "Dr. Grant's been getting me to do that, actually," he said.

"And how does that sit with you?" Norm asked. "Are you ready?"

"I think so," Malcolm said. "Though I'm not really sure what my future holds, to tell you the truth. I always envisioned my future revolving around Maggie. But I have to accept that isn't the case anymore. I suppose I'm still trying to find my touchstone. Does that make sense?"

Norm nodded. "It does," he said. "After my wife Nora died, I felt that way. But after you get past the grief and the sense of loss, you find the strength to go on. You have no choice, after all."

Malcolm admired his grandfather's wisdom, his fortitude. Indeed, both of his grandparents had gone through great hardship in their lives, and yet had lived through it and risen above it. And he figured that if they could do it, then so could he.

Antigonish, Nova Scotia

Maggie had grown frustrated and anxious about her inability to contact Malcolm. He never answered his phone and his voice mail box was full. She tried every day to reach him, and had begun sending emails to all of his email accounts. But she received no replies, nor any indication that he'd even seen or heard her messages. Maggie began to wonder if he was so angry with her for leaving her that he was simply ignoring her now. And the thought of that was the most distressing of all.

It was past six o'clock, and Maggie was exhausted. She didn't mind helping Marilyn out occasionally when she was short-staffed; but as her pregnancy progressed she found it increasingly difficult to do so.

"Hi there," called one of the mothers as she came down the stairs. Her name was Molly Harper, and she was a nurse at the local hospital. "How was my Daisy today?"

"She didn't eat much today," Maggie said. "I think she might be coming down with something," she said. "She seemed quite lethargic most of the day."

Molly frowned. "That's no good," she said. "Any fever?"

"Low grade," Maggie replied. "I made sure she had plenty to drink."

Molly nodded. "Thanks for taking such good care of her, Maggie," she said.

Marilyn, who was close by, spoke up. "You know, Maggie's a trained nurse."

Molly's face registered her surprise. "Really? So why are you working here then?"

"I'm only in Canada temporarily and can't apply for a job at a hospital," Maggie explained. She wished Marilyn hadn't said anything about her training.

"Well if you miss it, they're always looking for volunteers at St. Martha's," Molly said. "I work on the maternity ward there."

Maggie's interest was piqued. "Really? I'd love that," she said. "Though I don't have much free time working here," she added.

"You have weekends," Marilyn pointed out.

Maggie nodded. The thought of keeping her hand in the profession she'd worked so hard to be a part of appealed to her. "I'll think about it," she said.

Molly smiled. "Let me give you my cell number. That way you can call me if you have any questions about St. Martha's."

"That would be grand," Maggie replied with a smile.

Inverness

"So how did you enjoy the football match?" Dr. Grant asked.

"It was great," Malcolm said. "I mean Inverness lost, but it was still fun to watch."

Grant nodded. "Yeah I heard," he said. "I heard that the refs were pretty biased too."

"Well it does seem that way sometimes when you're rooting for one side," Malcolm said. "When you're playing it feels that way all the time."

"I'm sure," Grant said. "So you've played football?"

"No, I played hockey in college," Malcolm said. "Was pretty good too."

Grant nodded. "What did you like most about playing?"

Malcolm thought about this for a minute. "Not sure if there was just one thing," he said. "I loved the competition," he said. "Loved the thrill of the game. Hockey's a fast game, real physical."

"So I've heard," Grant said. "So you liked to play because you played well. It gave you a great sense of satisfaction."

"I suppose so," Malcolm said. "Of course at one time I loved the attention from women that I'd get. That all changed when I met Maggie, though."

"What sort of attention?" Grant asked.

"Well, you know," Malcolm said, a little uncomfortable. "Lots of women like the athletic types. They sort of make themselves ...available, if you know what I mean."

"You mean sexually available," Grant said.

"Yeah," Malcolm said.

"So you would have sex with women who watched you play hockey?" Grant asked.

"Sometimes," Malcolm said, starting to feel awkward. "It didn't happen all the time."

"Did you ever have a relationship with any of the women? Or was it a onetime thing?" Grant asked.

Malcolm frowned, wondering where the line of questioning was coming from. "Not really, no," he said. "It's not something I'm proud of Doc, believe me," he said. "But it is what it is. Part of who I was."

Grant nodded. He wondered if Malcolm had ever considered the possibility that he used casual sex as a way to distance himself from others. It was clear that Malcolm had been emotionally damaged most of his life; one -night stands were a common by-product of a dysfunctional personality.

"But you're not like that now," Grant pointed out. "You've changed a lot since then, haven't you?"

"Yeah," Malcolm said, not liking where this was going.

"It was Maggie that changed you?"

"It was for Maggie that I changed," Malcolm said. "She made me want to be a better person. She...she made me a better person," he said, finding it hard to prevent the lump from forming in his throat.

Grant could see that he was struggling, but felt that a catharsis was needed. "But she's not in your life anymore," he said. "And you're still the same man you were with her."

Malcolm frowned. "You trying to make a point here, Doc?"

"Always," Grant said. "You've been defining yourself by the relationships you have with others. First your father, and then Maggie. It's time for you to define who you are based on you and you alone, Malcolm. The people around us shape us, but ultimately we make ourselves who we are. Don't you agree?"

Malcolm was silent as he considered this. He'd never thought of things in quite that way before. "I guess," he said. "Trouble is, I'm not even sure who I am any more. I'm not a college student, I'm not a hockey player, and I'm not in a relationship..." he stopped as he fought against the tears that threatened to fill his eyes. "I don't know who I am right now. I don't know where I'm going, what I'm supposed to do."

"That is the challenge you must face, Malcolm," Grant said. "You have to find out just who Malcolm Sullivan is. And you're the only one who knows that. No one can tell you."

Malcolm nodded. "I know," he said quietly. "It's just that...I'm not quite sure how."

Grant smiled. "I think you do, Malcolm," he said. "You're not the same man who first came into my office three months ago. I think you're stronger than you realize. Have confidence in yourself, son."

Malcolm smiled. "Thanks Doc," he said.

Antigonish, Nova Scotia

Pat could see how restless Mick was becoming the longer they stayed in town. He knew Mick well enough to know that he was a man that was accustomed to being busy. Living out of a suitcase wasn't exactly Mick's idea of a good time. So one evening Pat invited Mick to his favourite watering hole, the

Piper's Pub. Situated on the campus of Francis Xavier University, Piper's was a popular place, frequented by both students and locals alike.

"Doug I'd like you to meet my cousin, Mick O'Toole," Pat said to the barman. "He's visiting from Boston."

"Good to meet you, Mick," Doug said, extending a hand over the bar towards Mick.

"Same here," Mick said. He looked around the place admiringly. "Nice place."

Doug smiled. "Thanks," he said.

"Mick owns his own establishment down in Boston," Pat said.

"Is that right?" Doug said.

Mick nodded. "Sure is," he said. "The Hart and Hound's her name."

Doug nodded. "Fine name," he said. "What can I get you gents?"

"Two pints of the black stuff," Pat said.

"Coming right up," Doug said.

As Mick looked around he began to feel nostalgic, missing his own pub. Pat must have noticed and put a hand on his cousin's shoulder.

"Don't worry," Pat said. "You'll be back behind the bar of the Hart before you know it."

Mick looked at him and snorted. "Not sure about that," he said. "This situation with Maggie is a God-awful mess."

Pat nodded. "It is," he agreed. "But soon enough things will work out. Keep the faith, Mick."

Mick wanted to, but was having a hard time doing so. It seemed that Jack Sullivan had covered every possible contingency. Men like Jack Sullivan always knew how to win.

"You don't know this Sullivan bastard like I do," Mick said. "He's one cold hearted man, Pat. He gets his way no matter what. He's not accustomed to losing, probably never has."

Pat listened to his cousin, seeing how bitter he was. "That isn't right," he said. "Why is it that men like him always get their way?"

"Money Pat," Mick said. "Simple as that."

"So Mick," Doug said as he set the pints down before them. "You looking for something to do while you're here?"

"Why do you ask?" Mick asked as he picked up his glass of beer.

"My regular barman's broke his wrist," Doug said. "I'm pretty swamped here without him. You'd be doing me a favour if you could put in a few hours."

Mick was surprised by Doug's offer, and very tempted by it. "I don't have Canadian citizenship," he said. "I'd love to, but don't think I can."

"Maggie's working without citizenship," Pat reminded him.

"Is she getting paid?" Doug asked.

Mick wasn't sure if he ought to answer. He barely knew the man. How did he know he wasn't a federal agent from Revenue Canada?

"She's getting paid under the table," Pat said, obviously trusting Doug enough to tell him.

"Nice," Doug said. "Any time we can stick it to the government, so much the better."

Mick laughed. "We have the same way sentiment south of the border," he said.

"So what do you say, Mick?" Doug asked. "I'd pay you under the table too if you want."

Mick considered this. "Let me think about it," he said. "Can I let you know?"

"Sure thing," Doug said. "But the sooner the better, okay? I really need someone soon."

"I'll tell you tomorrow, how's that?" Mick said.

"Good enough," Doug said.

Seventeen

Maggie smiled as she entered the room of a 12 year old boy named Peter who was recovering from an appendectomy.

"Good morning Peter," Maggie said as she approached his bed. "How are you feeling this morning?"

"Sore," Peter replied.

"That's to be expected," Maggie said as she poured him a glass of water. "The doctor will be in to see you in a few minutes. He can give you some medicine for the pain if you like."

Peter nodded. "You sound like my grandma," he said.

"I do?" Maggie asked.

"Yeah, she lives in Ireland," Peter said. "Are you Irish?"

"Sure am," Maggie said. "My name is Maggie."

"Nice to meet you, Maggie," Peter said. "How come your uniform is different from the other nurses?"

"Well I'm a volunteer," she said.

"What's that mean?"

"It means I don't get paid for coming here," she said. "I'm a nurse, but because I'm not a Canadian citizen I can't work for money."

"Then why don't you just become a Canadian citizen?" Peter said.

Maggie smiled. "I might do that," she said. "I do love Canada, after all."

"Except the winters, right?"

Maggie turned to see the young pediatrician enter the room. His name was David Johansson, and he'd been very friendly with Maggie from the time she'd first started volunteering. "I don't mine them," she said.

Dave lifted his eyebrows. "Guess you haven't been around for enough of them," he said with a smile as he picked up Peter's chart. "How you feeling this morning buddy?" he asked.

"Sore," Peter said.

"I can help you with that," Dave said, looking over at Maggie. "Can you get this patient some ibuprofen please? 10 mills."

"Of course," Maggie said, and left the room.

"Is Doctor Dave in there?" asked Hannah, one of the nurses on the floor.

"Yes he is," Maggie said as she went to fetch the meds. "Why?"

Hannah smiled as she walked with Maggie. "Just wondering."

Maggie looked up at her with a frown. "Don't give me that, Hannah," she said. "I know you well enough by now to know you are mad about Dr. Johansson."

Hannah's face turned pink. "I wouldn't say that," she said. "I think he's very cute. But I'm pretty sure his interests lie elsewhere."

"What do you mean?" Maggie asked as she measured the meds under Hannah's supervision.

"Come on, Maggie," Hannah said. "He likes you! Surely you've noticed the way he looks at you."

Maggie frowned. "You're daft," she said. "I'm seven months pregnant. What man in his right mind would look at me that way?"

Hannah shrugged. "Ask anyone," she said. "I'm right."

Maggie just shook her head and left to return to her patient.

Dr. Dave looked up as she entered the room. He was listening to Peter's heart, so Maggie simply stood by and waited for him to finish.

"Sounds good," Dave said. "I think you're gonna live, kiddo," he said to Peter with a smile.

Peter smiled. "That's a relief," he said.

Dave laughed. "Here's Nurse Maggie with your meds," he said, giving her a smile.

Hannah's words jumped to mind as she handed Peter the paper cup containing the ibuprofen. Dr. Dave was certainly a handsome man: tall with dark wavy hair. But Maggie knew that she could never entertain the attentions of another man. Malcolm would always be her one and only.

"Thanks Maggie," Peter said.

"You're quite welcome," Maggie said. "Is there anything else I can get for you?"

"I'm good, thanks," Peter said, settling down for a nap.

Maggie watched him for a moment and then left the room. She was accompanied by Dr. Dave.

"So what about it?" Dave asked.

"Excuse me?" Maggie asked.

"Your citizenship," Dave said. "I heard what you said to Peter. Have you considered it?"

Maggie shrugged. "Haven't thought much about it, actually."

Dave frowned. "You should," he said. "You're an excellent nurse. Seems wrong that you don't get paid for what you're doing."

"I don't mind," she said.

Dave walked with her, trying to find the words to ask the questions he'd wanted to ask for weeks now. "So where is he?"

"Who?"

"The father of your baby," he said.

Maggie stopped and turned to him. "What??"

"Did he abandon you?" he asked with a frown. "Men like that should be castrated, if you ask me."

"I *didn't* ask you," she replied. "And what happened to him is none of your business, *Doctor.*"

Dave wanted to say more, but Maggie walked away from him in a manner that lead him to believe she wanted him to leave her alone. He did so, at least for the time being.

Martha's Vineyard, Massachusetts

Jack Sullivan looked at his watch nervously as the chauffeur took the exit for Martha's Vineyard. "Would you relax?" Deb said.

Jack looked at her. "Leave me alone," he said.

Deb frowned. "Why did you ask me to come with you anyway?" she asked.

"Because I can't talk to the old man," Jack said. "And you have a gift of the gab, so ..."

"Are you saying I have a big mouth?" Deb interjected.

Jack smiled. "Well, sometimes having a big mouth is a good thing," he said. "Came in handy this morning as I recall."

Deb gave him a playful punch in the arm. "You're a pig," she said.

Jack chuckled and turned to look out the window. "I wish the old fart would just die already," he said.

"What an awful thing to say about your own father," Deb said.

Jack shrugged. "No love lost between us, I can assure you," he said.

"Sort of like you and Malcolm?" she asked.

Jack turned and looked at her. "I don't hate my son," he said.

"Is that why you wanted me to break up him and Maggie? Because you love him so much?" she asked sarcastically.

Jack frowned. "None of your fucking business why I wanted you to break them up," he said. "Not that you succeeded," he added.

Deb sighed and looked out the window. "I did my best," she grumbled. "And I delivered that package like you asked. You said that would do the trick. Did it?" she asked, looking back at him.

"I don't know," Jack said. "I have no idea where Malcolm is right now. Last I heard he was in Scotland."

"Why would he go there?" Deb asked.

Jack had not told his girlfriend about his part in Maggie's disappearance. Despite the fact that they'd been lovers for several months, he didn't trust Deb. "His grandmother's there," he said.

Deb nodded. "So tell me about him," she said. "Your father. How old is he today?"

"85," Jack said.

"Wow," Deb said. "And he still lives on his own?"

"Yes, he's got a cook and a housekeeper, so he's well looked after," he said. "The old codger's too damn stubborn to admit it even if he needed help," he said.

"So why don't you get along?" she asked.

"You ask too many goddamn questions," Jack said. "You don't need to know any of that. All I want from you is for you to chat up the old fart so I don't have to. Got it?"

Deb sighed. "Yeah, got it."

The house where James Patrick Sullivan, AKA JP Sullivan, lived was not as large as Jack's home, but still stately and grand nonetheless. It was on the coast, for JP loved to fish, and was an avid boater when the weather was fine. He was a widower, and had been for some 20 years now, his beloved Elizabeth dying shortly after the birth of their youngest grandson, Malcolm. Although an octogenarian, JP still held the position of CEO of Sullivan Construction, and still attended board meeting on a regular basis. His relationship with his only child, Jack, had been a troubled one for many years. In fact, JP was the only person who could intimidate Jack. And that was something that Jack hated more than almost anything else.

"Nice place," Deb remarked as the driver turned down a long driveway.

Jack didn't reply. The tension that he'd been trying to ignore had reached its zenith, the same tension that he'd always experienced around his father. "Guess we might as well go see the old coot," he remarked as the driver parked the car. "Remember, he doesn't like to be patronized, so watch it with the phony compliments, okay?"

"Whatever you say," Deb said, trying to ignore the veiled insult. She waited for the driver to open her door and then stepped out into the cool October air. Smoothing down the skirt she'd hoped would earn her a compliment from Jack, she looked around at the grounds. The house was made of stone, with two stories and a large wraparound porch. Deb could hear the sound of the ocean nearby, for the property sat right on the beach. "You should get a place out here," she commented as Jack joined her.

"I hate the beach," Jack said. "Come on, let's get this over with."

The door was answered by the housekeeper, who knew Jack well enough to be cool with him, yet polite. She showed Jack and Deb into a small sitting room that had a large picture window looking out over the beach. Deb looked around the room, her eyes drawn at once to the large photo of an attractive woman on one wall. "Is that your mom?" she asked.

Jack looked up at the photo. "Yes," he said simply.

Deb frowned, wanting to milk more information from him. "When did she die?"

"Long time ago," Jack muttered, looking at his watch.

ehHHhhhhhhhhhhhh

He loves doing this, he reflected. *He just loves making me wait, like I've got nothing better to do than...*

"Well who have we here?"

Jack and Deb turned to the doorway to see JP standing there with a cup of tea in his hand. He was a tall man, broad of shoulder with large hands that evidenced his love of gardening. His eyes were the colour of slate, like those of his son, and took in everything despite his advanced years.

"Hi Dad," Jack said, putting on his best smile. "Happy birthday. This is Deb Rogers."

"*So* nice to meet you, Mr. Sullivan," she said, shaking his hand.

"Yes, so it is," JP said. "Would you like some tea? It's quite nice outside. We could sit on the veranda. The season's so short, don't you think?"

Deb was quite surprised by JP's charm, for his son had inherited none of it. "That sounds nice," she said.

JP smiled. "You know the way, son," he said to Jack before leaving them again.

"I thought you said he was a miserable old curmudgeon," Deb said as Jack lead her to the veranda.

"He is," Jack said.

Deb lifted her eyebrows. "Sure you're not talking about yourself?" she remarked.

Jack said nothing in response and simply let her pass through the door before him.

"Look at this view!" Deb said as they reached a wrought iron patio set. "I love it here," she said, taking a seat.

Jack simply sat down, unable to enjoy himself in the slightest. It wasn't long before JP reappeared with a tray in his hands.

"Here we are," JP said, setting the tray down. "You like your tea with sugar, don't you son?" he asked.

"Yes, thanks," Jack said, taking a cup from his father's hands.

"And you Miss Rogers?" JP asked.

"Just milk for me, thanks," she said.

JP handed her a cup and then sat down beside her, looking at the beach. "Lovely out here, isn't it?"

"I was just saying that," Deb said. "I just love it."

JP nodded, noting how quiet his son was. "So how are my grandsons?" he asked Jack.

"Doing very well," Jack said. "Tom's in the middle of a big case, high profile. Rob's practice is booming. Kids are all well, Jeremy's started golf lessons as the Club, and -"

"What about Malcolm?" JP said. "You didn't mention him. Not that I'm surprised," he said.

Deb felt uncomfortable, and began to wish that she hadn't come at all. Something told her things were about to get ugly.

Jack frowned. "Quite frankly I don't know much about him right now," he said. "He had a car accident a while back but -"

"A car accident?" JP interjected. "I hope he's okay."

"Yeah he's fine," Jack said. "Well enough to travel to Scotland. That's the last I've heard, that he's there visiting his grandmother."

JP nodded. "You don't give that boy enough credit," he said. "You never have. You've always been harder on him than the twins. And he's a good boy. He just needs someone to guide him in the right direction. You've never taken the time to do that."

Jack frowned. "Malcolm's always been spoiled," he said.

"Spoiled?" JP said. "You sent him to boarding school when he was 8. How is that spoiling him? You've ignored him his whole life."

Jack sighed, and looked out at the water lapping lazily on the beach. "You don't know him like I do," he said. "You don't know how difficult he was growing up. How difficult he still is."

"Difficult?" JP said. "He's the only one of your three boys who ever comes to see me. He's the only one who visited me in the hospital when I had my hip replaced last year. If you ask me, that boy is the best thing you've ever done. But you resent him, don't you? You resent that he was ever born."

Jack turned back to his father, wanting to lash out at him, but knowing better. "Can we change the subject, please?" he asked with a sigh, glancing at

Deb, who looked like she wanted the floor beneath her to open up and swallow her whole.

JP nodded, seeing that he'd hit a nerve. "Sure," he said, taking a sip from his tea. "How's business?"

Jack was only too happy to report to his father how successful Sullivan had been in the past quarter. JP listened, knowing everything that he was being told already. He kept a very close eye on his business, and an even closer one on the company's president. JP was no fool. He knew his son well. He knew that the young woman who'd accompanied Jack was no doubt sleeping with him, despite the fact that she was young enough to be one of his own children.

"What the *hell* was that?" Deb asked as she and Jack were driving home later.

"That's my father on a good day," Jack said. "He was being polite for your benefit."

"So why don't you two get along?" she asked. "What happened?"

Jack considered favouring her with an explanation, but thought better of it. It was none of her business what had happened to place such a strain on the relationship. Even Jack's own sons had no idea what had happened.

"Don't ask," Jack said. "Come here," he said, pulling her onto his lap. "I've got something for you," he said, grabbing at her breasts as he kissed her neck.

Deb was not in the mood, but knew better than to refuse his advances. And so she let him have his way with her as the chauffeur pretended not to notice and simply drove along, minding his own business.

Eighteen

Inverness

It was a cool autumn evening when Malcolm and his grandparents made their way to the banks of the River Ness for the annual Inverness Fireworks Display. Featuring one of the largest bonfires constructed anywhere in the United Kingdom, the spectacular was one of the most popular events in the Highland Capital and attracted crowds of between 10,000 and 15,000. The entertainment started at 7pm around the bonfire featuring Fire Twirlers and a Pipe and Drums Band.

"You warm enough, Nanna?" Malcolm asked as they enjoyed the entertainment.

Betty smiled and reached over to touch his face. "I'm just fine," she said. "This blanket is keeping me toasty warm."

Malcolm smiled, and took her hand and kissed it. "Good," he said. He watched the pipers as they performed a rousing version Highland Laddie. He'd never listened to the pipes before coming to Scotland with Maggie; but it hadn't taken him long to grow to love them. The sound of them roused something deep inside of him, something that made him very proud to have Scottish blood flowing through his veins.

The bonfire was lit at 7:30 PM, and the fireworks started about 20 minutes after that. As they watched the fire words, Malcolm's mind harkened back to

New Year's Eve, when he and Maggie had watched a fireworks display from the balcony of their suite at the resort they'd visited in St. Lucia.

It had been a warm night, with a clear sky full of stars, the breeze wafting up from the beach. Malcolm and Maggie stood on the balcony with champagne flutes in their hands, waiting for the countdown to 2012 to begin.

"2012 is gonna be the best year of our lives," Malcolm said. "I can just feel it."

Maggie smiled. "Well 2011 has been rather good if you ask me," she said.

"Yeah, Bruins won the Cup, that was damn good," he said.

Maggie laughed. "You're terrible," she said.

Malcolm smiled and leaned close to kiss her. "I know," he said, kissing her again. Just then they heard the crowd below start the countdown. "10...9...8...7..6...5..4..3..2..1..Happy New Year!!" As the countdown reached 1 the sky overheard burst into explosions of colour.

"Happy New Year, baby," Malcolm said.

"Happy New Year," she said. They touched glasses, and then took a drink of their champagne. Malcolm then took Maggie's glass from her hand and set it down along with his own. "Come here," he said, pulling her close. He kissed her deeply, his hands moving down the back of her body to rest on her bottom. "Let's go inside and ring in the New Year," he whispered into her ear.

Maggie looked up at him with a smile. "Any idea how we could do that?" She asked.

Malcolm nodded. "I have a few ideas," he said.

"Show me," Maggie said.

Malcolm took her by the hand and led her into their bedroom, leaving the festivities behind them.

"Malcolm? Did you hear me?"

Malcolm was shaken from his reflections by his grandmother. "What was that, Nanna?"

Betty smiled wistfully, knowing exactly where Malcolm's mind had wandered off to just then. "I was just asking you if you wanted a cup of tea," she said. "I brought a thermos."

Malcolm smiled. "That would be great, Nanna," he said. "Thanks."

Boston

Hugh Wellman was starting to feel the pinch of unemployment. He thought his problems had been solved when he'd been hired at the Hart and Hound; but when the O'Toole family had been forced to leave Boston for an indeterminate length of time, his brief employment had ceased. The Hart stood closed, its regulars finding new watering holes, and Hugh's bank account grew smaller. He didn't have a lot of options open to him either, for he'd dropped out of school at the age of 16, and had been working odd jobs ever since. His job at Sullivan Construction had been a good one, for it paid well and afforded him benefits. He knew that the only reason he'd been hired was because of his size. At six foot seven inches, he was an intimidating fellow. Too intimidating, it turned out, for most employers were reluctant to hire him. He'd been pounding the pavement for several weeks when he was approached at the gym he worked out at by an old colleague.

"Hugh Wellman, you son-of-a-bitch, how have you been?" Asked Jay Norris. "Long time no see."

"Hey Jay," Hugh said, taking a moment to take a long drink of water. "Been okay, you?"

"Can't complain," Jay said. "Where you working now? Sucked that Sullivan canned you."

Hugh frowned. "No shit," he grumbled. "You still driving for the old bastard?"

"Sure am," Jay replied. "You find some work since you left?"

"Was working as a bouncer at..." he was about to say the name of the pub, but decided not to. "At this bar, but the place closed down a few weeks ago."

"Tough luck," Jay said. "They go out of business? Never heard of a bar going out of business in this town."

"No, the owners just had to leave Boston for few weeks," Hugh said. "Family emergency or something."

Jay nodded. "Gotcha," he said. "Well I've got to get going," he said, picking up his towel and water bottle. "See you around Hugh. Hope you find something soon."

"Yeah, thanks," Hugh said. "Me too."

Hugh finished his work out, showered, and then headed out to the dark parking lot. It was late October, and quite cold outside. He shoved his hands into his pockets as he headed to his car, frowning against the bitter wind. Reaching his car, he tossed his gym bag into the trunk. He checked his watch, deciding that he had time to visit his mother before visiting hours were over. Hugh got into the car, anxiety filling him as he thought of his mother. She'd had a hard life, raising Hugh and his younger sister, Emily alone after their father had exited their lives. The memories Hugh had of his father were bad, of trying to protect his mother from his drunken rages, of being beaten by his father for daring to do so. And now, his mother was suffering from a failing heart, which seemed fitting, since she'd been suffering from a broken heart most of her life.

Hugh stopped at a small convenience store on his way to the hospital to pick up his mother's favourite sweets, Kraft caramels. He wasn't sure if she was allowed to eat them, but it made her smile when he brought them to her nonetheless.

"How's she doing today?" Hugh asked the duty nurse as he reached their station.

"She's been in good spirits," the nurse replied. "Ate all of her supper tonight."

"Good," Hugh said, relieved to hear it. He headed down the corridor, a walk he'd made so many times he knew exactly how many floor tiles he stepped on along the way. The smells of the hospital, smells of illness, of death, still filled him with uneasiness. But his mother needed him, she counted on his visits, and he wasn't about to let her down now that she needed him most.

"Hi Mom," Hugh said, summoning a smile as he entered his mother's room.

Janet smiled, sitting up in her bed as he gave her cheek a kiss.

"Hello Hugh," Janet said. "I was starting to think you weren't coming," she said.

"I was at the gym," Hugh said, pulling a chair closer to his mother's bed. "But you know I'd never miss visiting you," he said, taking her hand.

Janet smiled. "You're a good boy," she said. "Your sister was here earlier," she said. "Brought me those," she said, pointing to the small bouquet of carnations on the table next to her bed.

"Your favourite," Hugh said. "Speaking of favourites," he said, pulling the bag of sweets from his pocket. "I got you something too."

Janet smiled when she saw the caramels. "You shouldn't have," she said.

"Are you kidding? I know how addicted you are to these things," he said with a smile.

Janet laughed. "I suppose I am," she said. "So any luck today? Did you hear back from that job at the docks?"

Hugh sighed. "Yeah, another dead end," he said.

Janet frowned. "I'm beginning to think that Sullivan fellow who fired you made sure no one else gave you a job," she said.

Hugh nodded. "I think you might be right, Mom," he said. "That would be something he'd do, the miserable bastard."

"Men like him make me sick," Janet said. "Rich beyond anyone's needs and selfish to the bone. But mark my words, Hugh, Jack Sullivan will be made accountable for his life one day, in this life or the next."

"I hope so, Mom," Hugh said. "That man has messed up the lives of a lot of people. He deserves to pay for what he's done."

"That nice family that gave you a job deserves to see him pay after everything he's put them through," Janet said. "That poor girl! What a monster he is to do such a thing to his own son."

Hugh nodded in agreement.

On the other side of the room, behind a privacy curtain, lay a victim of an automobile accident, giving testimony to a young woman representing a prestigious Boston law firm. The woman in the bed couldn't help but think that the paralegal was only half listening to her, for she seemed very interested in the conversation that was happening on the other side of the curtain.

Hugh was thoughtful as he left his mother's room. He knew that he'd soon need to remove her from the hospital, and had already looked into nursing homes. He was worried about how he'd pay the bills, even with his sister's help. He'd find a way, though; he had no choice. As he stood waiting for the elevator, Hugh checked his messages. The doors had just opened when a young woman came running towards him.

"Hold the doors please!" she said.

Hugh stepped inside and pressed the button to keep the doors from closing, allowing her to join him in the elevator.

"Thanks!" she said as the doors closed behind her. She gave him a smile. "I appreciate it."

Hugh nodded, looking away from her. She wasn't a terribly pretty woman, but she had a nice body, the sweater she wore just tight enough to show off her breasts. It had been a long time since Hugh had been sexually engaged with a woman, so he took another look before she put on her overcoat.

"Cold outside tonight," she said as they rode down the elevator.

"Sure is," he replied.

"Winter's coming," she said.

"Uh huh," he said, wondering why this well dressed young woman was trying to engage him in conversation.

"Visiting someone?" she asked.

"Yeah," he said.

"I was with a client," she said. "I'm a paralegal."

"I see," Hugh replied.

"Deborah Rogers," she said, holding her hand out to him.

Hugh looked at her well manicured hand, and then up at her face. He didn't really understand why she was making the effort to connect to him, but clearly she was. And he was so needy for female attention by now that he took her outstretched hand and shook it. Her skin was warm and soft.

"Hugh Wellman," he said.

"Nice to meet you, Hugh," Deb said, giving him a smile.

"Yeah, you too," he said.

The elevator stopped and they stepped out into the lobby together. Hugh couldn't help but notice that Deb was trying to keep up with his long strides as he walked along towards the exit.

"I'm sorry, but would you do me a favour?" she asked.

Hugh looked down at her. "What?"

"It's rather dark outside," she said. "Would you...would you mind walking me to my car?"

Hugh stopped in his tracks and looked down at her. How did she know that he wasn't the type of man she was seeking protection from?

"I guess I can do that," he said. "Where are you parked?"

"North side," she said. "Come with me."

Hugh followed her, his eyes travelling over her as she walked, enjoying the swing of her hips. She wasn't his type, but right now she'd do. *Don't be stupid*, he told himself. *Women like her don't do men like you.*

"Here we are," she said when they reached her red Audi. She gave him a smile. "Thank you so much," she said, opening the door of her car with her fob. "And if you ever need legal help, give me a call," she said, fishing a business card out of her purse. "In fact, just give me a call," she said. "I'd like to see you again, Hugh."

Hugh frowned. "Really?"

Deb nodded. "Yes, why does that surprise you?"

Hugh shrugged. "You're a pretty classy chick," he said. "I'm probably not the kind of guy you go out with."

"You're not," she said. "But I have a thing for big men like you," she said, looking him in the eyes. "Always have."

Hugh couldn't help but smile. "You don't say?"

Deb nodded. "I do," she said. "So call me. Okay?"

"Maybe I will," he said as she got into her car. She waved to him and then drove off. Hugh watched her, and then looked down at the car in his hand, surprised by the turn of events that he'd just been a part of.

Nineteen

S now had come to the Highlands, the first of the season. Malcolm had been dreading the 10th of November, Maggie's birthday, but it had come and he'd managed, somehow, to get through the day. He'd found strength in his time in Scotland, strength he didn't know he had. Working with Dr. Grant had helped him tremendously, and Malcolm found himself at a place he thought he'd never be - ready to resume his life.

And now that he felt more like himself than he had in months, he decided to check into the world once more.

After saying goodnight to his grandparents, who both went to bed by 11PM, Malcolm sat in the small living room and checked his voice mail and text messages for the first time in months. His voicemail box was full, which didn't surprise him; nor did the more than 90 text messages that were waiting for his perusal. He scrolled through them, looking for her name; but of course it wasn't there. He was surprised, however, to see her brother Will's name appearing over and over, always with the same message: *Call me!!* Malcolm frowned as he recalled the last time he'd seen Will, a man he'd once considered a close friend. *Why the hell should I call you?* He thought as he deleted the messages with a frown. *So you can call me a cheating bastard again?* His brothers had each sent him several texts, which pleased him. The one positive that had come from the end of his relationship with Maggie had been the blossoming of his relationship with them. He knew that it was too late to call them now, but made a mental note to do so the next day. Next he listened to his voice mails. Both Rob and Tom had called him, along with the Ferrari dealer who was anxious to find out how he was enjoying his new car. The last message was from Will. He listened to it, quite certain he knew what Will had to say. He couldn't have been more wrong, or more surprised: *Malcolm, this is Will. I know you're pissed at me right now, and I don't blame you. But you need to call me as soon as possible. It's about Maggie. I know where she is.*

Malcolm sat for a moment, unable to react. Had he heard the message correctly? He listened to it again, and he heard the same words: *I know where she is.* Was Will telling the truth? Or was he simply trying to drive the knife deeper into Malcolm's heart? *I have to know,* he decided, *I have to find out one way or another. I'll go crazy if I don't.* He found Will's number, not caring what time it was in Boston, and placed the call. It rang twice before Will picked up.

"Hello?"

"Will it's Malcolm."

"Malcolm! I'm so glad you finally called me back. What took you so long? I've been leaving messages for weeks now!"

Malcolm decided not to favour Will with an explanation for his silence. "You said you know where Maggie is," he said. "Are you being honest with me? Or just fucking with my head?"

"Why would I do that?" Will asked.

"Really? Do you really need to ask me that?" Malcolm said.

"Yeah...I guess you have a point," Will said. "About all that, what went down the last time we saw each other, I'm sorry Malcolm. Really sorry."

Malcolm said nothing right away, for he was having difficulty believing what Will was telling him.

"Where is she?" Malcolm asked finally.

"Antigonish," Will said. "Nova Scotia."

Malcolm frowned. "She's in Canada?"

"Yeah, she has been all along," Will said. "Our mother's been staying with her part time, and now we're all here. My dad and brothers and Alli and I decided to-"

"You're with her now?" Malcolm asked. "She's there with you?"

"Well no," Will said. "She and Mum are at our cousins' house. There wasn't room for all of us there so we're staying in a motel for now."

Malcolm's credibility was starting to wear thin. "Why did she leave me?" He asked. "Why hasn't she contacted me?"

Will was silent for a moment before responding. His answer wasn't what Malcolm wanted to hear.

"You're gonna have to ask her that yourself, mate," Will said. "She needs to be the one to tell you why she did what she did."

Malcolm didn't know what to say, what to think. Part of him didn't believe him. After so long without any knowledge of Maggie, without any hope of ever finding her again, this seemed too good to be true. Malcolm had only recently recovered from the trauma of losing her; would he be a fool to open himself up to disappointment now?

"I don't believe you," he said finally. "I have no reason to. You thought I betrayed her. You thought I cheated on her. Why should I believe you now?"

"I *should* have believed you," Will said. "I should never have thought you could hurt Maggie. And I'm sorry that I did. Please Malcolm, I swear I'm telling you the truth! I swear on my life that I am."

Will's passion seemed genuine, and yet Malcolm was still reluctant to open himself up to be hurt again. He wanted to believe, but couldn't quite bring himself to do so. "I'll think about what you've said," he said finally.

"Okay, but don't take too long," Will said. "Maggie is lost without you."

Malcolm frowned as he ended the call, Will's final words hitting him hard. They didn't leave his mind as he listened to the next call in his voice mail, which was from his brother, Tom.

"Hey Malcolm! When are you coming home? We're worried about you. Listen, I have to ask you something. What happened to Maggie's engagement ring? And did you ever talk to Dad about it? Call me back, okay?"

There was a similar message from Rob, asking about Maggie's engagement ring, and whether or not their father had known what had happened to it. Malcolm was confused, and the anxiety he'd been fighting for so long started to worm its way back into his gut. He looked at his watch. 1:23 AM, and decided to call Tom first. He used his cell phone number, not wanting to have to talk to his sister-in-law, who would undoubtedly be full of questions he wasn't prepared to answer.

"Hello?"

"Tom it's Malcolm."

"Malcolm! It's great to hear your voice! How are you? Are you still in Scotland?"

"Yeah I'm still at my Nanna's house," Malcolm said. "I'm okay, Tom, better than I was."

"That's great to hear," Tom said. "I've been worried about you. So has Rob. Have you talked to him?"

"Not yet," Malcolm said. "Why did you ask about Maggie's ring?"

"Well it's rather strange, actually," Tom said. "I was golfing with Dad a few weeks back and he said something that struck me as very odd. We were talking about you, I was saying how worried I was about you. He expressed the opinion that you should have forgotten Maggie as soon as she sent the ring back to you. I didn't know she had sent it back. Did she? And did you tell him that she had?"

Malcolm's mind harkened back to that terrible day when he'd return to the empty apartment to find an unmarked package waiting for him. He knew that he would never forget the feeling of emptiness that had filled him when he saw the ring fall out of the package onto the counter top. But he had told only one person about that: Gus. So how did his father know it had been returned? Unless Gus's theory was right, unless Jack was responsible for Maggie's flight from Boston.

"I never told him anything about the ring," Malcolm said. "He'd have no way of knowing that she sent it back to me unless he had something to do with it."

Tom was silent for a moment or two. "I think you need to come home, Malcolm," he said. "Right away."

"I think so too," Malcolm said. "I spoke to Maggie's brother a little while ago," he said. "He told me where Maggie is."

"What? Where is she?"

"Canada," Malcolm said. "Nova Scotia. She's been there all along."

"And has he known all along?"

"I don't know," Malcolm said. "I'm not even sure I believe him, after the way he treated me the last time we saw each other."

"Malcolm whether or not you believe him you still need to get home," Tom said. "Dad is involved in all this, I'm sure of it now."

Malcolm nodded. "I think so too," he said quietly. "And when I can prove it, he'll pay. I don't care if he's my father I'll make that son-of-a-bitch pay, I swear it."

Twenty

*Y*ou know where Maggie is?" Betty asked at breakfast the next morning. Malcolm nodded. "She's been in Canada all this time," he told his grandparents. "I still don't know why she left, but I'm all but certain my father is involved."

"Your father?" Norman asked. "Surely he's not *that* rotten," he said.

"Oh he is," Betty said. "It wouldn't surprise me in the least to learn that he's responsible for all this."

"So you're leaving today?" Norman said.

"Yes," Malcolm said. "I want to get to her as soon as possible. Will texted me the address where she's been staying." He frowned as negative thoughts entered his mind. "I only hope that he's telling me the truth," he said. "If I go all that way only to find it's all been a pack of lies...I'm not sure I could handle that."

Norman and Betty exchanged a look of concern.

"I don't think it is," Norman said. "From what you've told me of Will, he seems like a man of good character. I think he's telling you the truth, Malcolm."

Malcolm nodded. "I hope so," he said. "So will you be going back home too, then?" he asked his grandfather.

Norman smiled and looked at Betty. "Well, I think I'll stay on a little while longer," he said. He reached over and took her hand. "Your grandmother and I still have some catching up to do."

Malcolm smiled. "Are you kidding me?" he asked. "That's awesome."

"We wanted to tell you, but you had so much to contend with that we didn't want to give you more to think about," Betty explained, giving Norman's hand a squeeze.

"I think you two ought to be together," Malcolm said. "You both need someone in your life."

"Life's too hard to be without someone at your side," Norman said. "That's why you need to go and find your Maggie," he said. "And when those great-grandbabies of ours are born, you can bet we'll be on the next plane to come and see them."

"And spoil them rotten," Betty added.

Malcolm laughed. "Okay, you've got yourselves a deal."

Betty and Norman took Malcolm to the airport in Inverness later that morning, where they bade a tearful goodbye to him.

"I don't have the words to thank you both for all that you've done for me," Malcolm said as he hugged them each in turn. "I was such a mess when I got here."

"And look at you now," Betty said, giving him a teary smile. "I'm so proud of you, Malcolm," she said, touching his face fondly.

"We both are," Norman said. "It takes a big man to do what you've done. You just remember that we'll be here for you, no matter what."

"Thanks Grandpa," Malcolm said. "I love you guys so much," he said, hugging them both once more.

Malcolm took a short flight from Inverness to Glasgow, and then waited an hour for a non-stop flight that would bring him to Halifax, Nova Scotia. It was a difficult wait, knowing that at the end of his journey he would see Maggie. He refused to allow negative thoughts enter his mind, something he'd learned to do in his therapy. *I **will** see her soon*, he told himself, *and everything will work out...I will be with her soon and we'll never be separated again.*

Boston

"He said *what?*"

Tom nodded as he stirred his coffee. "You heard me," he said. "And according to Malcolm, he hadn't said anything about the ring. So what does that mean?"

Rob frowned, not wanting to consider what it meant. The two brothers sat in a downtown cafe, wanting to talk about the situation with their father. Neither had said anything to their wives, nor anyone else for that matter. If their father was involved in Maggie's disappearance, then they knew that they would have to tread very carefully.

"What are we going to do about this?" Rob asked. "You know the law, what options do we have?"

"We have to wait and see if our suspicions are correct," Tom said. "And if they are, we need to determine what exactly Dad did. He's not stupid, Rob. He'd have made sure his ass was covered. It won't be easy proving anything, he'll have made sure of that."

Rob nodded. "No doubt," he said. "Do you know when Malcolm's coming home?"

"No I don't," Tom said. "I told him he needs to get here soon. I just hope he's okay now. He was pretty messed up when he left. He sounded better, though. Didn't you think so?"

"Yes," Rob said. "He sounded stronger. He didn't deserve any of this. After the shitty childhood he had, losing his mother the way he did, he deserves to be happy."

"He will be," Tom said. "Once he finds Maggie and all this mess is behind him, he'll be happier than either of us. That's a guarantee."

Antigonish

Living in a motel was not Mick O'Toole's idea of fun. He was sharing a room with his twin boys, whom he loved dearly, but who liked to stay up late and watch television. Mick was a creature of habit, and he was finding the disruption to his life taxing and more than a little stressful. Irene had done her best to make things more comfortable for him, but she knew that he hated the situation they were in as much as she did. Irene missed her home, she missed her kitchen and her own bed. As much as she loved her cousins, their home was not her home. Pat and Noreen must have realized this, for one weekend they went to visit their son for the weekend. Irene took advantage of their absence to cook Mick's favourite supper. He was delighted.

"So when is Malcolm coming, anyway?" Quinn asked as they enjoyed their mother's roast beef dinner.

"I don't know," Maggie said. "I haven't heard from him. Have you, Will?"

Will shook his head. "I texted him the address here," he said. "But he didn't reply. So who knows if he even believed me?"

Maggie frowned, frustrated to hear this. "He has to believe it," she said quietly. "I can't live like this anymore."

"None of us can," Irene said. "I don't know how much longer we can impose on Pat and Noreen," she said. "I know they say they don't mind, but it's been a disruption to their lives as well."

"We should go back to Belfast," Aidan said.

"No, we'll not go back there," Mick said. "Malcolm will come, lass," he assured his daughter. "And once he does, he'll know what to do. I'm sure of it."

Maggie didn't want to hope, for she'd learned from bitter experience that hoping too often lead to disappointment and heartache. "I don't know what to believe anymore, Da," she said. "Perhaps he's angry. I know I would be, after all I left him with no word, no explanation. He has every right to be angry."

"He's not angry Megs," Will said. "At least not with you."

"Come on lads, let's clean up," Mick said as he stood up. "If you want to go to that movie you'd better get cracking."

"You're going to the movies?" Maggie asked as Aidan picked up her plate.

"Yeah, you want to come Megs?" Quinn asked.

Maggie smiled. "I'd love to, but I'm pretty tired tonight lads," she said. "Another time though, I promise."

"We'll stay back with you, Megs," Will said. "Alli was hoping to Skype with her sister tonight anyway."

"Okay," Maggie said.

Once the dishes had been loaded into the dishwasher, Mick and Irene took the twins to the movies while Will, Alli and Maggie stayed behind. While Will and Alli headed into the back bedroom, Maggie decided to work on her knitting. Now that she knew the gender of her babies, she'd busied herself making tiny hats, booties and blankets for her babies. Maggie found knitting soothing, for it occupied her mind just enough to remove her from her problems. She had just started the finishing touches on a pink bootie when the doorbell rang. Her first instinct was to ignore it, for the chances that it was someone trying to sell her something were pretty good. But when the doorbell rang a second time, followed by someone knocking on the outside door, she decided to see who it was. Deeming it safe to do so since Will was with her, she headed to the door. Upon reaching it, she pulled the lacy curtain back to peek outside. She screamed when she saw who it was.

"Malcolm!!"

Twenty One

With trembling hands Maggie unlocked the door, frantic to get to Malcolm. At last she opened it and finally, after many months apart, she was reunited with the love of her life.

"I've missed you!" Malcolm said as he held her tight. "I didn't think I'd ever see you again!"

"I'm sorry! I'm so sorry I had to leave you!" Maggie cried. "I've been miserable without you!"

Malcolm stepped into the small landing, pushing the door closed with one foot. He took Maggie's face in his hands and kissed her deeply. "I've been lost without you," he told her between kisses. "I didn't want to go on any more!"

For a few minutes they simply held one another, each of them crying, neither wanting to let go of the other, each one afraid that they'd wake up and find that they'd simply been dreaming.

Maggie led him into the house and sat down on the sofa, patting the spot beside her. "Look at you!" he said when he noticed her round belly. He sat down beside her and ran a hand over her. "Wow," he said softly. "They've really got big," he said.

"I know their gender now," Maggie said.

Malcolm looked up at her. "Do you? What are they?"

"One of each," she said. "Just like we wanted."

Malcolm smiled. "That's ...that's amazing," he said, quite overcome. He pulled her into his arms again.

"Malcolm!"

Maggie and Malcolm looked up to see Will standing in the doorway. He smiled and walked over to Malcolm, capturing him in a big bear hug when Malcolm stood up. "I'm so glad to see you!" he said.

Malcolm was rather surprised by Will's warm greeting, and returned his hug. "It's good to see you too," he said.

"I want to apologize again," Will said. "I should have known you'd never cheat on Maggie, here."

Malcolm shook his head as he looked back at Maggie. "No, not a chance," he said. "I need you to explain what happened," he said to her. "Why did you leave? Why couldn't I reach you? And why did your mother lie?"

Maggie looked at Malcolm and then back at her brother. "Would you let me talk to Malcolm alone, please?" she asked.

"Of course," Will said. "It's good to see you, mate," he said to Malcolm once again, and then left them to return to Alli.

Malcolm sat down beside Maggie again, and picked up her hand. "Now tell me," he said. "All of it."

Maggie nodded, and looked down at their joined hands. She knew that what she had to tell him would blow his world apart. She had to be the one to keep him from reacting in a destructive manner, for she knew he was capable of just that. And yet, he deserved to know the truth. All of it, no matter how ugly.

"The day you left for Australia," Maggie began. "I was accosted by two men, thugs you'd call them."

Malcolm was upset immediately. "Who? Who did that to you?"

"I didn't know their names," she said. "They didn't hurt me, but they took me to a car and made me get into the back seat. They were armed, Malcolm, so I knew that they meant business."

"You saw their weapons?" he asked.

"One of them, yes," she said. "They wouldn't tell me where they were taking me. They said that they didn't want to hurt me, but that they would if I didn't cooperate."

"When I find out who they were, I swear to God I'll kill them both," Malcolm said, growing angrier by the minute.

"You can't do that, and you know it," Maggie said. "What I'm going to tell you now is going to make you even angrier, Malcolm," she said. "But I need you to be calm, I need to you keep control of your anger. Can you do that?" she asked him, taking his face in her hands.

Malcolm looked into her eyes, seeing in them her desperate need for him to be strong. But he was already so angry; how could he possibly promise such a thing and mean it?

"I don't know," he told her. "Just tell me. I need to know the rest."

Maggie nodded, and dropped her hands to hold his. "They drove me to a quarry," she told him. "And when I was let out of the car, I saw that the equipment there had your name on it. Sullivan. It was a Sullivan Construction Company site."

Malcolm felt as though he'd been punched in the gut, and for a moment his hands tightened on hers. "My father was behind this, wasn't he?" he asked.

Maggie nodded, wishing more than anything that she could tell him no. The look in his eyes broke her heart, but she forged on, knowing he needed the whole truth.

"He was waiting for me in a trailer," she said. "He knew that we were engaged, and tried to tell me that you'd be disinherited if you married me. I told him that I knew he had no such power, and that bothered him. But he had an alternate plan, an even more diabolical plan."

Malcolm frowned. "What plan?"

Maggie sighed, and looked down at their intertwined fingers. "He brought out a folder of photographs. They were photos of people who'd been killed in construction accidents. He showed me some, they were horrible. I told him that as a nurse I'd seen accident victims before, and that they didn't shock me. It was then that he revealed his plan. He told me that I'd feel differently if it was my brother Will in one of those photos. He knew that Will worked for him, and said that if I didn't leave town, that he would meet with an accident." She stopped, waiting for his reaction, but he said nothing. She looked up at him, the look of anger in his eyes alarming her. "So you see I had no choice," she said, her voice breaking. "I hated to leave you, hated not to even tell you why. But if I didn't do as he said, he'd have killed my brother!"

Malcolm didn't say anything, but stood up and walked across the room. Even though he'd suspected that his father had somehow been involved, it was still immensely painful to hear it nonetheless.

Maggie looked at him as he stood at the fireplace, his back to her. Even without him saying a word she knew that he was tremendously angry. But more than that, he was in pain. She stood up and walked over to him.

"Please say something," she said, slipping her hand in his.

Malcolm looked down at her hand in his, and then into her eyes. "What do you want me to say, Maggie?" he asked. "You want me to stay calm, remember? But how can I? How can I stay calm when I know what that mother fucker did to you?" he asked, his voice rising in anger. "How can you expect me not to hunt him down like the mongrel that he is and kill him with my bare hands?"

"Because I know you're better than that," she said, taking her hands in his. "And there's more at stake here than revenge, Malcolm." She took one of his hands and placed it on her round belly. "Our children need you, Malcolm," she said. "I need you. If you do this, if you go after him, then what will become of us? You'll be put in prison, and we'll be left alone. I can't go on without you, Malcolm. It's been so hard," she said, breaking down.

Malcolm pulled her into his embrace, her words slicing through his anger. He closed his eyes, resting his face in her hair, letting himself be soothed by her presence, her scent, the feel of her body next to his. "I'm sorry," he said, kissing her hair tenderly. "I swear on the lives of our children, that you'll never be alone again. In fact, I want to get married as soon as possible, Maggie," he said, looking down in her eyes. "I know you want a church wedding, but we can do that later, when all this is behind us."

Maggie nodded. "We can go to city hall," she said. "And have a civil ceremony."

"Yeah, that's what we need to do," he said. "And as soon as possible. But first we need a place to live, a place big enough for your family too. I don't want them staying in a hotel, it's gotta be shitty doing that night after night. Besides, I know your father can't afford to do that for long."

Maggie smiled, touched that he'd think of her family. "You'd do that for them?"

"Of course," Malcolm said. "They're like my family now, Maggie. Soon they will be, and I want to protect them. If my father threatened your brother's life, then they're all in danger. I think they need to stay here with us until my father is dealt with once and for all."

Maggie nodded. "I think so too," she said. "Perhaps we could rent an apartment."

"No, an apartment won't be big enough," he said. "Think of it, there's eight adult plus two little ones on the way. We'll need a house, Maggie. And a big one at that. We'll hire a real estate agent tomorrow to find a place for us." He yawned, the long day of travel finally catching up with him. "Right now I need to find a place to crash," he said with a smile.

"I know you must be exhausted," she said, stroking his cheek. "There's a nice hotel outside of town," she said. "Let me go back a bag. I'm coming with you."

"I like the sound of that," Malcolm said. He sat down on the sofa while Maggie went back to pack a bag. Pulling out his phone, he made a quick call to his grandmother to let her know that he'd arrived safely and, more importantly, that he'd found Maggie.

"All set?" Malcolm asked, standing up as Maggie reappeared. "Let me take that," he said, taking the small suitcase from her.

"Did you rent a car?" she asked as she put on her jacket.

"No I had a taxi drop me off," he told her. "My stuff's still on the driveway. At least, I hope it's still on the driveway," he said.

Maggie laughed. "Not to worry. This town is quite safe."

They went outside and Maggie lead him to her car, realizing that she would have to tell him what had happened to her Porsche.

"I had to sell the lovely car you gave me," she told him as she popped the trunk. "I needed the money."

Malcolm nodded. "I understand," he said. "Where is it now?"

"At the dealership in Halifax, as far as I know," she said as he put their things in the trunk. "Unless someone bought it by now."

"Well if it's still there, we'll get it back," he said.

Maggie smiled. "I'd love that," she said. "But we're going to need something a little more practical now. Not much room in a Porsche for babies."

"Then we'll get a family car too," he said as they got into the car. "Something really safe, like a tank."

Maggie laughed. "Well I don't know if that's necessary."

"Are you kidding? Nothing's too safe for our kids," he said.

Maggie drove to the hotel where she and her mother had stayed on the night they'd first arrived in Canada. How different things had been then! It hardly seemed possible that she was now going there to spend the night with Malcolm. She glanced over at him as she drove, smiling when she saw him dozing off in the passenger seat. *Poor love must be knackered,* she thought, knowing that he'd undoubtedly been travelling all day, not to mention that he was still on UK time, some four hours later.

They checked in at the Antigonish Evergreen Hotel, which was decidedly slow given that it was mid- November. The room they were given was large and comfortable, with a king sized bed.

"Is it safe for us to fool around?" Malcolm asked as he helped Maggie with her jacket.

"Yes," she said. "Within reason of course," she added.

"What do you mean?" he asked.

"Well, some of the things we like to do won't be possible," she said. "But I'm sure there is a lot of things we *can* do."

Malcolm smiled, as his hands moved down the length of her arms. "Glad to hear it," he said. "It's been so long since I've touched you," he said.

Maggie grew excited by his words, by the look in his eyes. She helped him as he pulled her shirt over her head, needing his touch as much as he needed hers.

"My body isn't the same as you remember, I'm sure," she said as he ran his hands around to the back of her bra and unclasped it.

"No, but you're every bit as beautiful now," he said as he pulled her bra off of her body. "Even more so," he said, running his finger tips lightly over her bare breasts. He bent and kissed them softly as her hands moved to the fly of his jeans.

"Come here," she said, sitting on the bed and beckoning him over. Malcolm took a moment to remove his jeans before walking over to her. She pulled his shorts down and took his erection in her hands. "I've missed doing this to you," she said, looking up at him as she closed her mouth over him. Malcolm watched her, his hands meandering his hands into her hair.

"Feels so good," he said, lost in the moment. It was almost impossible to believe that a few short days ago he was ready to give up on ever finding her, and now she was here, making love to him.

"Get up on the bed, baby," he said, "show me that beautiful ass of yours."

Maggie smiled, and released him. She stood up, and let him help her remove the rest of her clothes before climbing up on the bed on her hands and knees. Malcolm ran his hands over her bare bottom, kissing her before he took her by the hips and pulled her closer. Maggie closed her eyes as she felt him push into her, the pleasure of their union making her moan softly.

"Is that okay?" he asked, still concerned about her condition.

Maggie looked over her shoulder at him. "Oh it's better than okay," she told him with a smile.

Malcolm laughed. "Good to know," he said, pulling out of her slowly and then pushing into her again.

They made love tenderly but with the passion built up over their long separation. And later, when they lay in each other's arms, they talked into the night.

"Feel this," Maggie said, taking one of his hands and placing it on her abdomen. Malcolm smiled as he felt the strong kick of one of their twins.

"Whoa," he said. "That was amazing! Does it hurt?" he asked, looking up at her.

"Not usually," she said. "Though lately they've been treating my internal organs like their playground."

Malcolm laughed. "There's another one!" he said. "Like a WFC match in there!"

Maggie laughed. And then her eyes filled with tears. "I missed you so much," she said, snuggling closer to him.

Malcolm kissed the top of her head. "I've missed you too, baby," he said. "I've never been so low as I was when I couldn't find you. I didn't even know if I wanted to live anymore."

Maggie looked up at him. "Oh my poor Malcolm," she said, stroking his face. "I'm so sorry I put you through all this!"

"Don't you dare apologize," he said, capturing her hand in his. "This was *not* your doing, Maggie. You did what anyone in your position would do. And I don't ever want you to feel responsible. Tell me something, how did your brother find out about all this? If you went to such lengths to keep anyone from knowing, how did he find out?"

"One of the men who took me to your father ended up at the Hart," she told him. "He'd been fired by your father, and he and Will became friends."

Malcolm frowned. "Will became friends with one of those bastards?"

"He didn't know about what had happened, remember," she said. "He simply knew that he was a man who was down on his luck, so he offered him a job as bouncer at the Hart. And I guess after a while he began to get to know my brothers and my father, he felt like he needed to tell them what he'd been a part of. And he did."

"Doesn't erase what he did," Malcolm said.

"No, but he will be able to testify about what happened," she said. "That's important."

Malcolm nodded. "I suppose so," he said. "I guess this happened after I left town. I think I would have noticed a new bouncer."

Maggie nodded. "I'm glad you went to Scotland," she said. "Being with your grandmother must have helped you."

"It did," he said. "And my grandfather came all the way from Australia to be with me too."

"That's wonderful," she said.

"Yeah I was blown away when he showed up," Malcolm said. "They talked me into going to therapy. And I've never had much use for that shit, you know that; but it really helped. Helped me put things into perspective and manage my emotions a lot better."

"I'm so glad," she said. "I was so worried about you after I heard about your car accident."

"Carrie told you?"

"No Mum did," she said. "But Carrie kept me updated. I was so tempted to come and see you, but I couldn't. I just couldn't take the risk."

"I know baby," he said, kissing her again. "But we're together now, and my father is going to pay for what he's done. You have my word on that."

They held each other close in the dark, and, before long fell asleep in one another's arms, feeling complete once more.

Twenty Two

The next day Maggie and Malcolm met Maggie's parents and brothers at a local restaurant for breakfast. Irene was so pleased to see Malcolm that she hugged him right in the middle of the restaurant, not caring who saw her.

"It's so good to see you two back together," Mick said. "It's clear to see that you belong together."

Maggie smiled, pleased to hear her father finally say so.

"We are going to get married right away," Malcolm said. "We both want a church wedding, but given the circumstances, we're going to do the city hall deal, as soon as possible. And then, once all this is behind us, we'll do it up right."

"I think that's a grand idea," Irene said.

"And we want to find a house for us all to live in for now," Maggie added, looking at Malcolm. "A real estate agent is looking for a place right now. Malcolm engaged him this morning."

"All of us?" Quinn asked. "You mean we're not going home?"

"Not yet," Mick said. "It's not safe for any of us in Boston right now, lad."

"Your dad's right," Malcolm said. "Until my father is behind bars, you're gonna have to stay here."

After breakfast, Malcolm and Maggie acquired a marriage license from the Deputy Issuer. After delivering the license to the justice of the peace who would be performing the ceremony, they met with the realtor whom Malcolm had hired.

The realtor, Jim Cummings, had three houses to show them. The first two they visited were too small for their needs, and Maggie and Malcolm were starting to get discouraged. But then they saw the third home, and knew at once that it was the one they wanted. With a sandy beachfront, ocean views and mountain views, the spacious 4000 square foot home had everything they were looking for. In addition, since it was a holiday rental, it was already furnished.

"How long would you be looking to rent?" Cummings asked.

"Not sure," Malcolm said as they admired the view. "A few months at least."

"Months?" Cummings asked.

"Is that a problem?" Malcolm asked. "If I need to pay more, I'll do it."

"I...I don't think it will be a problem," Cummings said. "It's just that... most people rent for a few weeks at a time, not a few months."

"Well our situation is rather unique," Maggie said.

"I see," Cummings said. "Let me give the owner a call," he said. "And I'll get back to you."

"Okay, but we'd like to move in as soon as possible," Malcolm said. "So the sooner you can get back to us, the better."

That afternoon, while Maggie had a nap, Malcolm phoned his brothers to catch them up on what was happening. Tom was in court, so he spoke to Rob first.

"I can't believe he did that," Rob said after Malcolm had told him all about Maggie's harrowing experience. "I'm not surprised that he's behind this, but I didn't think that he would stoop so low."

"He's going to pay, Rob," Malcolm said. "One way or another, I'll make him pay."

"How are you going to prove it?" Rob asked. "It's Maggie's word against his."

"One of the goons who was there has been working at the O'Toole's bar," Malcolm said. "He got canned by Dad, and got friendly with Maggie's brother Will."

"And he told Will all this?" Rob asked.

"Yeah, I guess he felt guilty or something," Malcolm said. "Whatever his reasons, he's gonna be able to help us make sure the old man pays. And I mean to make him pay, Rob. After everything he's put Maggie through, he deserves to rot in prison for the rest of his life."

"He does," Rob said. "But you know how resourceful Dad is. It may take more than the word of a disgruntled thug to put him behind bars."

Malcolm frowned, not liking what his brother was saying. "What then?" Malcolm asked in exasperation. "There has to be a way to nail him."

"Tom could probably think of a way," Rob said. "He knows the law better than either of us."

"True," Malcolm said. "Still, maybe it's time to bring out the heavy artillery."

"You don't mean..."

"Yeah, I mean it. Who better to scare the shit out of him? JP's the only person who can do that," Malcolm said.

"I don't know," Rob said. "Do you really want to get him involved in all this?"

"Yeah I do," Malcolm said. "I want that bastard to pay for what he did, and JP is the only one who can make sure that happens."

"Okay, I guess you're right," Rob said. "But I think before we talk to him, we need to get Tom's take on all of this. You don't want to tip your hand, after all. I think we're going to need to proceed very carefully, Malcolm. If Dad gets a whiff of what's going on, it's game over. You know how cunning he can be."

"Yeah you're right," Malcolm said. "But none of this can come down before the twins are born. I don't want Maggie getting upset right now."

"Of course," Rob said. "it will take a while to get all our ducks in a row anyway. So when is she due?"

"First of December," Malcolm said. "I gotta tell you Rob, I'm nervous as hell about becoming a dad."

"Yeah I was too with my first," Rob said. "But I've seen you with kids, Malcolm. You're a natural. You're going to be a great father."

Malcolm smiled, his brother's praise meaning a great deal to him. "Thanks Rob. That means a lot coming from you."

"Well I mean it. Listen I have to get going," he said. "Talk to Tom, and then maybe we can arrange a conference call or something to all talk together. What do you think?"

"Great idea," Malcolm said. "I'll call you back in a few days."

Malcolm ended the call, and then returned to the bedroom where Maggie was napping. He felt quite tired himself, having spent the last few days travelling and running around. So when he lay down and spooned up behind Maggie in the bed, it took him mere moments to fall asleep as well.

Twenty Three

Antigonish, Nova Scotia

hree days had initially seemed like a long time to wait to get married; but the time passed quickly as Malcolm and Maggie set their lives back in order. The owner of the house they both loved was more than happy to allow them to rent it indefinitely, which was a relief to the whole family who were quite tired of living out of suitcases. Maggie loved the house, but felt strange sleeping in someone else's bed. So Malcolm ordered new beds for every room, as well as linens. The urge to nest was setting in with Maggie, and she wanted more than anything to get her nursery set up. Her doctor had told her that twins can come early, and she wanted to be prepared for such an eventuality.

"What about this, do you like this?" Malcolm asked. He and Maggie were shopping for wedding rings, with their wedding coming up quickly.

"I like them all," Maggie said. "You pick."

Malcolm smiled. "You're easy to please," he said. "I just wish I had your engagement ring to give back to you. I can't tell you how horrible it was when you sent it back to me."

Maggie looked up at him. "I didn't send it back to you," she said. "I didn't even have it after I left town."

Malcolm frowned. "What do you mean, you didn't have it?" he asked. "Where was it?"

155

"Your father took it from me," she said. "Even when I asked him to keep it, he wouldn't hear of it. It must have been him who sent it back."

Malcolm's silence was ominous, and Maggie began to regret saying anything. She knew how tightly wound up Malcolm was, trying not to vent his anger. He was handing it remarkably well, however, all things considered.

"I like this one," Maggie said, deciding to deflect his attention. "Why don't we try them on and see how they look?"

"Isn't that bad luck or something?" Malcolm asked.

Maggie laughed. "Bad luck? You sound like my mother. Besides, don't you think we've had more than our share of bad luck lately?"

Malcolm nodded. "You're right," he said, giving her a kiss. "From now on, nothing but good luck," he said. He beckoned the clerk over and they tried on the rings. "Perfect fit," he said. He looked at Maggie. "Just like you," he said, kissing her again.

It was just like old times that night, as the family relaxed in their new temporary home. Aidan and Quinn were excited to discover that there was a hot tub on the back of the property, and spent a long time in it before Mick told them to get out or they'd never father children. Irene outdid herself with a fine meal that was enjoyed by everyone. There was a feeling of excitement in the air as the family anticipated the long awaited wedding of Maggie and Malcolm which would take place the next day. They decided to have the wedding at the house, with Pat and Noreen invited as special guests of honour. Irene had wanted to cook a big meal for the party afterwards, but Malcolm told her they wanted her to relax and made reservations at the finest eating establishment in the small town.

"Just think," Maggie said as she and Malcolm snuggled in bed together. "Tomorrow at this time we'll be married. I can't believe it, after all we've been through, it's finally happening."

Malcolm nodded as he stroked her long hair. "Part of me keeps thinking I'll wake up and find I'm dreaming," he said. "I had some pretty whacked out dreams when we were apart."

Maggie frowned, remembering the nightmare she'd had about Jack. "I know what you mean," she said. "I've never had so many bad dreams in my life."

Malcolm kissed the top of her head. "Well no more," he said. "Nothing but happy dreams from now on. New rule."

Maggie laughed. "So are you going to tell me where we're going for our honeymoon? Or do I need to tickle it out of you?"

Malcolm smiled. "Is that a threat?" he said. "Not even married and you're already bossing me around."

Maggie laughed. "So...no hints?"

"Nope," Malcolm said. "You'll just have to find out tomorrow night."

Maggie sighed. "Fine," she said with a yawn. "Goodnight love."

"Night baby," he said, kissing her again. "Sweet dreams."

The next morning was bright and cool, a perfect autumn day. Maggie woke up early, too excited to be able to sleep for long. Malcolm was still in a deep sleep, so she decided to let him sleep while she went into the bathroom to shower.

Malcolm was awoken by the sound of the shower and rolled over to look at the clock. It was early, but he decided to get up anyway. He knew that Maggie would be getting dressed in their room, and would tell him that it was bad luck for him to be there.

"Good morning," Maggie said as she entered the room. Malcolm had to smile when he saw how short the belt of her bathrobe was now.

"Good morning," he said, walking over and giving her a kiss. His hands rested on the sides of her round belly, and was rewarded with a kick of greeting from one of his children. "And good morning to you too," he said, bending to talk to her abdomen.

Maggie smiled. "They're very active this morning," she said. "It's like they know what's happening today."

"Maybe they do," he said. "They've heard us talking about it all week, after all."

Maggie laughed. "Yes, I suppose they have," she said. "I'm going to have to ask you to leave," she said. "I need to get dressed, and..."

"Bad luck, yeah I know," he said with a yawn.

"Didn't sleep well last night?" she asked as he walked to the bathroom.

"Nah, guess I was too keyed up," he said. "No worries. I'll sleep on the train."

"The train to where?" she asked.

Malcolm laughed. "Nice try sweetheart," he said, and then stepped into the shower.

Later

Malcolm stood waiting with Will, who was serving his best man, growing more nervous by the minute. He looked at his watch again, wondering what the holdup was.

"Relax mate," Will said. "She's not going to leave you at the altar."

Malcolm laughed. "Hope not," he said. "You've got the rings?"

Will stuck one hand in his pocket and pulled the wedding bands out to show him.

"Did you get it?" Will asked.

Malcolm nodded. "Didn't sleep last night, but I got it."

Will smiled. "She's gonna flip."

Malcolm smiled. "I'm counting on it."

The skirl of bagpipes announced the approach of the bride, and Malcolm and Will turned their attention to the other side of the garden, where Alli stood with a small nosegay in her hands, trying valiantly not to cry. She walked towards Malcolm, Will and the JP, followed by Mick, Irene and Maggie. Malcolm felt his eyes tear up as he saw his bride, looking utterly radiant in a flowing pale pink gown. Her hair was piled up on her head and bejeweled with tiny pink pearls. He watched, mesmerized as she walked up to him, her eyes reflecting the emotions that filled her heart.

The civil ceremony was brief, but Maggie and Malcolm had added their own personal touches to it, making it more meaningful to them. When the time came for the rings to be exchanged, Malcolm smiled and pulled a surprise out of his pocket for Maggie.

"I thought you might like this back," he said, holding her engagement ring between his thumb and finger.

Maggie's eyes filled with tears as she looked at it, then up at him. "How... how did you get it back? You said it was in Boston!"

"It was," he said, as he slipped it on her finger. "I flew down there last night to get it."

"You did?"

Malcolm nodded.

Maggie smiled, and reached up to touch his face. No wonder he was so tired this morning, she reflected.

They exchanged wedding bands, and then the JP asked them to join hands as he made the final decree.

"Malcolm and Margaret have made the declarations required by the laws of Canada. They have chosen to exchange rings as a token of the marriage vows, and it is my pleasure to announce that they are now legally husband and wife," he said. He smiled, and turned to Malcolm. "You may kiss your bride," he said.

Malcolm didn't hesitate to do so.

The Townhouse was a popular restaurant in the downtown area, and it was there that the wedding party and their small number of guests enjoyed a quiet reception. Irene had made a wedding cake for the occasion, and after eating lunch, Malcolm and Maggie cut the cake while their guests took photos and applauded.

"I'd like to propose a toast," Mick said standing up. He picked up a glass of champagne as all eyes turned to him. "I remember Malcolm when he first started coming into the Hart. And never would I have ever believed that one day he'd become my son-in-law. But he's come a long way in the past year," he said, giving Malcolm a smile. "And I'm sure that my little girl couldn't have found a better match. Maggie, I couldn't be happier for you than I am right now, and I know that in a few more weeks, when my grandchildren are born, you two will be wonderful parents. So here's to you," he said, holding his glass up high.

Everyone took a drink of their champagne, and then Malcolm stood up.

"Thanks Mr. O'Toole," he said.

"No, no more of that Mr. O'Toole," Mick said. "You call me Mick from now on, or Dad if you prefer."

"And you call me Mum," Irene said.

Malcolm smiled. "It'll be my pleasure," he said. "Never got to call anyone that before," he said, looking down at Irene with a smile. "I'd like to say a few words now that I have all your attention," he said. "Words can't really express how I feel right now. I'm ...so honoured to be a part of this amazing family. I never dreamed I'd be so lucky. But now, now that Maggie's my wife, I know that I'm the luckiest man in the whole world." He bent to kiss Maggie, who was in tears by this point.

After wedding cake and tea and coffee, the newlyweds went home to change, and then headed to the train station in Truro, and hour's drive from Antigonish. Maggie's curiosity was finally satisfied when she saw the destination of the train they boarded: Montreal.

"I can't believe we're going to Montreal!" she said as they sat in the comfortable first class section of the VIA train.

Malcolm smiled. "Well believe it baby," he said. "I just hope you can take the excitement," he said. "Don't want you going into premature labour or anything."

Maggie laughed. "I think I can handle it."

Twenty Four

Malcolm and Maggie spent their honeymoon taking in the sights of Old Montreal, eating at Montreal's world famous restaurants, and relaxing in their lavish hotel room. Malcolm knew that Maggie was at the point in her pregnancy when she needed a lot of rest, and given the stress she'd been through over the past few months, he was determined to see that she got it.

One afternoon Malcolm insisted that his new bride spend the afternoon at the hotel's spa. Maggie didn't object, and received pampering like she'd never known at the hands of the resident experts. While she was enjoying her massage, manicure and pedicure, Malcolm spoke to his two brothers in a long overdue conference call. After getting caught up with each other, the three brothers put their heads together to tackle the big issue at hand: their father.

"Personally, I don't think we should go to the police," Tom said. "I know he's broken the law, but if I know Dad, he'll only lash out if backed into a corner."

"Are you suggesting that we let him get away with what he's done?" Malcolm asked. "Cause there's no way in hell I'd agree to that."

"I'm not suggesting that," Tom said. "I'm suggesting we use a different tactic."

"Are you talking about JP?" Rob asked.

"Yes," Tom said. "At least let him in on what's happening. He may have a better suggestion than all of us."

"JP hates Dad," Rob pointed out. "He'll just call the cops on him."

"Why is that, I wonder?" Malcolm asked. "What did he do to piss off the old man so much?"

"I think a lot of it has to do with your mother," Rob said. "JP loved Judith. We all did, she was a great lady."

"You mean...the way Dad treated her?" Malcolm asked, not quite sure he was ready to open up that old wound.

"He treated her great until she got pregnant with you," Tom said. "And then..."

"I know the whole story," Malcolm said, sensing his brother's hesitance. "My grandmother told me that Dad wanted my mother to have an abortion."

"That really upset our grandmother," Tom said. "She was a very religious person, and it broke her heart that Dad would suggest that. She was already upset when his marriage ended to our mother, and then that was kind of the last straw."

"So he hates Dad because of Grandma?" Malcolm asked. "Is that it?"

"That's my best theory," Tom said.

"We should ask JP," Rob said. "Think he'd tell us?"

"Never know until you try I guess," Malcolm said. "So what do you think he could do for us?" he asked, steering the conversation back to the matter at hand. "You think he'd have an idea?"

"Couldn't hurt to ask him," Rob said.

"We have a witness, don't forget," Malcolm said. "Hugh Wellman's ready and willing to testify against Dad."

"That will help, no doubt," Tom said. "I just hope this guy is smart enough to keep his mouth closed, though. If Dad finds out he's been talking...well let's just hope he doesn't."

"He won't find out," Malcolm said. "Hugh's not stupid."

"Let's hope not," Rob said. "A lot is hanging on his testimony. He can back up everything Maggie says."

"And we'll need that, I'm afraid," Tom said. "Otherwise it's just Dad's word against hers. And that's not going to end up in Maggie's favour."

"You're right," Malcolm said. "But with Hugh it won't be just her word. He's the key."

Twenty Five

Boston

"So tell me about yourself," Deb said as she and Hugh sat at a small cafe.

"Not much to tell," Hugh said. "Born and raised here in Bean Town," he said. "Been working since I was 16. Kind of a loner."

Deb nodded, as she sipped her low fat Latte. "So what do you do? Your profession I mean."

"Well, I'm sorta between jobs right now," he said. "Had a sweet job, but lost it a few months back."

Deb frowned. "Sorry to hear it," she said. "What happened? Cut backs?"

"Nothing like that," he said. "Just worked for a prick, that's all. Then I got a job as a bouncer, but the place is shut down right now."

"A place here in town?" she asked.

"Yeah," he said. He took a drink of his coffee, not wanting to give her any details. He barely knew her, and wasn't about to start divulging sensitive information to her about the O'Tooles and their situation. "What about you? You said you were a lawyer or something?"

"Paralegal," she said.

"What's the difference?" he asked.

"Well ...lawyers can practice on their own," she said. "Paralegals work under the supervision of a lawyer. Less schooling."

"Gotcha," he said. "You're not from Boston, are you? Can tell by your accent."

Deb smiled. "Guilty as charged," she said. "I'm from Wisconsin, actually. Went to school here and decided to stay."

Hugh nodded. "So how come a classy girl like you is still single?"

Deb shrugged. "I guess I'm picky when it comes to men," she said, giving him a smile. "You're single too. Why is that?"

"I was with this woman for about 2 years when she dumped me for some jerk she works with," Hugh said.

"What a terrible thing to do," Deb said. "How long ago was that?"

"Let's see," Hugh said, thinking back. "Almost six months now."

"Six months is a long time to be alone," she said, placing a hand on his thick forearm. "A man like you needs a woman in his life."

Hugh couldn't deny that, neither could he deny the way her touch made him feel. He shifted in his seat. "You wanna get out of here?" he said. "Go someplace and get a drink? And I don't mean coffee," he said. "It's kinda dead in here."

Deb smiled. "Sure," she said. "I'd love to."

They ended up in a dance club, which was quite crowded given that it was Friday night. Hugh wasn't much of a dancer, and would have preferred remaining at the table they'd managed to procure; but Deb managed to coax him onto the dance floor with her.

"I can't dance," he told her as she took his hands. "Two left feet, you know?"

Deb laughed. "Nonsense," she said. "Just move to the music," she said, as she wiggled her body in a rather provocative manner. Hugh watched her, not even trying to hide the fact that he was doing so. He decided that he would take the earliest opportunity to get into Miss Paralegal's pants, her legal briefs as it were. It seemed to him as though she was asking for it, the way she was moving, the way she was dressed, the way she looked at him. It was his opinion that if women didn't want to be banged, they shouldn't lead a man on as though they wanted him. And to his mind that's what Deb was doing. So when the music changed tempo, he pulled her to him, letting his hands roam down her back to her shapely bottom.

"This is more my style," he said. "Nice and slow."

Deb could feel his hands on her bottom, could feel the beginnings of an erection through his pants. And it excited her. She'd never been with a man like Hugh, so rough and dangerous. She imagined that sex with him would be the same, and the thought of that sent a rush of arousal through her. Sex with Jack was so predictable, so traditional, so...boring. Running her hands up into his hair, she pulled him down to her and kissed him on the mouth. Hugh returned her kiss, and it wasn't long before she felt his tongue in her mouth, aggressively exploring as his hands kneaded her bottom. She knew that he would take her with very little encouragement, and as much as she was physically attracted to him, she didn't want to give him the wrong message.

"Sorry," she said, breaking their kiss. "I couldn't resist."

"Don't apologize," he said, sensing that she was regretting her overture. "Maybe I should take you home. It's getting pretty late."

Deb nodded. "I think so, yes," she said. "Thank you."

Hugh drove Deb to her apartment complex, unsure how things were going to play out. She was sending him mixed signals, making him crazy with lusting her and then backing off like a shy school girl. He'd have no trouble at all having sex with her at this point, even though it was only their first date. It certainly wouldn't be the first time he'd done so. But he sensed that she wasn't like that, that she had more self control and more self worth than the women he usually associated with. He decided to let her control the way things unfolded, all the while hoping they unfolded in the way he wanted them to.

"Nice building," Hugh said as he parked the car. He was hoping she'd take the hint and invite him in.

"Would you like to come up for a bit?" she asked, as though reading his mind.

"Sure," he said, turning off the car. "Lead the way."

Deb led him into the building, giving the doorman her usual patronizing smile. Hugh followed her to the elevator, not at all surprised by the richness of the place she called home. The elevator was empty when they stepped inside. "You must pay a fortune to live in a joint like this," Hugh commented.

Deb shrugged. "I guess it's pricy," she said. "But I love it here. The view of the harbour is spectacular."

Hugh didn't say it, but the view of the harbour was the last thing on his mind as he followed her down the corridor to her apartment. He was too busy admiring her behind as she stood at the door unlocking it.

"So here we are," she said as they stepped inside. She tossed her keys into a ceramic bowl that sat on a small cherry wood table in the small hallway at the entrance.

Hugh followed her, looking around at the luxurious apartment. It was a far cry from the small apartment he rented, an apartment he wouldn't be able to afford for much longer unless he found a source of income soon.

"Come here," she said, beckoning him towards the balcony. She opened the door, a rush of cold air blowing past them as they stepped outside. "See what I mean?" she said, turning to him.

Hugh nodded, setting his hands on the metal railing. "Pretty sweet," he said, admiring the harbour lights below.

Deb nodded, moving beside him, resting her hands on the rail beside his. She couldn't help but notice how large his hands were, and wondered if the rest of him was as big.

"So where do you live?" she asked.

"Southie," he said. "Not exactly the Harbour district."

Deb smiled. "But you love it there, that's what counts."

Hugh turned to her. "You think so?" he said. "You might not think so if you saw the dump I call home."

Deb was uncomfortable, and looked away, as the huge social gulf opened up between them all of a sudden. But she pushed past it and moved closer to him. "It's cold out here," she said.

"Yeah, sure is," he said. He hesitated for a moment, and then put his arm around her. Deb didn't object, and snuggled against him.

"That's better," she said.

"Yeah," he said, wrapping his other arm around her and pulling her closer. The scent of her perfume filled his senses, the feel of her body against his doing little to dampen the lust he'd been fighting all evening. "You smell good."

Deb looked up at him. "You like it? It's Chanel's latest -"

Her words were cut off by Hugh's mouth on hers. He kissed her deeply, his hands travelling down her back to grab her bottom aggressively. Deb held on to him, the ferocity of his kiss making her weak in the knees. Finally he broke the kiss, and moved his mouth to her ear.

"I think we should go inside," he whispered into her ear. "Let me warm you up some more."

His words sent a thrill through her, and she had to resist the urge to simply follow the primitive urges he was drawing out of her.

"Okay," she said.

He took her hand and led her back into the apartment. Deb stopped to close and lock the door, and turned back to him. She knew that she needed to be the one to rein things in before they got out of control. Hugh would have no trouble at all taking things to the next level in a hurry if she permitted it.

"I need to say something," she told him before he had a chance to make a move.

"What?" he asked, feeling as though he already knew what she was going to say.

"I am *very* attracted to you," she said. "But I'm just not prepared to get too ...physical yet. We barely know each other. I hope you can understand my feelings and respect them."

Hugh sighed. "I guess," he said. "Though you might have cooled things down before now. You've been sending some pretty strong signals my way."

"I'm sorry," she said. "As I said, I'm very attracted to you, Hugh. So much so that it would be very easy for me to just throw caution to the wind and spend the night with you. But I'm not that kind of woman. I need to know a man more than I know you before I get that intimate with him."

Although Hugh had expected this, he was disappointed nonetheless. "Gotcha," he said, feeling foolish suddenly. "I guess I'd better go home, then."

Deb watched him, her feelings starting to get very muddled. Her purpose had been clear when she'd first approached Hugh, but she hadn't counted on actually having feelings for the man. But she did, and that made her situation all the more uncomfortable.

"I hope you'll call me again," she said, watching him as he headed to the door.

Hugh stopped. "Do you want me to call you again?" he asked, not looking at her.

"Yes," she said at once. "I do. Very much."

Hugh looked back at her for a moment. "I'll think about it," he said, and then turned and left her apartment.

Deb stood looking at the door as it closed behind him, confused and unsettled by what had happened. Somehow she'd lost control of the ebb and flow of things, somehow he'd obtained the upper hand. She realized then that Hugh Wellman had more to him than met the eye, and that she'd been underestimating him all along. *You **will** call me again*, she decided as she walked over to lock the door. *You've got me under your skin now, Hugh...you won't be able to resist calling me again.* Deb tried to ignore the fact that perhaps, just perhaps, she had it all backwards; and that it was *her* who had *him* under her skin. She pushed such nonsense aside, and drew a warm bubble bath to soak in before bed.

Martha's Vineyard

"Well isn't this a nice surprise," said JP as he welcomed Rob and Tom into his home.

"We wanted to come and see you on your birthday," Tom said. "But things were just a little too hectic."

JP nodded. "I understand," he said. "Life's busy with kids and jobs, I remember. Come on in."

Rob and Tom followed their grandfather into the large living room. "Have a seat," JP said as he took his favourite spot by the fireplace. "Cold one out there," he said.

"Sure is," Rob agreed as he sat down on the small wicker sofa near his grandfather's chair. "Hate to think of how cold it'll be in a few more weeks," he said.

JP nodded, looking at his two grandsons. "How have you been? How are the kids?" he asked.

"Good," Tom said. "Busy as ever with school, friends, all the extra stuff they do."

"Always seems likes something," Rob said with a smile. "Between dance classes, hockey practice, riding lessons..."

"Kids these days are too busy if you ask me," JP said. "When do they get to be just kids?"

Rob and Tom exchanged a look. "I agree with you, Grandpa," he said. "It's the wives who insists on these extras."

JP nodded, far too much of a gentleman to express his opinion about his grandsons' wives. "So where is your brother? Your father told me he was in Scotland."

"He's not there anymore," Rob said. "He's been back for a few weeks now."

"Actually, it's him that we want to talk to you about," Tom said. "Malcolm."

JP frowned. "What about him?" he asked. "Is everything all right with him?"

Rob and Tom exchanged a look.

"No, everything is not all right with him," Tom said. "There's a ...situation we want to talk to you about."

"We need your opinion, Grandpa," Rob said. "We need your help handling this situation."

JP nodded. "Tell me about it," he said. "And tell me how Malcolm is involved."

Tom hesitated, and looked at his twin as though for guidance.

"This isn't going to be an easy thing for you to hear," Rob said. "But we both think you need to know. Malcolm does too. He'd be here today if he could, but he can't, and we'll explain why."

JP frowned, growing equally concerned and confused. Malcolm's father had not mentioned anything about Malcolm being in some sort of difficulty; and yet, would he have cared enough to do so?

"Just tell me, boys," JP said. "Tell me what's wrong with Malcolm."

Rob and Tom took turns relating the past history of Jack's animosity towards Maggie. They told of Malcolm's engagement to Maggie, and then, finally, related the events of that day at the airport when operatives of their father had abducted, confined and taken Maggie to the quarry where Jack awaited her. JP listened in silent shock as he listened to his grandsons describe the nefarious plot his only child had devised to tear Malcolm from the woman he loved. JP wasn't surprised by the level of malice that Jack was capable of, but it angered him deeply that Malcolm had once again been the object of that malice.

JP stood up and walked over to look into the fire. "Where is Malcolm now?" he asked. "Has he found her? Has he found Maggie?"

"Yes, he found her," Rob said, standing up with his brother to walk over to join their grandfather. "He found her with the help of one of Dad's henchmen, ironically."

JP looked up at him. "Really? How did that happen?"

"Dad fired the guy," Tom said. "And he ended up working at the pub that Maggie's parents own. They hired him as a bouncer, not knowing what part he'd played in Maggie's disappearance. I guess after awhile, he felt compelled to tell her family what he knew."

JP said nothing as he digested this. Emotions raged though him, a jumble of them all vying for supremacy: shock, rage, disappointment even shame. *I raised him*, he thought. *He is what he is because of me....*

"Grandpa? You okay?" Rob said.

JP walked back over to his favourite chair and sat down heavily. Each of his grandsons were concerned by his silence, and worried that the old man night be having a cardiac event.

"I'm not going to let him get away with this," JP said at last. He looked up at Rob and Tom. "He *won't* get away with this. And when I'm finished with him, he'll rue the day he ever tried to ruin Malcolm's life."

"What are you going to do, Grandpa?" Tom asked. "If you go to the police with this, you know that Dad will get his back up and do something desperate. And desperation often makes people do terrible things."

"And besides that, Malcolm doesn't want anything to happen before Maggie has the babies," Rob said.

JP's face registered his surprised. "Maggie is pregnant?"

Rob nodded. "She's having twins in December," he said.

"And Malcolm doesn't want anything upsetting her until she's given birth," Tom said.

"That's understandable," JP said. "Very well, we'll wait. That will give us time to get our plans in order. And mark my words, your father is so arrogant he won't even see it coming."

Twenty Six

Nova Scotia

Malcolm and Maggie returned to Nova Scotia after spending two weeks in Montreal. As much fun as she'd had, Maggie was exhausted by the time they'd arrived back at the house.

"I can't believe you went to Montreal," Aidan said as Maggie and Malcolm gave out souvenirs to the family. "You don't even speak French, and the Habs are there. You hate them, Malcolm."

Malcolm laughed. "Yeah, well I sucked it up for your sister's sake," he said, looking at Maggie with a smile. "Though it was tough, I'm not going to lie to you."

"Mail's here," Will said as he entered the room. Mick's Uncle Ted had been forwarding the mail from Boston for weeks, enabling the family to keep up with their bill payments. "Something here from the bank, Da," Will said, handing Mick an envelope bearing the name Bank of America. Mick took the envelope and left the room. Maggie couldn't help but notice how worried her father looked, and looked at her mother. Irene's eyes followed her husband out of the room, and then returned her attention to the others.

"Everything okay, Mum?" Maggie asked as Malcolm talked to the boys about the sights they'd seen in Montreal.

"Nothing for you to concern yourself with," Irene said.

Maggie frowned. "Don't do that," she said. "If there's a problem, I want to know. I want to help."

Irene glanced at the doorway where Mick had left and looked back at her daughter. "Things are just a little tight since we had to close the pub," she said. "Your Da's worried about how he's going to pay the mortgage on the place."

Maggie hadn't considered that, but it made perfect sense. The source of income that enabled Mick to keep the pub open was gone. Keeping the bank from foreclosing would be a challenge.

"Malcolm can help him out," Maggie said.

"You know your Da would never accept help," Irene said.

"Even if it means losing the Hart?" Maggie asked.

Irene sighed. "We can't change him, love," she said. "He is what he is."

Maggie knew that to be true, but wasn't content to leave it at that. "Well I'm knackered," she said. "I think it's time for bed."

Irene smiled. "You go on," she said, giving her a kiss on the cheek. "You need plenty of sleep these days."

Maggie nodded, and then headed upstairs to bed.

"It sounds like you had a bonnie time in Montreal," Irene said as Malcolm joined her for a cup of tea.

"We did, yeah," he said. "It was awesome being able to take her," he said with a smile. "Of course she kept having to go to the ladies, and needed to get off of her feet every couple of hours."

Irene smiled. "Yes, I remember those last few weeks carrying twins," she said. "It's exhausting."

Malcolm nodded. "She's a trooper though," he said, the pride and love he felt for his new wife evident.

Irene smiled. "Only a few more weeks, then," she said. "The nursery looks lovely. You've done a nice job."

"Thanks," he said. "I've had a lot of help. Those two kids are gonna be spoiled rotten by all the attention they'll get from their uncles," he said.

Irene laughed. "Aye well I think their grandparents will give the uncles a run for their money in that department. Have you finally decided on names, then?"

Malcolm nodded as he took a sip of his tea. "Yeah we have," he said. "But Maggie's warned me to secrecy. She wants the names kept strictly on the QT."

Irene smiled. "I see," she said. "Well that's her prerogative I suppose."

"And there's one thing I've learned, Mum," he said. "Never argue with a pregnant lady."

Malcolm stayed downstairs a bit longer, but then decided to go to bed. He picked up the suitcases and headed upstairs. He found his new wife sitting on the edge of the bed, brushing out her long hair with an expression on her face he knew well.

"What's wrong?" he asked, setting the bags down and then coming over to sit beside her.

Maggie set her brush down on the table beside the bed and looked at him. "I'm worried about my father," she said. "Mum says he's having trouble with the mortgage on the Hart. I'm worried he's going to lose the place. That would break his heart."

Malcolm nodded. "What makes you think that will happen?"

"He's not making any money," she said. "He closed the pub when he and the lads came up here. If the pub stays closed for much longer, he may not be able to keep up with the mortgage payments."

Malcolm hadn't considered this. For him, the thought of mortgage foreclosure was unheard of. But then he was from a vastly wealthy family, and money had never been an issue.

"Why don't we help him out?" he suggested.

"I thought that too," Maggie said. "But Mum said he would never accept any help. He's a very proud man. She's right."

Malcolm considered this for a moment. "Well...what if he didn't know about it until it was too late?" he said.

Maggie frowned. "What do you mean?"

"I mean what if someone helped him without him knowing it?" he said. "I could do that. I *want* to do that, Maggie. Your family is my family now," he said. "And it's because of what my father did to you that they're in this mess."

Maggie smiled, and reached up to touch his face. "You're a wonderful man, you know that?"

Malcolm took her hand and kissed it. "Thanks baby," he said. "Do you know the bank your dad has the mortgage with?" he asked, standing up.

"Bank of American on Washington," she told him, watching him as he sat at the computer in their room. "You're going to do it tonight?"

Malcolm shrugged. "Why not?" he said. "It's easy when you do it online," he said, sitting down at the computer.

Maggie pushed herself off of the bed to watch him. "How can you do that?" she asked. "It's not your account."

"Doesn't matter," he said. "I deal with that bank all the time. If I tell them I want to make a payment on your father's mortgage, they're not gonna say no. Bankers never say no when you want to give them money."

Maggie smiled. "I suppose not," she said. "But don't you have to talk to someone to do that?"

"Yeah," he said. "I'm sending the bank manager an email to call me first thing in the morning. I'll do it then."

Maggie bent to kiss his cheek. "Thank you love," she said. "You don't know what this means to me."

"Sure I do," he said, pulling her down onto his lap. "Your family is important to you. And if I can help you help them, I'll do whatever I can."

Maggie smiled. "I love you, do you know that?"

Malcolm laughed. "Yeah, I think I got that," he said, and pulled her close to kiss her. "Love you too, babe," he murmured between kisses. His hands travelled up under her blouse, sending shivers down her spine. Even though she was eight months pregnant, he still found her as desirable as ever. Maggie pulled her blouse over her head with his help, eager for him to continue.

"You don't mind that I have this big belly now?" she asked as she reached around and unclasped her bra and then pulled it away from her body.

"No way," he said, running his hands up the sides of her body to take her bare breasts in his hands. "You're every bit as sexy to me now as ever," he said, teasing her nipples with his finger tips.

"I think you're wearing too much clothing," she said, noting the rather sizable bulge in his pants. "Stand up and let me help you out of these jeans," she said, getting off of his lap.

"Whatever you say," he said, standing up. He unbuttoned the top of the fly of his jeans and watched her do the rest. She yanked at his hips, pulling the denim from his body.

"Well what have we here?" she said, running her hand over the large erection pressing against the fabric of his shorts. She slipped her hand inside and grasped his erection, making him moan with appreciation. "Now let me sit," she said, sitting in the chair. "And you come here."

Malcolm was more than happy to let her take control of things, and stood before her. She pulled his shorts down, releasing his stiff penis, and then bent to run her tongue along the length of him.

"Shit that feels so good," he said, closing his eyes as she grasped him with her hand as her tongue teased him. She drew him into her mouth, sucking him deeply as her hands stroked the length of him. Malcolm ran his hands into her hair, watching her fellate him, knowing that he'd need to stop her soon if things were going to go any further. And he definitely wanted that to happen.

"Come over to the bed," he told her. "I think you need to go for a ride."

Maggie pulled his penis from her mouth and looked up at him with a smile. "You do, do you?"

"Absolutely," he said, walking over to the bed and lying down on his back. Maggie took a moment to remove her pants and panties, and then joined him on the bed. Taking his hands to support her, she straddled his body, lowering herself onto his slick, hard penis.

"This was a very good idea," she sighed as she felt him filling her.

"I do try," he said with a smile.

The next morning Malcolm spent an hour on the phone with the Bank of America, who were only too happy to accommodate one of their most affluent clients. Malcolm decided to pay the entire mortgage on the Hart and Hound, some fifty thousand dollars, deciding that it was money well spent. Maggie was just coming out of the shower when he concluded his phone call.

"So you spoke to the manager of the bank, then?" she asked, rubbing her wet hair with a towel.

"Yep, it's a done deal," he said, standing up.

"So their payment is taken care of?" she asked.

"*All* their payments are taken care of," Malcolm said. "I paid the rest of the mortgage."

Maggie's eyes widened in shock. "You paid for the whole mortgage?"

"Yeah, no big deal," he said. "I figure it's the least I can do, considering how important that place is to me. I met the love of my life there, after all."

Maggie smiled. "You're so sweet," she said, giving him a kiss. "My parents will be in shock when they find out."

"I told the manager to tell them an anonymous benefactor paid it," Malcolm said. "I know how awkward they'd feel if they knew it was me."

Maggie couldn't dispute what he'd said, but knew that her parents were clever enough to figure out that Malcolm was the benefactor.

"Well I'm hungry," she decided.

"What else is new?" he asked her with a smile.

Maggie gave him a swat on the behind in response as he headed into the bathroom for his shower.

Boston

The music from the stage show blared over the drunken patrons as the scantily clad dancers swayed and shook their bodies to the beat. Their efforts were met with shouts of encouragement, the level of noise growing louder as each piece of clothing was removed and dropped to the floor.

Hugh Wellman watched the strippers, a collection of empty beer glasses surrounding him on the sticky table top. It had been more than a week since he'd last seen Deb. Despite her request, he had not called her, and had begun to think that he'd made a foolish mistake ever getting involved with her in the first place. She wasn't his type, not even close. And yet he somehow couldn't get the scent of her out of his mind. More than likely it was simply the fact that he'd been celibate for quite some time; not by choice, but strictly by circumstances. He'd hoped when Deb had shown interest in him that he'd have found an end to his sexual drought, but such was not the case. Deciding he didn't need the aggravation of being teased and lead on any more, he'd stopped calling her. She'd sent him several texts in the past week, but he'd ignored them all, hoping she'd get the hint and leave him alone. But Deb Rogers was nothing if not persistent.

As he sat watching the show on the stage reach its conclusion, Hugh heard his cell phone, its ring barely audible amidst the din that surrounded him. He took it out of his pocket and looked at the number, not surprised to see that it was Deb. Deciding he needed to end this once and for all, he answered the call.

"Yeah?"

"Hugh? Is that you?"

"Who else would it be?"

Silence. "Why haven't you returned my texts?"

"Didn't have nothing to say."

"Is everything all right? You have me worried."

Hugh frowned. "Look, this ain't gonna work," he said. "You and me...we're just too different."

More silence. "Can you come over to my place?" she asked. "I'd like to talk about this in person."

Hugh rolled his eyes and cursed under his breath. "Nothing to talk about," he said. "What do you want from me, anyway?"

"If you come over to my place, I'll tell you."

Hugh frowned and looked at his watch. It was almost midnight, and no doubt the night doorman would give him all sorts of trouble just getting in the front door. "If I come you gotta meet me downstairs," he said. "That doorman of yours gives me the stink eye when I come over."

"Deal," she said. "I'll meet you in the lobby in 20 minutes."

"Make it thirty," he said. "I gotta get a cab. I'm kinda loaded."

"Okay, thirty minutes then," Deb said. "See you then."

Hugh shoved his cell phone back in his pocket, and stood up. He pulled out his wallet and left a tip for the waitress and then made his way outside. It was quite cold outside, but the alcohol in his system didn't allow him to notice as he stood outside calling for a cab. There were patrons outside, making the most of the dark and the lateness of the hour to conduct shady business. Hugh ignored them and walked to the curb, the pungent aroma of marijuana surrounding him. A taxi cab pulled up after a few minutes, and he climbed in the backseat. When he gave the driver the address, the man looked at him rather oddly through the rear-view mirror. But he said nothing, and simply drove to the Harbour District, hoping he'd get paid for his troubles when he got there.

Deb was waiting anxiously when he arrived. She was wondering if he'd even show up, given the terseness of the conversation they'd had earlier. But when he walked through the door, all her anxieties dissolved. She went to him at once, the smell of alcohol rolling off of him.

"I'm so glad you came," she said, taking him by the hand.

Hugh said nothing, and let her lead her to the elevator. They stood alone in the elevator, the tension between them palpable. Hugh watched her, trying to deny the feelings she aroused in him. But he couldn't. His eyes travelled over her, noting how the shirt she wore clung to her breasts. Deb could feel his eyes on her, the way he was examining her both exciting and frightening her.

"So how have you been?" she asked finally, unable to stand the silence between them.

"Okay," was his simple reply.

Deb nodded. "Find anything yet?"

Hugh shook his head.

"Oh, sorry to hear it," she said as the doors opened on her floor. She led him down the corridor to her apartment, keenly aware of how closely he was following her. As she stood unlocking the door she could feel the heat from his body behind her, smell the sweet scent of alcohol on his breath.

"Come on in," she said, trying to keep things light. But Hugh was in no mood for lightness, and said nothing as he followed her into the posh apartment.

"So what did you want, anyway?" he said once they'd reached the living room.

"I wanted to talk to you," she said. "I want to know why you didn't call me this week."

Hugh shrugged. "Didn't feel like it."

Deb frowned. "Did I do something wrong?" she asked. "Was it because of ...the way things ended last time?"

"You mean the way you gave me the brush off?" he asked.

"Is that what you think I did?"

"Yeah. I don't like being jerked around," he said. "I don't know the way you usually treat the men in your life, but if that's it, then you can forget about me right now."

Deb listened to him, seeing that underneath his coarse exterior, he was hurt. She'd hurt him when she'd rejected his advances. And that surprised her.

"I'm sorry," she said. "I...I've never been with a man like you before, and..."

"A man like me?" he asked, walking over to her. "What exactly do you mean by that? A man who isn't rich? Who's uneducated? Who doesn't have a fancy job or an expensive car?"

Deb started to regret her invitation as he drew closer to her. He was angry and he was drunk, and sometimes that combination could be dangerous.

"Well, those may be true," she said, choosing her words carefully. "But that isn't what I meant."

"What did you mean, then?" he asked, standing right in front of her, towering over her as he looked down into her eyes.

"I mean I've never been with a man who makes me feel the way you do," she said, deciding to lay it on the line. "You make me feel ...afraid and excited all at once. You exude power, and you don't even try. There's just an animal magnetism about you that I find extremely exciting. I haven't been able to stop thinking about you all week, Hugh. I can't stop thinking about what it would be like to be have you in my bed."

Her words surprised him. They aroused him, and he took her by the shoulders and pulled her to him. "You want me in your bed?" he asked. "You want me to fuck you, Deb? Is that what you're saying?"

Deb nodded, her mouth dry, her heart racing. "I do," she said.

That was all Hugh needed to hear.

Twenty Seven

Nova Scotia

"I'm afraid I don't understand," Mick said. "I received a letter recently telling me that my mortgage payment was past due, and not you're telling me my mortgage is paid? All of it?"

"Yes Mr. O'Toole, that's exactly what I'm telling you," said the woman on the phone.

"How is that possible?" Mick asked.

"The balance of your mortgage, a sum of fifty-one thousand, eight hundred eleven dollars, was paid by an anonymous benefactor," she told him. "That's all I can tell you, sir."

Mick was certain that an error had been made. Who would pay out that much money for another person? Who had that kind of money to pay out all at once? And then he realized who it was. "I see," Mick said. "Thank you."

"Not at all sir," the woman said. "Thank you, and congratulations."

Mick ended the call and handed Irene's cell phone to her. The look on his face was one of shock.

"What's happened?" she asked. "What were they calling about?"

"You heard," he said, sitting down at the table with her. "The mortgage on the Hart, it's been paid off."

Irene thought she'd heard that, but didn't think it could possibly be true. "What? But how?"

"An anonymous benefactor," Mick said. "Paid the whole thing off, all in one payment. Now who do we know with that kind of money?"

Irene's eyes widened. "You don't think it was Malcolm, do you?"

"Who else?" Mick said. "Our son-in-law certainly has enough money to do it. Hell, that wouldn't even be a drop in the bucket for him."

Irene thought back to the conversation she'd had with Maggie the previous evening. Had Maggie put him up to it? Or had Malcolm done it on his own? He'd certainly demonstrated tremendous generosity in the past; it would be like him to do such a thing.

"Well if he wanted to remain anonymous, how do we find out?" Irene asked. "It's not like he's going to say anything."

"Maggie will tell us," Mick said.

"Maybe," she said.

"How do I look the man in the eye knowing I'm beholden to him now for that much money?" he asked. "It's bad enough we're living here under his roof, now this."

Irene frowned. "If the man wants to do this for us, just let him. He knows what a bind we're in, and I'm sure he feels responsible since it's because of his father that we are. Let him do this, Mick. Don't let your pride get in the way."

Mick frowned. "What's that mean?"

"It means don't let this act of kindness be spoiled by your pigheadedness," she said. "Think of it this way; would you rather lose the Hart? Or let your son-in-law help you?"

The thought of losing his beloved Hart was unthinkable to Mick. He'd worked hard to be able to take over its ownership. And yet, being indebted to his daughter's husband was more than his pride could handle.

"You know bloody well I can't lose the Hart," he grumbled.

"Then swallow that Irish pride of yours and let it go," she said. "Just this one. Can you manage that?"

Mick sighed. "I don't suppose I have a choice now, do I?"

Irene smiled. "You're right. You don't."

Boston

It was quite late in the day when Hugh woke up. He was disoriented at first, for it was not his own bed that he awoke in. He smiled when he thought about how he'd spent the previous night. They'd slept very little, for Hugh had thoroughly slaked his lust by taking Deb several times. They'd finally fallen into an exhausted, sweaty sleep sometime near dawn. Hugh couldn't remember the last time he'd slept so well. He rolled over and looked at the clock on the night table, not surprised to see that it was after noon. He was alone, and reasoned that Deb must be in the shower. Getting up, he decided to pay her a visit, certain that she wouldn't mind the company.

As he walked across the bedroom, he heard a cell phone start to ring. He didn't recognize the ring tone, and figured that it must be Deb's. He looked around, for the ring tone was a rather irritating one, and he wanted to silence it. Her phone was on the floor under the bed, next to the tattered panties he'd unceremoniously ripped from her body the previous night. He reached down and picked it up, stopping and staring at the screen when he saw the name of the caller: Jack Sullivan.

"Oh, you're up," Deb said from the doorway.

Hugh looked up at her as she stood there with a towel wrapped around her and a smile on her face. He help up her phone and showed her the screen. "Something I should know?" he asked.

Deb's face betrayed her, but only for an instant. She was good at lying, always had been. "He's a business associate," she said.

Hugh felt his emotions churning violently as he started to put together the pieces of a very ugly picture. "What kind of business, exactly?" he demanded.

"Legal, what else?" she replied casually. "I was hoping you'd join me in the shower," she said, moving to wrap her arms around him, but Hugh moved away. Deb frowned. "Something wrong?"

"You tell me," he said. "You never mentioned that you knew Sullivan," he said.

"Why is that a big deal?" she asked, growing nervous by his building anger.

"You know damn well why," he said. "I told you I was fired by Sullivan, I told you that and you never thought to mention that you know the man?"

"I really don't see what one thing has to do with the other," she said.

"No, you wouldn't," he said. And then he remembered the night he'd met her, the night he'd told his mother all about what Jack Sullivan had done, about the O'Tooles and how they'd left Boston. A sick feeling invaded him as he began to understand exactly why a woman like Deb Rogers had been interested in him. He grabbed her roughly by the arm. "You heard everything, didn't you?" he said. "You've been using me all along! You and that bastard Sullivan planned all this, didn't you? *Didn't you?*"

"Stop it!" she cried, trying to yank free from his iron grasp. "You're hurting me!"

"Tell me the truth, goddamn it!" he said. "Tell me the *real* reason you wanted me to call you. And don't give me any bullshit about being attracted to me, cause we both know that's a fuckin lie."

Deb didn't know what to say. In hindsight, she was foolish to think that she could manipulate a man like Hugh, for he was far cleverer than she gave him credit for. But as much as what he was saying was true, she knew that there was more to it now than she'd anticipated. She felt something real for him, despite the devious manner in which she'd pushed herself into his life.

"Okay, I'll admit it," she said finally. "At first, yes, I was just trying to get to you. I wanted information, and was prepared to get it any way I could."

Hugh released her, as though touching her now revolted him. "You fucking bitch," he said. "You pretend to be so classy, so much better than a guy like me, when you're really just a two-bit whore."

His words struck Deb deeply, and she felt tears spring to her eyes. "Please hear me out," she said, reaching for him, but he refused to let her touch him, and started looking for his clothes. "I admit that my initial interest in you was less than admirable, but now, now it's different. Now I care about you, for real, and..."

"Just shut the fuck up, would you?" He said, pulling on his jeans. "I don't believe anything that comes out of that lying mouth of yours, so spare me the bullshit. You've had your fun, slumming with the bum from Southie," he said, pulling his undershirt on next. "You've used me and now you're gonna go running back to your pal Sullivan and tell him everything, isn't that what you've been planning all along?"

"It *was* what I was planning," she said. "But now things are different. Now I have feelings for you, now I don't know what I'm going to do."

Hugh buttoned up his shirt, not saying a word. He felt foolish for having trusted her, for letting her manipulate him. He wasn't a man who was easily used, and yet she'd done a masterful job of it. "I'm outta here," he said, picking up his jacket from the chair at the end of the bed.

"Hugh please wait!" she said, running after him and placing herself in his path. Her towel fell to the floor, and she hoped that the sight of her naked body would quell his anger. It didn't.

"Get outta my way," he said. "I don't want to hurt you, but if you try and stop me from leaving, I will."

Deb hesitated, unsure if he was bluffing. But then she remembered that he used to work for Sullivan as a body guard, a muscle man, a man who made problems go away. She stepped aside and let him pass, helpless to stop him. The sound of the apartment door slamming signalled his departure. Deb sat down on the end of the bed, her body shivering. She sat for a moment or two, trying to decide what to do. *I've made such a mess of things,* she thought as tears started down her face. *What am I going to do?* Her thoughts were interrupted by the sound of her phone ringing, and she started at the suddenness of it. Brushing the tears from her face she walked over and picked up her phone, seeing that it was Jack calling again. She knew that she couldn't avoid him any longer, and accepted the call.

"Where the hell were you earlier?" were the first words she heard from her long time lover.

"In the shower," she said. "Did you want something?"

"Yeah, I need to talk to you," he said. "Get your ass over to my office. Now."

Deb frowned, the manner in which he spoke hurting her, not for the first time. "Okay, I'll get there as soon as I can," she said. "What's this about, Jack?"

"You'll find out when you get here," he said, and then hung up.

Deb felt anxiety welling up inside of her, knowing that whatever it was he wanted to see her about, it wasn't good. Her day was about to get worse. Much, much worse.

Nova Scotia

Maggie's cousin Noreen had invited the mothers of the children that Maggie had helped care for to her home for a baby shower for Maggie. Irene was also present, as well as Alli. Maggie knew about the shower, and hoped secretly that Carrie would be present. She'd been talking to her a lot lately, now that everything was out in the open, and missed her greatly. But she knew that it was a long way from Boston to come, and didn't expect her to make such a long trip for a Sunday afternoon party.

The living room of Noreen's house had been transformed with blue and pink streamers and balloons, the furniture rearranged to make room for chairs for the guests as well as a large table for the gifts. Maggie was given the seat of honour, a rocking chair that had a large bow on it and turned out to be a gift from her brothers. The guests had just taken their seats when the doorbell rang.

"I'll be right back," Noreen said, excusing herself from her guests. Irene had made a plate of treats for Maggie, who did her best to sample all the treats that her mother and cousin had worked so hard to make. But when she saw who entered the living room with Noreen, her plate ended up on the floor.

"Carrie!!" Maggie exclaimed as her best friend ran over to hug her. Both women were in tears as they embraced, Carrie laughing when she was unable to put her arms around Maggie.

"Oh my God look at you!" Carrie said with a smile. "You're so round!" she said, putting her hands on her friend's round belly.

Maggie laughed. "Only two weeks to go, what do you expect? I can't believe you're here!" she said, hugging her again. "Did you drive?"

"Dave did," Carrie told her as she took a seat beside Maggie. "He's gone to the house, your mom gave us the address. Malcolm has no idea he's coming," she said with a smile.

"He'll be so happy to see Dave," Maggie said. "I hope you're staying for a bit."

"We're spending the night, but that's all we can manage," Carrie said. "I wish we could stay longer."

"Next time," Maggie said. "When the babies come."

The shower was lovely, with plenty of good food and pleasant company. Maggie received a lot of things that she needed for the babies. The best gift, however, was the surprise appearance of her dear friend, Carrie. Seeing her again made her realize how much she'd missed having Carrie in her life, and the two friends vowed to see each other again very soon.

Malcolm had been very surprised when Dave showed up at his doorstep, and the two long time friends spent the afternoon getting caught up. Dave was quite struck by the change in his best friend. Malcolm had grown up a great deal in the months they'd been apart. He had no doubt that Malcolm was not only ready for fatherhood, but that he'd be a very good father. It was hard to believe given the man that Malcolm had been only a year earlier. Clearly Maggie's presence had been what it took to enable Malcolm to realize his full potential.

Boston

The office was very quiet when Deb arrived. Jack's secretary wasn't working, as it was Sunday, and so Deb headed directly into the office. Jack was inside, practicing on his indoor putting green when she entered the room.

"How's the putt?" she asked.

Jack ignored her question as he lined up his shot. Deb watched the ball as it landed in the hole. Another perfect shot.

"I had an interesting phone call last night," Jack said, walking over to his desk. He sat down on the edge of it, his putter in his hands. "And you'll never guess what they told me," he said, rolling the club between his hands.

Deb looked down at the putter, a little unnerved by the manner in which he was toying with it. "What did they tell you?" she asked.

"They told me that they'd seen you at a dance club recently," Jack said, his grey eyes glacial.

Deb felt as though her insides had turned to ice. "Yes, I like to go dancing," she said, fighting to keep her voice even. "Is that a problem?"

"I don't give a damn what you do, quite frankly," he said. "Unless you're doing it with another man."

Heart hammering within her, Deb faced him. "Another man? Jack, what are you talking about?" she asked, hoping her tone sounded more confused than terrified.

Jack moved quickly, so quickly she didn't have time to react. He brought the club head of the putter to her throat, the cold metal matching the look in his eyes.

"Don't fuck with me," he said. "I know you were with Hugh Wellman. I have photos to prove it."

"Oh, *him*," she said, stepping away from the end of the putter. "You see, I had a plan, I was using him to get information, and..."

"You expect me to believe that?" he said, dropping the club and grabbing her roughly by the arm. "You had a *plan*? You're not smart enough to have a plan," he said. "I know he was at your apartment last night," he went on, squeezing hard. "Did you fuck him, Deborah?" he asked, slapping her face with his other hand. "Did you suck his dick?" he asked, slapping her again.

"Stop it!" she cried. "Please stop!"

Jack released her, shoving her hard enough to throw her to the floor. "You're a waste of my time, do you know that?" he said. He grabbed her by the hair next, and pulled her face up to look at his. "We're done," he said. "And your cushy apartment, I'm having you evicted. You'll regret crossing me, Deborah. I'm sure you already do." He released her again, and she fell to the floor, crying and shaking with emotion and fear. "Now get the hell out of here, you pathetic slut."

Deb got up slowly, blood seeping from the corner of her mouth. She summoned her shredded dignity and left the office, wiping her mouth with the back of her hand. It wasn't the first time that Jack had hit her, but he'd never done so with such anger before. *I was a fool to think I could hide this from him,* she thought as she stabbed at the elevator button. *But if you think you've won Jack Sullivan, think again.*

Nova Scotia

Carrie and Dave stayed very late at the home of their best friends. Maggie was very tired by the time they left, but didn't want to go to bed and miss visiting with Carrie.

"So when do you expect to return to Boston?" Dave asked as they sat by the large fireplace in the great room.

"Not sure," Malcolm said. "My brothers and I have been trying to figure out the best way to deal with our father. It's a tricky situation," he said.

"No kidding," Carrie said. "I still can't believe he did that to you, Maggie."

Maggie nodded. "I'd really like to put it behind me, but we can't do that, not yet. But for now we're focusing on our babies," she said, looking at Malcolm. "They are our priority now."

"Absolutely," Malcolm said, giving her a smile. "I can't wait to meet the little guys."

"It's so exciting," Carrie said. "I can't believe you two are having twins!"

"Well I certainly can," Maggie said.

"It's like a cage match in there sometimes," Malcolm said.

Dave and Carrie laughed.

"Hopefully they'll get along better when they're born," Carrie said. "Otherwise you'll have your hands full."

"I think we'll have our hands full no matter what," Maggie said.

It was nearly 2AM when Dave and Carrie left for their hotel.

"You call me as soon as you go into labour," Carrie said. "I want to be there when your babies are born."

"I would love that," Maggie said. "I think Malcolm could use the support in the delivery room too."

Carrie laughed. "Then count me in," she said. "I would love to be there to see your children enter the world."

Maggie smiled. "Thanks, Carrie," she said. "That means a lot to me. To both of us."

Twenty Eight

Boston

Deb Rogers was sure she'd hit rock bottom. Her relationship with Jack Sullivan was over; and although she was not heartbroken, she was upset to be losing out on the financial benefits that went along with her association with him. She'd become accustomed to the fine things that came along with being Jack's lover, not the least of which was the fine apartment she'd lived in for over a year. She knew she would never be able to afford it on her paralegal's salary, and had relied on his financial support to help her make her rent. He'd only agreed to do so when Malcolm had moved in, and he'd enlisted her help to break up Malcolm and Maggie. She'd failed to do so, which had not pleased Jack.

And then there was Hugh. Deb had intended to use him to help Jack, to please Jack. She was often rewarded when she did something that pleased him. But that too had blown up in her face, and Hugh wanted nothing to do with her. Not only that, her brief association with him had caused her nothing but problems, a chain reaction of events that had landed her where she was now, packing her belongings in boxes. She'd been given to the end of the week to leave her apartment, but had not yet found another place that met her rather rich tastes.

It was almost midnight, and Deb had just got into bed when her phone started ringing. She thought twice about answering it, but when she checked the caller ID, she was alarmed to see that it was her boss. *What could he be calling about at this hour?* She wondered. She remembered that one of their clients was in the hospital; had she taken a bad turn? Picking up her phone, she accepted the call.

"Hello?" She said.

"Deborah, it's Dale. Sorry for the lateness of the call," said her boss.

"It's okay," she said, sitting up in bed. "Is everything all right?"

"No, I'm afraid not," Dale said. "I'm afraid I'm going to have to terminate your employment at my firm," he said. "Effective immediately."

Deb was sure that he was joking, for Dale Cameron tended to be something of a cut up.

"Dale, come on," she said. "It's too late at night for kidding around."

"I'm afraid I'm not kidding, Deb," Dale said. "I'm really sorry, but I'm totally serious. I have to let you go."

"But...but why?" Deb asked, her heart starting to race. "What have I done to deserve this?"

Dale was silent for a long time, as though struggling to find a response. "That's all I can tell you," he said. "I'm sorry Deb. Goodnight." At this point he ended the call.

Deb sat in her bed, staring at the screen of her phone. What had happened to cause Dale to fire her? They'd worked well together for almost 5 years now. What was the *real* reason he felt compelled to end her employment? And then she had an idea: Jack Sullivan. Could he be the reason? Did he have that much pull? *I have to know,* she thought. *But how? How do I find out the truth?* Deciding that she could do nothing until morning, she turned off the light and tried to sleep, knowing that sleep would not come easily to her now.

Nova Scotia

Maggie and Malcolm sat on a gym mat, surrounded by other couples, practicing deep breathing exercises. Maggie had been attending childbirth classes for months now with her mother; but now that Malcolm was back, he was anxious to learn as much as he could in the short time left before the arrival of the babies.

Maggie could tell that Malcolm was nervous about the prospect of child birth. But to his credit he was doing a good job of hiding it, and participated in the classes with enthusiasm.

"They give you drugs, right?" Malcolm asked as they walked to the car later. "You don't feel anything when you're going through all that, do you?"

"That's a personal choice," she said. "And even if I do decide to get an epidural, you can't get it until a certain point in the labour."

Malcolm nodded. "You're gonna get that, right?" he asked as he opened the car door for her.

"I don't know," she said. "Part of me would like to try to do it without drugs."

Malcolm frowned, not liking the sound of that. "Why would you do that?" he asked. "Judging by those videos we watched, it's gonna hurt. A lot."

Maggie smiled. "Yes, it will," she said. "That's something you're going to have to accept, love. Giving birth is hard work, that's why they call it labour. But I'm prepared for it, you don't need worry."

Malcolm didn't say anything as he started up the car. He was quite certain that nothing would prepare him for seeing the woman he loved in so much pain. But it wasn't his call to make. If Maggie wanted to tough it out, that was her choice. All he could do was sit by her side and support her.

After their class, Malcolm and Maggie went out for dinner. As much as they loved their family, they craved time alone, something they didn't get a lot of these days. So when they had the chance to share a quiet meal alone, they were very happy to take advantage of it.

"I can't finish this," Maggie said, pushing her plate away. "It's delicious, but there's just no room."

Malcolm smiled, but said nothing. He was tempted to remind his wife that she'd be having a snack on the way home and another before bedtime. But he knew that she was rather sensitive about her weight at the moment, so he said nothing.

They'd just been given their bill when Malcolm's phone rang. He was surprised to see the name that appeared on the screen of his iPhone: James Sullivan.

"Hello?"

"Malcolm my boy, it's good to hear your voice," said JP.

Malcolm smiled. "It's good to hear yours," he said. "How are you, Grandpa?"

"I'm well thanks, quite well," JP replied. "Except that I'm quite concerned about you, Malcolm."

"You are?"

"Yes," JP said. "Your brothers paid me a visit recently. They told me all about what your father did to your Maggie."

Malcolm looked over at his wife, who was picking at her dessert. "They did, eh?"

"Yes, and I was appalled," JP said. "But you've found her, they told me you'd found her."

"Yeah I did," Malcolm said. "We got married a few days after I found her."

"That's wonderful," JP said. "I'm happy for you, son. I just want to let you know that I'm not going to let your father get away with what he's done. I know you want to wait until the birth of your twins, but I promise you that I am going to help you ensure that your father pays for what he's done."

Malcolm was quite overwhelmed by his grandfather's words. "Thank you," he said. "It means a lot to have you on my side."

"You don't need to thank me, Malcolm," said JP. "I'm just doing what family does. You have a miserable excuse for a father, and I'm just trying to make up for that, in whatever way I can."

Malcolm nodded. "I appreciate that."

"Well I'll let you go," JP said. "I'm looking forward to meeting your Maggie soon," he said. "As well as my new great-grandchildren."

Malcolm smiled. "I look forward to that too," he said. "Thanks for calling, Grandpa."

"Goodnight son."

"Goodnight."

Malcolm ended the call, and looked up Maggie. "Wow, I sure didn't expect that," he said.

"It was your grandfather?" she asked as Malcolm took out his wallet to pay the bill.

"Yeah, but not Norman," he said. "My other grandfather. My father's father."

"Oh...I didn't know you two were close," she said.

"We're not," Malcolm said. "At least, we never have been, not really. He's always been kind of distant. I was afraid of him when I was a kid, actually."

"What was he calling about?" Maggie asked.

"He's going to help nail my dad," Malcolm said. "He and my dad have never got along," he said. "And now he's going to help us nail him. And if there's anybody my father is intimidated by, it's JP."

"JP?"

Malcolm smiled. "Yeah, that's what he goes by," he said. "We all call him that, though not to his face of course."

Maggie laughed. "Well that's great," she said. "I hope he has some good ideas. Your father's ruthless, but clever."

Malcolm nodded. "Yeah he is, but don't worry," he said. "Nobody knows him better than JP. And nobody knows better how to screw him over than JP. It's gonna be awesome."

Boston

Deb slept little, for the wreckage of her life weighed heavily on her mind. Getting fired was the last straw, the final nail in the coffin. But it had also served to push her into action, and as she got dressed, she rehearsed in her mind what she would do to get her life back. She knew that Jack was angry with her for what he saw as her betrayal, but he'd gone too far. Deb was certain that he'd somehow been responsible for the loss of her job, and to her that was simply going too far.

The offices of Sullivan Building and Construction occupied five floors of one of Boston's largest office buildings. Deb knew that Jack's secretary, Annie, would undoubtedly have been instructed not to allow her entry into Jack's office, but that didn't concern her. Annie was easily bullied, for Deb had plenty of experience doing just that. So when the secretary looked up at her with undisguised loathing in her eyes, Deb simply gave her a patronizing smile.

"Hi Annie, how's it going?" she asked.

"Is there something you want?" Annie asked, not falling for Deb's false pleasantries.

"I need to talk to Jack," Deb said. "Would you tell him I'm here?"

Annie smiled. "No, I'm afraid I can't do that," she said, savouring the moment.

Deb's false smile faded quickly. "Why the hell not?"

"Well, for one thing, he's in a meeting," Annie said. "And for another... well, I don't think he'll want to see you. As a matter of fact, he left word for me *not* to let you in. So there you go."

Deb scowled, and leaned over the desk. "Okay, I'm trying to be nice to you, but clearly you can't be anything but a bitch," she said. "I'm going to wait in his office," she said, leaning closer to Annie. "And you're going to let him know that I'm here," she said. "Got a problem with that?"

Annie was sorely tempted to chuck her tea in Deb's face, but decided to take the high road. "I do have a problem with that, as a matter of fact," she said. "If you try to gain access to Mr. Sullivan's office, I'll have security up here before you can say bottle blond."

Deb ignored the insult and stood up straight. "You go right ahead and do that," she said. "And let Jack know I'm here. I'm quite certain he'll want to see me." She turned and left, walking towards Jack's office while Annie placed a phone call to security.

Deb entered Jack's office, looking around at the familiar surroundings. She'd lost count of the number of times she'd given Jack sexual pleasure in this office, the number of times he'd struck her almost equal. She frowned, wondering how she'd stayed in a relationship with a man like Jack for so long. But the answer to that was easy: Jack's money. Deb liked money, she liked being bought fine things, taken to expensive restaurants. It was worth the unpleasant sex and occasional abuse, in her opinion.

"What the hell are you doing here?" Jack asked, appearing in the doorway. A security guard accompanied him, looking at Deb threateningly.

Deb looked at the guard, then back at Jack. "We need to talk," she said. "Alone," she added.

Jack looked at the guard and gave him a nod. "I'll give you ten minutes," he said. "But that's it."

Deb waited for the guard to leave and close the door behind him before she spoke. "It might surprise you to know that I lost my job," she said.

Jack walked over to sit behind his desk. "Is that right?" he said. "What a pity," he said, sitting down and giving her a smug look.

"I know you were behind that," she said. "Just like you're behind me being evicted."

Jack simply smiled. "You can't prove that," he said. "You can't prove anything."

It was Deb's turn to smile. "No? Well that's where you're wrong," he said. "You see, I happen to know what you did to your son," she said. "I know what you did to Maggie. And if you don't make things right with me, then I'll go to the press and tell *them* what I know. How do you like *that*, Jackie?"

The smile left Jack's face immediately. "What the fuck are you talking about?"

"Don't try to deny it," she said. "I know you threatened Maggie's family," she said. "I know you ran her out of town. Just think of the headlines, Jack: Business Magnate Arrested on Charges of Extortion. Doesn't that have a nice ring to it?"

Jack's scowl deepened. He had no idea how she knew, but she knew nonetheless. And there was simply no way he could allow her to go to the press with what she knew. Even a rumour of such malfeasance could spell disaster for his company. "What do you want?" he finally said.

Deb smiled triumphantly. "I already told you," she said. "My apartment, my job," she said. "Effective immediately. You can do that, Jack. You're a powerful man."

Jack nodded, his mind working a mile a minute. "Yes I am," he said. "Okay, consider it done. But how do I know you won't go to the press anyway?"

"You have my word," she said. "You'll just have to accept that, Jack."

Jack nodded, knowing he'd do no such thing. "I suppose so," he said. "Now get out," he said. "I have work to do."

"Fine," she said. "But make sure that you do what you promised. I'd hate to make your life ...unpleasant."

Jack smiled. "That's very considerate of you," he said. "Now get out."

Deb said nothing more, but left the room convinced that she'd won.

Twenty Nine

*J*ack kept his word. He called the apartment complex and had Deb's lease renewed, and called the law firm where she worked and made arrangements for her to continue her employment. He decided that he needed to be very careful where she was concerned henceforth. He didn't know how she'd learned of what had gone down at the quarry all those months earlier, but decided that since she knew, he needed damage control. Jack was a resourceful man, and knew that he would land on his feet. He always had. But for now, Deb would get her way. Anything just to keep her quiet.

He was on his way home, after a rather unpleasant day, when he heard from an old friend.

"Bob, good to hear from you," Jack said, pleased to hear a friendly voice.

"Sullivan," said Bob Harmon, an old frat brother of Jack's. "How's business?"

"Excellent," Jack said. "We've had a fantastic quarter. Couldn't be better."

"That's great," Bob said. "I've been meaning to call you for a while now, Jack. Last time we spoke you suggested getting our youngest together, Malcolm and Robin."

"I did," Jack said. "How did that work out?"

"Well, quite frankly, your son was very rude to Robin," Bob said.

Jack frowned. "He was, was he?"

"Damn right," Bob said. "Told her he wasn't interested, and hung up on her. Robin's a beautiful young woman, Jack. Your boy would be doing well to date a girl like her."

"I know," Jack said. "I...I don't know what to tell you, Bob. He's difficult, has been his whole life."

"Makes me wonder why you'd suggest he date my daughter," Bob said. "She's a good girl, Jack. Not like the girls your son usually associates with."

"Give my apologies to Robin," he said. "I'll have a word with my son. He's out of line talking to her that way, and I'll tell him so."

"That's fine," Bob said. "Just don't ask him to call her. I don't want him involved with her after all."

"I understand," Jack said, feeling embarrassed. "Again, I'm sorry, Bob. I really thought things might work out for them."

"Robin's too good for him," Bob said. "I hope you're not offended by me saying that, but it's true."

"It *is* true," Jack said. "I couldn't agree more. And you have my word, Malcolm will hear about his from me. I guarantee it."

Jack ended the call, the bad day he'd been having now worse.

Nova Scotia

"That feels *wonderful*," Maggie sighed as Malcolm massaged the small of her back. "You have very talented hands."

Malcolm smiled. "I've heard that before," he said.

Maggie laughed. "I'm sure you have," she said. "You may have missed your calling," she said.

"Maybe so," he said. "Your back is in knots, baby," he said, applying pressure with his thumbs.

"Carrying two babies will do that," she said.

"Yeah I'm sure," he said. He reached over to the bedside table to get some more massage oil. "You know, there may be other parts of your body that are in need of attention," he said.

Maggie smiled, and looked over her shoulder at him. "You think so?"

Malcolm nodded, rubbing the oil between his hands. "Like this amazing ass of yours," he said, running his hands over her bottom. "I've always been a big fan of this ass."

Maggie laughed. She closed her eyes, enjoying what he was doing. "Okay... before you go too much farther, I need to stop you."

Malcolm's hands froze in place. "Why? Something wrong?"

"I need to use the loo," she said. "Help me?"

Malcolm smiled. "Sure," he said, and got off the bed. He came around to the other side of the bed and helped her off the bed. "Don't be long," he said, giving her a soft kiss on the mouth.

"I'll do my best," she said.

Malcolm sat on the edge of the bed to wait as Maggie headed into the bathroom. He hadn't been waiting long when his cell phone rang. Deciding to take the call, he picked up his phone from the table, deciding he'd cut the call short as soon as Maggie reappeared.

"Hello?"

"Malcolm, it's your father."

All the anger, the enmity, the craving for revenge came rushing back at the sound of his father's voice. His body grew tense, his grip on the phone tightened. "What do you want?" he said.

There was silence for a moment on the line. "What do I want? I haven't spoken to you in months," Jack said.

"So?"

"So I wanted to talk to you," Jack said. "I needed to talk to you."

"What about?"

"Are you still in Scotland?" Jack asked. "Because if you are, you need to get your ass back..."

"I'm not in Scotland," Malcolm said.

"Oh. Where are you?"

"None of your fucking business," Malcolm said. His eyes turned to the bathroom door where Maggie had appeared. The look on her face told him that she'd heard much of the conversation. She walked over to sit beside him on the bed.

"That's a nice way to speak to your father," Jack said. "I've been concerned."

"Yeah, sure," Malcolm said. "What's the real reason you called? And don't give me that horse shit about being concerned about me. We both know that's a bunch of crap."

Jack was silent for a few moments, and Malcolm had begun to think he'd hung up.

"Who is it?" Maggie mouthed.

"My father," Malcolm mouthed back.

Maggie covered her mouth with her hands, her eyes wide with fear. *What does he want?* she thought anxiously. *Why is he calling? Does he know we're together? Does he know we're here?*

"I got a call from an old friend of mine," Jack said finally. "His daughter called you a while back, girl by the name of Robin. You remember that?"

"Maybe, I don't know," Malcolm said. "Why?"

"Because she was rather offended that you blew her off," Jack said. "Bob's an old friend of mine. Would it have killed you to go out with her? It's not like you're in a relationship anymore."

"I don't need you setting me up," Malcolm said. "Just stay out of my life, can you do that?"

"What the hell is your problem, boy?" Jack asked. "Do you have any idea how much money your hospital bill was? How much trouble I went to get you out of that Mickey Mouse hospital and into Mass General?"

"Yeah, I know," Malcolm said. "I also know you went golfing in Seattle when I was in a coma," he said.

"It was a business meeting," Jack said. "You really are something, so goddamn spoiled, so goddamn selfish. You spent too much time crying on your granny's shoulder in Scotland, boy. Now you're more of a pussy than ever."

Malcolm stood up, unable to contain his anger. "You listen to me, you son-of-a-bitch," he said. "I've spent my whole life being criticized by you, being bullied by you and trying my damnest to live up to your expectations. But you know what? I'm done. I don't give a damn if you're my father, we're done. Don't call me, don't expect me to call you, and don't get any more of your fucking cronies to try and set me up with their pathetic daughters."

"I see," Jack said. "Well that's fine with me. You've been nothing but a burden since the day you were born. If you want out, then you're out. Go out into the world, find a job. Go ahead. See how well you do in the real world. You won't last a day."

"I'll do just fine," Malcolm said. "I don't need your fucking company or you, so leave me the hell alone." He ended the conversation and threw his phone across the room. He ran his hands through his hair, trembling with anger. And then he remembered his wife. He turned back to her, the look on her face alarming her.

"What did he want?" she asked, looking up at him, eyes wide with fear. "Does he know we're together? Does he know where we are??"

"No, no he doesn't know anything," he said, taking her hands. They were trembling. "He has no idea we're together, Maggie. There's no way he can know."

Maggie nodded, but the terror didn't leave her eyes. "What if he traced the call? What if he's on his way here right now?"

Malcolm was horrified to see the terror in his wife's eyes. "Listen to me," he said, taking her by the shoulders. "There's nothing he can do to hurt us, Maggie," he said.

"Then why was he calling? What did he want?" she asked.

"He was pissed off because I didn't want to go out with the daughter of some old friend of his," he said. "He thought I was still in Scotland."

"Maybe you should have let him believe that," she said.

"Maybe," he said. "But he has no idea where I am. He has no idea where you are," he said. "And he won't find out, not until this is all over. And by then it will be too late for him to do anything about it. So please, don't worry," he said.

"I'll try," Maggie said. "But I can't make any promises, Malcolm."

Malcolm nodded, and opened his arms to her. As he held her in his arms he closed his eyes and forced the negativity from his mind. *He can't hurt us now... he's never going to hurt us again...I'll make sure of that, as God as my witness.*

Thirty

Boston

*L*ife was good for Deb Rogers. Having been reinstated at her job, she decided to do some shopping. Her apartment was hers again, and she decided to celebrate with some new furniture. And yet, she somehow didn't feel satisfied.

More than a week had passed since the night she'd spent with Hugh Wellman, a night she knew she'd never forget. He'd been everything she'd hoped he'd be as a lover. She was sure that she would forever compare any other lover she took to him, and was quite certain they'd never measure up, figuratively and literally. But Hugh hadn't wanted her once he'd found out that she was connected to Jack Sullivan. Not that she could blame Hugh for that; learning he'd been used by her was a hard pill to swallow for a man like Hugh. Deb had texted him a few times, but, not surprisingly, he ignored them all. She'd been tempted to try and find out where he lived, and show up at his doorsteps, but was unsure how he'd react upon seeing her there. *You know how he'd react,* she thought with a frown. *He'd probably kill you...he could certainly do so quite easily.*

Deb decided to pick up dinner at Mike's on her way home. It was crowded, as usual, as Mike's was a popular place. As she stood waiting for her take out order, she couldn't help but notice a rather handsome man who was also waiting for his own. He gave her a smile, which Deb returned. She noted how well he was dressed, and figured him to be a professional of some sort. Trying not to be too obvious she glanced at his left ring finger to see if he was married. He wore no ring. *So much the better,* she thought.

"Order number 89," the teenage girl at the counter called.

"That's me," the man Deb was admiring said. He walked over to the counter, giving Deb another quick look as he did so. She moved a little closer to see how he paid for his meal, impressed when she saw him pull out a Platinum American Express card.

"Better bundle up," she said as the man turned to leave. "It's cold out there."

The man nodded. "Sure is," he said. "Hope you've got someone to keep you warm tonight."

Deb shook her head. "Nope," she said, making a sad face. "I'm going home to an empty apartment."

"What a coincidence," he said. "So am I."

Deb smiled. "Now, why do I find that hard to believe?" she said, laying it on thick.

The man shrugged. "I don't know," he said. "But it's true. I don't suppose you'd like to have some company?"

Deb had never been a woman to say no to a rich man, particularly when the man was handsome. "I'd love some," she said. "Just let me pick up my order."

Nova Scotia

Maggie was up early the next morning, her uneasiness making her sleep a restless one. She made her way downstairs in the quiet house and made herself some tea. It wasn't long before Malcolm joined her.

"Did I wake you?" she asked as he poured himself a cup of tea.

"No," he said. "Can't sleep when you're not there I guess," he said with a smile. He sat down across from her and studied her face for a moment, knowing that she was still rattled from the phone call the previous night. For a few moments they sat in silence, simply sipping on their tea.

"You okay, babe?" he asked, reaching over to take her hand.

Maggie, who'd been absorbed in thought, looked up at him. "Yes of course," she said.

Malcolm didn't buy it. "Sure about that? You're awful quiet."

"I didn't sleep very well," she said. "I'm tired."

Malcolm nodded, quite sure that she was. "Just so you know, I'm gonna block his number so he can't call me again," he said. "That way we won't have to deal with his bullshit anymore."

"For now," she said.

Malcolm frowned. "What do you mean?"

Maggie sighed, and looked out the window. "Well...so long as we're staying here, he can't bother us. We're safe. But when we go back to Boston, he'll be there. And none of this has been resolved, Malcolm. I don't know how it can be given who he is."

Malcolm frowned. "When we go back to Boston, he'll be behind bars," he said. "Do you think I'd take you and the little guys there if he could harm any of you?"

"I'm not saying that," Maggie said.

"Sure sounds like it," Malcolm said.

Maggie looked back at him. "I'm sorry," she said. "It's just that...we've been living in this idyllic wee paradise up here," she said. "We're married now, we have a lovely home, we're so happy. It's just easy to forget about all that nastiness and pretend like it isn't just waiting for us to sort it all out. Today was just a hard dose of reality, one I'd just as soon not have had just now."

Malcolm didn't know how to respond. He too had fallen into the illusion that everything was perfect, that their troubles were behind them. But hearing his father's voice had shattered that fantasy. Seeing the fear in his wife's eyes had made it all too clear that their troubles were far from over.

"I know," he said. "And I'm sorry. I don't know what else to say."

"You needn't apologize, love," she said. "This wasn't your doing."

"No, but he's my father," Malcolm said. "I should never have left you alone. None of this would have happened if I'd just stayed with you."

"You don't know that," she said. "If he felt this strongly about splitting us up, he would have found another means to do it."

"Maybe," Malcolm said.

"I just wonder if...we could stay here," Maggie said. "It's beautiful here, safe, clean, quiet."

"Boston is home," he reminded her.

"Your home," she said.

Malcolm frowned. "It's not your home too? We met there, we fell in love there, we went to school there, all our friends are there- how can you say it's not your home?"

Maggie looked away. "It stopped being my home on that day," she said quietly. "You weren't there, Malcolm," she said. "You didn't see the coldness in his eyes when he showed me those pictures. I can never go back to Boston without remembering that."

"You can't give him that kind of power over you, Maggie," Malcolm said. "If you do, then he wins. He *wanted* you out of Boston, remember? If you never go back, then he wins. Is that what you want?"

"Of course not!" she said. "I'm just so scared."

Malcolm was frustrated. He was at a loss to know how to allay her fears. All he knew was that he needed to keep her stress level down, and their conversation seemed to be doing the opposite.

"I know you are, baby," he said. "If you want to stay here, then we'll stay here," he said. "I don't care where we live, so long as we're together."

Maggie smiled. "Really? Do you mean it?"

Malcolm nodded. "Absolutely," he said. "All I want is for you to be happy, babe. And if living here does the trick, then this is where we'll live."

Maggie gave his hand a squeeze. "Thank you," she said through her tears.

Boston

Deb checked her cell phone as she rode down the elevator on her way to work. She'd enjoyed a very pleasant evening with her new friend, Brad. Brad had turned out to be a lawyer for a small corporate business. He was single, as she'd hoped, and, in her opinion, utterly charming. They'd talked into the wee hours of the night, and exchanged phone numbers when he'd finally gone home. She'd been reluctant to text him first, but didn't need to worry as he'd texted her as soon as he'd arrived home. It pleased her that he'd clearly succumbed to her charm, for it was the boost to her ego that she desperately needed after being dumped by two men in short order recently. She smiled as she saw his text: *Good morning Milady*. She'd never been called *milady* before, but decided that she liked it. Brad was unlike any many she'd ever dated in his intelligence and sophistication. *I guess bad things do happen for a reason*, she mused as she sent a witty text back to him. *If Jack had never dumped me, I wouldn't be available to see Brad. Though that didn't stop you from sleeping with Hugh*, she reminded herself with a frown. *But that doesn't count*, she told herself. *That wasn't a real relationship ....it was just...sex. The best sex you've ever had...*

Deb stepped off the elevator, gave her usual patronizing smile to the doorman, and headed off to the parking garage. It was still early, and the garage was rather empty. She reached her own car, opened it, and got inside. She noted that there was a car on the other side of the garage idling. It bothered her that people did that, that they felt the need to idle their car in a heated garage. Don't they read the papers about green-house gas emissions? She thought peevishly as she started up the car. She drove past the idler, giving him a stern look as she did so, and the put him out of her mind completely as she made her way to work.

The man in the garage waited for her to leave, and then left the garage as well.

As she drove along, Deb's phone rang. She picked it up, pleased to see that it was none other than Brad. Seeing his name on the screen of her phone brought a smile to her face.

"Good morning handsome," she said. "Shouldn't you be in court by now?"

"I am," he said. "I'm just waiting for the judge to arrive. I wanted to hear your voice. I hope you don't mind."

"I don't mind at all," she said. "I'm pretty happy to hear your voice too."

"I'm glad to hear it," he said. "By any chance are you free for lunch today? I should be wrapped up here by noon."

"I think so," she said. "I don't have my calendar in front of me, but I'm sure I can swing it. Where do you want to meet?"

"How about Radius?" He suggested. "I have an in there, so we can get a table no problem."

This pleased Deb no end, for Radius was one of Boston's finest eateries. "Sounds wonderful," she said. "I'll see you there at noon."

"Until then, milady," he said.

Deb could only manage a rather embarrassing giggle before he ended the call. *Radius...must have money if he eats there enough to have an in*, she mused. *So much the better!*

Nova Scotia

Maggie slept late the next day, her sleepless night taking its toll on her. Malcolm, however, was up early, unable to sleep. It bothered him that his wife was still so terrified by what had happened, so much so that she was acting in a manner most unlike her. Malcolm had always known Maggie to be sensible and level headed, but her fears where Jack were concerned were causing her to be the opposite. Her desire to remain in hiding seemed irrational to him, but he didn't say so. He knew that she was acting out of fear, a fear that she'd borne alone for many months while they were estranged. So rather than try to make her see reason, he decided to go along with her wishes, no matter how illogical they seemed to him.

It was very early when Malcolm arose from bed, but he knew that he wouldn't sleep any more. Besides, he'd recently begun jogging in the early morning as a way to keep himself in shape. It also served as a quiet time alone where he could sort through his thoughts. He'd learned how important this was while in Scotland, and wanted to keep up the practice.

"You're up early," Will commented when Malcolm appeared in the kitchen.

"So are you," Malcolm said. "I'm going jogging."

"Care for some company?" Will asked.

So much for the solitude, Malcolm mused. "Sure thing. Let's go."

Will had no trouble keeping up with Malcolm's pace, for he was a man in strong physical shape. He'd wanted to speak to Malcolm alone, and found it hard to find the time to do so when the house was always full. He decided to wait until they stopped before speaking his mind.

It was a cold morning, with frost painted on the roof tops, as they two men jogged through the quiet neighbourhood. So when Malcolm suggested they stop at the local Tim Horton's for coffee, Will agreed whole-heartedly.

"Wish we had this place back home," Malcolm said as they walked into the crowded coffee shop. "Never had a better cup of coffee than here."

Will smiled. "I know what you mean," he said. "It's addictive."

Malcolm laughed. "Yeah, so are the doughnuts. Maggie's totally hooked on the Boston Creme."

"Seems fitting," Will said with a smile as they stood on queue.

"Don't know about that," Malcolm said. "She's not crazy about the thought of living there anymore. My father's ruined it for her."

"She'll get over it," Will said. "She's tough. I think she's just scared right now, and extra-emotional because she's pregnant."

"Maybe so," Malcolm said as they reached the head of the queue. The elderly lady behind the counter gave him a smile, recognizing him from his previous visits.

"Good morning Hazel," Malcolm said. "How are you doing this morning?"

Hazel smiled. "Just fine thanks," she said, "you?"

"Great," Malcolm said. "This is my brother in law, Will," he said.

"Hiya," Will said.

"What can I get you lads?" Hazel asked. "Your usual, Malcolm?"

"Yes ma'am," Malcolm said. "What'll you have?" He asked Will.

"Just black for me," he said. "Medium."

"And what about the little missus?" Hazel asked with a smile. "Shall I pack a couple of her favourite up for her?"

Malcolm smiled. "Yeah, what the hell," he said. "Not like she's dieting."

"I won't tell her you said that, mate," Will said.

Malcolm laughed as he handed Hazel his Tim Horton's card. "Deal."

The two men found a nearby table to enjoy their coffee.

"So I have some news I wanted to tell you about," Will said. "I haven't told anybody else but Alli."

"What is it?"

"I've been offered a job with a construction company in Bangor," Will said. "They'd posted an advert online saying they needed pipe layers. I contacted them and talked to the guy on the phone. They want me to come down next week."

Malcolm was surprised, for he'd had no idea Will had been looking for work. But it wasn't really that unexpected, given the fact that he was a young man who'd been wanting to start a life with the woman he loved for some time now.

"That's great," he said. "I'm happy for you. I'd be lying if I said I won't miss you, though."

Will smiled. "Yeah, I'll miss you too mate, I'll miss everybody. But it's time. I'm 24 years old. I need to get out on my own, make my own way."

"I get that, believe me," Malcolm said. "I have to tell you though, Maggie won't like it. She'll be worried."

"I know," Will said. "But it's something I have to do. Bangor's not far from here, it's not like I'm going back to Boston. I can't keep running from your father me whole life."

Malcolm nodded. "I know," he said. "I'll talk to her," he said. "She'll have to see things your way, Will. You have the right to your own life."

Will nodded. "I appreciate that, Malcolm," he said. "You're a good brother."

Malcolm smiled. "Right back at you, dude."

As they walked back to the house, Malcolm thought about how he would tell Maggie that her older brother would be leaving them in the very near future. She was already stressed and afraid; how much more so would she be when Will was gone? And yet, there was nothing Malcolm could do to stop it from happening. Will was entitled to a life of his own, a life where he wasn't beholden to his sister for his very existence. Somehow she'd need to see that. Somehow he'd have to help her see it.

Thirty One

*S*moky air filled the bar, the music pulsating through the floorboards, rattling the dirty windows. Hugh Wellman had been grateful to find employment as a bouncer, and didn't question the squalidness of the establishment. He'd been desperate; for the bills from the nursing home where his mother now lived were still coming in regardless of his state of employment. So far he'd been kept busy, for the bar, which had the unlikely name of the Lucky Strike, was frequented by an unruly assortment of characters from the rougher side of Boston. He'd broken up more fights in the short two weeks he'd been employed there than the entire time he'd worked at the Hart and the Hound. Of course, the Hart was frequented largely by university and college students, not gang members, drug dealers and hookers. That made a significant difference.

It had been almost three weeks since Hugh had last seen Deb Rogers; but she had texted him many times since then. At first it was several times a day. It got to the point that Hugh turned off his phone; but that didn't stop her from continuing to call and text him. But then, quite suddenly, she stopped trying to reach him. Hugh was surprised, but relieved that she'd finally given up. She was not a complication he needed in his life.

Hugh's attention was drawn to a commotion at one of the tables. This was not unusual, for it happened at least once a night. He headed over to see what was going on, frowning when he saw that one of the barmaids, Morgan, was involved. The customers whose bill she'd just delivered were unhappy, and refusing to pay for drinks they were sure they hadn't ordered.

"Is there a problem here?" Hugh asked as Morgan stepped aside.

"Yeah, this bitch says we owe 30 bucks," one of the men said. "No fuckin' way we owe that much."

"Well one of you is lying," Hugh said. "And I know it ain't her," he said, nodding in Morgan's direction. "So either pay up, or we can settle this in the alley out back. What's it gonna be?"

The two men looked at each other, neither of them particularly wanting to tangle with Hugh, but not bright enough to know when to back off.

"I say we let my little pal here settle this," one of the men said, pulling out a knife. "What do you say to that?"

Hugh didn't really want to have a hassle; it was closing time, and all he wanted was to get home.

"I say you're a fuckin idiot," Hugh said, kicking the man's chair out from under him. The man's chin hit the table, and his knife skittered out of his hand, nicking one of Hugh's forearms. The manager arrived at this point and, with the help of the bartender, escorted the two customers out the door.

"Come with me," Morgan said, "you're bleeding, you need to get that cleaned up."

"It's nothing," Hugh said, wiping the blood on his arm with his hand. "Just a scratch."

"Stop trying to be a hero and just come with me," Morgan said.

Hugh frowned, and followed her into the kitchen.

"Sit down," Morgan instructed as she fetched the first aid kit.

Hugh sat down at the small table and watched her as she rifled through the shabby looking tin for some supplies. "You don't need to do this," he said.

Morgan sat down across from him and pulled his arm straight. "You want it to get infected?"

"No," Hugh said.

"Then let me do this and stop complaining," she said, glancing up at him as she cleaned the scratch.

Hugh resigned to the inevitable, and simply watched her. Morgan was very young, barely legal by his estimation. She'd always seemed out of place to Hugh, never more as now as she showed him compassion.

"There," she said, as she finished applying a bandage. "Was that so bad?"

"Never said it was bad," Hugh said. "Just unnecessary."

Morgan laughed. "Now I have to get going before I miss my bus," she said.

Hugh stood up. "Young girl like you shouldn't be taking the T this time of night," he said.

Morgan shrugged as she stood up too. "I do it all the time," she said.

"I'll drive you home," Hugh said. "It's the least I can do after all your tender loving care," he said with a hint of a smile.

Morgan smiled. "Okay," she said, not relishing a long wait in the cold. "Deal."

The rooms that Morgan rented were several blocks away, above a laundry mat in what Hugh considered a rather bad part of Southie. And that said a lot.

"I'll walk you up," Hugh said as he parked his car on the street, making sure he locked it. "How many times you been mugged on your way home?" he asked her as they walked up to the building.

"Never," she replied as she fished her keys out of her backpack. "I can look after myself."

Hugh said nothing in response, and simply followed her into the building.

"This really isn't necessary," Morgan said as they walked up the stairs. "I know this place looks like a dump, but there's a lock on the door. People can't just wander in from the street."

"Good thing," he said. "Cause the people in this part of town you don't want wandering in."

Morgan was about to respond when the sign on her door stopped her in her tracks. It was an eviction notice.

"What the hell?" she said, ripping it from the door. She noticed that her lock had been changed as well. "Look at this! One bad cheque and that skinflint kicks me out!"

Hugh took the notice from her hand. "That sucks," he said. "What are you gonna do?"

Morgan thought for a moment as she stared at the locked door. "I don't know," she said quietly. "I mean...it's the middle of the night. Where am I supposed to find a locksmith now? Not that I'd have the money to pay him."

"You can crash at my place if you want," Hugh said. "I won't try nothing. Promise."

Morgan looked up at him. "I know," she said. "I don't want to put you out," she said.

"What else are you gonna do?" he said. "Sleep on the floor out here?"

"No," she said. She looked at the lock on her door once more, and then made up her mind. "Thanks Hugh," she said. "You're all right."

Hugh was embarrassed when he remembered what a mess his small apartment was, which happened just as he was turning the key in the lock.

"Sorry about the mess," he said as he kicked aside a newspaper that was lying just inside the door. "I'm not the neatest guy in the world."

"Don't worry about it," Morgan said, looking around. "I'm just happy to have a place to sleep." The apartment had a long corridor, with a small kitchen at one end and an open area at the other that served as both living room and dining room. There was one bedroom adjacent to the kitchen, with a small bathroom beside it. "You have a lot of room," she commented as she unzipped her jacket.

"Are you joking?" he asked as he hung up his own jacket on the back of the door. He took hers from her and did the same to it. "I have to go outside to change my mind."

Morgan laughed. "Good one! But seriously, you should see my place. I have one room and a bathroom. That's it."

Hugh frowned. "And you pay how much?"

"Nine hundred a month," she said, wandering into the living room.

"That's larceny," Hugh said as he followed her. "You should get out of that place ASAP kid," he said. "That landlord of yours is ripping you off. Big time."

Morgan had considered this before, but felt trapped. She knew almost no one in Boston aside from the people she worked with.

"Come on," Hugh said. "I'll show you were you can sleep."

Morgan followed him down the hallway to the bedroom. It was small, with a double bed on one side. She looked up at him, feeling awkward. "So...where are you gonna sleep?"

"I don't sleep much these days," he told her. "So the couch is fine for me."

Morgan frowned. "Why don't you sleep? Insomnia?"

"Something like that," he said. "I'll let you get to bed. Bathroom's just outside."

"Thanks Hugh," Morgan said. "I really appreciate this."

Hugh turned and looked at her for a moment. She seemed so sweet, so sincere; but his experience lately with women had left such a bad taste in his mouth that he was reluctant to trust anyone just yet, no matter how kind they seemed to be. "Goodnight," he said simply, and then left her, closing the door behind him.

Morgan woke up early the next morning, the unfamiliar bed making it difficult for her to sleep in as late as she'd have liked. The first thought that entered her mind was that she no longer had a place to live. It had been difficult to find a place to live that was close to her job. Finding another would be next to impossible. As she made the bed she wondered how much Hugh paid in rent for his place, which seemed huge compared to her own. After she made the bed she started picking up the clothes that were on the floor, feeling as though she needed to do something to repay Hugh for his kindness. *What a slob,* she thought with a bemused smile as she sorted the clothing into piles of clean and dirty. Once she'd put the clean ones away and deposited the dirty ones in the laundry hamper, she headed into the kitchen to see what Hugh had in the way of groceries.

Hugh had fallen asleep in front of the television, which was not unusual for him. What was unusual for him was being woken up by the smell of food cooking. He sat up on the couch, running a hand through his tousled hair just as Morgan appeared in the room with two plates in her hands.

"Good morning," she said, giving him a smile. "Are you hungry?"

"Yeah," Hugh said as he stretched his long arms. "You cooked?"

Morgan nodded as she set the two plates down on the small table in the corner of the room. "You don't have much in the way of food, but I managed to scrape something together."

Hugh couldn't remember the last time he'd had a woman cook for him. He prided himself on being a very self-sufficient man. But he'd be lying if he didn't admit to being pleased by Morgan's gesture.

"I hope you don't mind," she said as Hugh sat down with her.

"Why would I?" he said. "Been a long time since I'd have a home cooked meal. Breakfast for me is usually coffee and a doughnut from Dunkin's."

Morgan smiled. "That's not the healthiest way to start the day," she said.

Hugh shrugged as he picked up his fork. "No, I guess not."

They ate together in silence for a few moments, each of them still a little uncomfortable with the situation they'd found themselves in.

"So what are you gonna do about your place?" Hugh asked her as they finished up and took the dishes to the kitchen. He was shocked by how clean the place looked.

"I don't know," Morgan said. "It's not easy finding a place," she said. "I don't have a car, so I need to live close to work. That's about the only place I could afford. But apparently I can't even afford that."

Hugh considered this as he put the dishes into the sink. "Well I don't think you should be giving that asshole any more money," he said. "I hate to say it, but he saw you coming."

Morgan nodded as she watched Hugh wash the dishes. "You're probably right," she said. "So what do I do?"

"You don't have folks in town?" he asked.

"I can't go back to my folks," she said. "I'd rather live on the street."

Hugh looked at her, sensing that it wasn't simple pride that made her feel that way. But he wasn't about to pry.

"Well, you could stay here if you want," he said as he handed her a clean plate. "Bring your stuff here, just until you figure out what you're gonna do. He'll put your stuff out on the street if you don't get it out of there."

Morgan was surprised by his suggestion and considered it in silence as she dried the plate in her hands. "You'd do that for me?" she said finally. "You hardly know me."

Hugh looked at her. "I know you enough to know you need help," he said. "Besides, you can cook and you don't mind cleaning up after me. That's worth the price of rent any day."

Morgan laughed. "Well then I accept," she said. "You're a good guy, Hugh. Thanks again."

Nova Scotia

Maggie's reaction to Will's decision to leave Nova Scotia troubled Malcolm. Deeply. He expected her to be sad, given the fact that the two siblings were very close. There was no doubt Maggie would miss Will, as well as Alli to whom Will had recently become engaged. But there was more to her reaction than sadness. She was terrified by the thought of Will moving away, terrified that something horrible would befall him as soon as returned to American soil. She hadn't come out and said it in those terms, but Malcolm knew her well enough to know that was going through her mind. And once Will and Alli had gone to Maine, Malcolm decided he needed to talk to his wife about her fears.

"Ready for bed?" Malcolm asked as Maggie joined him in their bedroom.

Maggie nodded through a yawn as she climbed into bed with him. "I'm done in."

Malcolm smiled as she snuggled into his arms. "You okay, babe?" he asked, kissing the top of her head. "I know how hard it must have been to say goodbye to Will."

Maggie said nothing for a moment, for she'd be struggling with her emotions all day. "I think he's making a mistake," she said. "But I can't tell him that. He's too stubborn."

Malcolm frowned. "Baby he's a grown man," he said. "He needs to make a life for himself, for him and Alli. You can see that, can't you?"

Maggie turned to look at him. "Yes, of course I can," she said. "And I'm thrilled that he'd engaged to her, she's like a sister to me."

"So what's the problem?" he asked. "And don't tell me there isn't one. I know you better than that. You've been upset since Will told you he was leaving a week ago."

"I'm going to miss him," she said.

"Yeah I know that, but there's more to it," Malcolm pressed. "You're afraid something's gonna happen to him, aren't you? That my father is going to track him down or something. I'm right, aren't I?"

Maggie tried to hold back the tears, but it was no use. The worries she'd been battling all week were simply too much to contain any longer. "Yes, you're right," she said. "I'm afraid that your father will find out where he is, and that he'll have something terrible happen to him, just as he said he would."

Malcolm frowned. "Maine isn't Massachusetts," he told her. "My father has a lot of pull, but he can't do anything even if he did know where Will was."

"You don't know that," she said. "Your father is a ruthless, dangerous man. Who knows how far he'd go?"

Malcolm sighed. Her paranoia was making it impossible to reason with her, but he didn't want to point that out to her. She was supposed to be avoiding stress now, after all.

"You're right, he is," Malcolm said. "But I also know that your brother is a smart guy. If he sniffs trouble, he'd not going to hang around to wait for something to happen. Bangor is only six hours away. He's not going to put Alli in a position of danger."

"I suppose not," Maggie said.

"You've got to get past this," Malcolm said. "You need to avoid stress."

"I know," she said. "And I'm trying, Malcolm. Truly I am."

Malcolm smiled, and took her face in his hands. "You're the most amazing woman I know," he said. "Have I ever told you that?"

Maggie shook her head.

"No?" he said. "What the hell is wrong with me?" he said, and then kissed her softly on the mouth.

Maggie sat downstairs, watching the news. Upstairs the twins were asleep. Malcolm had taken Maggie's brothers out to a movie, and her parents were at Pat and Noreen's for their weekly euchre night. It was quiet in the house, and Maggie relished it after a long evening of looking after two babies. But then the sound of breaking glass made her jump in her seat. With heart pounding, she stood up, and muted the television. She stood perfectly still, straining her ears to try and determine what had caused the crash.

"Malcolm? Is that you?" she called.

There was no answer.

Maggie tried to master her fear, but it was impossible given the circumstances. And when the lights went out, she couldn't help but scream...

"Maggie, wake up! Wake up!"

Maggie woke with a start, and looked up into the eyes of her rather startled husband.

"You were screaming," Malcolm said, his eyes troubled.

Maggie sat up with his help. "I...I was having a nightmare," she said.

"No kidding," he said. "Please tell me it wasn't about my father."

Maggie looked at him. "I don't know," she said. "If it was, I never saw him. It was just...scary and weird," she said with a frown. "I'm glad it's over," she said, wrapping her arms around his neck.

Malcolm held her in his arms. He was concerned by the frequency of her nightmares, but was helpless to do anything about it. Like it or not, so long as the situation with his father remained unresolved, Maggie would have night mares. And there wasn't a blessed thing he could do to stop them.

Boston

Hugh and Morgan spent the day packing up her belongings in boxes Hugh had collected at the bar. He had seen at once that she had not exaggerated the smallness of her apartment, and found himself growing claustrophobic as they day went on.

"Any suggestions for the furniture?" she asked as Hugh closed up a box of dishes. "Don't think they'll fit in your trunk."

"Probably not," Hugh agreed. He looked at the three small pieces: a futon, a small dresser and a bookshelf. "I've got a buddy who has a pick up," he told her. "He might be able to move 'em for us."

"Great," she said. "But unless he can come today, my landlord won't let me leave it here," she said. "He's a real prick."

"Sounds like it," Hugh said, looking around the place. "How long you been living here?"

"A little over a year," she said. "I moved here after I dropped out of college."

"Why'd you do that?" he asked.

"Didn't have the money to continue," she said with a frown.

Hugh wasn't surprised, given her current living conditions. "Be right back," he said, heading to the bathroom.

Morgan continued packing the small collection of books from her bookshelf, and didn't notice someone at her door until he spoke.

"What's going on here?"

Morgan turned to see a rather greasy looking little man standing in the doorway.

"I'm moving, what does it look like?" Morgan said.

The landlord, Eddy, frowned. "You still owe me money, girl," he said. "You think you can just leave when you're owing me money? I don't think so sweetheart."

Morgan frowned. "I don't have the money," she said. "You know that, Eddy."

Eddy nodded, looking her up and down. "Well maybe we can...come to some sort of arrangement," he said. He gave her a smile that made her skin crawl. "You do something nice for me, and I let you stay. What do you say?"

"I say go fuck yourself," Hugh said from the bathroom door.

Eddy looked up, startled by Hugh's unexpected appearance.

"Who the hell are you?" Eddy asked, trying to mask his fear.

"None of your goddamn business who I am," Hugh said, walking over to where Morgan stood. "Morgan doesn't owe you a cent, you got that?"

"She owes me a month's rent," Eddy said. "Her last rent cheque was no good. Either she pays me or I call the cops."

"You go ahead," Hugh said. "And while they're here I'll tell them how you just tried to solicit sex from her as payment for her rent."

Eddy's eyes widened. "I never did!"

"I heard you, you slimy piece of filth," Hugh said. "An arrangement? Who do you think you're fooling with that?"

Eddy's eyes darted from Hugh to Morgan and back to him. "There's no way you can prove it," he said.

Hugh folded his arms over his chest as he stared down the greasy little man. "Sure I can," he said. "We both heard you, that's two against one. Plus there's no smoke alarms in this flea trap," he said. "That's a fine of a thousand dollars. And I'll bet there's not one smoke alarm in this whole fuckin' building, is there you cheap bastard?"

Eddy was beginning to get rather nervous by this point. "Fuck you!" was his only response.

Hugh moved quickly, and before Eddy knew what was happening, he found himself pinned up against the wall.

"Now you listen to me you piece of shit," Hugh said. "You're gonna let this young lady leave here free and clear," he said. "And you're gonna give her back her security deposit too," he said. "How much was it?" he asked Morgan.

"Five hundred bucks," Morgan said.

"You're gonna give that back to her," Hugh said, applying pressure to Eddy's throat. "And you're gonna let my buddies pick up the rest of her stuff tonight. If you do that, then I won't call the cops. If there's a problem when my buddies come by, then expect a visit from the boys in blue."

"Fine, fine!" Eddy squeaked. "Just let me go!"

Hugh released him, and looked back at Morgan, who looked a little shocked by the turn of events.

"You've got an hour to get her money," Hugh said, looking back at Eddy. "Cash. Every five minutes beyond an hour, add another fifty bucks."

"Are you kidding?" Eddy said. "That's bullshit!"

"You sure about that?" Hugh asked, pulling his phone out of his pocket.

"No, no I got it," Eddy said. "I'll get the money." He gave one last look at Morgan and then left.

"Whoa," Morgan said. "You're scary when you want to be."

Hugh smiled. "Yeah I guess so," he said. "Let's start taking these boxes to the car," he said.

Morgan nodded, and picked up a box and followed him out the door.

After they'd finished loading as many boxes as Hugh's car would hold, they left the apartment to get some lunch. Morgan sat beside Hugh looking at thick wad of bills that Eddy had given her.

"I don't think I've ever held this much money in my hand in my whole life," she said with a smile.

Hugh glanced at her as he drove. "Well don't be flashing that around," he said. "There's plenty of people who'd roll you for it."

Morgan laughed, amused by his turn of a phrase. "I won't," she said, sliding the thick envelope of cash into the back pack between her knees. "Thanks for fixing things with Eddy," she said. "I don't know what I'd have done if you hadn't been there."

"The guy's a slime ball," he said. He frowned as a question formed in his head, one he wasn't sure he wanted to know the answer to. "Has he ever done anything to you?" he asked. "Has he ever touched you?"

"No," Morgan replied. "Thank God."

Hugh nodded. "Lucky thing," he said. "I'd probably have to rip his nuts off if he had."

Morgan smiled, surprised by his comment.

They reached a small diner and parked on the street.

"You better bring that with you," he said to Morgan, indicating her backpack. "Don't want anybody breaking into the car to steal it."

Morgan agreed, and pulled the backpack out of the car and slung it over her shoulder. As they walked down the street towards the diner, they passed a homeless woman sitting with her back against the wall of an abandoned store, a shabby paper cup in front of her. Inside were a few coins. Morgan stopped when she saw her, making Hugh turn and see what she was doing.

"Morgan, let's go," he said.

"Just a minute," she said. She set the backpack down on the sidewalk and carefully opened it and withdrew a fifty dollar bill from the envelope. She handed it to the woman with a smile. The woman took it, shocked by the young woman's generosity. She wasn't the only one. Hugh stood not knowing what to say as the homeless woman grabbed Morgan's hand and squeezed it, tears in her eyes. He'd never seen such a selfless gesture in his life. He knew for a fact that Morgan had nothing, that the five hundred dollars in that envelope represented all the money she had in the world; and yet she'd given fifty dollars, one full tenth of her boon, to a perfect stranger. Clearly there was a lot more to this young woman than met the eye.

"You keep doing that you'll have nothing left," Hugh said as he opened the door to the diner for her.

Morgan shrugged. "I don't plan on it," she said. "But I couldn't just walk past her, Hugh. She looked so sad, so ...lost."

Hugh was about to tell her that the homeless were unseen by passersby every day, but decided not to. He'd been one of those passersby more times than he could count. But now he wasn't sure he'd be able to pretend not to see them any more, not after what he'd just witnessed. Not after she'd forced him to see them for the first time in his life.

Thirty Two

Nova Scotia

*M*alcolm woke up to the sound of the alarm clock. He frowned, wondering why he'd done such a thing, and then remembered that he was playing hockey that morning.

"Malcolm turn it off," Maggie said sleepily, rolling away from the offensive noise. "It's too early to get up."

Malcolm leaned over and shut off the alarm. He threw back the covers and got out of bed with a yawn. Maggie turned back and looked at him questioningly.

"What are you doing?" she asked.

"I told your brothers I'd play hockey with them this morning," he said.

Maggie had been pleased when Malcolm had agreed to this, for the twins had been after him for weeks to join them and their house league team for a game. But being woken up at the crack of dawn wasn't nearly as pleasing to her.

"Have fun," she said, and turned over and went back to sleep.

Malcolm smiled, and then went to get dressed.

It was close to nine when Maggie woke up again, and only did so because she needed to use the bathroom. She'd returned to her bedroom, put on her bathrobe and slid her feet into her slippers when her phone rang. She was pleased to see that it was Carrie. She sat down on the side of the bed to take the call.

"Hi Maggie! How are you? I hope I didn't wake you up."

"Not a chance," Maggie said. "I never sleep in any more. The twins make sure of that."

Carrie laughed. "So how are you feeling?" she asked.

"Pretty good," Maggie said. "I've been taking it easy, Malcolm's seen to that."

"Good," Carrie said. "Poor Malcolm must be living on pins and needles these days."

Maggie laughed. "Actually he's been pretty calm," she said. "Since he's been coming to the classes he feels a lot more involved. Of course when the real thing actually starts, it's a whole different story."

"Oh he'll be fine," Carrie said. "After everything you two have been through, child birth will be a piece of cake."

"Well I don't know if I'd go that far," Maggie said. "So what's new with you? How's work? How's Dave?"

"Work's fine," Carrie said. "Same old same old, you know how it goes," she said. "Dave's great," she said. "In fact, he's part of the reason I'm calling. He popped the question last night!"

"Oh Carrie!" Maggie said. "I'm so happy for you!" She said, wishing she was there to give her best friend a big hug.

"Thanks Megs," Carrie said. "I still can't believe it actually," she said. "He had the ring, did the whole big production. I had no idea it was coming."

Maggie laughed. "That's wonderful," she said. "Have you set a date?"

"Not yet, but we're thinking next summer," Carrie said. "You guys will be back in Boston by then, right? I'm counting on you being my matron-of-honour."

Maggie didn't know what to say. How could she tell her best friend that she never wanted to return to Boston?

"I'm not sure we'll be living in Boston by then," Maggie said. "But we'll definitely be there for your wedding."

"You guys *are* coming back to Boston, aren't you?" Carrie asked.

Maggie sighed. "I don't know," she said. "Nothing has been resolved with Malcolm's father. And so long as that's the case, I won't set foot there, Carrie."

"So what is the status of all that anyway?" Carrie asked. "Does Malcolm have a plan?"

"His grandfather does," Maggie said. "Apparently there's been bad blood between Jack and his father for years," she said. "And the old man is more than happy to help out. I don't know what he's got in mind, neither does Malcolm. But nothing is going to happen until after the babies are born. Malcolm has made that clear."

Carrie didn't want to press the issue, for it was clear that Maggie still had some major issues to deal with.

"Well I hope things work out soon," Carrie said. "And I'm sure they will, Megs. Malcolm will make sure of it."

"I know he will," Maggie said.

"Well I'm at work, and my break's over," Carrie said. "I just wanted to tell you my big news."

"I'm so glad you did," Maggie said. "I'm really happy for you guys. Give Dave my best."

"Will do," Carrie said. "I'll talk to you soon, okay Megs? And be sure you call me when you go into labour."

"I will," Maggie said. "Thanks for calling, Carrie. Goodbye."

"Bye Megs."

Maggie ended the call. A lump formed in her throat as she thought of her friend and how much she missed her. How she would love to go dress shopping with Carrie, to help her plan her wedding, to simply share in her joy in a real way. But Carrie was in Boston, and Boston was a place that Maggie couldn't think of now without growing fearful and tense. The city that she's once loved had become a place full of danger. And that broke her heart. She gave into her sadness and had a good cry, grateful at least that Malcolm wasn't home to see it happen.

Maggie had a shower and got dressed. She was just about to leave the bedroom when Malcolm arrived.

"How was your game?" Maggie asked as Malcolm put his hockey bag in the closet.

"Pretty good," Malcolm said. "Still trying to break in the new equipment."

Maggie nodded. "I'm sure you'll manage," she said.

Malcolm said nothing, thinking wistfully of his hockey bag sitting back in their apartment in Boston. "You had breakfast yet?" he asked.

"Not yet," she said. "I heard from Carrie earlier," she said. "And guess what?"

"She and Dave are engaged," Malcolm said with a smile.

"He called you?"

"Yeah, just before I got home," Malcolm said.

"Isn't that wonderful?" Maggie asked.

"Sure is," Malcolm said as he pulled off his shirt.

His seeming lack of enthusiasm puzzled Maggie and she sat down on the bed. "You don't seem that happy," she said.

Malcolm turned to his wife, unsure if he ought to say what was on his mind. "I'm very happy for them," he said. "Just kinda bummed that we're not there to celebrate with them."

Maggie nodded. "Yes, I feel the same way."

"He asked me to be his best man," Malcolm said. "But I'm not even sure I can be. How can I throw him a stag party when we're 12 hours apart?"

"Well given the circumstances I don't think he'd expect you to."

"But that's not right," Malcolm said. "He *should* get a stag party. Every groom should."

"You didn't," she pointed out.

"Well our circumstances were different," he said.

"Yes, and they still are," she said. "Nothing has changed."

"I know," he said. "Believe me, I know."

Maggie frowned. "You make it seem like that's my fault," she said.

"How am I doing that?" he asked.

Maggie said nothing, which only exasperated him even more.

"I'm going to have a shower," he said, annoyed by her silence.

Maggie watched him leave, and then got up to go make breakfast, her mood having worsened considerably.

Boston

Jack Sullivan was having a bad day. It had begun with a message from his father informing him that he would be attending the budget meeting that was planned for that afternoon. JP had been a regular at the monthly board meetings; as CEO he felt compelled to do so, despite his advanced years. But it had been years since he'd attended a budget meeting. The fact that he wanted to attend one now, out of the blue, concerned Jack considerably.

On his drive into Boston, Jack spilled coffee in his lap when his driver was forced to apply the brakes suddenly for a motorcyclist that swerved in front of the car quite suddenly. By the time he arrived at his office, he was in a foul mood. His father was already there, waiting for him when he got there.

"Good morning Jack," JP said, enjoying the miserable mood that was emanating from his son's very pores. "You look like you spilled something."

"Yeah I know," Jack grumbled as he slammed his briefcase onto the desk. "What brings you into town today, Dad? It's a mighty cold day out there. You should have stayed home."

JP frowned. He hated being patronized, especially by his son. "I'm old Jack, not infirm. I wanted to come to the budget meeting. Is that a problem?"

Jack shrugged as he hung his overcoat up in the closet. "Of course not," he said. "Pretty dry stuff though," he added. "Lots of spread sheets, that sort of thing."

"I've been to budget meetings before," JP said. "I know what goes on, Jack."

Jack frowned, and bit back a response. "Suit yourself," he said. "You want coffee? Annie's probably got some made by now."

"That would be delightful," JP said. "I'll take it black."

The conference room was down the hall from Jack's office, and was already full when Jack arrived with his father. He was annoyed when JP's appearance was met with applause from the collection of financial professionals gathered around the chrome, rectangular table.

JP smiled as he took his seat. "Thank you gentlemen," he said. "Please, enough."

Jack sat at the head of the table and waited for the others to fall silent before he began. He was about to speak when Annie entered the room with a cup of coffee and a Danish for JP.

"Here you are sir," Annie said, setting the cup and plate before the elderly man. "It's apple, your favourite," she told him with a smile.

JP gave her a wink. "You're an angel," he said. "Thank you so much."

Annie had always liked JP, and had often bemoaned the fact that his son was nothing like him. "Can I get you anything else?" she asked JP, pointedly ignoring Jack.

"Not a thing, my dear," JP said. "I thank you."

Annie left the room, ignoring the fact that Jack was giving her an annoyed look.

"Can we start now?" Jack asked in a tone of undisguised exasperation.

"Please do," JP said. "I'm very interested to learn about what's been going on here."

Jack frowned, feeling rather uneasy by his father's unusual interest in the budget. "Phil, you're up," he said, looking at a man to his left. "Your report please."

Phil stood up and passed out a copy of the quarter's expenses to each person seated at the table. JP pulled out his reading glasses and commenced reading over the rows of numbers. There was no doubt that the company was doing well; profits were steady and rising. Everything seemed normal, and quite expected, except for one column: expenses. JP frowned, and looked up at his son who was absorbed in reading the report. *What have you been spending this company's money on now, Jack?* He thought. *And how is this connected to what you did to Malcolm?*

The meeting lasted about an hour as they went over the figures, looked at some charts and projections on the smart board, and generally patted themselves on the back for all the money they were making. Once they'd concluded, and the money men started filing out, JP remained seated. Jack noticed this, and walked over to where his father sat.

"So? Satisfied?" he asked, parking his behind on the table beside his father.

"No, not entirely," JP said. "I have some questions. Some rather serious questions."

"Oh? Such as?" Jack asked, trying to be causal.

"These *special projects,*" JP said. "I'd like some clarification on what those projects are."

Jack said nothing, his mind working feverishly to think of a clever response that his father would buy.

"Well part of that is the box at the Gardens," Jack said. "It's pricy, but good for business."

JP nodded, knowing full well that the box didn't account for even half of the amount listed. "And these consultations expenses," he said. "They seem pretty high to me. Exactly who have you been consulting with and for what reason?"

"Legal mostly," Jack said. "Listen Dad, I don't have time for this interrogation right now. I'm a busy man."

JP looked up at his son with a smile. It was clear that Jack was being evasive, and that made JP feel all the more certain that there was a lot his son was hiding.

"I know that son," JP said, deciding to back off for the moment. "Perhaps when you get a chance you can draw up a detailed list for me," he said. "Or have Annie do it. I'm just...curious," he said with a smile.

Jack did his best to return the smile, but it wasn't easy to do given the uneasy feelings welling up inside of him. HIs father was no fool. Jack knew that he would have to be very creative in order to hide those aspects of his life that he'd best keep hidden from his father.

"Okay Dad, I'll get right on that," Jack said at last, standing up. "But I have to go right now, I'm expecting a call."

JP stood up. "All right son," JP said. "I look forward to seeing your report soon."

Jack said nothing and watched as his father put on his coat and then left.

"Damn it," Jack said once JP had departed. "Damn you to hell, old man." He frowned, the tension in his temples tightening, growing into what he was sure would be a rather nasty headache. He left the room, headed for his office. "Get me some aspirin," he said to Annie, and then went into his office, slamming the door behind him.

Elsewhere in Boston

Deb had gone out with her new friend Brad every night for two weeks. They'd been to dinner, to the movies, and had spent the night at each other's apartments more than once. Deb was, quite plainly, head over heels. Brad was the man she'd been waiting for her whole life. He was handsome, intelligent, charming, witty and, above all, rich. The way he threw money around reminded her of Jack Sullivan, except that Brad didn't feel compelled to tell her how much he'd spent on her, or suggest an appropriate payment for it later on. No, Brad was perfect.

"Have I told you how beautiful you look today?" Brad asked as they sat eating lunch in an exclusive downtown eatery.

Deb smiled. "You have," she said. "But I don't mind hearing it again."

Brad smiled, and reached over to take her hand. "Good," he said. "Because I can't stop saying it."

Deb couldn't suppress a giggle. She felt like a silly school girl when she was around him. He made her feel like no other man ever had. And even though she'd only known him a couple of weeks, she felt as though she could easily give her heart to him. In fact, she was quite certain that she already had.

"Last night was incredible," Brad said, reaching over and taking her hand. "I haven't been able to stop thinking about it. About you."

Deb felt her face grow warm at the memory of their night together. Brad had been a tender yet passionate lover.

"I know," she said. "Neither have I."

Brad held her gaze, the look in his eyes so earnest. "I hope I don't scare you when I say this," he said, running his thumb slowly over her palm. "But I do believe I'm falling in love with you."

Deb felt a thrill go through her at his words. "That doesn't scare me," she said. "In fact, I feel the same way, Brad. I'm falling in love with you too."

Brad smiled, and then reached over the table to kiss her. Deb didn't care that they were in a crowded restaurant, she didn't care that she needed to be back at work in less than an hour and would probably be late. Nothing seemed to matter when Brad was kissing her. So when he suggested they blow off work that afternoon and go for a long drive in the country, Deb agreed whole-heartedly. She had no idea where they were going, or when they'd return to Boston. But she didn't care. So long as she was with Brad, life was good.

They drove for about an hour until they were well out of the city limits. It was quite dark out, and Deb was getting hungry. She looked at the clock on the dashboard. It was almost 6 o'clock.

"Maybe we should think about heading back," Deb suggested. "I'm hungry, aren't you?"

"Yes sure," Brad said. "But would you mind if I pulled over for a moment? I really need to...you know, relieve myself."

Deb smiled. "Of course I don't mind," she said. "Just don't be out there too long," she said. "It's pretty cold out there."

"I'll be as fast as humanly possible," he said, pulling the car onto the soft shoulder. "Be right back," he said, leaning over and giving her a quick kiss before he left her to go answer the call of nature.

Deb watched him as he disappeared into the nearby woods. She pulled her phone out of her purse to check her messages, amused by how embarrassed he was to have to resort to such measures. Most men would simply relieve themselves on the side of the road; but not Brad. He had class. As she entered her password, she noticed out of the corner of her eye the glare of headlights. She glanced up, noting the approach of a vehicle. It was large, for the lights were high off the ground. Deb looked back at the screen on her phone. But the lights were too bright, and she looked up again, squinting as the vehicle drew closer. "Lovely," she muttered as she tried in vain to read her messages. She looked up, waiting for the vehicle to pass. It was then that she noticed that it was heading straight for her. She didn't even have time to scream before the gravel slinger slammed head on into Brad's Mustang, crumpling it into so much scrap metal.

South Boston

It was well past midnight when Morgan and Hugh arrived back at his apartment. When they reached the front door, they were met by two rather dodgy looking men. Morgan was fearful until she realized that they were Hugh's friends, the men who'd brought the rest of her belongings.

"What the hell are you guys doing here at this time of night?" Hugh asked after introducing Morgan to Mitch and Steve. "I told you to come get my keys at work," he said as the two men started unloading the truck.

"I couldn't," Mitch replied. "Me and Steve were working. Had a job to do for the boss."

Hugh frowned, and glanced in Morgan's direction, wondering if she had any inkling of the kind of *work* his friends did.

"The landlord won't be happy if we start moving stuff in at this hour," Morgan said.

Hugh shrugged as he hefted a large box. "Tough," he said. "He'll get over it."

It took the four of them about forty minutes to move everything up to Hugh's apartment. By the time they were finished, it was almost 2AM. Morgan was hoping to get to bed, as it had been a long day; but when Mitch and Steve parked themselves on the sofa, she knew that this wouldn't happen.

"Thanks for bringing my stuff over," Morgan said as she sat down.

"Yeah no problem," Mitch said, checking Morgan out. He looked at Hugh and then back at her, and then back at Hugh. "So you two are living together, eh?"

"Yeah, but don't get any stupid ideas," Hugh said. "We're friends."

Steve looked at Mitch and smirked. Morgan felt her face grow hot, and looked away.

"How's your mom doing, Hugh?" Mitch asked.

"Not so good," Hugh said. "Not eating much these days." He frowned as he realized that he hadn't been to see her that day since he was kept busy helping Morgan pack.

"What's wrong with your mother?" Morgan asked.

"Heart," Hugh said. "She's been in the nursing home for months now."

"Sorry to hear it," Morgan said. "Is she here in Boston?"

Hugh nodded, stifling a yawn. "I'm beat," he said, standing up. "You guys can hit the road now."

Mitch and Steve were quite accustomed to their friend's bluntness, and were not offended by it.

"Okay, we'll leave you two alone," Steve said with a smile.

Hugh gave him a dirty look but it simply rolled off of Steve like water off a duck's back.

"Thanks again," Morgan said, pleased that Hugh had asked his friends to leave.

"No problem," Mitch said. "You take care."

Morgan watched as the men left, and then headed down the hallway to the bedroom. She was surprised to see how the men had rearranged things. Her futon was at the far side of the room, and Hugh's bed had been moved closer to the door. Between the two beds the men had set up the dressers, which, she noted, divided the room in two.

"Figured you'd get some privacy this way," Hugh said as he joined her in the bedroom. "At least a little bit."

Morgan looked up at him. "That was very considerate of you," she said. "Thank you."

Hugh wasn't accustomed to people with manners, people who showed appreciation and consideration of others, and simply nodded in response.

"I'm going to get ready for bed," Morgan said, digging through one of her suitcases for nightgown.

"Knock yourself out," Hugh said with a yawn. He waited for her to leave before stripping down to his shorts. He climbed into bed, and was asleep before she returned to the room a few minutes later.

Thirty Three

Morgan was woken up a scant few hours later by the sound of a cell phone. It wasn't hers, as she had left it in the living room over night to charge. She sat up in bed, waiting for Hugh to wake up and answer the phone, but he didn't. Eventually the caller gave up, and the room fell silent again. Morgan hadn't even closed her eyes when the phone rang again. Exasperated by now, she got out of bed, deciding to wake Hugh up. Clearly he was a rather sound sleeper given the loudness of the guitar riff that served as his ring tone. She turned on the light beside her bed and walked over to where Hugh was sleeping.

"Hugh wake up," Morgan said, standing beside his bed. "Hugh!"

"Huh? What...what's going on?" Hugh said as he opened his eyes. He looked up at her, startled. "What's wrong? Why'd you wake me up?"

"Your phone," Morgan said. "It's been ringing. Didn't you hear it?"

Hugh sat up as the phone started up again. He frowned, a feeling of dread settling into him as he got out of bed and walked over to the dresser to pick up the phone. When he saw his sister's name on the screen, the dread skyrocketed. "Yeah? Emily? What's wrong?" he said as he held the phone up to his ear.

Morgan watched him, gathering enough from the conversation to know that Hugh's mother was in trouble.

"What is it?" she asked as Hugh ended the call and started throwing on some clothes.

"My mother," Hugh said. "She's going down fast. I need to get to the home."

"I'll come with you," Morgan said, and went to her own dresser to find clothes.

"You don't have to," Hugh said as he zipped up his jeans.

"I know I don't have to, but I want to," she said. "I'll be right back."

Hugh finished getting dressed as she went to the bathroom to do so, running down the hall in her bare feet. The screen on his phone told him that it was just past four, which meant he'd had less than two hours of sleep. It was going to be a long night.

Hugh and Morgan arrived at the nursing home less than thirty minutes later. Hugh knew the way well, having visited his mother every day for months. *I didn't visit her yesterday,* he reflected as he walked through the familiar corridors. *I didn't get to see her...I didn't get to say goodbye...*

Hugh's brother in law, Jeff, was outside Janet's room with Hugh's nephew and niece.

"How is she?" Hugh asked Jeff.

"Not good," Jeff said. "I'm sorry, Hugh. You'd better get in there. I don't think she's gonna last much longer."

Hugh frowned and looked at Morgan. She looked up at him, her eyes full of sympathy. She reached over and gave his hand a squeeze. "Go," she said. "I'll be right here."

Hugh nodded, and then left her to go to his mother's side.

"Are you my uncle's girlfriend?"

Morgan turned to see a young girl of about 10 years of age standing beside her.

"No," Morgan said. "I'm just a friend."

Jeff was familiar with the sort of people his brother-in-law usually associated with, and as surprised to hear her say this. She didn't seem at all like the sleazy women he usually socialized with; she seemed sweet and innocent. Jeff couldn't help but wonder about the nature of the unlikely friendship.

On the other side of the door, Hugh sat beside his mother. She was unconscious, and had been for several hours. HIs sister Emily stood on the other side, unable to stop the steady stream of tears that ran down her face.

"How long has she been like this?" Hugh asked, looking up at his sister briefly.

"Since midnight," Emily said as she brushed the tears from her face. They watched their mother for a few moments in silence, unnerved by the sound of her breathing as fluid backed up in her lungs. There was nothing they could do, nothing anyone could do. She was dying, and both Hugh and his sister knew it was only a matter of time now.

"I didn't get to see her yesterday," Hugh said, looking down at his mother again. He frowned. "I promised her that I'd come every day, and I didn't come yesterday."

Emily had noted changes in her brother over the past several months. She attributed part of it to their mother's condition, but sensed that there was more to it than that. Hugh and she were not close, had not been since they were children, for she had disapproved of his line of work and the people he chose to associate with. But in the times when their visits to their mother had coincided, she'd seen changes in her brother, positive changes. And that gave her hope.

"Don't beat yourself up," Emily said. "Stuff happens. You were here every day, Hugh, and don't think she didn't appreciate it. It meant the world to her."

Hugh nodded, fighting against the grief that was threatening to overwhelm him. "I just wish I'd had the chance to say goodbye to her."

Emily pulled a chair up beside Hugh's, and, after a moment, took his hand. They sat together in silence, waiting for the inevitable.

"So how do you know Hugh?" Jeff asked.

"We work together," Morgan said. "He's a bouncer at the bar where I wait tables."

"He's a bouncer now?" Jeff asked. "When did he stop working for Sullivan?"

Morgan, who had no idea that Hugh had ever worked for one of Boston's biggest companies, shrugged her shoulders. "I have no idea," she said. "I've only known him a little while."

Jeff thought it strange that she was here with him in the middle of the night if they'd only know each other a short time, but didn't say anything for the moment. He was prevented from doing so when his wife emerged from the room and rushed into his arms, weeping. Jeff knew that Emily's mother was gone, and consoled his wife as best he could. He was joined by their two children, who cried as well realizing that their grandmother was dead.

Morgan stood for a moment, feeling awkward and out of place. And then she remembered Hugh. Tentatively she pushed open the door and walked into the room. She saw Hugh sitting beside his dead mother, a look of utter desolation on his face. A lump rose in her throat and she walked to him.

"I'm sorry," she said, putting a hand on his shoulder. "So sorry."

Hugh looked up at her, and then wrapped his arms around her and cried. Morgan held him, stroking his dark hair as he gave in to his grief.

Later, after they'd left the home, Hugh and Morgan joined Emily and her family at a local IHOP for breakfast. Discussing the funeral of a loved one is never easy, but it was necessary. The fact that their mother had already spoken to them both about what she wanted helped a little.

"I'm not working right now, Hugh," Emily told him. "I can get the arrangements made."

"I'd appreciate that," Hugh said as he stirred his coffee slowly. "Just tell me what it costs you, I'll give you half."

"Sure. I can let you know in a couple of days," Emily said.

Hugh was silent as he drove home with Morgan, which didn't surprise her. But given his usual disposition, she worried about how he would deal with this tragedy.

"I'll call Carl and let him know you won't be in tonight," Morgan said as they drove home.

"No, don't do that," he said. "I'm working."

Morgan frowned. "Hugh, your mother just died," she said.

Hugh cut her off. "I know that, damn it," he said. "I'm not gonna sit around feeling sorry for myself. I'm gonna work."

Morgan tried not to be hurt by his abrasiveness, but it was difficult. She was tired, she'd been through an emotional wringer, and yet he seemed to not appreciate any of that, nor the fact that she had provided him with emotional support when he needed it most. She said nothing for the rest of the ride home, as she did her best to hide her tears from Hugh.

Nova Scotia

Evening was falling as Maggie and Malcolm walked through the quiet neighbourhood that they'd come to think of as home. It was a cold night, with a dusting of snow on the ground and the rooftops. Malcolm held his wife's hand as they navigated the winding bike trail that ran parallel to the coast.

"You okay babe?" Malcolm asked.

"Yes," Maggie said. She smiled. "You've asked me that twice now, you know."

Malcolm looked at her. "Have I?"

Maggie nodded.

Malcolm smiled with a shrug. "Well we're getting down to the wire," he said. "I just want to keep a close eye on you."

"I see," she said. "You don't need to worry. I'm fine. It's nice to get some fresh air."

"Yeah but it could be a little less fresh, if you know what I mean," Malcolm said. "Freakin' freezing out here."

"Just wait until the snow really piles up," Maggie said. "Noreen tells me sub-zero temperature are not unusual at all in the winter."

Malcolm nodded. "Can't wait," he said.

The local Tim Horton's was quite busy when they arrived, but Malcolm managed to find them a table. Maggie sat down and unbuttoned her coat as Malcolm headed to join the queue.

Maggie looked around, feeling comfortable and safe amidst the locals. She knew the names of many of them, and smiled at them as they gave her a friendly wave. *This is the perfect place to raise a family,* she reflected. *The perfect, safe place.*

"Your usual, Mrs. Sullivan," Malcolm said as he set the tray on the table.

Maggie smiled. "I really need to cut back on these," she said, picking up a Boston crème doughnut. "I will never get back in a bathing suit at this rate."

Malcolm laughed. "Are you kidding? Running around after two kids will be the best work out you could have."

"True," Maggie said. She picked up her hot chocolate and sipped at it. "Christmas will be wonderful this year," she said with a smile. "Just think, we'll have our two wee babies with us."

Malcolm nodded as he sipped his coffee. "Crazy," he said. "Hard to believe last Christmas we had that big blow up with your dad. Remember that?"

"How could I forget," she said. "And then we went away to St. Lucia. That was lovely."

"We should go back there with the kids some day," he said. "But not before we take them to Scotland. My nanna will be going crazy waiting to meet them."

Maggie smiled. "I'm sure," she said. "Have you spoken to her recently? Is your grandfather still there?"

Malcolm nodded. "I have feeling those two are gonna end up getting married," he said. "How awesome would that be?"

"Very awesome," she said.

Their conversation was interrupted by Malcolm's cell phone. They both grew tense, worried that it would be Jack again. But it wasn't. It was Jack's father, JP.

"Hi Grandpa," Malcolm said. "How are you doing?"

"I'm quite well thanks, Malcolm," JP replied. "How are you and Maggie?"

"Great just great," Malcolm replied. "Just waiting for the big arrival, now."

"When is Maggie's due date again?" JP asked.

"December 14th," Malcolm said. "Coming up fast."

"Indeed," JP said. "I look forward to meeting them and Maggie soon."

Malcolm looked up at Maggie. "Well I'm afraid that's not going to happen in the near future, Grandpa," he said. "My father has made sure of that."

"I'm sure I can help you out with that, Malcolm," JP said. "In fact, that was the reason I called you. I want to talk to you about something concerning your father."

"Oh? What would that be?" Malcolm asked.

"I attended a budget meeting recently," JP said. "I didn't tell your father I was coming, I just showed up. He hates it when I do that."

Malcolm laughed. "Yeah, I'm sure," he said. "Did you learn anything interesting?"

"Well yes actually," JP said. "Your father's personal expenses. There were considerable discrepancies, discrepancies that I have questioned him about."

"And did he give you any answers?" Malcolm asked.

"Not yet," JP said. "I'm sure he thinks I've just forgotten about it. He seems to think that I'm a senile old fool, after all. But I haven't forgotten. I've been doing some investigating, and, thanks to my insider, I've discovered a few things."

It didn't surprise Malcolm at all that his grandfather had an insider spying on his father. And JP was correct: Jack *did* think he was a senile old man.

"What did you find out?" Malcolm asked, deciding to put the call on speaker at this point so Maggie could hear too.

"There was a lot of money spent on legal consultants," JP said. "And when I dug a little deeper, I found out that the legal consultant was his girlfriend, Deborah."

Maggie and Malcolm looked at each other in shock.

"Are you talking about Deborah Rogers?" Malcolm asked. "She's his *girlfriend?*"

"Yes," JP said. "You didn't know?"

"No!" Malcolm said. "I had no idea."

"Do you know her?" JP asked.

"Yeah, she lives in our building in Boston," Malcolm said. "She used to flirt with me, as a matter of fact. She seemed to be trying to get between me and Maggie."

"Your father probably put her up to that," Maggie said. "He wanted us broken up since the day we met."

"Why is that, Maggie?" JP asked once he realized that Maggie had joined the conversation. "What issues does he have with you?"

"I'm wasn't rich," Maggie said. "My family isn't rich. He figured I was only interested in Malcolm for his money, no matter what Malcolm told him."

"That's despicable," JP said. "So he used this woman to try and break you up, but when that failed he resorted to more nefarious means."

"Exactly," Malcolm said. "But he didn't win, Grandpa. We're married now, and he has no idea where we are."

"Good," JP said. "I suggest you keep it that way for now. And as for his expenses, I mean to confront him about the amount of money he's been spending on this floozy. From what my contact tells me, it looks as though he's been paying for her apartment for quite some time now."

"You think he'll admit it?" Malcolm asked. "He's pretty good at lying about things he's trying to hide."

"No he'll deny it," JP said. "And that's fine for now. We don't want to tip our hand just yet. I'll put it on the back burner for a later time."

"Good," Malcolm said. "We don't want him getting suspicious."

"No, my thinking exactly," JP said. "Well I'll let you go now," he said. "I will keep you up to date on what I learn. I promise you that this will all be behind you soon," he said. "I intend to see to that personally."

Malcolm smiled at Maggie, happy that she'd heard his grandfather's promise. "Thanks Grandpa," he said. "That means a lot to us."

"Think nothing of it my boy," JP replied. "Considering how you've been treated by your father your whole life, it's the least I can do."

Thirty Four

The funeral of Janet Wellman was a small, understated affair. There was a reception at Emily's house afterwards, where a light lunch had been laid out for the small gathering of relatives who'd come to pay their respects.

"Thanks for the help," Emily told Morgan as they cleaned up afterwards.

"You're welcome," Morgan replied. "I'm happy to do it."

Emily closed the dishwasher and turned to her with a smile. "You know, it's so good to see Hugh with someone like you," she said. "He's certainly dated his share of losers over the years."

"Well we're not actually together," Morgan said. "Not in the way you're thinking. We're just friends."

"Friends who live together," Emily said.

"Yes, but...but not in that way," Morgan said. "I needed a place to stay after getting evicted, and he let me stay with him until I can find a place of my own."

Emily nodded, a little disappointed. "I see," she said. "So are you from the Boston area?" Emily asked.

"Yes," Morgan said as she helped Emily wrap up leftovers. "Lived here all my life."

"You have family in the area, then?" Emily asked.

Morgan didn't like talking about her family, but didn't want to appear rude. "My mother and her husband live in Roxbury," she said.

"And your dad?" Emily asked.

"I haven't seen my father since he left my mother, my brothers and me," Morgan said. "I was six."

"Sounds familiar," Emily said as they finished up. "I left home when I was 17 to get away from my father. He wasn't exactly what you'd call a loving, compassionate man."

Morgan didn't comment, but reflected to herself how much like her own story Emily's was. And Hugh's. Knowing this about him shed a little more light on the inscrutable man she lived with.

Hugh was his usual taciturn self as they drove back to their apartment later on. Morgan knew that the death of his mother had affected him deeply, far more so than he was willing to admit. She knew him well enough by now not to press the issue, and was content to sit in silence with him as they drove home.

It had been snowing all evening, and the streets were quite slick. Hugh drove slowly, far more slowly than he liked, and by the time they arrived at their apartment building it was dark.

"It's fuckin' freezing out here," Hugh grumbled as they walked through the alleyway that lead up the street. "If I catch the asshole who took my parking spot I'll rearrange his face."

Morgan smiled, amused by his comment. But her smile soon faded when she noticed a gang of rather surly looking men blocking their egress. Hugh noticed them too, and stopped to assess the situation. He turned to Morgan, not surprised by how scared she looked.

"What'll we do?" she asked.

"It'll be okay," he said. "They'd be stupid to mess with me."

Morgan nodded, but wasn't convinced. While he was intimidating, he was but one man, while there were at least five of them.

Hugh walked up to the men, with Morgan at his side. Slowly they turned to face him, their eyes moving to Morgan as they sized her up in a way that made her skin crawl. She took a step closer to Hugh, slipping her hand into his as she did so.

"What's up dude?" one of the gang members said, as they stepped into their path.

"Nothing," Hugh said. "Step aside."

"What's your hurry?" another of the gang members said, stepping closer to Morgan. "We're friendly, ain't we?" he asked his colleagues.

"Sure, real friendly," a third agreed.

Hugh frowned. "Well I'm not," he said. "So if you don't want any trouble, you'll step aside."

One of the men stepped up to Hugh and looked at him. "What are you gonna do?" he said. "There's one of you. There's five of us."

Hugh hesitated for a moment, and then drove his fist into the man's face, smashing his nose with one blow. The others were shocked for a moment, and did nothing. But then the one closest to Morgan grabbed her and held her captive, pressing a switchblade to her throat.

"Give us your money, mother fucker," the man with the switchblade said as two of the others helped their leader whose nose was bleeding copiously all over the snow.

Hugh looked at the man, and then into Morgan's terror filled eyes. He knew the type of men these were, and knew that they wouldn't hesitate to kill Morgan if he refused. Pulling his wallet out of his pocket, he pulled the few bills he had inside and handed it over. "Let her go," he said as the men took the money.

"Well hold up," the man who held Morgan captive said. "Maybe I'm not done with her yet," he said. He grabbed a handful of her chestnut hair and sniffed it deeply. "I think I'll have some fun with this nice piece of ass."

Hugh knew that if he made a wrong move, that Morgan's life could be jeopardized. And yet, the thought her being mauled by the filthy hands of her assailant was more than he could bear. But before he could decide upon a course of action, Morgan herself acted. She drove the heel of her boot into the top of his foot, causing him to scream in pain. Taking advantage of his predicament, she thrust her elbow into his face, and then jumped away from his grasp, as the knife fell to the sidewalk.

Hugh was impressed with her courage, and grabbed the man by the throat. "Run," he told Morgan as he slammed the man into the building. "Run!"

Morgan took a moment to pick up the knife and then ran down the street, adrenaline pumping through her. She reached the apartment building and opened the door. She took a moment to collect herself, to calm the shaking that had beset her. *What should I do?* She thought anxiously. *Should I call the police?*

Morgan wasn't sure if what was transpiring down the street was something Hugh would want the police involved in, and so she decided not to call them. It was the right thing to do.

"You come around here again and I'll kill you," Hugh said as he held the man captive against the bricks. "You got that?"

The man nodded, and looked over his shoulder, hoping for some help from his friends. But they'd decided to cut their losses and leave him to fend for himself. "Let me go, man!" he pleaded. "I didn't hurt your woman none!"

"But you wanted to," Hugh said, squeezing a little more. "You filthy piece of shit, you wanted to do more than hurt her," he said. "I swear, if I see any of you mother fuckers around here again, I'll kill you. I swear to God I will."

"That's cool man," the man said, finding it hard to speak due to the pressure on his larynx. "I'll tell them, I swear, just let me go!"

Hugh wanted very much to keep squeezing, to squeeze the very life out of the man. The emotions he'd been battling for days now, since the death of his mother, only served to augment the rage he felt. The look in Morgan's eyes was one he knew he'd not soon forget, and it had aroused emotions in him he didn't even know he felt. But under all the rage he knew that killing this man was wrong, that he was better than that now, that Morgan was making him want to be better.

"Get the hell out of here," Hugh said, releasing the man at last. "And remember what I said. I'll fuckin' kill the lot of you if I ever see you again." The man, who was barely out of his teens, nodded, and then turned and ran off to find his cowardly comrades. Hugh watched him go, an uneasy feeling inside of him that he'd not seen the last of them. And then he headed home.

Morgan was standing in the foyer waiting for him when he arrived. When she saw him at the door she ran to open it for him, relieved beyond measure that he was all right. Without a word he wrapped his arms around her and held her close. Morgan, though surprised by his gesture, welcomed it, and pressed her face into against his chest, her arms wrapped around his waist. It was at this point that her tears came.

"It's okay," he said, letting her cry. "It's over. They're not gonna hurt you, Morgan. I'd kill them first."

Morgan looked up at him, his words startling yet strangely touching. "You would?"

Hugh nodded. "I didn't know it until now," he said. "But when that bastard had that knife held to your throat, it was all I could think of. The thought of you getting hurt," he said, lifting a hand to wipe the tears from her face, "made me want to kill him."

Morgan knew Hugh enough to know that he wasn't a man who expressed his emotions easily. But his words, however crude, spoke volumes to her. She smiled at him. "That's the most romantic thing anyone has ever said to me," she told him.

Hugh couldn't help but smile. "Romantic?" he said. "I just said I wanted to kill someone, and that's romantic?"

Morgan nodded.

"Really?"

"Yes really."

Hugh was shocked that, behind all his crudeness, all his threats, she could see what he was really saying. Any other woman would be too hung up on the violence to see the intent behind the threat of it; but not Morgan. She accepted and understood him like no other woman ever had.

"If you say so," he said, and bent to kiss her. Morgan kissed him back, running her hands into his unruly hair.

"Let's go home," Hugh whispered into her ear.

Morgan smiled. "Okay, let's go."

A few hours later...

Hugh watched Morgan as she slept in his arms. He was surprised by the way things had turned out, but happily so. He kissed her forehead as she slept, and then climbed out of bed to go use the bathroom. Morgan's eyes opened as he left her, and she frowned when she discovered him gone. Pulling back the covers she got out of bed to find him, pulling a blanket around her before she did so.

"Hugh?" she called. "Where'd you go?"

"In here," he said. "Just checking the scores."

Morgan walked down the hallway to the small living room, where Hugh was sitting on the couch, remote in hand. "Bruins playing tonight?" she asked as she joined him.

"Yeah," he said, pulling her close. She shared the blanket with him, snuggling against him as he found the late news. "Big game too. Sorry I woke you," he said. "I tried to be quiet."

"You *were* quiet," she said. "It got cold in the bed when you left."

Hugh smiled, and kissed the top of her head. "Well I can warm you up some more in a minute," he told her.

Morgan laughed, and then let him watch the news in silence, knowing how important the Bruins were to him. But before the sports news began, there was a local piece about a fatal car accident that occurred outside of the Metropolitan Boston area.

"More on the strange accident that took place earlier this week near Ipswich," the reporter said. "You'll recall how a car that was parked on the shoulder of a quiet stretch of road was struck head on by a larger vehicle. The sole casualty of the accident has been identified by coroners. Deborah Rogers, age 28, was in the Mustang at the time of the collision. And now on to the sports..."

Hugh sat in stunned silence as the sports scores were flashed on the screen. He didn't even notice that the Bruins won a decisive game over the Rangers, and his lack of reaction to the 6-0 thumping made Morgan look at him.

"What's wrong?" she asked. "You look like you've seen a ghost."

Hugh turned to her slowly. "That woman who was killed in that freak accident," he said. "I knew her."

Morgan's eyes widened. "You did? I'm so sorry," she said.

Hugh frowned. "Something tells me that was no accident," he said. He remembered how the friends who'd helped him move Morgan's belongings had mentioned that they'd had a job to do for their boss. He knew who their boss was: Jack Sullivan. Had he arranged for Deb's death? It certainly seemed like something he'd do, for Hugh knew his style quite well. *Will O'Toole needs to be told about this*, he decided. *Malcolm needs to be told about this.*

"What do you mean?" Morgan asked. "You think she was murdered?"

Hugh nodded, but told her nothing of his suspicions. The less she knew, the better. "I'd bet money on it," he said.

"Wow," she said. "How did you know her?"

"We dated for a short time," he told her, turning off the television. "Turned out she was just using me," he added.

Morgan frowned. "I'm sorry," she said again. "That sucks."

Hugh nodded. "Yeah, well, I don't want to talk about her anymore," he said, pulling her onto his lap. "In fact, I don't wanna talk at all anymore," he said, pulling her close and kissing her.

The alleyway was long and dark. Hugh could barely see anything, but an overwhelming sense of dread propelled him forward. He knew that Morgan was near, and he felt certain that she was in danger. He called her name into the menacing shadows, but received no response. Hugh pushed forward, groping his way against a cold wall of brick on his right side. He peered into the dark and called her name again. This time he heard her voice.... Hugh, don't come any closer!

Hugh's fears redoubled upon hearing this, and for a moment he froze. But then a scream pierced the darkness, and he knew that he needed to reach her no matter what. He called her name, screamed her name, but heard nothing. His heart did double time as he started running, on and on, until at last he reached a dead end. He turned around, confused and frustrated. And then he saw Morgan. She was lying in a pool of blood, her throat slashed. Hugh ran to her, but before he could reach her a man stepped out in front of him, barring the way. His face was obscured by the shadows, but he spoke, and Hugh knew the voice at once. You're too late Wellman. Too late. Hugh reached out and grabbed at the front of the murderer, pulling him out of the shadows to reveal his face. Jack Sullivan....

"Hugh wake up. Wake up!"

Hugh awoke with a start, his heart racing, his body bathed in sweat. The light went on and he squinted at it, and then at Morgan.

"You were having a nightmare," she said, running her fingers through his tousled hair.

Hugh stared up at her, almost unable to comprehend the fact that she was actually there. The terror and rage of losing her was still surging through him, and for a moment he could only look at her.

"You okay, sweetie?" she asked, growing concerned by his silence.

Hugh lifted his hands to capture her face. "Yeah," he said at last. "I'm fine."

"What were you dreaming about?" she asked.

Hugh shook his head. "Doesn't matter," he said, wanting to push the horrifying images from his mind. He pulled her down to him to kiss her, his need to connect with her consuming. He made love to her with a sense of desperation, and when they lie in one another's arms later, Morgan snuggled up close to him, sensing his need to remain connected.

"Wow," she sighed. "That was incredible." She looked up at him with a smile. "You're really an amazing lover, you know that?"

Hugh smiled. "So are you," he said, kissing the top of her head. "I kinda had you pegged as a virgin when I first met you," he said. "You seemed so ... innocent somehow."

Morgan said nothing for a moment, and simply occupied herself with tracing her finger tip through the hair on his chest. "Well, you know different now, don't you?"

Hugh sensed he'd touched upon a sensitive issue with her, and frowned. He wanted to ask her more, but didn't want to upset her. "You know I'm an old man, right?" he asked her.

Morgan laughed. "You could have fooled me," she said. "How old are you, anyway? Thirty?"

"Thirty one," he said. "How old are you? Please tell me you're at least 18."

Morgan smiled. "Yes, I'm 22," she told him.

"Just a kid," he said, kissing the top of her head.

"Yeah whatever," she said. "You gonna tell me about your dream?"

A frown creased Hugh's brow. "Not sure you'd wanna hear it," he said. "It was bad. Real bad."

"Was I in it?"

Hugh looked down at her and nodded.

"Oh," she said. "Maybe I don't want to know."

Hugh said nothing as he played with a strand of her hair. "I think I need to tell you about something I did," he said. "Something I'm not proud of."

Morgan looked up at him. "What?"

"Well I told you how I used to work for Sullivan Construction," he said.

"Yeah," she said.

"Well sometimes the boss asked me and some other guys to do things that were, well, not quite legal," he said.

Morgan looked up at him. "Such as?"

"I never killed anybody, if that's what you're worried about," he said. "But I did other things that weren't too nice. There's one that still bugs me, one I'll have to learn to live with. That's the one I want to tell you about, cause believe it or not, you're involved in it now too."

Morgan frowned. "How am I involved?" she asked warily.

"Let me tell you what happened first," he said. "Then you'll get it."

So Hugh told her the whole story of how he and his two friends, the very same friends who'd helped move Morgan's furniture only recently, had abducted a young woman named Maggie O'Toole. He described the meeting at the quarry, and how his former employer, Jack Sullivan, had black mailed Maggie, using the life of her beloved brother as a bartering tool to force her out of his son's life. Morgan listened in shocked silence as Hugh told the story, and then how he'd come to be employed by the very same O'Toole family after being fired by Sullivan. Finally he told her how he'd gone to Maggie's brother and father, and had told them the entire story.

"That's an incredible story," Morgan said. "I can't believe he'd do that to his own son!"

"The man's a monster," Hugh told her. "Remember that woman who was killed in that freak accident in Ipswich? The one I'd dated?"

"You think Sullivan was responsible for her death?" Morgan asked.

"Yep," he said. He went on to explain how Deb had been involved with Jack, and how she'd cheated on him. Finally he told her about the night that his friends Mitch and Steve had moved in her things, how they'd been occupied earlier in the day. Morgan began to grow fearful by the end of his narrative.

"So what does any of this have to do with me?" she asked anxiously.

"Sullivan is gonna figure out sooner or later that it was me who Deb was fooling around with behind his back," he said. "And he could even figure out that I was the one who told the O'Tooles about what he did to Maggie. He'll be gunning for me, Morgan. And after seeing what he did to Deb..."

"You don't think that he'd try to kill you too, do you?" she asked, the fear evident in her eyes.

"He might," he said. "And I don't want to put you in that kind of danger. I think we need to get out of Boston. The sooner the better."

"But where would we go?" she asked.

"I don't know," he said. "All I know is that I don't want to put you in any danger, and as long as we're close to Sullivan, you are. We both are."

Morgan considered this for a moment. "That's what you dreamed about, isn't it?" she asked. "Your nightmare was about him. About Sullivan."

Hugh nodded. "You're right," he said. "But maybe that's not a bad thing. Maybe it was the kick in the ass I needed to realize that we're not safe."

"But we have no money, Hugh," she said. "Where would we go?"

Hugh thought for a moment. She was right: they had very little money. "Well, maybe we can sell our stuff," he suggested. "You know, pawn it."

"I guess," she said. "But...where would we live? How would we live?"

"We'll get by," he said. "I'll take care of you, Morgan," he said, stroking her face. "I'll find a way. I swear it."

Morgan smiled, tears springing to her eyes. "I know you will," she said.

Thirty Five

*J*P Sullivan was a creature of habit, and he had been in the habit of taking a morning stroll each morning. And despite the fact that it was frigid outside, he walked for thirty minutes before returning home to have his morning coffee and read the paper. When he arrived in the breakfast room, his paper was waiting for him along with a hot cup of black coffee and a bran muffin. That was how JP liked his life; predictable, orderly and simple.

"Brisk one out there this morning, Sherry," he said as his housekeeper helped him off with his coat.

"Yes I can see that," she said with a smile. "But you never let that stop you, do you sir?"

JP chuckled. "Well Massachusetts has a pretty long winter," he said. "If you avoid the cold, you don't spend much time outside."

"Yes, very true sir," Sherry said, unfolding the paper for him as he took a seat at the small wooden table. "Enjoy your paper."

"Thank you my dear," JP said. He took a sip of his coffee as he scanned over the headlines. There was nothing that interested him, just the same bad news about the economy, about the Middle East, about the environment. *The world's going to Hell in a hand basket,* he thought with a frown as he turned to the local news. He did a double take when he saw a photo of someone he knew: Deborah Rogers. His eyes read quickly over the text that followed her photo, an uneasy feeling filling him as he did so: *Deborah Rogers, age 28, has been positively identified by coroners as the sole victim of a bizarre car accident on Back Hamlet Road. Ms Rogers, a paralegal at Cannon, Emerson and Finch, had been left in the car by her companion, Mr. Bradley Stone. According to Mr. Stone, when he returned to the car after a few minutes, it had been crushed by an oncoming car. The vehicle in question has not been identified, and the police have no leads on the case. If you know something about this incident, contact Crime Stoppers at...*

JP stopped reading at this point. He set his cup down rather shakily as he stared at the photo of Deborah. He couldn't shake the feeling that his son had had a hand in the death of her, for he knew from his mole at Sullivan that they'd had an ugly break up recently. But would Jack stoop that low? Was he that beyond redemption that he'd murder a woman who'd been his lover mere weeks earlier? *And what would he do to Maggie if he found her if he's capable of this?* He thought. JP was not a man who had trouble making decisions, but the situation he'd stumbled onto had him stymied. He felt certain that Jack would deny any involvement in Deb's death, but would undoubtedly be on the defensive henceforth. *Malcolm has to be told about this,* he decided. *He needs to be warned.* But JP didn't know where Malcolm was, and this sort of information wasn't something you would discuss over the telephone. *So how do I warn him?* He thought in dismay. He thought for a moment, stirring absent-mindedly at his coffee. And then he had an idea. He stood up from the table and headed over to the telephone on the far side of the room. He picked it up and called his grandson Tom, who was a lawyer. If anyone would know what to do, it would be him. It was Saturday, and so he found Tom at home.

"Hi grandpa. How are you?" Tom asked.

"Not too well, Tom," JP said. "In fact, I'm pretty shaken up right now."

"Why? What's wrong? Are you ill?" Tom asked, the concern evident in his voice.

"No, nothing like that," JP said. "You think you could swing by here, Tom? I really need to talk to you about something."

"Of course," Tom said. "I'll be over in an hour."

"Thank you son," JP said. "I'll see you then."

Bangor, Maine

Will O'Toole was used to getting up early, so on the weekend, when he was off work, his body simply refused to sleep in. Some people might be annoyed by such a seeming betrayal, but Will had grown to accept it, and put the time to good use. Leaving his sleeping fiancée he'd rise early and go jogging. He'd come to enjoy early morning jogs when he'd started the custom with his brother-in-law, Malcolm. And since moving to Bangor, had kept up the practice whenever he could.

Will and Alli lived in a small house in a quiet subdivision in Bangor. Close enough to see the ocean, they'd come to love the small town they now called home. Will had just started down the bicycle path that ran through the subdivision when his cell phone started to ring. Will considered letting the call go to voice mail, but given the fact that his sister was due to give birth any day, he didn't. But the name on the screen wasn't Malcolm Sullivan; it was Hugh Wellman.

"Hello?" Will said, a little surprised to be hearing from Hugh after so long.

"Hi Will. It's Hugh Wellman," Hugh said. "How's it going?"

"Good, very good," Will said. "What about you?"

"Well I've been better actually," Hugh said. "Listen Will, I really need to talk to you about something, but it's not something I can talk about on the phone. But believe me, it's real important."

Will frowned, Hugh's words alarming him. "What's all this about?" he asked. "You're kinda freakin' me out here."

"Believe me, you'll be more freaked when I tell you," Hugh said. "Can we meet somewhere? Soon?"

"Well I'm not in Boston any more, Hugh," Will said.

"I didn't figure you were," Hugh said. "I'll come to you, Will. You tell me where, and I'll be there."

Will hesitated, not sure he ought to tell Hugh where he was. After all, it wasn't that long ago that this man had been a part of a nefarious scheme to split Maggie from Malcolm. *But then he became your friend, he told you everything, he helped them find each other again...*

"I'll send you a text with my address," Will said. "It's gonna take you a while to get here from Boston, so don't leave too late okay?"

"I've got stuff to do today," Hugh said. "But I'll leave first thing in the morning."

"Okay," Will said. "See you tomorrow then."

Will ended the call, and then sent a text to Hugh. He frowned as he sent it, worried about what had Hugh so agitated. He was sure that it had something to do with Jack Sullivan. But what? What now? *I guess I'll find out later on today,* he decided, and then resumed his jog, considerably less relaxed than he'd been minutes earlier.

Martha's Vineyard

Tom and Rob Sullivan were shown into their grandfather's home by his housekeeper, who led them into the study where JP was waiting for them.

"Thank you for coming so quickly," JP said as his grandsons shook his hand in greeting.

"Well you sounded pretty upset on the phone, Tom said as the three men sat down, "I figured it was important."

"It is," JP said, picking up a newspaper from the small table between the chairs. "Tell me, do either of know who your father has been dating for the past several months?"

Rob and Tom exchanged a look, their grandfather's question coming out of left field.

"Some paralegal, I think," Tom said.

"He didn't bring her around much," Rob said. "But I met her once. She was a lot younger than him if I remember right."

"Yes, she was a lot younger," JP said. "Younger than either of you, as a matter of fact."

"She *was* a lot younger?" Tom asked. "Why are you talking about her in the past tense, Grandpa?"

"Because she's dead," JP said, and presented them with the article he'd read that morning about Deborah's death.

Rob took the paper and his twin read along with him. JP watched as their faces registered their shock as the words of the article sunk in. They looked up at him when they'd finished the short article.

"That's ...strange," Rob said. "What a strange way to die."

JP nodded in agreement. "But more than strange, suspicious. At least to me. And here's something you may now know; your father broke up with Ms Rogers several weeks ago. And apparently it was a nasty break up."

"He dumped her?" Tom asked.

JP nodded.

"Any idea why?" Rob asked.

"She cheated on him," JP said.

"How do you know all this, Grandpa?" Rob asked. "I can't see Dad telling you any of that."

"No, he wouldn't," JP said. "I happen to have a source who works very closely to your father," he said. "She keeps her eyes and ears open, and has been very helpful over the years."

Rob nodded, knowing immediately who it was, and was sure his brother knew it too: Annie.

"You think there's a connection between Deborah's death and her break up with Dad, don't you?" Tom asked.

"I do," JP said. "In fact, I wouldn't at all be surprised if he was responsible for her death. Indirectly of course," he said. "He'd never get his hands dirty."

Neither Tom nor Rob wanted to consider what their grandfather was suggesting, but it was hard to deny the likelihood. And if he was capable of eliminating a woman he'd once been intimately involved with, then he was far more dangerous than even they'd realized.

"There has to be a way to find out for sure," Rob said. He looked at his brother. "Is there some way of identifying the vehicle that struck the car she was in?"

"I'm sure if there is, the police are already doing it," Tom said. "Paint traces might tell us something, but not enough for an indictment. Not a chance."

Rob frowned, knowing that his brother knew what he was talking about.

"Whether or not we can prove it is not really the point," JP said. "The fact that your father is capable of such cold-bloodedness is the real issue at hand. Your brother's wife is in danger. If your father finds out that she married Malcolm... well you know what could happen. I don't need to spell it out for you."

"Do you really think he'd kill Maggie?" Rob asked.

"She's pregnant, Grandpa," Tom said. "Do you think he's capable of kill-ing a pregnant woman?"

"*He* wouldn't kill her," JP said. "But he'd have her killed. Just as he had Deborah killed. Just has he would have had Maggie's brother killed if she hadn't done what he told her to. There's not a doubt in my mind. And don't think it doesn't pain me to say such a thing about my own son."

The three men sat for a few moments, the enormity of JP's words hanging in the air.

"So what should we do?" Rob asked.

"We should tell Malcolm," JP said. "And as soon as possible. Before your father learns of their marriage. Before he has a chance to do something monstrous."

Boston

Hugh and Morgan spent the day packing up the belongings that they needed to take with them on their trip to Maine. The rest they planned on tak-ing to the local pawn shop. Mitch had agreed to let Hugh borrow his truck for the day, and came up to help them move some of the heavier items downstairs.

"Looks like you're leaving town," Mitch observed as he and Hugh dis-mantled Hugh's punching bag. "What's going on?"

Hugh looked over at Morgan, who was taking the few framed photos Hugh had off of the walls.

"We're eloping," Hugh said. "Leaving town tomorrow."

Morgan nearly dropped the photo she was holding when she heard Hugh say this, and figured he'd only done so for Mitch's benefit.

"Eloping?" Mitch asked, the incredulity clear in his voice. "Are you shit-ting me, man?"

Hugh shook his head, and walked over to where Morgan stood. "Nope," he said, putting his arm around her. "We're eloping, aren't we baby?" he said, kissing her on the cheek.

"That's right," she said, going along with him.

Mitch looked at them, starting to think he'd missed something. "I thought you told me you two were just friends," he said, looking at Hugh.

Hugh shrugged. "So I lied," he said. "Sue me."

"You knocked up?" Mitch asked Morgan.

Morgan felt her face go red with embarrassment. "No!" she said.

"Don't be an asshole," Hugh said. "We're eloping because we love each other. Is that so strange?"

Mitch considered this for a moment. "Guess not," he said. "Just kinda sudden is all."

"When you're with the right person, you know it," Morgan said, giving Hugh a smile.

"Whatever," Mitch said. "Let's get the rest of this stuff down to the truck," he said to Hugh. "I've got shit to do tonight."

It took several hours for Hugh and Morgan to pawn their household, for the owner of the shop was a rather tight fisted man who tried to low ball them for every item they presented him with. At the end of the day, they walked away with a little over two thousand dollars. It wasn't as much as they'd hoped for, but such was the nature of the transaction. It was almost nightfall when they returned to their empty apartment.

"*Now* it looks big," Hugh commented as they stood in the empty living room.

Morgan smiled. "So what are we gonna do for a bed tonight?" she asked.

"Well the mattress from my bed is still back there," he said.

"Yeah, but there's nothing on it," she pointed out.

Hugh nodded. "True," he said. He looked at his watch. "We might as well start driving up to Maine," he said. "We can crash somewhere along the way."

"Okay," she said. She looked around the apartment one last time. It had only been her home a few weeks, but she'd been very happy here. She'd fallen in love here.

"Let's go babe," he said, taking her hand. "Time to put this place behind us."

Morgan left with him, closing the door behind her.

On the way out of town, Hugh pulled into a drive through ATM to deposit the cash he'd been given by the pawn broker. As he put the car into neutral at the ATM, Morgan made a decision. She opened her backpack and pulled out the envelope of cash that her former land lord had given her weeks earlier. "Here," she said, pulling the cash out and handing it to Hugh. "Take this too."

Hugh looked at the wad of cash and then up at her. "You sure?"

Morgan nodded. "We're in this together, right?" she said.

Hugh nodded. "Yeah," he said. He took the cash from her, and then leaned over to kiss her. "We sure are."

Morgan smiled, and then watched him as he leaned out of the window to get an envelope to deposit the money with. As he did so, his unzipped jacket opened up, and Morgan saw that he had a gun stashed in the inner pocket. She sat back in her seat, her heart drumming hard. She'd had no idea that he owned a gun, and the discovery that he did unnerved her.

Hugh sat back in the car, looking at the deposit slip. He had almost six thousand dollars in the bank now. It would see them through for a little while, but he knew that he'd need to find a source of income soon before the funds were depleted completely.

"Wanna get something to eat before we hit the road?" Hugh asked, looking at Morgan briefly before he pulled out of bank parking lot.

"Sure, if you want," she said.

Hugh came to a stop at the street and turned to her. "Something wrong?" he asked, seeing the look on her face.

"You have a gun," she said simply.

"Yeah, so?" he said, pulling out into traffic.

"I...I didn't know you had one," she said.

"I don't make a habit of flashing it around," he said.

"Where was it? Where did you keep it?" she asked. "I never saw it in the apartment."

"It was in a box up in the bedroom closet," he told her, unsure what the big deal was. "You got a problem with guns?"

"You could say so, yes," she said.

"Oh. Well, sorry," he said. "But I feel safer when I'm travelling if I have it with me."

Morgan didn't reply, but simply turned and watched the city passing them by, trying not to think about the past.

It was almost midnight when they arrived at the Maine border. They were both tired and decided to stop for the night. They found a Days Inn off the 95 and were lucky enough to find a vacancy.

Hugh carried an overnight bag that they'd prepared while still in Boston as they rode up the elevator. He could tell that Morgan was still not herself, and he frowned. *What's the big deal?* He thought as they rode up the elevator.

He watched her as she yawned, wondering if he ought to ask her about her obvious hang up.

"Tired?" he asked her.

"Uh huh," she said through a yawn.

"Yeah, long ride will do that," he said.

"Yeah, sure," she said.

Hugh didn't want to press her, given the lateness of the hour, but knew that he'd need to do so at some point. He'd never been in a relationship with someone like Morgan before, and he didn't want to do anything to mess things up.

"You okay?" he asked her as he set the suitcase down to unlock the door to their room.

"Yeah, just tired," she said.

"I think there's more to it," he said as she walked into the room. He followed her in. "It's the gun, isn't it? It's got you scared."

Morgan unzipped her jacket and hung it up before responding. "I'm not scared, Hugh," she said. "I trust you completely." She turned to him. "Surely you know that."

"So tell me why you freaked out when you saw it," he said.

"I didn't freak out," she said with a frown. "I just don't like guns. Lots of people don't. What's the big deal?"

"I don't know," Hugh said. "That's what I'm trying to figure out."

Morgan sighed, and ran her hand through her hair. "Hugh I'm tired," she said. "Can we talk about this another time?"

"Yeah, sure," he said. "Let's go to bed."

It was a few hours later when Hugh was woken from a deep sleep by the erratic movements of Morgan. He turned to her, wondering if he ought to wake her up. Deciding to do so, he turned on the light above the bed and shook her gently by the shoulder.

Morgan woke up with a start, and looked up at him.

"You were rolling around in your sleep," Hugh told her. "Bad dream?"

"Yeah," she said, glad that it was over. "Sorry."

"You don't have to apologize," he said, pulling her close. "It was about the gun, wasn't it?"

Morgan frowned. "I don't want to think about it."

Hugh nodded, as his finger tips stroked her shoulder. "What happened to you?" he asked. Clearly something had happened to make her so afraid of guns. "Who hurt you, Morgan?"

Morgan didn't want to get into the past, but judged that Hugh deserved to know.

"It's a long story," she said. "You sure you want to hear it?"

"Of course," he said. "I care about you, I want to help you if I can."

Morgan took a deep breath, gathering her nerve and her thoughts before she launched into her sad tale.

"I was 6 years old when my father took off," she said. "I barely remember him, and I'm not even sure why he left. My younger brother was 3. My mother remarried after a very short time, less than two years later. The man she married, my step-father, was a hunter. He had a lot of guns."

"Is that why you don't like them?" Hugh asked. "Because of him?"

"Yes, but not just because he had them, but because of what he did with them," she said. "He never liked me and my brother, and resented us from day one just because my mother gave us attention. So he used to like to play games with us. Games using his guns. Games like Russian Roulette."

Hugh looked down at her in shock. "He did that to you?"

"Well he did it a couple of times, yes," she said. "Turns out he didn't have any bullets in the cartridge, but we didn't know it at the time. He'd laugh at how scared we were, and my mother was too much of a chicken shit to do anything. The fact that she was stoned half of the time didn't help either."

Hugh could feel himself growing angrier as she told her story, but he let her continue.

"When I got older, the games changed," Morgan said. "He'd get me alone and make me take off my shirt, and he'd have his hunting rifle in his hands to make sure I did it. Sometimes he'd make me touch his junk. I was so afraid of the gun in his hands that I'd do it without question. Eventually my brother and I were taken away and put into foster care. But I was almost 13 by then." She took a moment to calm herself, as the memories were dredging up emotions she'd just as soon never experience again."

Hugh held her closer, an overwhelming sense of protectiveness filling him. "You ever see your mother?" He asked.

"No," she said. "I don't want to see her. She left me and my brother to fend for ourselves. What kind of a mother does that?"

"A terrible one," Hugh said. "I'm just glad you got out of there. You deserve so much better, Morgan. You know, if our paths ever cross, I'll kill him. I swear to God I will."

Morgan looked up at him. "I don't want you to do that," she said. "Even if he deserves it, you'd be put away for life. And then where would that leave me?" She reached up and stroked his face. "I need you, Hugh. I love you."

Hugh was surprised by her admission, but knew that she was being totally honest with him. Other women had claimed to love him before. He'd even thought himself in love before. But now he knew otherwise. Now he knew what love really felt like, and it was unlike anything he'd ever felt in his life.

"I love you too," he said, and pulled her to him once more.

Thirty Six

Bangor, Maine

It was Sunday morning. Will and Alli had just arrived home from morning mass when the doorbell rang. They'd been expecting Hugh, so they weren't surprised by it. And yet, they'd both grown anxious waiting to hear what he had to say, what he deemed so urgent that he was willing to drive over 200 miles to tell them.

"I'll get it," Will said. "Why don't you put some coffee on, sweets?"

"Sure," Alli said.

Will went to the front door and opened it, surprised to see a young woman with Hugh. She was holding his hand.

"Will! It's good to see you man," Hugh said, giving Will a smile.

"Yeah, you too," Will said.

Hugh turned to Morgan. "Morgan this is Will O'Toole," he said. "Will, meet my girlfriend Morgan."

"Pleased to meet you, Will," Morgan said, holding out her hand for Will to shake.

"Same here," Will said. "Come on in. It's pretty cold out here."

Hugh and Morgan followed Will into the small house.

"Alli, meet Hugh and Morgan," Will said as Alli joined them in the front room. "This is my fiancée, Alli," he said.

262

"Nice to meet you," Hugh said. "And congrats," he added, looking at Will.

Will smiled. "Thanks mate," he said. "Come on in the kitchen," he said. "Alli's made some coffee."

Everyone adjourned to the kitchen, where Alli had put out a plate of fresh muffins on the table. After she poured coffee for everyone, she joined them at the table and waited expectantly for Hugh to begin.

"So what brings you up here?" Will said. "What's so important that you drove all this way to talk to me?"

Hugh glanced at Morgan briefly before launching into his story. "It has to do with Jack Sullivan," he began.

Will and Alli grew tense at once.

"What about him?" Will asked. "What's he done now?"

"Let me tell you about something that happened in Ipswich first," Hugh said. "There was a car accident on one of the back roads," he went on. "This guy stopped on the side of the road to take a piss in the woods, and left his girlfriend in the car. When he got back, the car was totalled. According to the cops, it had been struck head on by a much larger vehicle that was travelling in the wrong lane. The woman in the car was crushed, and it took the coroner a few days before they could identify her."

"How terrible!" Alli said.

"Who was she?" Will asked. "And what does this have to do with Sullivan?"

"She was his ex-girlfriend," Hugh said. "A woman by the name of Deborah Rogers. He'd broken up with her a few weeks earlier. You see, he found out that she'd been cheating on him. And I know that's true, because it was me she cheated with."

"You were involved with this woman?" Will asked.

"Yeah, for a short time," Hugh said. "Turns out she was planning to use me. But that's beside the point. The point is, on the day this accident happened, two former colleagues, guys who still work for Sullivan, told me that they had a job to do for the boss."

Will started to understand, and a cold feeling started to well up inside of him. "Are you saying that Sullivan arranged for her death?" he said.

Hugh nodded.

"That's a pretty big jump to make, don't you think?" Alli asked.

Hugh looked at her. "I used to work for Sullivan," he said. "I know him well. And I know his style. This has him written all over it."

"But there's no way of proving it, is there?" Will said.

"Unfortunately not," Hugh said. "If only there were, your sister's troubles would be over. But he never does anything himself. He's careful to make sure he can't be connected to anything dirty. But I'd bet my last dollar that it was him. And if he's capable of doing that...well I don't need to finish do I?"

Silence fell over the two couples as they considered this.

"Jack Sullivan is a ruthless, dangerous man," Hugh went on. "Morgan and I left Boston because we're not safe there. If he knows I was the man who slept with his girlfriend, that's enough to have him gunning for me. But should he ever find out that I told you about that day at the quarry, then my life won't be worth shit."

Will nodded, a frown on his face. "There's something you don't know, Hugh," he said. "Malcolm and Maggie are married now. In fact, they're expecting twins any day now."

"I didn't know that," Hugh said, looking at Morgan. "Well then it's a good thing I came then," he said. "Cause if he finds out somehow, your sister's is serious danger."

"We're going to have to tell Malcolm," Will said. "I don't know what he's going to do about it, but he has to know."

Hugh nodded. "Where are they, Will?"

Will hesitated and looked at Alli. Hugh could see that he was still unsure if he could trust him, and that bothered him.

"Look, I know you're still not sure you can trust me," Hugh said. "And given my history, I don't blame you. But I'm not the same man I was when I helped Sullivan, not even close. I've worked hard to change, and, thanks to Morgan here, I have."

Morgan smiled, and put her hand on his. "You've done it yourself," she said. "I was just there to encourage you. Don't sell yourself short. You're a good man, Hugh Wellman."

Will watched the exchange, surprised by the genuineness of the affection Hugh and Morgan clearly felt for one another. Hugh was not the same man who'd walked into the Hart and Hound so many months earlier. He'd worked hard to put his past behind him, a past that Will suspected was far more challenging than he knew.

"They're in Nova Scotia," Will said. "We'll go this afternoon. I'll drive."

Antigonish

"I'm stuffed," Maggie sighed, and pushed her plate away from her. "I really wish I could finish this, it's delicious, but there's just no room."

"Don't push yourself," Malcolm said, pulling her plate towards her. "You always pay for it later."

Maggie smiled as she watched him polish off the rest of her omelet. "You know, you're not going to be able to do this for much longer," she said.

Malcolm glanced up at her. "What do you mean?"

"I mean that once these babies are born I'll be able to eat an entire meal again," she said. "All in one sitting."

Malcolm laughed. "Yeah well I'll need to go on a diet by then anyway," he said.

Maggie smiled, and then noticed another pain deep in her pelvis. She'd been very uncomfortable during mass, and was all but certain that she'd begun labour. But given the fact that she'd already had a false alarm, she didn't want to raise the alarm just yet.

Malcolm's phone rang as the waitress came to clear their dishes. He looked at the screen to ensure that it wasn't his father. It wasn't, though. It was his brother Tom.

"Hey Tom," Malcolm said. "How's it going?"

"Not bad, how about you?"

"Good, really good," Malcolm replied. "Just enjoying brunch with my beautiful wife."

"How's she doing?" Tom asked. "No sign of the twins yet?"

"Not yet, no," Malcolm said. "Any day now."

"Nervous?" Tom asked.

"A little, yeah," Malcolm said. "Excited mostly."

"You guys will be great parents," Tom said.

"Thanks Tom," Malcolm said.

"Listen Malcolm, Rob and I really need to talk to you," Tom said. "It's really important. It's about Dad."

Malcolm looked up at Maggie, who seemed distracted. "What about him?"

"I don't want to talk about this on the phone," Tom said. "We want to come see you. Is that okay?"

Malcolm grew anxious. His brother was worried that their telephone conversation could be compromised. What was it that he had to say?

"I guess so," Malcolm said at last. "You've kind of got me worried, Tom," he said.

"Sorry Malcolm," he said. "But this is serious. Very serious."

Malcolm nodded, looking at Maggie again. But she wasn't listening, in fact she seemed to be in pain. "I'll text you my address," he said. "I've gotta go."

Malcolm ended the call, and then sent a quick text to his brother. Then he turned his attention to his wife. "What's going on, babe?" he asked. "You okay?"

"No," she said. "I think this is it, Malcolm," she said. "I think this is the real thing."

Malcolm nodded, trying to remain calm. "You sure?"

"I've been having contractions since I woke up," she told him. "So yes, pretty sure."

Malcolm frowned. "Why didn't you say something?"

"I wanted to make sure it wasn't a false alarm," she said. "But it isn't. I'm sure of it."

"Okay," Malcolm said. "Let me pay the bill and then we'll go. Call your mom while I take care of this, okay?" he said, picking up the bill and sliding out of the booth.

Maggie called her parents while Malcolm paid the bill, and then they proceeded to the hospital.

Bangor, Maine

As they made preparations to head up to Nova Scotia, Morgan realized that she wouldn't be able to cross the border. She had no passport.

"I didn't know we'd have to go to Canada," she said. "I've never had a passport. Never needed one before now."

Hugh felt terrible. He was torn between his desire to get to Malcolm and Maggie, and the love and protectiveness he felt for Morgan. "I don't want to leave without you," he said, looking at her. "No freakin' way."

Morgan smiled, and put her hand on his. "I'm sorry," she said. "You need to get there as soon as possible, remember? It'll take me weeks to get a passport. You can't wait that long."

"Will and Alli can go," he said. "I'll wait here with you, and then when you get your passport, we'll go up." He looked at Will. "I'll stay here with Morgan," he said. "You two go up ahead, and we'll come once Morgan has her passport."

"I think that's a great idea," Will said. "Malcolm and Maggie need to be told about this as soon as possible."

"Agreed," Hugh said. "We'll come up as soon as we can, but it's more important that they be told."

Will and Alli didn't take long to pack a bag, and by mid afternoon they were on their way.

"If you put a rush on the passport you'll get it faster," Will told Morgan as they stood outside. "It shouldn't take long."

Morgan nodded. "Thanks for letting us stay here," she said. "We'll take good care of the place."

"I know you will," Will said with a smile. He turned to Hugh. "I'll let Malcolm know your part in all this," he said. "He needs to know how much you've changed."

"I appreciate that," Hugh said. "Just hope when he finally meets me he doesn't want to beat me senseless for my part in all this."

Will smiled. "I'll make sure he doesn't," he said. "Malcolm's a smart guy. He'll be able to see the bigger picture, Hugh. No worries."

Hugh wasn't so sure, but said nothing. He and Morgan stood in the driveway and watched as Will and Alli pulled away, waving to them as they drove away down the street.

Nova Scotia

"Are you *sure* Megs?" Carrie asked.

"Yes, absolutely," Maggie said. "I'm in the hospital right now. They've checked me in. This is it, Carrie."

"Okay, I believe you," Carrie said. "I'll get there as soon as I can. How far apart are your contractions?"

"Well they were about 9 minutes apart, but they've slowed down a wee bit," Maggie said. "But I'm not going anywhere. I refuse to go home until these babies are born."

Carrie laughed. "How's Malcolm holding up?"

"Good," Maggie said. "He's trying to get a hold of his grandparents in Australia to let them know that the babies are on the way."

"Grandparents?? I thought it was only his grandfather," Carrie said.

"Yes, well his grandmother made the trip with him when he left Scotland," Maggie said. "They're quite close now. It's lovely."

"That's awesome," Carrie said. "And from what you've told me, they'll be thrilled to have two great grandbabies."

"I'm sure they will be," Maggie said. "Well Mum's back so I'll say goodbye."

"Okay Megs. Good luck! I'll see you soon," Carrie said.

"Bye for now," Maggie said, and then ended the call.

"Was that Carrie?" Irene asked as she took off her coat.

"Yes," Maggie said. "She's on her way."

"Grand," Irene said as she took a seat in the chair beside Maggie's bed. "Where's Malcolm?"

"He's trying to get a hold of his grandparents," she said. "He's quite frustrated that he hasn't been able to reach them yet."

"Well there's plenty of time still," Irene said. "You have a long wait ahead of you I think."

Maggie nodded. "I know," she said. "But this is it, Mum. I'm not leaving this hospital without these babies in my arms."

New Brunswick

"So Morgan seems nice, don't you think?" Alli asked as she and Will made their way east.

"Yeah she does," Will said. "Seems like a good match for him. He needs a nice girl in his life, poor bugger."

"He's had a rough life, hasn't he?" she asked.

"Sure has," Will said. "But this girl seems to have brought out the best in him. I hope Malcolm can see that there's more to Hugh than the thug who took Maggie to that quarry," he said.

"You told Hugh that he would," Alli reminded him.

"Of course I did," Hugh said. "What else was I supposed to say? That Malcolm will probably hate him and want to kick his ass?"

"True," Alli said. She sighed. "I'll just be happy when all this mess is over," she said. "Then we can plan our own wedding, get started with our own lives."

Will nodded. "It won't be long, love," he said. "I promise."

Nova Scotia

"Breathe babe, that's it," Malcolm said. He held her hand as she laboured through a contraction. It had been a very long day, and Malcolm could see how exhausted and frustrated she'd become.

"These babies are never going to come out," Maggie said as her contraction subsided. "It's been so long!"

Malcolm didn't know what to say to make her feel better. It *had* been a long day. It had been mid-morning when she'd been admitted, and now it was nearly midnight.

"First babies always take their time," Irene said, sitting on the other side of the room. "You need to be patient, love. They'll be along."

Maggie frowned. "Yeah sure," she grumbled.

"Why don't we go for a walk?" Malcolm suggested. "The nurse said that might help move things along."

"Okay," Maggie said, letting him help her up.

"I'll give Dad a call and let you know how you're doing," Irene said. "He's been texting me for updates."

"We'll be back shortly, Mom," Malcolm said as he helped Maggie out of the chair.

Irene waved them off and picked up her cell phone to call her husband.

At Malcolm and Maggie's home...

Quinn and Aidan had just gone up to bed when the doorbell rang. Mick was on the phone with his wife, and hesitated about going to the door. But when the ringing persisted, he decided to see who it was. Carrying the phone with him, he headed downstairs and looked through the window beside the door. He was shocked to see Will and Alli standing there. Mick opened the door at once, and welcomed them in.

"What a surprise!" Mick said, embracing his first born. He turned to Alli next, and gave her a hug. "What are you two doing here at this time of night?"

"We've been driving all day, Da," Will said as they stepped into the foyer. "We need to talk to Malcolm. Right away."

Mick grew concerned at once. "Why? What's wrong?"

"It's a long story, Da," Will said. "Is Malcolm here?"

"No, he's not," Mick said. "He's been at the hospital all day. Maggie went into labour this morning."

"She did?" Alli said.

"Aye," Mick said. "I'm going over to take your mum out for a bit," he said. "I can take you with me if you feel the need to talk to him right away."

"We do," Will said. "It's not something that can wait."

Mick nodded. "Very well, then let's go. You can tell me what's going on in the car."

St. Martha's Hospital

Maggie leaned her head against Malcolm's chest as he rubbed his hands up and down her back. He hated seeing her in pain, and couldn't wait for the entire experience to be over. Things were picking up a bit, as the walking seemed to be helping out after all. As they continued to walk, they were both surprised to see Mick, Will and Alli walking towards them.

"Will! Alli!" Malcolm said as they reached him and Maggie. "What are you doing here?"

Will was torn about telling Malcolm what he knew, for now that Maggie was in labour he questioned the timing of his news. "I heard my niece and nephew were about to arrive," he said with a smile. "Didn't want to miss that!"

Malcolm knew Will well enough to know that he wasn't being totally truthful with him. He turned to Maggie, who was talking to Alli and Mick. "Alli, Dad, would you take Maggie back to her room? I think she needs to get off of her feet."

"Sure thing," Alli said.

Malcolm gave Maggie a kiss. "I'll be right back," he said, grateful that Maggie was too preoccupied with her labour to question the sudden and unexpected appearance of her brother.

"What is it?" Malcolm said to Will once Maggie was out of ear shot. "Something's happened, hasn't it?"

Will nodded, not at all surprised by Malcolm's question. "I'm afraid so," he said. "But I'm not sure this is the best time to get into it. I didn't know Maggie was in labour. Not sure I want to burden you right now."

Malcolm frowned. "You drove all the way from Bangor to tell me something," he said. "Obviously you think it's important. Tell me. I need to know, Will."

"It's about a woman named Deborah Rogers," Will said. "You know her?"

Will's words could not have surprised Malcolm more. "Deborah Rogers?? What about her?"

"She's dead," Will said. "And I have good reason to think that your father is responsible."

Malcolm said nothing initially. The shock that Deb was dead was considerable. But to hear that there was a chance his father had been involved with her death much more so.

"How did she die?" he asked. "And what makes you think my father had anything to do with it?"

"It's a long story," Will said. "And Hugh Wellman is a part of it."

"Hugh Wellman?" Malcolm said. "You mean that bastard who took Maggie to the quarry? *That* Hugh Wellman?"

Will nodded. "You have to understand how much he's changed," he said. "He's not the same thug who took Maggie that day."

Malcolm wasn't so sure, but let Will continue.

Will told Malcolm the whole long, complicated story, including Hugh's involvement with Deborah. By the end, it was quite clear that Malcolm was more than a little shaken.

"Can you see now why I felt it was important to talk to you about this?" Will said. "If your father is responsible, if he was behind Deborah Rogers' death, then he is far more dangerous than any of us realized."

"I can't believe this," Malcolm said. "It's just too much to swallow. Could he actually do such a thing? Really?"

"I don't know," Will said. "But Hugh seems to think so. And think of it, he worked for your father Malcolm. He knows a side to him that you don't. He drove all the way from Boston to tell me, so I think he's pretty convinced."

Malcolm frowned. "So how come he didn't come tell me himself?" he said. "Too much of a chicken shit to face me?"

"His girlfriend doesn't have a passport," Will explained. "Otherwise he'd be here right now."

Malcolm said nothing. He didn't want to consider what Will was suggesting. He had too much to deal with at the moment. His wife was in labour, his twins were on the way. His head was spinning. And now he had this to contend with?

"You know what? I can't deal with this right now," Malcolm said. "I have a wife who needs me at her side," he said. "I'll think about it later. Maggie needs me," he said, and then left Will to return to his wife. Will let him go, knowing that Malcolm was right. He had a lot to contend with right now. *But he knows,* he told himself. *And once the babies are born and things have settled down, he'll know what to do. I'm sure of it.*

Thirty Seven

Halifax International Airport

The flight from Boston to Halifax, Nova Scotia is usually a little over an hour in duration. However, given the fact that the flight from Boston had been delayed three hours due to a blizzard, Rob and Tom Sullivan didn't arrive in Halifax until very late. And then, to make matters worse, there was freezing rain in Halifax, making the long drive to Antigonish protracted and dangerous. After attempting to navigate the dark, unfamiliar roads, they decided to stay at an inn along the Trans Canada. As anxious as they were to talk to Malcolm, neither were prepared to risk their lives. They decided that they'd get up early and make the long trip to Antigonish. A few hours wouldn't make a difference after all.

"Did you get a hold of Malcolm?" Tom asked his brother as he emerged from the bathroom.

"No, I didn't figure I'd try this late," Rob said. "It's after midnight."

Tom nodded with a yawn. "Yeah, I suppose we'd better wait. You know, I still can't believe what JP told us. Did you think Dad was capable of such a thing?"

"No," Rob said. "But then again, we really haven't paid much attention to what goes on in his life, have we? We're both so wrapped up in our own families, our own professions, that we've been pretty unobservant where he's concerned. Seems he's living a whole secret life we know almost nothing about."

Tom nodded thoughtfully. "I have to wonder if Mom knew about this side of him," he said. "It would explain why they fought too much when we were kids."

"Yes it would," Rob said. He looked at his watch with a yawn. "Well we should get some sleep," he said. "I don't know about you, but I'm beat."

"Me too," Tom said. "I'll arrange for a wakeup call," he said. "Seven too early?"

"Nope," Rob said. "Seven's good."

St. Martha's Hospital - Antigonish, Nova Scotia

Malcolm had decided not to tell Maggie about what Will had told him. He knew that he wouldn't be able to avoid telling her indefinitely, but pushed that aside for the time being. Irene had been delighted to see Alli and learn that her son was in town, and left Maggie's room with Mick and Alli to see him.

"Still no word from my grandparents," Malcolm said as he set his phone on the small table beside the bed. "I'm starting to get worried."

"Well there's a huge time difference, remember," Maggie said.

"That's true," Malcolm said.

"What was it that Will wanted to tell you?" Maggie asked.

Malcolm hesitated for a moment, not wanting to tell her, but not wanting to give her any hint that it was something troubling either. "I'll tell you later," he said.

Maggie was about to question him, when a contraction stopped her. They were coming more frequently, and with greater intensity now, and she was hopeful that she'd soon be able to deliver. Malcolm held her hand and encouraged her, as he'd been doing all day, as she laboured.

"I want to get up and walk again," she said once the contraction had subsided. "It helped move things along last time."

"Okay, whatever you think will help get these babies here," Malcolm said, helping her to her feet. He took her hand and they walked out of the room and into the corridor.

While they were out of the room, Maggie's friend, Molly, arrived to check on her. She'd been with her for the past several hours, and was hoping she'd still be on duty when the twins finally arrived. While she was refilling Maggie's pitcher of water, she heard a cell phone ringing. As she returned from the bathroom she saw that the phone was on the table beside the bed. She set the pitcher down and picked up the phone, surprised that Malcolm had left it behind. When she saw the name on it, she picked it up at once, knowing that Malcolm had been trying to reach his grandfather all day. She hesitated for a moment, wondering if she ought to pick it up for Malcolm. She'd come to know Maggie quite while when she was volunteering at the hospital, so she decided to accept the call.

"Hello Malcolm Sullivan's phone," she said.

There was silence at the other end for a moment, and then a man's voice spoke. "Who is this?"

"My name is Molly," she said. "I'm ..."

"Where is Malcolm?" the man interjected.

"He just stepped out into the corridor with his wife," Molly said. "Would you like me to bring the phone to him? He's not far."

Silence.

"Never mind," he finally said. "I'll call back later," the man said, and hung up.

Molly looked at the phone in surprise, and then shrugged her shoulders and set it back down on the table. She left the room, making a mental note to come back in fifteen minutes to check on Maggie.

Bangor, Maine

It was past midnight when Morgan finally heard from Will.

"Did you get to talk to Malcolm?" he asked.

"Yeah, but the timing probably wasn't the best," Will said.

"What do you mean?" Hugh asked.

"His wife's in the hospital about to give birth," he said. "He's pretty stressed out about that. I probably shouldn't have laid that on him too."

"He had to know," Hugh said.

"Yeah I know," Will said, stifling a yawn.

"How did he react when you mentioned my name?" Hugh asked.

"Just about as you'd expect," Will said. "But I'm sure once he sees how you've changed, he'll feel differently about you. I'm sure of it."

"We'll see I guess," Hugh said. "Morgan and I will be there as soon as the passport comes. Keep me posted though, eh?"

"I will," Will replied. "Goodnight."

Boston

Jack Sullivan sat on the edge of his bed, his hands shaking. Had he heard the woman correctly? Did she say Malcolm was with his *wife*?? *No, there's no way he could have found her,* he thought resolutely. *There's no way she'd have let him find her. Not after everything I said to her, not after all the threats.*

Jack stood up and began to pace in his enormous bedroom, his mind working a mile a minute. If Malcolm indeed had married Maggie, then undoubtedly she'd told him everything. *Damn that bitch! Damn her to hell! Who does she think she's dealing with? Does she really think she's going to get away with this?* He hesitated for a moment before walking over and picking up his cell phone again. This time he called one of his trusted associates, Mitch Gardner.

"Gardner, I need you at my house in half an hour," Jack said, not caring what time it was. Mitch was paid well to be available at a moment's notice, 24/7.

"Whatever you say, Mr. Sullivan," Mitch replied. "I'll be right over."

Jack ended the call without even saying goodbye. He stood for a moment, his rage building, and then threw his cell phone across the room, shattering a picture on the wall upon impact.

St. Martha's Hospital - Antigonish

Maggie had finally entered transition, the final and most difficult stage of labour. Malcolm supported her as best he could through the almost incessant contractions, but really felt as though he was doing very little. But what could he do? As much as he wanted to help her, he couldn't. She was on her own. The nurse kept close by, reminding Maggie not to push, encouraging her to breathe, and occasionally checking her to see if she was ready to deliver.

"*Please* tell me it's time!" Maggie said. "I can't take it anymore!"

The nurse, an older woman named Nora, smiled as she examined Maggie. "Good news," she said. "You're fully dilated. I'll let Dr. VanDyk know at once."

Nora left and Maggie turned to Malcolm. "Thank God," she said.

Malcolm smiled, and kissed her forehead. "Won't be long now," he said.

Dr. VanDyk entered the room along with Nora. She gave Maggie a smile. "So those babies are finally ready, are they?" she said as she positioned herself at the foot of the bed.

"We were beginning to think they'd never arrive," Irene said.

Dr. VanDyk laughed. "Well babies come when they're good and ready," she said as Nora lowered the end of the bed. "Now Maggie, on your next contraction, I want you to push as long and as strongly as you can, okay?"

Maggie nodded as Malcolm helped her sit up. She winced as a contraction hit her, and bore down, holding Malcolm's hand for support.

"That's very good, Maggie," VanDyk said. "Push hard, good girl!"

Malcolm and Irene encouraged Maggie as she delivered the first of the twins a short time later.

"It's a girl!" Dr. VanDyk announced as she held up the tiny baby girl.

Maggie was overwhelmed with emotion as she set eyes on her daughter, and took her eagerly from the nurse. "Oh my God, she's precious!" she said, kissing the baby's brow.

Malcolm could only nod, his own emotions more powerful than he'd anticipated. "She's perfect," he said, running a finger down the side of his daughter's face. "Just like her mom."

Irene stood by with tears running down her face, her eyes fixed on her tiny new granddaughter. "She's beautiful," she said with a smile.

Maggie looked up at her mother, grateful that she'd been able to share the experience with her.

"Let's get her cleaned up," Nora said, taking the baby from Maggie. "Her twin will be making his appearance soon." Malcolm watched as his daughter was weighed, measured and cleaned up. She weighed in at an even six pounds, and had a smattering of blond hair on top of her head.

"Here you go, Daddy," Nora said, handing the baby to Malcolm with a smile.

Malcolm took the baby from her, holding her the way she showed him. He looked down into her face, marvelling at the fact that she was his, a part of him. "Happy birthday sweetheart," he said, kissing her on the tip of her perfect wee nose. "I'm gonna spoil you rotten," he said, "but you're not allowed to date until you're 40, got it?"

Irene and Maggie laughed.

"That's a wee bit extreme, don't you think?" Irene asked.

Malcolm shook his head. "Nope," he said.

It wasn't long before Maggie's contractions began once again, and Nora took the baby from Malcolm so he could support her. It amazed him that she had any energy left after the long day of labour, after already giving birth once; but she persevered, and within a few minutes, gave birth to a son. He too had blond hair, and weighed six pounds, fifteen ounces.

"You're amazing, you know that?" Malcolm said as Maggie held their newborn son in her arms. "I'm totally blown away right now." He looked at their son with a smile. "He's one good looking kid," he said.

Maggie looked up at him with a smile. "Must take after his daddy," she said.

Malcolm smiled and leaned down to kiss the baby. "Hey champ," he said. "Can't wait to show you how to take a slap shot."

"Would you like to hold him?" Maggie asked.

"Thought you'd never ask," he said, and took the baby from her arms. He looked up at Irene who stood on the other side of the bed holding her new granddaughter in her arms.

"What do think, Grandma?" he asked. "Ever see such good looking kids?"

Irene laughed. "Well their mum was as good looking, that's for sure," she said. "Are you going to tell me their names now?"

Maggie looked up at Malcolm. "I suppose we ought to name them, shouldn't we?"

"Yeah, they can't be called baby girl and baby boy Sullivan all their lives," he said.

Maggie laughed. "No, definitely not."

"Well? Tell me!" Irene said. "I'm dying from the suspense!"

"Well, this is William Michael Sullivan," Maggie said, looking down at her son. "And you're holding Judith Irene."

Irene's smile grew and her eyes misted over as she looked down at her tiny namesake. "I'm honoured," she said, and gave little Judith a kiss.

Once Maggie was moved onto the maternity ward, Irene decided it was time for her to leave, for she knew how much Maggie needed to sleep. She'd called Mick and let him know the news, and had promised to bring home pictures of their grandchildren.

"I'll be back in the morning with Dad and the lads," Irene said. "Dad sends his love and says he can't wait to meet the wee bairns."

"Did you tell him their names?" Maggie asked.

"No, I thought you might want to tell him and the lads," Irene said. "Will is going to be so thrilled," she said with a smile.

Maggie nodded, and then hugged her mother goodbye.

"I'm so happy for you," Irene said as she embraced her daughter. "You're going to be a wonderful mother."

"Thanks Mum," Maggie said. "I learned from the best."

After Irene had departed, Malcolm sat down beside Maggie's bed, yawning mightily. "I can't even imagine how tired you must be if I'm this beat," he said.

Maggie smiled. "Maybe we ought to try and get some sleep while we can," she said.

Malcolm nodded, looking over at the two cribs where the twins were asleep. "Guess they wake up pretty often at this age, eh?"

"Every couple of hours at first, yes," she said. "But it gets better as they grow bigger, as their tummies are able to hold more."

"Makes sense," he said, yawning again. "Okay I'm gonna try and catch a few zees," he said, settling into the chair and pulling a blanket up over him.

"So am I," she said. "I've never been so tired in my whole life." She closed her eyes, and drifted off to sleep with a smile on her face.

Boston

Jack paced up and down in the huge foyer of his empty house. It was very late, past midnight. He wasn't concerned about that, however. He knew that he wouldn't sleep, not given the rage that was coursing through him. *How? How did he find her?* He thought with a deepening scowl. *Is she really that stupid that she'd tell him where she was?*

While he was waiting for Mitch to arrive, he decided to go online, onto the company website. He meant to track down Will O'Toole, find out what site he was working at, and ensure that he met with an unfortunate accident.

Then you'll regret fucking with me, he thought as he entered his executive password. *Then you'll see how foolish it is to cross me.* But as he entered Will's name, he was met with some news that he did not expect: Will had resigned the company. In fact, he'd resigned several months ago. This discovery only added to Jack's ire, and it took an enormous effort not to throw his tablet across the room.

Jack was startled by the sound of the security gate, and stood up at once. He set his tablet down on the chair he'd been sitting on and crossed the large foyer to activate the gate, knowing that it could only be Mitch who was calling at this hour. He waited impatiently for the doorbell to ring, more anxious than ever to talk to Mitch. He needed answers, and he was hopeful that Mitch could provide them.

Soon enough, the doorbell rang, and Jack answered it at once.

"Come in," Jack said, shivering as a cold December blast entered the house along with Mitch.

"What's going on, boss?" Mitch asked. He didn't dare voice his opinion of being yanked from a warm bed with a friendly woman to venture out on this bitter cold night; he knew better than that. "You look pretty shook up."

"I am," Jack said. "Let's sit down. I have a job for you."

"Sure," Mitch said, hoping he'd at least be offered a hot drink for his troubles. But the hired help was asleep, and Jack wasn't exactly known for his hospitality.

"Did you know that Will O'Toole quit?" Jack began.

"No I didn't," Mitch replied, finding the question a little out of left field. "When?"

"According to HR, three months ago," Jack said. "Gave no notice, just left."

"Huh," Mitch said. "Guess he had his reasons."

"What reasons?" Jack said. "What business does a man like him have quitting a job where he's making twenty-five dollars an hour?"

Mitch didn't see the point his boss was labouring to drive home. "Maybe he found something what pays more," he suggested.

"Maybe," Jack said. "But it doesn't matter. What matters is finding him. I want you to track him down, Gardner. Track him down and have a serious talk with him."

"You're pissed at him because he quit?" Mitch asked.

"No," Jack said. "His sister is now married to my son," he said. "Despite everything, the bitch married him."

Mitch nodded. "O'Toole might not be easy to find," he said.

Jack frowned. "Hire help if you need it," he said. "I just want this done."

"You know boss, Hugh may know where he is," Mitch commented.

"Hugh?" Jack said. "You mean Wellman?"

"Yeah," Mitch said. "He worked at the bar that O'Toole's old man owned until they closed it down."

Jack was silent as he digested this, anxiety worming its way through his gut.

"What do you mean, they closed it down?" Jack asked.

"I don't know much more than that, boss," Mitch said. "All I know is Hugh lost his job a few months back, and was kinda down on his luck for a while until he found that job at the Lucky Strike."

Jack's frown deepened, the anxiety inside him forming a tight ball. *I never should have let Wellman live,* he thought. *He knows too much...*

"Find him," Jack said. "Find Wellman. Find him and have a conversation with him, but make sure he tells you where to find Will O'Toole."

Mitch didn't know what to say, or how to respond. Hugh Wellman had been his friend for years. He'd helped him more times than Mitch could count, bailing him out of jail, lending him cash when needed it, even letting him crash at his place back when Hugh worked for Sullivan. But how could he refuse? Mitch had a serious gambling problem, and had accumulated considerable debt over the years. He needed his job, and wasn't likely to find another one easily.

"Have you seen him recently?" Jack asked.

"Huh?"

"Wellman, have you seen him lately?" Jack asked in exasperation.

"Yeah, I saw him last week," Mitch said. "Helped him and his woman. They were pawning all their stuff 'cause they were leaving town. Eloping."

Jack frowned. "Did you say he was leaving town?"

Mitch nodded, stifling a yawn. "Seemed to be in kinda hurry too," he said. "Didn't even know the girl that long either."

Jack pondered this for a few minutes, his mind sorting out the pieces of the puzzle. "Find him," Jack said. "Find him and use him to find O'Toole."

"You want me to ...talk to both of 'em?"

"Yes," Jack said. "And then after you've done that, I want you to find Maggie O'Toole. It's time she was shown just what happens when she tries to play in the big league. Make sure she understands."

Mitch nodded. "Whatever you say, boss," he said.

To be continued....